ETERNALS

Liminal Books is an imprint of Between the Lines Publishing. The Liminal Books name and logo are trademarks of Between the Lines Publishing.

Copyright © 2025 by S.F. Chaudhry

Cover design by Morgan Bliadd

Between the Lines Publishing
1769 Lexington Ave N, Ste 286
Roseville MN 55113
btwnthelines.com

First Published: July 2025

ISBN: Paperback 978-1-965059-54-8

ISBN: Ebook 978-1-965059-55-5

Library of Congress Control Number: 2025940949

ETERNALS

S.F. Chaudhry

To those who know, the pen is always mightier than the sword

Prologue

Location: Planet 8 – Nova, The Final Frontier

From the outside, the planet Nova seemed to be shrouded in a veil of darkness, dead and long forgotten. On the contrary, the concealed planet was more alive than ever.

Far beneath the ink-black mists lay a thickening sense of fear and panic. Cloaked beings rushed to and from, searching for any mode of escape to prevent their inevitable doom from striking. As fast as they hurried, the planet's inhabitants were too late.

Large spaceships hovered over the black atmosphere, harshly illuminating the scurrying fleets amongst the rubble and dust. They wrought just as much destruction as the troops on the ground with warships swimming through the clouds, shooting down any fleeing vessels. The ships rained havoc upon Nova with missiles and bombs as a lone voice blared over an intercom:

"Surrender to The Committee or meet your peril."

There's a sense of surrender in the form of cowardice. The people of Nova who were still alive took whatever course of action they deemed appropriate as they moved faster, desperate not to meet their ends like this.

Meanwhile, Committee troops dressed in navy blue uniforms continued to descend from above and assault the civilians of Nova. They wore visors to conceal their identities, not that the Novans needed to know the faces of the beings waving plasma guns, blasters, rays, and other weapons at them.

The impending attacks only provoked the Novans to work faster, getting into small ships and taking off with whatever was salvageable. Some Novans took up weapons of their own in an attempt to defend themselves.

All of this was understood by The Committee as a sign of retaliation. The monotone intercom echoed somewhat sadly as if whoever the voice belonged to was being forced to invade Nova and now threaten death. Yet, the voice's tone was emotionless as it concluded rather stiffly, "Then you give us no choice. Destroy the planet."

As soon as the command was given, a sense of frenzy rippled across the planet. Time seemed to stop as every single Novan imagined their planet being blown to bits, obliterating them with it. Nova was their home; no one should be able to just rip it away from them.

The foreign armies who pledged allegiance to The Committee were small but successful. The soldiers gathered as many Novans as possible, rounding them up in groups and threatening them into doing as they said.

One group consisted of trembling women and children cowering behind pointed weapons, silently pleading for mercy. For life. Not this. Not war.

A little girl with almond eyes as purple as the singed flags of her planet watched in horror as a missile dropped from the skies into her home.

"Papa!" she exclaimed, her eyes widening. She crumpled into sobs, throwing her arms around her mother's neck.

Her cries quickly dissolved as one of the troops' commanders, a young woman, strode toward her and her mother. The woman, who could not have been more than twenty, wore disgust on her features.

The girl whimpered, pressing her stuffed doll to her chest.

The woman grabbed the doll, trying to take it away, but the child held onto it fiercely.

"Please don't take my doll," she pleaded softly. Water bubbled in her eyes as she pressed it to her chest. "Papa got it for me. It's my favorite one."

The commander only sneered, reaching for her belt, and pulling out a switchblade. "Then he should have complied with us." She held the blade to the child's neck. "Would you like to join him?"

A sob tore out of the child's throat.

Aggrieved, her mother addressed the commander. "Don't you think you have taken enough? It's only a toy. Let her have it."

The woman pressed the edge of the blade further into the child's neck, hard enough to draw blood.

The child's mother tensed. "It's alright, *canazi*," she said softly to her child. "I'll find you a new one."

The nickname seemed to do the trick, as the child handed the last piece of her father over to the soldier. Her mother glared as the woman snatched the doll from the child's hands, using her blade to tear it apart.

The commander walked to the head of the group that was now surrounded by soldiers, eyeing her captives with contempt. As she surveyed the crowd, she put her hand on the hilt of a sword that rested in a sheath strapped to her side. She raised her chin, looking above the Novans. "There is no mercy for scum that do not comply. Since you do not wish to comply, I do not wish mercy upon you."

She stepped back, allowing a soldier to step in her place. He nodded toward his commander before cocking his gun. The loud metallic sound stifled screams and whispers, in various dialects, of the people in the crowd.

A woman who would've been considered human by appearance, were it not for her dewy pastel blue skin that looked like raindrops clung to it and golden shoulder-length hair that was loosely covered with a grimy cloth, moved in front of the invader with the gun.

"*Quaeso, ne feceris. Bellum nobis non vis, non solum superesse volunt,*" she squeaked through trembling and bruised, blue lips. Fear shone in her aquamarine irises. "Please, don't do this. We do not want war; we only want to survive."

The soldier sneered as he spat onto the woman's face. "If you wanted to survive, then you should have joined us. You brought this upon yourself." He gestured to the armed beings that surrounded the innocent Novans. "Kill them all."

The woman clasped her hands together. "Please, don't do this." While fear clamored in the chests of her fellow Novans, she stood tall. She wouldn't show defeat or desperation to the tyrants who had come to ruin Nova's peace and freedom. Despite her will for strength, the words came out rather lamely, "At least don't kill the children."

The man mimicked a face of pity as he pressed the tip of a blaster to her chest. The woman shut her eyes in an attempt to brace herself as he laughed sardonically. "You're pathetic, the lot of you. So, you will be the one to die first."

Bzzt.

The woman made an odd sound, one that resembled a grunt, and fell onto her back as a pool of blue liquid spilled out of her chest. And just like that, she was dead.

The same soldier stepped over her with a snarl of disgust and pressed the trigger multiple times, not stopping until nearly everyone in the herd dropped dead. He only lowered his weapon to spit, aiming at the fear stricken Novans who could only wonder helplessly who would be next.

Onlookers screamed and fled, only to find themselves trapped by the invading army. Men, women, and children cowered beneath the uniformed soldiers whose weapons were aimed right at them, ready to shoot with no hesitation once given the command. The soldiers forced the crowd to separate as their king was dragged out from his palace.

Finally, the people who claimed to be The Committee stepped onto the dusty and blood-splattered planet with the help of a smaller vessel. The commander with the sword joined the approaching figures as they walked toward the King of Nova, ignoring the hate and despair written on Novan faces as they surveyed their success.

It was evident from the way the seven figures were dressed that they meant business. Each one wore a black uniform consisting of a simple tunic and durable pants, with holsters at their side to accommodate any desired form of arsenal. Each uniform had a crest over the left shoulder in the shape of a wispy sun. Despite their diverse appearances, their facial features were contorted into unanimous and almost robotic expressions, with thin flat lips and empty, unreadable eyes.

The King helplessly took in the mayhem: his planet, once brimming with diversity and great economic success, so easily reduced to nothing by the horrors of war. Houses and living complexes were blown to pieces with furniture reduced to mere piles of rubble. Stores no longer existed under smoldering boulders. It was devastating for a planet that once teemed with all forms of life to be reduced to nothing but ash and blood.

The King of Nova swallowed a gasp, utterly horrified as he looked at the sickening sight of his domain. Terror stricken, eyes reflecting infernos and carnage and the taste of death heavy in his mouth, he asked numbly, "Why are you doing this?"

At first, the monarch received no reply. After a few moments, one of the seven responded emptily, "We are The Committee, and we wish to unite the galaxy. We've already shown you that we won't hesitate to obliterate your weak planet to achieve our goal."

The sword-bearing woman continued, "Either you can wish to have no acquaintance with us and be annihilated or accept us and live fruitfully under our protection from here on out. The choice is up to you, but quite frankly," she pulled the sword out of its sheath, "we are satisfied either way."

The King of Nova pressed his lips in a firm line as he contemplated the decision at hand.

On one side was his honor and dignity. Nova was his family's bloodline, passed down from before even the birth of his grandparents' grandparents, and was supposed to be the legacy of his kin. A king was never supposed to surrender his birthright. That was the highest form of treason.

But on the other hand, the lack of mercy was suffocating him and his world. There was nothing left of his planet for him to fight for. Not that he'd get the chance to restore Nova or its people as their fate hung at his word.

He couldn't help but feel guilty as he looked over his people, huddled in masses with weapons pointed right at them. Soldiers from enemy lines yelled harshly at them as they waved guns and blasters in weeping faces, waiting for the verdict that would determine life or death for an entire civilization. Parents cast pleading looks toward their ruler on their grimy, bloodied faces as their terrified children cried in their laps.

Not far from the King's line of vision lay the scattered bodies of dead Novans, limp and faded. Mothers, fathers, sons, daughters, people. Lifeless.

That's what his planet was. Unsalvageable. He was unable to look into the eyes of anyone as he sighed in defeat. "We surrender. Just don't kill them, please."

The man who stood in the center of the seven twitched his lips upward slightly. "Good," he said, turning to his comrades, "let's get these people onto the ships. And off this deranged planet. I want reconstruction here now."

He turned to look at the former ruler, "As for you, I'm afraid that your services are no longer required by the Committee. You have been indefinitely removed from office."

Chapter 1

Location: Planet 2 – Kosmir, The Final Frontier
10 YEARS LATER

Seven beings sat around a large circular table with their backs pressed against their seats. Various expressions decorated their faces, ranging from intrigue and confusion to fear and dread. They were all silent, however, with gazes directed toward a glowing orange sphere that was as old as history itself.

Together, this unity formed The Committee, the most feared yet most highly respected beings amongst the stars, all with one sole objective: to save the universe.

In The Committee's eyes, the universe was filled with a plague—a lack of universal control. Where there is no control, there is chaos. Chaos was known to unfold to catastrophe, which bred war. The unity of The Committee cannot afford war, for the act of it has taken so much from them, and they would sacrifice anything and everything to prevent another war from happening again.

War brought instability, and the universe should be anything but that. Hence, the need for sole universal control. One ruler for all terrains to eliminate all forms of dispute whether political, economic, or social. One set of rules for everyone regardless of race, class, and gender.

However, with every attempt at peace, there was resistance, and they'd stretched their universal domain and goals to eliminate all who opposed their ideologies.

Countless rebels and fugitives had refused to see the fruits of their efforts, so they had been properly eliminated. However, that wasn't to say that there weren't rebels still scattered across the cosmos.

The ancient artifact was connected to the screen by a device that conducted searches throughout databases from all of the nine realms. Within minutes of scanning, a profile was projected onto it.

A hushed silence swept through the members of the organization. An image of planet Earth appeared, accompanied by the profile of a seventeen-year-old girl named Marah Morana.

The quiet was soon overcome with conversations amongst the seated, sounds of disbelief and perplexion conflicting with each other. How could someone from Earth have the capability to destroy everything that they stood for?

"That's not possible!" somebody shouted.

The sudden outburst encouraged everyone else to talk at once, tones reflecting a wide variety of emotions, silence long forgotten.

The member of the group who was seated at the center of the table stood up. Her shoulder-length hair, the color of bones, mirrored the frost in her irises as she smacked her hand down onto the table. The gesture allowed energy to race furiously across the table, mimicking the glow of malevolence in the Chairwoman's eyes. She clicked her tongue while raising her brow. "Done?"

Silence answered the Chairwoman's probe.

She then began to speak, in a tone that threatened anyone who dared to talk over her, "I know it is quite alarming for a human to be decoded as an enemy, but please, one at a time."

She sat back down, an indirect gesture for someone to start talking.

The members around the table nodded. The mortal seated across from the woman cleared his throat to speak.

The woman sent a nod to the Legionnaire.

"How can she, a mere human, be a threat to Kosmir? We are all beings with abilities that a human could only dream of! This must be a mistake!"

A masculine voice, betraying no emotion of shock, argued once Legionnaire Nial had finished. "There's no way the information can be wrong. This is the Poten we're talking about—it has been used for decades, centuries even, and never once has it made a mistake. The Poten predicted Nova would be the source for rebels and was it wrong? From the beginning, most rebellions were petty Novans. Even now, a Novan leads the rebellion."

He turned to the Legionnaire to his left, who hadn't spoken since the revelation. "What do you think, Jasna? You've been studying the Poten for years; surely you can make some sense out of this?"

Legionnaire Jasna sat with his back straight and brows furrowed as he looked into the Poten's light and then the screen. His eyes reflected the device's golden-orange glow as he spoke slowly but surely, "I do not know. One cannot understand the outputs of creation. We must accept it, logical or illogical."

Legionnaire Mizra, the youngest at the table, raised a hand from the sword that sat by her hip to her side. She pondered her thoughts before speaking, "The only question is why a human, of all beings, would pose a threat to us. We haven't done anything to the planet Earth, and humans are the lowest of all forms. They possess no special abilities; it doesn't add up."

"When does life ever make sense?" the white-haired woman, who had been first to speak, retorted. "Is the Poten ever wrong?"

Legionnaire Mizra shook her head. "Exactly, Chairwoman. The human is a threat to our successful control of the galaxy and must be taken out immediately. All we need to do is establish our eternal reign over Kosmir. We need to get to the girl before the rebels find out about her."

The white-haired woman hummed, "It's highly unlikely that they would have this information. We have the Poten. They have nothing to stop us. Even if they," she exaggerated, "somehow had some ability to do so, we can end this problem before they can get their hands on her."

The Chairwoman stood up now, and all attention was focused on her. She spoke carefully, experience weighting her words, "We must retrieve this girl before the rebels get hold of her. We cannot let anyone, especially a human—the lowest of all life forms in the galaxy—get in the way of the takeover of Kosmir."

Her audience of Legionnaires dipped their heads and brought closed fists over their hearts. "As you wish, Chairwoman Kate."

"Good," Chairwoman Kate concluded, to sounds of approval. "Ready up a team to locate this human so we can extract her and eliminate her before the rebels can find her. In the meantime, I'll interrogate our prisoners. Meeting adjourned. Get to work, we have much to do."

What The Committee failed to notice was the figure hiding in the vents, who just so happened to have heard every single word.

Chapter 2

Location: From the streets of Kosmir to the hidden uprising

The concealed figure listened carefully as The Committee discussed a potential threat to their dictatorship of a government. The figure's ears perked up. This person, whoever he or she was, would be essential to the rebel cause. *This person could be exactly what we need to save Kosmir!*

But from Earth?

The cloaked figure didn't get the chance to ponder the given information as The Committee continued talking. She leaned closer to the vents, still staying far enough back to avoid detection should anyone happen to look in her direction.

The sound of shuffling feet and metal being scraped against tiles indicated that the meeting was over. This meant that the hidden figure had to get out of there to avoid the possibility of being caught. If she were to be found, she would most likely be put to death—which was the last thing she and her cause needed.

She soundlessly scrambled through the air vents all the way to the shaft, which served as an exit to the outside world. Before exiting, she peeked outside to make sure that no one was looking in her direction.

Being careless compromised safety. Safety was costly and the figure knew it needed to be spent judiciously. Unfortunately, it seemed that every day there were more limitations on protecting her safety.

Long gone were the days of protestors who supported the rebel cause, but weren't actively in it, standing outside The Committee's headquarters. The Committee branded the rebels as the ultimate enemy, turning many angry souls into a distasteful silence.

But not her.

She pushed the grate and slipped out of the vents. After returning the grate to its original place, she wasted no time in heading toward her place of sanctuary. Luckily, the sun was beginning to set, which was to the girl's advantage, since fewer people would be roaming about should any of them see who she was.

She kept her hands curled in her pockets and her head dipped down as she walked on city streets. She hastened her pace as a gust of wind blew past her, causing a shiver to roll through her frame. Just as she bunched up the material of her hood, she heard the sound of a weapon humming to life.

Curiosity killed the cat, and the girl couldn't help but play the same risky game. She came to a halt, looking across the street where officers dressed in blue armor and guns threw open the door to a local shop and forced out a boy who had to be no older than sixteen.

The woman stiffened as she locked eyes with the boy, query after query forming in her head.

Are you okay? What's going on? she desperately wanted to ask.

The boy recognized her through her apparel and gave her a look to not interfere.

She knew that he was right—if she were caught then they would all be in trouble. Still, it didn't settle right with the blue-skinned Zonan to leave him behind and subject to the enemy's mercy.

"You're under arrest for suspicion of rebelling against The Committee," one officer announced.

Unfortunately for the cloaked woman, lurking about would only draw unwanted attention.

The boy flashed her a tight-lipped smile before contorting his features into a sneer as he was harshly picked up and his hands were slapped with cuffs.

She bore eye contact just enough for him to get the message before continuing on her path. While doing so, she couldn't help but think back to what she had just witnessed. The idea of it happening to her encouraged her to hasten her pace.

A breeze billowed past her, forcing her to tug her hood closer to her face. As she did so, a piece of paper flew straight toward her chest.

Narrow chocolate-colored eyes darted to the left and then the right as she scanned her surroundings, ensuring that no one was watching her. Once she was positive that the coast was clear, she caught the paper before it could collide into her and looked at it.

The paper had a picture of her face and the phrase "WANTED" scribbled in big black letters. She dipped her head down, crumpling the paper into a small ball and shoving it in her pocket. She could worry about that later. Right now, she was needed elsewhere.

She tugged the hood farther down her face, making sure to conceal her forehead and the stone-like marking that signaled her out before heading deeper into the planet's streets.

As she resumed her pace, she occasionally looked over her shoulder to calm her suspicious nerves, a habit she was forced to adopt. She eventually came to stop before crossing.

Nobody willingly used this street. That was what made it the perfect route in and out of her cause's headquarters. Still, with eyes everywhere, the blue-skinned Zonan couldn't just waltz right in through the front door. The building in front of her was an old, abandoned warehouse, at least from the outside. If someone were to get a glimpse of her entering, they'd definitely report her and expose the entire operation.

The cloaked woman inhaled sharply as she cast her gaze left and right to ensure that no one was eyeing her. Concealed by her dark-colored hood, she strained her eyes upward in search of any cameras perched on rooftops. Cameras, which The Committee claimed were for the protection of all Kosmirians, were really a tool to keep tabs on all of the citizens, especially ones that appeared to be rebel-like.

Once she was sure the path was safe to venture forth, she hurried to the warehouse across the street. She gently pressed the buzzer at the door.

"Code?"

"*Et aeterni.*"

The doors parted in half with a creaking sound, revealing an elevator. A smile tugged on Kiera's lips as she pressed the third button among five, and the elevator doors closed softly.

From the looks of the rusty architecture, it would be easy to assume that no one had been inside the facility for years, if not decades. From the interior, it was quite the contrary. The elevator softly chimed as the figure stepped out onto tiled flooring and withdrew her cloak. Her smile widened as she stepped toward bustling life.

Beings of different species and all ages from amongst the stars moved to and fro, reporting news of any valuable information that they had gathered. Some were scanning monitors, running their own diagnostics on whatever information could be utilized to aid their fight against The Committee. The rebels were anyone who didn't have anything left to lose.

They were usually widows, orphans, or those who chose to remain alone in The Committee's empire. Usually, the rebels were a more balanced group, but many had started families and intertwined lives, and their cost of protection was to give up the fight. Perhaps, it was to the rebels' benefit that the leading forces were the youth.

She cleared her throat to speak, bypassing formality with urgency. "I have urgent news. I need to speak to Leia and Natira right away."

A rebel immediately fetched the two operatives, and Kiera gestured for them to follow her to the closest empty room.

Natira was the first to break the silence. "What's going on?"

Kiera cut to the chase, "I found the asset. Her name is Marah Morana."

The oldest out of the three, Leia Halim, wore a tight smile at Kiera's news. Knowing how long they've waited for this news, she ran a hand down a braid that fell to her mid-back as she probed, "Where is she?"

Kiera's smile dissipated as the grim truth slipped out of her mouth: "Earth."

The joyous moment quickly snapped in half. "Earth?" Leia and Natira chorused in disbelief.

Kiera nodded, knowing of Earth's reputation. She found herself repeating the Chairwoman's exact words. "When has the Poten ever been wrong? We need to get to her before they do."

Leia and Natira looked like they wanted to disagree, but said nothing since Kiera had a point.

"So, a human is supposed to be the biggest threat to The Committee's existence," concluded Natira tightly. "Was there anything special about her that you could see?"

Kiera rested her arms across her chest. "She had a weapon, but weapons aren't what makes one special." The Zonan continued as she met the gaze of her friends, "It's not one's abilities or powers, but something about their character. Say Marah has the character and the ability to help us; how do we know that she will be willing to do so?" She paused. "I mean, we can't force her to fight this battle if she doesn't want to. After all, this isn't her fight."

Leia's Novan lilac eyes darkened. "It is now. The Committee knows about her, and they're probably planning to kill her so she can't be of use to us. She's in danger, whether she likes it or not. We can't force her, but we can explain the situation to her. I think she will understand and help us. If not, we'll have to try and get her to." She sighed, rubbing her temple. "We need as much help as possible if we want to end The Committee's reign. It's not going to be any easier sitting and hoping that Marah will work with us, but we have to try."

The Nantak, Natira folded her arms across her chest, meeting Kiera's eyes. "You observed her. Do you think she has what it takes to help us?"

Kiera was silent as she pondered the question. That's the thing, isn't it? But does it matter if she's not? If she wants to help, that would be good enough for me. But if she's doesn't, then that's that, isn't it?"

The purple-eyed Novan and the Nantak clad in black nodded. "You need to tell the others," said Leia, "then you need to go."

Kiera stood and returned to the main room where all eyes were on her.

"I went to spy on The Committee," she announced, "to gather some sort of intel on anyone that might be key to taking them down. I overheard some valuable information. They identified a being that serves as a great threat to them. Her name is Marah Morana, a seventeen-year-old girl." She sucked in a breath as she cast her eyes to the tiled floor. "From Earth."

The room broke into murmurs and whispers. How could the person who would have such high significance to one of the most important causes in the universe's history come from such a primitive planet?

One of the rebels spoke up. "How can you be so sure? It's Earth! They still haven't grasped the concept that there are other beings besides them! And humans don't have any abilities! There's no way she can help us—this has to be a mistake! Are you absolutely positive that a human can contribute to our cause?"

Kiera sighed. "I'm just as surprised as you are. A human helping a rebel cause? That's like bringing a toaster to war. But you and I both know that the Poten doesn't make mistakes, and it's feeding The Committee the information that they need to conquer the galaxy. There has to be something special about her if the Poten chose her. There was some more information on her that I couldn't make out, but it had The Committee scared. We can use that to our advantage. As much as I'd love to talk this out, we always knew that there was someone capable of ending The Committee. We never knew who, so we can't make assumptions, can we?"

She was answered with murmurs and whispers of agreement.

"And since The Committee already has her location, I have no doubt that they are going to attempt to eliminate her, which means that we have to act first. Ready me a ship to her location," she ordered with a slight nod.

"I have *The Fortem* ready to go at your word," informed one of the people in the crowd, whose emerald skin was decorated with pink locks of shoulder-length hair.

Kiera nodded. "Excellent," she concluded. "Have Joven prepare a room for Marah."

Rebels began scattering to their posts and assembling into their teams. Each rebel needed to be at optimum efficiency; the slightest error could jeopardize not only the mission but the entire cause. Kosmir, the largest planet in the galaxy, would be doomed. They all swore to defy The Committee for as long as they lived, and they intended to do so.

Kiera walked towards the ship; determination set in her blue features. Her cloak billowed from the wind of the ship as she entered it. "You ready?" she greeted the pilot.

"Always," laughed the pilot as she flipped a switch on the ship's center console, causing *The Fortem* to roar to life. "Where are we going?"

Kiera grinned as she pressed a button on her watch, projecting a holographic keyboard in front of her. "Marah Morana."

The alien sounded out the name, typed the letters out into her corresponding language, and double-clicked the button. Instantly, a hologram of the planet Earth appeared and zoomed into smaller masses of land. Kiera watched, intrigued, as a point formed on the map with a city name that sounded funny on her alien tongue: "It appears the target location is Sacramento, California, Earth."

The pilot hummed as she pulled a lever back, opening the facility's ceiling. With a click of a button, thrusters pushed *The Fortem* up and out of Kosmir's atmosphere.

Earth was in close proximity to Kosmir's moons, Qamar and Lux, and with Tessa's skilled flying, Kiera knew she'd catch a glimpse of the planet soon.

She leaned forward in her seat as her eyes glazed over various hues of purple, blue and black. The vessel was minutes from Earth. She couldn't help but harbor worry.

Earth wasn't like most planets. Earth wasn't even aware that there were other planets like it in its solar system. Kiera doubted humans were even aware of other solar systems. She was never one to judge, but she couldn't help wondering if what she had heard was a mistake.

"Let's see what you're all about," Kiera hummed while pressing a different button on her watch, causing a projection of Marah Morana to appear. Colored pixels depicted black and white hair and eyes the color of the greenest grass freckled in the sun's golden rays. The girl appeared to be running with a piece of metal in her hand.

This intrigued Kiera.

As she leaned forward to try and get a better look at the unfamiliar object in Marah's hand, Tessa announced that she was preparing for landing.

The rebel nodded and turned the hologram off, directing her attention to the window. It displayed the milky blue and green hues of the planet that she knew so little about. *There's so much blue; what's inside?*

"Strange, isn't it?"

Tessa turned to look at Kiera.

"The humans live on such a large planet. A planet of so many colors. It's amazing. They must really care for their planet."

"Still doesn't make them any less strange."

Kiera laughed as the mounds of colors took on lines and new shades, indicating that she was getting closer to answering the questions she had about Marah Morana.

The landing wasn't as soft as Kiera had anticipated; then again, the alien didn't expect Earth to have the technology for magnetic flooring to prevent such a landing. She stood up as the hatch in the back of the vessel opened, "Use the camouflage tech, but keep your comm on. Humans are supposedly everywhere."

Kiera didn't wait for Tessa to reply as she headed to the back, pausing as she looked out of the door to a surplus of greenery in different forms. *Is the humans' need for oxygen so great that they require an abundance of foliage? Interesting.*

The rebel hopped off the ship, landing on soft soil that made the bottoms of her shoes sink. She turned back to the pilot, flashing a thumbs-up, and within seconds *The Fortem* was no longer visible.

She looked down at the strange soil that clung to her boots and picked it up with her fingers. The substance stretched out in all directions, she noticed. Its softness starkly contrasted with the stone walkways of Kosmir to which she was accustomed.

She clicked a button on her watch and zoomed in on the location of Marah Morana, pointing north. Draping her hood back over her head, she trekked off in search of the rebellion's possible savior.

Chapter 3

Location: Planet 1 - Earth, The Final Frontier
Sacramento, California

The autumn atmosphere was crisp and warm, at a temperature where the sun's rays were heavy enough to beg skin to not be covered but just light enough to send an occasional breeze rustling by.

The day was just as ordinary as yesterday, and all of the days before it. The sun shone brightly from above, soaking everything underneath in its golden rays. Birds perched on branches chirped their melodies and the trees continued their transformation from summer to fall.

A figure stalked through the woods; one hand fastened around the grip of a bow and the other green-sleeved hand resting loosely against her side.

She trod forward, purposely stepping on amber and yellowish-green leaves that made crunching sounds as the soles of her boots scraped against the colored roughness. An autumn breeze billowed past her, sending leaves rustling into the air.

The girl began to smile as the leaves danced around her, a vivacious cacophony of red, orange, yellow, and green picked up into the wind current and flew past her vision. The hood of her coat lifted and fluttered against the back of her head, causing wisps of her hair to brush her shoulders.

Her eyes fell shut as a warm sigh softly slipped out of her lips. She inhaled as she dug her boots into the ground, and then exhaled, a blissful sensation of pure tranquility. It was just her and nature.

However, the aura of serenity was short-lived as a snort rippled through the air.

The figure stilled as her eyes shot open. *A boar.* Judging by the increasingly loud thumping sound, the girl realized that the animal was heading right in her direction; the playful mood was long gone as Marah Morana crouched low behind a tree, taking care not to make a sound.

Somewhat hidden, Marah slowly raised her bow while slipping her other hand over her shoulder to pluck an arrow out of its quiver. She soundlessly drew the arrow back against her bowstring, maintaining a firm grip as she waited for the animal to appear.

Marah's eyes narrowed, focusing straight ahead of her where the sound of snuffling was emanating from. She adjusted the level of her bow, preparing for the boar to come out from behind the trees.

Live on your own, they said, it's easy. Have they seen the price of meat these days?

She drew the bow fully back as another snuffling snort reached her eardrums. It was close.

She slowed her breathing, preparing to lose the arrow.

Three.

Two.

One.

And shoot!

The boar charged out of the undergrowth, its flesh colliding with Marah's arrowhead piece. It sprawled as it crashed to the ground, loudly squealing.

Marah remained where she was, her hand unconsciously moving toward her quiver in case the animal wasn't alone.

As she was about to go retrieve the carcass that would fill her freezer, the sound of multiple snorts and squeals, accompanied by the crashing of multiple bodies coming through the brush reached her ears.

Neither she nor the boar was alone.

Knowing it was foolish to tangle with a herd of wild boars and their sharp tusks, Marah took off in the opposite direction the boar had come from. As she darted between trees and scanned the woods for any other potential threats or resources, she heard the solitary crunching of a footfall upon leaves. The sound was light, suggesting that the foot belonged to some*one*, instead of some*thing*.

Marah bolted. No one ever came into these woods.

She sucked in a breath, fingers turning red from how tight she was holding her bow. She waited with bated breath as the sound of footsteps came closer. There was something strange about the footsteps: the person would take a step and then pause, as if confused about where they were.

Not many people would want to come here. Possibilities? A random dude, a hunter, or have I been trespassing all this time?

Marah considered bolting. She saw this ending in one of two ways. If the person were a hunter, they'd probably shoot first and ask questions later. Or they might realize that she wasn't an animal—at least, not one to be eaten—and leave her to her own devices. *Unless they're a cannibal.*

She almost scoffed. *What are the chances of that?*

Or the person could be an officer. *Juvie doesn't sound comfortable at all. Orange is definitely not my color.*

The sound of crunching leaves became louder, despite the slow movement. The lightness of the footsteps suggested to Marah that whoever the person was did not want to be found, or at least not easily. This meant that the person was looking for something - or someone.

"Marah Morana?" the person muttered in a feminine voice. "Am I in the right place? Is this tracker working?"

Marah felt herself shrink. Whoever this person, they obviously knew her. How, was something she would like to know. She spoke stiffly, trying to conceal the panic within her as her hands opened and closed unsurely, "Come out where I can see you."

She was met with silence. Her ears didn't pick up the sound of footsteps anymore, which drew her to the conclusion that the mystery person was no longer moving. There were two possibilities as to what was going to happen next. The first being that the person would admit their business and then be on their way. The second being that the person wouldn't say anything—and then she'd probably get kidnapped.

Marah decided to call out again, unsure if the person had heard her the first time. "Who are you and what are you doing in my woods?" Not that the woods were hers, but they might as well have been since she was the only person she knew who used them.

Still no response.

"I have a weapon and I'm not afraid to use it." The girl hoped she sounded as confident as she thought she did.

She was met with silence. Again.

This is totally not creepy.

She turned her head slightly, hazel eyes trying to make out some of the mysterious person's appearance. When she caught a glimpse of skin the color of seafoam, Marah quickly dropped to her heels as she contemplated what she knew was impossible. *Supposed to be impossible, at least.*

"You're seeing things," she whispered in disbelief. "There's no way a person could have skin whatever color that is."

She furtively looked back and was met with what was definitely a blue forehead that had some kind of marking on it. At first, she wondered if the being that she was looking at was a girl that was really into, and good at, cosplay when the art looked too good to be real. For one, the blue paint didn't really look like paint. Paint tended to run off in places or have varying amounts of concentration, but the blue the woman coated herself in was perfect. Too perfect even for someone who must've spent hours applying it.

The woman lifted her wrist to reveal a band that Marah could only describe as a watch that displayed a projection of her face. She gulped, willing herself not to take off running.

Crouched behind a tree, she watched the being survey her surroundings, no doubt looking for her. The being confirmed Marah's suspicions when she heard them say: "The tracker confirms that I am close to Marah."

Marah must've not been as good at hiding as she thought since the alien then raised her voice while facing her direction, "I know aliens like me look scary, but I can assure you that I mean no harm. Can you please stand up from behind the tree?"

An alien? They're real? Marah stood up slowly and found herself taking a step toward the creature. Intrigued, she ignored her gut feeling to run the hell away without looking back.

She took another step forward and bit her lip. The more steps she took, the more her stomach began to churn. She yawned, feeling tired all of a sudden. It was a strange feeling. She had woken up no more than a few hours ago; it was impossible that she could be tired already. It was as if her bodily processes were slowing down against their will.

Except, that was exactly what was happening.

Sleep, murmured a foreign-sounding voice inside her mind.

Marah shook her head as she argued with the voice. "I'm not tired."

As soon as she had spoken, she swayed on her feet, dragging an arm to a tree to keep herself standing upright.

The alien remained perfectly still, watching her curiously as she bent her fingers in a rhythmic manner.

"What are you doing to me?" Marah's words spilled out in loose fragments as she continued to move forward, despite the fuzzy feelings in her chest. "What are you?"

She staggered, nearly tripping over her feet. As black dots freckled her vision, she flung out an arm against a branch to regain her balance. The hood of her coat fell off as she shook her head in an attempt to clear her sight.

The human immediately regretted doing so, as all she ended up with was more darkness and bile creeping up her throat.

Sleep.

Marah bent over as her vision spun in circles and she tried to fight the voice's command. She huffed as she slowly stood back up, pressing a hand and a knee against the bark of a tree until she felt steady enough to move.

Though the trees in front of her began to sway, and her numb limbs continued to protest, Marah took a step toward the blue-skinned creature.

Sleep, the voice commanded, slightly less patiently than before.

Marah was now facing the creature, who definitely didn't look human. "Stop it," she tried to say, but her voice was slurred, and before she knew it, darkness sank into her mind and caged her.

Chapter 4

Location: From the lowest planet in the stars to the home of
the orphans

Kiera looked down at Marah Morana, who she was dragging behind her. She returned to the area where she had landed, and *The Fortem* materialized out of thin air.

She boarded the ship and set the human in a seat, pulling a belt over Marah's unconscious body to prevent her from falling out of it.

"Do you think that she will be able to help us?" the pilot asked, as Kiera buckled her own belt.

Kiera sighed softly. "I don't know," she admitted. "You and I both know that the Poten doesn't make mistakes. There's something about her, I can feel it." Unsure who she was trying to convince, she opted to let hope die on her tongue, "We should get going before The Committee gets here."

The pilot flashed a look at Marah Morana before revving up the engine. "For Kosmir's sake, I pray that she can help us."

Kiera said nothing as *The Fortem* picked up and sailed out of Earth's atmosphere.

The Zonan leaned back in her seat, indulging in her thoughts. Something was nagging her, and she couldn't help but look back at the human and wondered if this was all a mistake.

"Tessa?"

"Yeah, boss?" the pilot hummed.

"If we're right about her, what happens?"

"If she's the threat The Committee makes her out to be, then we can avenge everything and everyone that we lost. Who knows? Maybe we'll save the universe."

Kiera nodded, staring off into space as bits of meteors whirred past her vision. "And if we're wrong?"

"Then we kidnapped someone who will probably put us all in danger. She'll either prove to not be what we need, or we let her go back to Earth, where we can't guarantee that she won't expose us. Either way, it's a risk, if you ask me."

Kiera nodded, turning to face Tessa. "Knowing all of this, is it a risk you would be willing to take?"

Tessa smiled cheekily. "For everything and everyone that we lost, we either succeed in avenging them or we die trying. What part of our lives isn't a risk?"

Kiera smiled a tiresome smile, satisfied with the answer.

Minutes after The Fortem exited Earth's upper atmosphere, Earth had its second alien encounter.

The Committee descended upon the most insignificant of the galaxy's realms in an invisible aircraft, hovering above the apartment complex that the Poten deciphered to be their source for extraction. Inside, Legionnaire Mizra, a lissome woman which suited her position as well as her sport, gripped the hilt of a sheathed sword as she looked down on the ant-sized people of Earth.

The youngest of the Chairwoman's Legionnaires dreamed of this day for years. Her mother had used the sword strapped to her side to aid the conquest of Nova and given it to her to continue The Committee's legacy the day she became of age a year ago. When her mother died last year, she eagerly accepted Chairwoman Kate's offer to take her place and waited for the day when she could be assigned something grand for The Committee.

Mizra only wished that the conquest she had finally been awarded had been grander than Earth. It was the reason the other Legionnaires passed the job on to her. As distasteful as the world was, she would continue the work of her mother's sword.

"This," she breathed out unimpressed as she stared at contrasts of blues and greens that were peppered in wispy whites and concrete grays, "is pathetic. They have nothing special about them except for their aptitude to fight and corrupt each other."

She walked toward the aircraft's doors, footsteps signaling the doors to open for her. Shoulder-length denim blue hair was tied together behind her ears before she jumped out of the ship, into a freefall, and soundlessly landed atop the building's roof. Clad in her uniform and sword now in hand, her mauve irises scanned the scene, utterly unimpressed.

Children occupied a box of water while their parents sat on lounge chairs or on some flimsy device basking in the sun.

It was pathetic, she thought. If the mission had been to conquer Earth, it would've only taken seconds. The humans she observed had no care for who could be lurking among them or what capabilities they possessed.

She looked past the scene to see an endless row of transportation—smaller than the box of water, but still box-like in shape—sitting, unmoving.

Those in the middle of the streets, she noted, moved based on flashes of color while those on the sides couldn't be bothered to move with any flash of color.

No wonder humans are so primitive; they can't even make their transportation work properly. Now, to find the human.

"You," the Kosmirian declared, advancing toward the closest human in sight.

The man had the audacity to not respond, focused on an even smaller box in his hand.

The Legionnaire would've assumed it to be a phone, but it seemed to lack all the things her phone could do.

Scoffing, she thrust out her sword, knocking the device to the ground.

The man made a sound of shock before whirling around to face her. He eyed her strangely, which Mizra took offense at. She flicked her wrist, lifting the blade to the human's neck. Now, she had the attention of everyone.

"How dare you," she seethed. "Can humans not even hear properly?"

The man shoved her blade down. "What's your deal, cosplay?"

She ignored the man's insult. "Where can I find Marah Morana?"

"Apartment 38."

"Where?"

The man blinked. "Downstairs, duh. Also, take it easy with the sword."

"Mind your place, human." The woman turned away from the man and descended down the filthiest and most basic stairs she had ever seen in her life. The dimly lit room displayed no apartment, rather an elevator that revealed a child gawking at her.

"Move," she yanked the child out before taking her place. "Apartment 38," she stated, waiting for the doors to close.

Instead, she remained where she was. She cleared her throat as the child stared at her in confusion, "I said, take me to apartment 38."

She knew Earth had insignificant technology compared to Kosmir, but this was too much. She was moments away from cursing everything and everyone on this damn planet when the child she threw out piped up, "You have to press the button."

The answer seemed so obvious and yet a waste of time.

Mizra held up her hand when the child moved to step inside. "Simply tell me what I need to press."

"If my math is correct," the child started.

Mizra groaned, "What are you humans effective at?"

"38 is less than forty so it will be on the third floor."

Mizra didn't bother concealing her exasperation, "What button do I press?"

The child held up three fingers which the Kosmirian took to mean the button with a three on it.

"Good riddance," she exhaled as the doors finally shut and she experienced the slowest elevator ride in her lifetime.

Sighing, the Legionnaire rested her hands on her hips as she waited for the elevator to come to a stop. Once the elevator showed the slightest indication of stopping, she pushed the doors open with her bare hands and stepped into the corridor.

She followed a directory down the hall, not stopping until she spotted a door marked 38. She kicked down the door and stalked onto wooden flooring. With the rhythm and manner of a soldier, her eyes scanned her surroundings as she moved past cabinets and kitchen furniture and headed into the central space of the room, where a sofa and table sat in front of a TV. She inspected an open book on the table that listed the human's agenda and threw it onto the floor. Resting against a bookcase were books of varying color and thickness and shaped figures.

The act purposefully made a sound. Mizra remained still, waiting for the so-called threat that was Marah Morana to emerge.

With no response, Mizra could only assume the human was still sleeping. She swatted the door to the side with her sword and looked upon an empty room. She ransacked the apartment turning everything upside down looking for her. With the human nowhere in sight, she tapped the wristband on her wrist and said the human's name.

A beam extended from the band, scanning the entire apartment and revealed a set of footprints that detailed what Marah had done until Mizra's arrival. The only set of footprints that mattered were the ones that led out the door. Shoving her mother's sword in its sheath, she stormed under the sun all the way to the woods where the footsteps abruptly disappeared with no reasonable explanation.

Except, for one.

Aggravated, Mizra raised the band which depicted footsteps that belonged to a familiar Zonan. Sighing, she double tapped the band and waited for a mere second for the ship that had brought her to this useless world to pull her back up and take off for Kosmir.

Chapter 5

Location: Kosmir

Where am I?

Marah Morana's eyes slowly fluttered open as she took in unfamiliar surroundings. She didn't recognize where she was or how she got here, and the confusion was evident in her scrunched-up facial features. As she slowly processed what had happened, she recalled whatever memories she had of the day.

My alarm clock wouldn't shut the hell up and then I went to the woods for a little hunting and saw an alien?

Marah rubbed her eyes, remembering only darkness from there.

Disoriented and woozy, her body responded to the unfamiliar environment a second faster than her mind. She reacted instinctively, letting her eyes flutter shut for a few moments so she could rid herself of black dots that threatened her vision.

However, reality seeped in through her other senses. The room had no smell, unlike the airy moisture of the woods that she was accustomed to. There were no sounds to lock onto, except for her shallow breathing that was in tune to her racing heart. Once she could open her eyes without seeing spots, she moved to sit up.

As she did so, a pained wince had her moving a hand to the back of her throbbing head and noticed that her bow was on a table next to her.

She frowned. She didn't own a table that looked like it belonged in a hospital. She looked down, and the curve of her frown deepened as she found herself sitting on a bed that didn't belong to her.

"Where the hell am I?" Marah swung her legs off the bed and moved to grab her bow. The first thing she noticed was that the door was entirely clear, which allowed her to look over the people in the facility with her as they walked past.

Only, the people didn't look like people. They looked odd, with multi-colored skin and facial features that Marah knew had to be inhuman, a lot like the alien she swore she saw back in the woods.

Did the alien bring me here?

Fear slowly creeping through her veins, Marah's breath caught in her dry throat. With her back pressed against the farthest wall from the door, she could only whisper, "This is definitely *not* California."

Am I dreaming? How?

The human sucked in a breath in an attempt to regain her composure. She knew that panicking wouldn't get her anywhere and, if anything, could put her in danger. The more she looked at these strange people with tails, antennas, and vibrant skin colors, the more she knew that she had to get the hell out of here.

Except she was in alien territory—pun fully intended—with no clue as to how she was supposed to get out.

Do they not see me?

Marah tentatively walked toward the door, unsure if anyone was watching her. *Did they take my blood or implant an egg in me, and now they are going to observe what happens to me? I knew the government was a liar. How the hell do superheroes on TV act like this is nothing?*

She continued to walk, expecting to be stopped, but to her surprise, nothing happened. She couldn't help but look past the door, where aliens walked past her without paying her the slightest of attention. She took another step forward. The doors pulled apart from each other, causing her to flinch, closing her eyes in anticipation of something to happen. After waiting for a few moments, she opened her eyes to find herself all alone.

There was no loud blaring of an alarm. There was no sign of a bunch of aliens ready to shoot her down without asking any questions. Nor was there any shock that was going to render her unconscious for whatever the aliens had planned for her next. Just an open door.

Marah breathed out quietly in disbelief. "Well, that was easy."

Hesitating, she turned back to the window and saw everyone still engaged in their own activities. Which meant that there was a high chance that she could escape easily without getting caught by whoever brought her here.

Her stomach churned as she rocked back on her heels, unsure of what her plan for escape was. *If I'm being honest, I didn't think I would get this far.*

"If you act like you know what you're doing, you can get out easily," she reassured herself. "You've seen this happen a billion times in the movies. Hold back and you'll get stuck." She tightened her grip on her bow, grateful to have her most trusted ally.

She sucked in a breath, trying to calm the butterflies in her stomach, "On three."

"One."

She exhaled slowly. "Two."

"Three!"

Marah bolted out of the door and ran as fast as her legs would take her. She wasn't sure which way she was going, but she dismissed the worry. She kept running along the hallway's tiled flooring, spotting a sign she presumed meant exit. *And that's my ticket out of here!*

Her feeling of relief was short-lived as a voice behind her called out, "Hey, stop!"

Marah didn't need to turn around to know that the voice was addressing her. She grimaced. *So much for an easy escape.* She wasted no time in spurring her legs on to move faster, running wherever the hallway took her, for better or for worse.

She didn't bother replying, huffing as her steps became heavier and more forceful. *This is really not my day.*

And as far as I know, this is only the beginning.

She came to a halt as the hallway opened to a multitude of people—for simplicities sake, that's what she had decided on calling them—since quite frankly, she had no clue what on Earth was going on. *For starters, am I even on Earth?*

The sound of footsteps echoed against her eardrums, reminding the human of her dilemma. She ducked through the crowd, hoping that whoever was chasing her wouldn't catch up to her. She paused briefly in search of an exit.

A male with short, floppy hair skidded to a halt at the sight of her. "Marah!"

Reactively, Marah spun around to a face that was in no way human and shook her head frantically.

"Kiera, Natira," he called out, gaining the attention of a being Marah recognized from earlier today and another girl with choppy, white hair in a leather jacket. "I have an update on Marah!"

With that, all eyes were on Marah. She turned on her heels, pushing past beings with tails and other features she didn't know how to describe while the two beings that were called out followed her.

"Marah, wait!" one of them appealed.

Marah did not wait. Instead, she ran faster. Her heartbeat thudded faster and louder as she scanned her surroundings in search of an exit.

She made a sharp right turn, trying to throw off whoever was following her. Instead, the sound of thudding footsteps resumed, indicating that her chaser was getting closer. Just as she was about to run through the glass doors, the alien Marah swore she had seen back in the woods appeared out of thin air in front of her.

Marah skidded to a halt to avoid crashing into the being. She was definitely the same alien from before. Disbelief was thick in her tone as she eyed the blue-skinned alien warily. "You again? Why did you bring me here?"

The alien made no effort to answer her question. Instead, a voice shouted from behind them, "Kiera, do you have her?"

As Kiera replied, Marah made a move to run the opposite way only to be cornered by a figure who had to be Natira wearing a no-nonsense look.

Kiera said nothing as she moved to touch Marah.

This time, Marah was faster as she dodged the touch. *Not this time!*

She pushed Kiera away from her and moved to get to the doors, but the blue-skinned girl grazed the human's arm. That was all it took for Marah to feel fuzzy all over once more as she trudged a couple of steps forward, mumbling, "Not this again!"

The effects were much faster than the first time as she swayed on her feet. Thinking became hard, and her eyes rolled to the back of her head as her frame slackened against Kiera.

A voice called out: *Wake up, Marah.*

Were it any other dream, she imagined she'd have some reaction of protest. Instead, her mind seemed eager to wake. She usually relished sleep, so she assumed that this was the first part of their experimentation on her taking effect.

Coming to, she heard a voice say, "I don't know when she'll wake, Natira, human biology isn't the same as ours."

With that, Marah's eyes flashed open as she bolted upright, ogling the three non-humans in front of her. "Get the hell away from me!" she exclaimed as she frantically reached for her bow and held it defensively in front of her.

She moved toward the door only for a girl who resembled a human, with the exception of the mauve tints of her irises, to stand between her and the door. Seriousness was written all over the girl's features, from the tightness of her plump lips to a semi-wrinkled nose. Her knitted brows stood against skin the shade of sunlit sand.

She scanned the girl from top to bottom. *Purple eyes—that's witchcraft. Does that mean I'm about to become a witch? No thanks, I sure love being human, thank you very much.*

Marah was paralyzed in disbelief as she looked at the three beings who looked less and less human than the one with blue-green skin; one had silver tattoos, and the other had purple hair.

No friggin' way.

Words spewed out of her mouth unconsciously as the human tried to make sense of the scene in front of her, "What the hell? What the hell? What the hell?" She ignored the slight tremble that wouldn't leave her skin, "What the—"

Marah was cut off by the gray-eyed, clad-in-black girl in the middle, who spoke rather stiffly, "Hell? You've made that very clear."

"Any other words you'd be more comfortable with?" retorted Marah.

"There are worse things than hell," was all the girl with platinum hair and black clothes replied.

Marah bit her lip, still unsure where to look or who to look at. "Still doesn't explain what's going on. This has to be some sort of dream. Did I really get kidnapped by aliens?" Her eyes narrowed. "Are you with the Secret Service or something?"

"What's a secret service?" With a look of confusion, Kiera leaned toward Natira and inquired, "Do the humans call us the secret service?"

Natira shook her head. "I believe the term they coin for us is extraterrestrial. Or the abbreviation, alien."

"It's not an abbreviation." Marah hesitated, inching further away from the beings in front of her. Maybe it was. Everything she knew was now false, she supposed she may as well know nothing. She was still unable to believe what she was witnessing.

She was quiet for a few moments before speaking slowly, "So you're aliens. This is real?" She pressed herself against a wall, fingers unconsciously pulling on her quiver strap as she mumbled for herself to wake up.

The one clad in purple replied to Marah's discomfort. "Well, Marah," she spoke kindly, "my name is Leia. You already met Kiera on Earth, and this," indicating the tough one in the middle, "is Natira. Yes, this is real. And, yes, aliens did kidnap you."

Bitterness filled Marah's tone as she looked up at the ceiling. "Great. So, the government is a liar, totally saw that coming." She faced her three kidnappers, "What's next, the sky isn't actually blue?"

Kiera raised a finger. "Actually…"

Marah looked at Kiera, eyes widening.

Leia resumed, "I'm from the planet Nova. Natira is from Nantak. Kiera is Zonan. And now, you're on Kosmir."

Natira swiped a lock of platinum hair behind her ear as she made eye contact with Marah, who forced her gaze to meet the alien's eyes, not the silver tattoos that peeked out of leather sleeves.

Kiera awkwardly waved. "Hello…well…formally this time. You're probably wondering why we brought you here."

Ah yes, that would be the million-dollar question.

Kiera paused, unsure of how she was supposed to explain.

Marah's brow quirked, getting the impression that the aliens in front of her were as clueless as her. She wasn't sure if that was a good thing or not.

Finally, the Zonan spoke. "We brought you here because your life is in danger."

Marah rolled her eyes. "No judgment here, but I don't exactly feel safe at the moment." She didn't hide the venom in her tone as she continued, "And my life is in danger because?" She crossed her arms across her chest and pinched herself. *Ouch. Nope. I'm still here on this alien planet. Fantastic!*

Natira inspected her chipped fingernails as she began to explain, "Your life is in danger because The Committee, a very dangerous group of people, want to hurt you so they can continue their plan to take over the universe."

"That sucks," interrupted Marah, "but how does this involve me? I'm human, not alien."

"They have the Poten." Kiera's response did nothing to wipe the confusion off the human's face. "It's a technology that is used to find potential threats to their government. You are on that list."

Marah scoffed as her gaze moved from the three aliens. "And why the hell would I be on this list? Up until this very moment, I didn't believe in aliens." *Can I go home now, or do I have to sit here and listen to this? I have way better things to do. I wonder if I make a joke about all of this, they'll laugh. Not going to lie, these people look like they could really use one.*

Leia shrugged. "Beats us. However, what's important is that you are on this list, for whatever reason that may be. Which puts you in direct danger, but also means that we need your help to take them down."

"My help?" Marah would have laughed if Leia's face didn't look like she was dead serious.

The violet-haired girl nodded. "Yes, your help. We are a rebellion group determined to end The Committee. And we have reason to believe that you are the key to taking them down."

She paused, awkwardly proposing the question that would change Marah's life, "So, what do you have to say?"

Marah was incredulous as she shook her head. "This isn't my fight. I'm supposed to be on my planet, living the same life I've lived for years, not dragged into some intergalactic space fight." Hostility and stiffness seeped into her voice. "Can I go now? Or am I being held hostage?"

From the start, Leia had the body language of a leader and now her words did. She was as firm as she was frank, "Marah, I know this is a lot to take in. I can't imagine what you're feeling, being that we kidnapped you and are now asking you to leave your home and fight for and against aliens. This is very…"

"Crazy? Insane?"

"I suppose so. But," she met the human's eyes, "we really need your help. You are what the rebellion needs."

Sensing that her words weren't appealing to Marah, the Novan made a last-ditch attempt. "What happens when The Committee decides they want to take over Earth?"

Marah defended herself as hazel eyes met purple ones. "Then they do. Look, I don't know much about whatever this is, but I don't really care." She pointed her bow's upper limb at Kiera, "You brought me here from my own home, and I don't really even know who you are—or where I am for that matter—and now you want me to just agree with you on your whole takedown of some all-knowing, high-powered government?" She remained defiant. "No thanks. All I want to do is be back home in my regular life, where all of this is a fever dream, and I am completely unaware of how many *Buzzfeed Unsolved* conspiracies are true. So, if you'll excuse me, I need to go home. Now." The last word rolled off rather rudely, but Marah didn't have the heart to care.

She was tired and overwhelmed with the surplus of broken realities. She moved a hand to her head and rubbed at the slight throbbing from *whatever the hell that alien did to me*. She stepped forward and Leia followed suit, still adamant about not taking no for an answer.

The Novan wore empathy. "This is a lot to take in, we know and we're sorry. But, we need your help. We need you. If I were you, I'd be acting the same way. We can address all of your questions and fill you in on anything you'd like to know. You're not totally in the dark, you," she countered on her fingers, "you know our names, you know where you are—the planet Kosmir. Habitants of this planet are called Kosmirians, but most identify themselves via their birth planet. You also know that you're wanted," she cringed, "and we are the only ones who can protect you from The Committee."

"Because some sort of supercomputer said so?" Marah responded to the head nods by saying, "That's like bringing a hole puncher to a gunfight."

Letting Marah's words sink in, Leia nodded. "Yeah."

Marah stifled a groan. *Do aliens not understand the meaning of the word, no?* None of this made any sense, nor was she eager for it all to make sense. She had no desire in leaving her home to live with the beings that kidnapped her. *Plus, who wants to fight a war?*

One thing was clear, the chances of her being allowed to leave were slim to none. There was only one answer and Marah hated that it wasn't the right one. Sighing sourly with a shrug, she gave in. "I don't think I have a choice, so alright. But, once all of this is over, I get to go home."

Leia nodded. "Sure, that's fair."

Kiera opened her mouth—to ask a question, Marah assumed—but she decided against it. There was a moment of awkward silence with the three aliens looking at each other and

Marah at them, each waiting for someone to say something.

Marah watched Leia move on from the hard part of convincing her. "So, this is the rebel base, where we do everything. We can give you a room to stay in and you can get settled. Then we can fill you in on everything else later."

"Sure," was all Marah said, looking away from the rebels. "The superhero movies make this much cooler, but alright."

Immediately Kiera questioned, "I'm fairly certain that I will ask questions about Earth a lot, and my first one will be: what is a superhero?" She eyed Marah with curiosity.

Marah wore confusion. "You guys are aliens, and you've never heard of a superhero? It's someone, a human or alien, who usually has powers, like you three." *This is ridiculous.* "How have you never heard of a superhero before?"

She was met with blank looks and a retort from Natira. "Superhero? That sounds childish and boring."

Marah rolled her eyes indignantly. *Well, aren't you a ball of sunshine?* "C'mon, this is classic Earth stuff. They even have people with powers who fight bad guys, just like I assume you all do. Y'know?" She wore a pointed expression, unable to believe the fact that aliens didn't know how many movies involved aliens.

The three girls looked at her as if she was the alien here. Which ironically, she was.

"Oh, come on!" Marah set her bow down and looked at the aliens with disbelief. "Some creature that either looks like a human or you know," she winced, struggling to find delicate wording. "Things, er, people who can do oddly-specific and special things that no one else can? Heroes, aliens even, are in…like…every other movie on Earth."

Nothing but silence.

She sighed, giving up. She sat back down on the bed, deciding to ask a different question. "What do you know about Earth? This stuff is like everything for us."

"About as much as humans care to know about us," Natira replied flatly. "The Committee doesn't find your species relevant."

Marah glanced at Kiera who winced. "The people who you say want to kill me? Cool."

She mentally cringing at the awkward silence that ensued. "So, what's our plan for this whole thing? Take down The Committee?" She pulled out an arrow from her quiver and fiddled with it. "How does this whole thing work?"

Leia took a seat. "So, we three are the leaders of the rebellion organization," she explained. "We are of all ages, but mostly on the younger side. Many of the adults that were protesting against The Committee built lives for themselves. Now, to protect their families, they no longer can. Everyone here has nothing left to lose."

Marah nodded, though she disagreed. The rebels could lose their fight and then she would lose her chance to go home. "If that's the case then why bother rebelling?"

Kiera rubbed the mark on her forehead. "Every government is subject to rebellion. Rebellion will always and must always exist to have justice and liberty. It needs to be constant, everlasting, even to be successful, don't you think?"

"As for The Committee," shrugged Natira, "they think they can establish universal peace by hurting other worlds and people. Other rebellion groups have risen, only to be destroyed by them. A few years ago, we learned that they possessed a weapon that told them who was truly dangerous to them." She looked at Marah as if to analyze her, to test the weight of her words. "Some called it a prophecy, others a myth. That there was someone out there in the universe who had what it took to defeat The Committee once and for all."

"And that's supposed to be me?"

Natira leaned back, crossing arms that revealed silver tattoos. "That's what Kiera says."

Marah noted the Nantak's sensitivity about her joining this not so merry crew. She pretended to ignore it; wringing her hands together as she picked at the head of an arrow. *They shouldn't need me.*

"And The Committee?"

"Ten years ago, The Committee invaded the planet Nova and bombed the planet." Leia ran a finger over a silver thumb ring. "They came once to deliver a threat then again to fulfill it. They destroyed the main city and said they would destroy everything and everyone unless the King surrendered. The King did, but the surrender came at the expense of millions of deaths. I was a child with a doll who lost everything, including the members of my family—one after the other."

Marah's lips fell into a firm line. She didn't know what to say for these beings, kids like herself, who lived in war and pain. If this was what The Committee does, what chance did she stand? *Where do I fit in? I don't share their pain or motivation; I'd be dead weight to carry.*

"This is what The Committee does. Many of us plan to avenge our planets and loved ones. Today, their leader is Chairwoman Kate."

All three aliens made a sour expression at the mention of the Chairwoman's name.

Kiera spoke after an uncomfortable pause and Marah was relieved by the warmth in her voice as she guided the conversation elsewhere, "So that's us. We three run this place, and the others are rebels who are just like us. They gather the information that we need, fight, and whatnot."

"So, what do I do?" Marah stood while putting the arrow back in her quiver.

"Well," asked Kiera, "what makes you special? Here, we use weapons and our abilities to train for war, what about on Earth?"

Marah looked down. "We don't prepare for war on Earth. We go to school for decades to pick a profession just so we can work until we die."

Natira retorted with an arched brow, "That sounds horrible."

The human dryly laughed, "It is." The humor left her tone as she answered Kiera's question, "I don't think I'm special. I don't know why. I was hoping one of you guys could answer that."

Leia rose from her seat, "We can figure that out as we go." She eyed the contraption in Marah's hand, "That's a weapon, isn't it?"

"Oh," said Marah, as she held out the bow so the three could see it better. "I guess. It's a bow and arrow. I shoot and hit whatever I aim at. That's about it." She shrugged. "I don't miss." *Most of the time, anyway.*

Chapter 6

Location: Where fists fly

Marah had never felt more out of place as she stared at the room that she was now standing in. "This is just an empty room?" Her words trailed away as someone, presumably Leia, did *something* to make the room become filled with an array of training equipment.

The four white walls became painted with bullseye targets, a wrestling ring, hanging punching bags, and other things that Marah couldn't name. Small moving robots that had the height of a trash can with glitching eyes hummed softly as they skittered toward the four women. The robots beeped, moving around Marah as if they were trying to figure out who she was.

Kiera chuckled softly as she bent down to pet one of the robots. "Easy there, Lucky. Emme, Marah's going to be helping us."

"I'm sorry, who are you talking to?"

Patience swept Kiera's words as she stood back up while the robots skidded about, "We use artificial intelligence to regulate everything.

Emme here manages the place and keeps us hidden. She and these guys are like a suit of armor."

"Huh. Magic," Marah breathed out.

Natira looked at the human with the slightest trace of irritation. "Technology, not magic. Think of what you might want, and the robots will make it appear." She paused to tap a red robot, "Targets on the north wall, please."

Marah tilted her head, nudging the wispy black streaks from her face to better see the row of gray targets neatly appeared in front of her.

"The targets you see on the wall over there are holograms, to be exact, but they work the same way as real ones. Hit them and they disappear. They can't hurt you."

"The targets can move if this is too easy," offered Leia. "Let's start slow and then work our way up."

Marah nodded, still hesitant. She took a couple of steps forward to get some space. *No pressure, just do your thing. Don't mess up and look stupid.*

She scanned the room, unsure of which target she should start with first, especially with the three aliens behind her who were definitely judging her. Marah resisted the urge to look at her audience, as they awaited some promise of the hero they needed.

She settled on the wall in front of her, lined up with perfectly spaced targets. She took a step back and inhaled. Now that she could breathe a little bit easier, she could deliver. After all, the first step to shooting an arrow is to have a steady heart and a steady mind. Only then would the rest of the body follow.

Marah reached over her shoulder to pull out a black-tipped arrow and set it against the bowstring, pulling the arrow far enough back to drive it where she wanted. Once she had enough tension, she exhaled, releasing the arrow. It hit the target right in the center—a perfect bullseye.

Moving to the next target, she plucked out another arrow. She pulled it back, resting the arrow against the bow as she inhaled, steadying her aim. She didn't hold her breath for too long, letting the arrow fly. She didn't have to look to know that the arrow made a perfect hit.

She took another arrow from her quiver and lined herself up in front of the target. She drew the arrow with ease and didn't need to think before letting it fly. It hit the target instantly.

Marah's fingers moved with muscle memory, pulling arrows from her quiver, drawing back, aiming, and then releasing one after the other. She repeated this as she headed down the line of targets, speed building up as the sound of arrows penetrating the wall become faster and louder.

Thwick.

Moments later, twelve arrows had been shot into the wall, all twelve of which were perfect hits.

Energy pooling in Marah's veins, the human swiveled back to face her audience hoping that there was some promise in her.

Leia smiled with a twinkle in her eyes, "How about moving targets?"

Marah raised a brow with a hint of a smirk as she drew her bow again but didn't raise to aim. *Moving targets? That's child's play.*

This time, the small robots veered closer to Marah and held up little target signs of their own.

Aww.

Straightening her spine as she put all her weight on her toes, Marah sent arrows flying in every direction. Within mere seconds, each robots' target had an arrow pierced right through.

She wore victory across her lips as she twirled an arrow between her fingers. The feeling was cut off when a blast of purple streaked past her vision, knocking her down. Her mouth fell open as she looked up to see Leia levitating off the ground with outstretched fingers, each hand holding up a ball of purple energy. Her eyes flickered, glowing with light.

Marah unconsciously blurted, "What. The. Hell?"

I really do say that a lot, don't I?

She brushed her hair behind her ears, and she stood up, refraining from cursing as she winced lightly. Out of the corner of her left eye, she noticed Natira posed in a fighting stance.

"Am I using my bow or am I fighting hand-to-hand combat? Also, a warning would be much appreciated next time." *What am I even supposed to do?*

The human received no reply as she ducked to avoid another attack of purple.

"Your choice," offered Leia as she moved to put Marah between her and Natira, who hadn't moved yet.

Marah jerked to the side as another ball of purple was thrown in her direction, stumbling over from the suddenness of it. She caught her weight with the hand that wasn't clasping the centerpiece of her bow.

She watched in awe as Leia's fingers danced, sparking purple pulses of energy. Within seconds, the pulses were directed toward Marah. The sparking gave her an idea.

Marah pushed herself off the ground, reaching into her quiver for an arrow and sending it toward the ball of energy. The arrow got caught in the ball, which exploded into a small cloud of dust with the sound of electricity crackling.

That actually worked?

The distraction from her shock caused her to be swept off her feet with a jab to the ankle. Her bow clattered to the ground, leaving Marah defenseless.

Natira allowed Marah to stagger back to her feet before throwing punches toward her, forcing the human to move backward as she attempted to defend herself.

Marah tasted uncertainty on her tongue as she threw a fist toward the Nantak's chest, a gesture to show that she could punch harder but not inflict any damage. After all, they were only sparring.

Natira, in turn, easily blocked Marah's fist. Her movements were sharp and precise as she thrust her right arm forward.

Not realizing Natira's true intent, Marah was sent back down to the floor. Before she even grasped the concept that she had fallen as her opponent's leg slammed into her.

Just as she was about to stand back up, Natira stood over her, keeping the human down. "You lack refinement," she remarked stiffly. "Try again."

Marah paused, looking up at the alien for confirmation as she stepped back to give the human some space. She stood, this time leaving her bow as she brought her hands in front of her.

Whatever patience Natira had for the apparent chosen one had seemingly run out as the alien delivered a spin-kick toward her chest, causing Marah to wince from the impact. Determined to prove her worth, Marah kicked a leg up that the Nantak easily dodged with a twist, and all she struck was air.

Natira's footwork was nimble as she stalked around Marah, sharp eyes an invitation to attack.

Marah stepped forward before attempting to throw a punch that hit Natira. Whether it hurt or not, Marah had no clue, as Natira's face remained stoic.

Before Marah could throw another punch, a fist collided into her chest harshly, sending her tumbling to the ground.

Marah winced, pain from the blow and the landing stinging as bitterly as Natira's clipped tone, "You need to do better. You need to be faster. If you are going to fight in a battle like this, you will easily be killed."

Killed. Even though death had brought this cause together, it hadn't occurred to Marah that she too could fall like the rebels who wanted to avenge their ancestors.

"This isn't useful to any of us! You're supposed to be something powerful. You're supposed to be something great; to take down the biggest dictator in the universe. This is the best you've got? Try again."

Marah stood back up with a slight wince. "Sorry to disappoint," she retorted, "but I'm human, okay?" She bent down and picked up her bow. "I can't do all sorts of cool magic tricks like you guys, hell, I'm not even supposed to! I don't know what you expected when you kidnapped me, but that's on you."

Natira opened her mouth but Marah wasn't finished.

"And if that's a problem, then you can win your war by yourselves."

She turned on her heel and walked out of the room. This time, no one made an attempt to stop her. *Good for them,* she thought bitterly.

Marah wasn't sure where she was going, nor did she care. She just kept going, letting her boots thud against tile as her thoughts cooled themselves down. If she were on Earth, she would've shot targets until the anger ripped itself apart. Here, she couldn't go and do that. *What can I even do here?*

She gritted her teeth. *Who did she think she was? Here I am doing them a favor and they want to get upset at me on day one? What a great bunch of people...aliens...whatever they are!*

Even though the alien could've handled that a whole lot better, the dark-haired girl had to admit that Natira did have a point.

This was serious business. The rebels were counting on her to be like them and help them fight their war. Even though she didn't want any part in this, she was going to fight, which meant that she needed to be able to defend herself. Especially when she had the disadvantage of lacking a powerful ability.

Still, Marah was more than bothered as she furiously wiped hair from her eyes. Anger ticked her features, and the more she focused on how angry she was the angrier she grew.

Eyebrows furrowing even more, she welcomed the feeling, knowing that once she faced and dealt with it, she'd be able to use it to calm herself down - though it didn't help that her cheeks were flushed red from the embarrassment of how she had not only messed up but walked out.

They came and took me without listening to what I had to say, forced me to say yes, and now they want me to be just like them. How am I supposed to be like the rebels, who quite literally have the power to actually do something?

This was a world of aliens and evil governments. Neither of which Marah had ever given thought to being real. And now, her life spun a one-eighty, having to fight with and against the very same magic she had discarded as a figment of her imagination.

"Is this a bad time?"

What do you think?

Marah whirled around to find the alien who had brought her into this mess standing somewhat shyly in front of her. She couldn't help but roll her eyes. "I don't think there's such a thing as a bad time, since I'm stuck here until your war is over."

She immediately winced as she registered how harsh her words had sounded. She sighed, not wanting to create more bitterness between herself and the people she was now stuck living with. "I'm sorry, I didn't mean to offend you." *Not entirely.*

Kiera waved the apology off. "It's fine." Her warm chocolate eyes flickered to Marah's. "I actually came here to apologize. You fight well. I can't fight like that to save someone's life," she confessed, "let alone mine. I rely on my powers entirely, and I'll admit that hand-to-hand isn't my best. Don't let Natira bring you down. She's not very, um," she paused, shrugging, "what's the word?"

"Kind?" Marah suggested curtly.

Kiera wore a strained smile. "Yeah, that. She's suffered a lot because of The Committee; well, for her whole life really. More than anyone else I know. She came from planet Nantak, Nova's sister planet. The Committee destroyed the planet and its people when their Queen decided not to let them waltz in and take over. The Committee retaliated of course. They killed almost every Nantak - it was a small planet, so it wasn't hard. Natira is the sole survivor. Because of how much she's had to suffer at their hands, she's very determined not to let another planet share Nantak's fate." She looked away, realizing how all of this might sound to a stranger who was probably prone to apathy. "It's hard because we don't know what they're planning, which is why we can't just get inside, guns blazing."

Marah nodded awkwardly. "If The Committee is as dictator-like as you say, I understand. Earth has had a couple of dictators of its own. Governments formed two sides and waged wars to end the reign of empires all the time."

Kiera dipped her head down. "In this universe, there are nine planets. Earth, Stella, Romana, Artemis, Litnick, Zona, Nantak, Nova, and Kosmir. The first planet they conquered was Nova. Then they moved to Nantak, and then Zona. Zona was a much larger planet than Nova and Nantak, so the siege took a long time, being that they were a new force with goals that the universe hadn't seen before. They bombed the planet for months, killed some of us, and threatened to kill others if the King didn't comply with their demands." She shrugged, "Hearing about you, the savior to suffering, she got really excited. We all are."

Marah's eyes glistened as she took a seat on the tiled floor. Even though she had been forced into this, she couldn't help but want to know more. "It's alright, I guess. Tell me more about The Committee."

Kiera obliged, sitting cross-legged on the floor in front of Marah. She rubbed her eyes before speaking. "The Committee brings death and destruction to whatever planet it sets its sights on. Mine was no different, like I said. There was chaos everywhere. I remember it all like it was yesterday. The first day they came, they didn't bring any warning. They dropped a bomb over one of our countries and waited for the impact. The bomb landed in a school full of innocent children, all younger than the age of eleven. We were in the middle of a science lesson when we heard a loud blasting sound. Children started to scream as the sky flashed a bright white, like lightning. But it was worse. There's a saying on Earth about it," she frowned, "I don't remember it."

Marah nodded. "I think I know what you're talking about. Lightning always strikes before thunder?"

"Yes," Kiera thanked her, "that's the one. The teacher paused her lesson and looked out of the window. The light was blinding, but when it stopped...I'll never forget how sick I felt seeing those large ships hovered over our skies, dark and dreary ships that obviously meant harm. There was nowhere to escape, not with the fleets of soldiers that descended from the dark sky shooting people down dead."

The Zonan paused.

"You don't have to share more than what you're comfortable with," Marah offered softly.

Kiera shook her head with a wry smile. "It's alright. I've come to terms with it. Sometimes, when one reopens old wounds, their hearts bleed. Either they'll bleed themselves to insanity, or they'll stem the flow and survive. We all bleed at some point, don't we?"

"Yeah," agreed Marah, "we do."

"I remember when the first bomb dropped. No one saw it, but we all heard it. I thought that if they were going to bomb, which is a traditional practice of war amongst the stars, they wouldn't bomb a school. I was wrong."

Kiera wiped her eyes, and Marah couldn't help but feel bad for her. Her anger toward Natira was long forgotten, and the hatred she had for Kiera for kidnapping her and bringing her here had softened.

"They didn't care," the Zonan said with a sniffle. "And the next thing I knew, a bomb broke through the ceiling and crashed all the way down to the ground, killing everyone in the entire building, except for me."

Marah had her hand pressed over her mouth, utterly horrified. She didn't know what to say. Even though she knew an apology wasn't warranted and that none of her words could ease the pain that Kiera had endured for so long, her words were soft as they parted her lips. "I don't know what to say. It might not mean much to you, but I'm so sorry. That's horrible. Worse than horrible. I can't imagine how that must have been."

Kiera smiled kindly. "I would say that you don't need to apologize, but we both already know that. I appreciate your sympathy, though. Sometimes nights come and I can't sleep, wondering if I was meant to die with the rest of my family."

Marah's heart clenched inside her chest. She wanted to tell Kiera otherwise, but her words probably wouldn't mean much since they had only met today. *Besides, I probably got on her nerves at least once today.*

But that didn't mean Marah had to be a heartless monster. "I don't believe in accidents," she offered kindly. "On Earth, we have a saying. Sometimes accidents are done on purpose. When it comes to fate, I personally believe that we don't control it. I don't know about religion here, but on Earth we believe that our fates are predestined. Everything happens for a reason. After all, you said that because you're still here, you have the chance to avenge all the lives that were lost."

There was absolutely no way that Kiera's survival was just luck. Just like Natira. I mean, look at what they're doing here.

Kiera's words only made the girl struggling to understand all of this think about herself even more. There were beings who wielded such power and capability, but for some reason, a computer thought that she was to be the chosen one.

Well, you did say that everything happens for a reason. But sometimes, technology can make mistakes. Just because someone is chosen, doesn't mean that they're the best bet. God writes blessings and tragedies; this could be either-or. I mean, what's stopping a computer from glitching?

Realizing that the two couldn't just sit there in silence, Marah tried to change the topic. "What can you do with your powers? They're interesting."

It wasn't a lie. Marah had grown up with a love of sci-fi and superheroes, so to be on a team where her teammates were exactly that felt surreal. So many things on Earth that had been considered true were probably incorrect. Like Leia. Leia's ability was strange to Marah not because of *what* she could do but rather *how*. Science told her that energy couldn't be created nor destroyed, so how did Leia's powers work? *Did she absorb the energy in the room, and then disperse it when you shot the arrow, proving science correct?*

A sudden doubt poked at Marah's head. *What if I'm not meant for something like this? What if I can't help these people?*

"I can sense people's emotions with my mind," Kiera said in reply to Marah's question as the stone-like marking on her head glowed a soft white. "Not always, though; all powers have limitations. Just before, I sensed you feeling guilty. Now, I sense..." She closed her eyes, trying to concentrate.

Marah felt awkward. *Hopefully, she's not reading my thoughts.*

Kiera's answer caused a wave of relief to flood through Marah. "I sense doubt. But that's understandable. I'm unsure as to what you're doubting, but given all of this, I can guess. I can control emotions to make people fall asleep or stop moving."

Marah arched a brow, smirking slightly. "Really? You'll have to show me sometime. Oh wait, you did. Twice."

Kiera chuckled as she continued, "I can also teleport short distances. Nothing really fancy, but I can go from this room to the training room, for example. As for Leia, you already saw. She creates energy and uses it as a weapon. She can also fly. She's pretty much the leader of this operation. she's strongly supported this movement these past few years. Natira is more on the complex side."

Before Kiera could explain what she meant by that, Marah felt a tap on her shoulder. The girl frowned. She was leaning against a wall. *There's no one next to me.*

"Hey."

The voice came out of nowhere, startling Marah and causing a yelp to tear out of her lips. She looked behind her to see Natira's face and hands poking out of the wall. She looked at the alien strangely but then remembered where she was.

Natira raised a brow, amused by Marah's reaction. "What? Never seen someone walk through a wall before?"

"I think we both know the answer to that," replied the human. "You can't just walk through walls whenever you feel like it and scare the crap out of me!"

Natira laughed. "Sure, I can. It's called phasing. I can walk through anything and everything. Except for people. Sometimes. Learned that the hard way."

Hazel eyes widened despite Natira's casualness. Marah turned to Kiera for an explanation.

The Zonan shook her head. "You really don't want to know."

Natira sat down, resting her elbows on her knees. She snickered as she gestured to Marah with two fingers decorated in rings. "You know what they say, no guts no glory. Literally."

Marah stared at Natira. "I have no clue how to respond to that, so I'm going to pretend that you didn't just say it. If you can walk through anything and everything, why don't you walk through The Committee walls and get them from the inside?"

Natira leaned her head against the wall. "If I could, I would. Besides, The Committee isn't a small group. You deal with one, and then you have to deal with ten more. Leia and I went to try and figure out if they were going to attack any other planets, but we didn't get to catch anything."

She turned her head and faced the human. Sincerity was thick in her tone, ash eyes meeting hazel ones. "I'm sorry for what I said earlier. I shouldn't have. You just found out that aliens are real and signed up for war. I didn't realize that all of this would be overwhelming, and instead of helping you adjust I lashed out at you." She offered a small smile, "I'm sorry, Marah."

Marah returned the smile, "It's alright. I understand how important this is to all of you." The statement wasn't entirely true, Marah couldn't wait for all of this to be over so she could go home.

Natira smirked as she stood up, offering a hand to Marah. "In that case," her eyes gleamed, "shall we start over?"

Chapter 7

Location: Where the hurt sprout wings and fly

Natira began to explain as the two returned to the training room. "Let's try weapons practice instead. Here, we have all different types of weapons, so you're going to have to learn how to use some of these."

"I have a specific thing going on," Marah said thinly, holding her bow protectively. "I'm strictly a bow and arrow type." *I'm not like you guys. I'm not trained for this.*

"As handy as your bow might be," said Natira, shrugging off her jacket, "if your bow is destroyed or you don't have access to it, you can't always rely on your fists to save you. This is a blaster, a very common weapon." The Nantak pulled out a blaster from a holster on her thigh— it was a sleek black device that resembled a basic pistol with a clear slide that stored glowing, moving purple goo. The barrel extended into a thinning cylinder that ended with a gray knob.

"This is the slide," she ran a bronze finger over the top of the gun where goo churned, "this holds the plasma that makes a powerful blast when it's shot from here," she tapped another finger to the knob-like sphere. She looked at Marah who nodded before continuing.

She held the weapon up, wrapping four fingers around the grip and the thumb flat on the part of the grip that was facing her. "If you press this button twice, you shoot. Like your arrow, aim is everything."

"That is so cool," exclaimed the human as Natira showed her the weapon in more detail.

"Emme, can you give us something to practice shooting with?" said Natira, turning away from Marah as she began to geek out, as hinted by the widening smile on her face.

Though Emme didn't vocally reply, a hologram took the form of a person as it materialized, getting depth and volume so it looked real. Once the cut-out finished loading, Emme chimed, "Will that be all?"

The alien nodded. "That's good for now, thanks Em."

She raised her right hand and Marah stepped to the side to give Natira some space. "With weapons," Natira explained, "you want to use your dominant eye for aim and shoot with the opposite hand. Otherwise, your hand-eye coordination will be off." She tilted her head to the side and cracked a knuckle as she determined her aim. Once she was satisfied, she pressed down on the trigger. Plasma shot through the dummy, right in the chest. "Another thing: your kill zones are the head, the neck, and the heart."

She held the weapon to the supposed chosen one, "Your turn."

"Head, neck, and heart," repeated the human as she took the blaster from Natira, "got it." While doing so, she couldn't help but look at the silver markings that littered Natira's skin. "Those markings on your hands—what do they mean?"

Natira looked down at her forearms as she answered, "These are the markings of my people. Nantaks, the people from my planet, are born with some. Others are gained over time. When one was born on

Nantak, they were given the mark of a lotus flower on their right hand. It represents the beauty of life." She pointed to her left wrist, where a foreign script was engraved into her skin, "This one is written in the Nukum language. It translates to love. Some don't have a specific meaning, but they tell a story anyway. Mine tell the stories of the days that I got them, or things that I felt back then. It was traditional to get tattooed on our birthdays, a sign of growth."

Marah spoke after a couple of moments. "I like them." Not wanting to make things awkward, she focused back on the lesson. She raised the blaster with her right hand, so it was slightly lower than her shoulder level and pressed down on the trigger, sending a well-aimed blast of plasma at the same dummy. Natira had made a head shot while Marah's pierced right through the heart.

The sound provoked Marah to yelp as she turned to face Natira. "Holy hell, did I really just do that?"

The alien nodded.

Marah wore a child-like smile as she practically fangirled, "That was so cool, let's do that again!" She giggled as she pretended to shoot the blaster, mimicking its sounds. "Pew! Pew! Pew! Take that!"

Natira snatched the weapon out of Marah's hand. "I think that's enough of that. I don't know what you just did, but don't do that again. Once you're good at this, I'll give you one of your own. Let's try hand-to-hand."

The human pouted before getting into a stance and then asked, "Quick question, how does everything work around here? Like where do you guys sleep and everything? How do you plan your next move of attack against The Committee and Chairwoman Kate?" She hesitated. "There is a plan, right?"

The sooner the better.

Natira half-smiled. "You catch on quick." She threw a fist toward Marah, taking the girl by surprise. "Most share rooms. Some on this floor and some on other floors. So, just a heads up what may look like a closet may have someone sleeping inside. We have separate quarters here."

Marah caught the punch just in time. "We?" she raised a brow.

"Leia, Kiera, myself," she met Marah's eyes, "and now you. You'll have your own room, of course, and we have already prepared some clothes and necessities for you." Natira swiped toward Marah's ankle, who noticed it quick enough to allow Natira to only hit the air. "Show me how you punch."

Marah wrapped her thumb around the rest of her fingers and directed her knuckles forward.

"Good form," Natira stated as she dodged the thrown fist. "But you hesitated. "As for your other question, we do have a plan." She withdrew from Marah and made a gesture that meant to follow her. The two began to walk in a circle, facing each other. "Tip: always be in a position where you can easily attack. Sometimes you want to get close to your enemy, but sometimes you don't. If you're ever in a fight and you have no clue how to fight the person, build up some time to think. But don't think too long," she jabbed toward the black-haired girl, "because your opponent will use the time to take you down."

Marah used her leg to prevent Natira from kicking her and pushed it, sending the alien a couple of steps backward.

"Good. I'm not sure if Kiera told you, but the rebels that you saw in the room when you were trying to escape are often spies. They work twenty-four seven to gather as much data as possible. And before you ask—yes, our clock and calendar are just like on Earth. If we can find The Committee's plans, then we can stop them from becoming more powerful. That's the hard part, because we make strategies based on their plans, so we can defend and gain an advantage."

Marah threw her head back to avoid a punch in the face. "Why's that?"

"Because there are cameras all over, watching everyone and everything."

Marah grunted as she threw a leg toward Natira's ankle but missed. "So, you can't just show up with an army at their front door." She threw another fist, only for Natira to catch it and twist, sending her down to the ground. This time, just as Marah was about to fall, she swept her leg under Natira, bringing her to the ground with her.

"Good," commended Natira. "Use whatever you can to bring your opponent to the ground. Any other questions?"

Marah jumped to her feet, ready for another round. "Yeah, how long has this whole operation been running? With you guys, anyway." Her blood pumped rapidly though her body as she felt bold enough to attempt to snap-kick Natira's leg.

"We joined three years ago, but we took over leading last year after the former leader was captured. We didn't meet under the best of circumstances." Natira hesitated, as if her thoughts battled each other, before caving in. "The Committee saw the only living Nantak left in the universe as something to auction off to the trafficking rings."

Marah's features softened, granting Natira an opportunity to shove her.

"If you're going to talk while fighting, don't get distracted," Natira warned her.

"Sorry." Marah resumed her stance.

"You learn a lot as a prisoner. How to test people's limits, what mercy is, and how to survive. I had escaped and found Leia, who was crying because her cousin had just kicked her out of their apartment."

The survivor took a swing toward Marah's chin. "Regular fights won't be long. You have to be quick on your feet and in your head. As I was talking, you could have attacked me several times; otherwise, I would have attacked."

Marah nodded, averting her gaze from Natira. She agreed to help the rebels, but fight and potentially die? That was a big stretch.

"Per The Committee's order, all beings were grouped into buildings based on their home world. The Committee didn't care much about two children, and finding out that I had escaped would be a ticket back to hell. We lived in alleys until ships full of Zonan refugees came. We met Kiera, who agreed to sneak us into her room so she wouldn't be lonely. Fast forward a couple of years and we found this place and made it home."

That's awful. Their lives are so sad, and yet they're still going.

Sweat beads formed on Marah's forehead as she wobbled, cutting her off from speaking. Determined to beat the tattooed alien this time, she sucked in a breath, supplying her body with the oxygen that her lungs were all but begging her for. Doing so, a burst of energy flooded through her as she stood up, countering all of Natira's attacks, working to defend herself instead.

Marah had to admit, the platinum-blonde knew how to fight. *Which makes sense given everything that's happened to her.*

As for her, all she had was her archery skills and a few martial arts classes from a couple of years ago. Her mother had encouraged her to take on extracurriculars for college applications, and she was not going to join boring medical clubs that would apparently help her get a career. She wanted to choose what to dedicate her life to.

Lost in thought, Marah slipped on her own feet and stumbled to the floor. She accepted Natira's hand back up and attempted to pick up a few things from Natira until the Nantak broke the silence. "What about you?"

Marah's arm was twisted behind her by Natira, black locks of hair whipped behind her. "Me?"

"Yeah. What's your story? You know a little bit about us, but we don't really know much about you. We all have our stories, what's yours?"

Marah answered with a huff as the Nantak demonstrated different punching techniques. "It's nothing compared to yours. It's a bit childish if you ask me. My father left me when I was fifteen."

Nantak eyes flickered to human ones as the alien apologized.

Marah shrugged the condolence off. "It's alright. There wasn't much to miss." She laughed a humorless laugh. "I would sneak out of the house and practice shooting. I had watched a movie and fell in love with archery. I demanded my parents let me practice in exchange for good grades. My father didn't care much about grades or my hobby. He just existed. My mother, on the other hand," she paused, unsure if she wanted to run down the path of memory lane, "was obsessed with my grades. She wanted me to be something amazing and spend the rest of my life studying, like her. That didn't appeal to me. I wanted to be free to explore the world."

And now you're exploring two worlds, would you look at that?

"I told her that I didn't want the future she was planning for me, and she got upset." Marah looked away, "She told me to pack my stuff and leave."

"Because of a difference in opinion?"

"She said that if I didn't follow her rules in her house, I didn't deserve to live in it. So, I packed up and left. That's pretty much it really. As I said, it's not super sad or death-involving."

Natira pulled away from Marah, signaling they were done. "Well, that's something we have in common." She spoke bluntly, poking fun, "Tragic backstories." She sighed, wiping her forehead. "Alright, that's enough for today. I'm tired."

Marah chuckled as she wiped sweat off her face. The two shook hands, concluding their spar. "I suppose that wasn't too bad for a human?"

Natira laughed as she elbowed Marah's shoulder. "You pick up quick. You're not a bad fighter. With a few months of training," she had the audacity to wink, "you'll be as good as me. Besides, we have other things to do."

"Like?"

Natira seemed hesitant. "If you're going to fight, you're going to need a suit," she revealed.

Marah laughed as she followed Natira out of the training room. "I knew it! You guys are literal superheroes!" She hung her bow across her shoulder and cracked her somewhat sore knuckles. "You just don't want to give me the satisfaction and admit it."

Natira rolled her eyes. "There's nothing to admit. C'mon."

She led Marah down a long corridor and headed inside a room on the left-hand side.

Marah followed, unsure of what to expect.

She thought of the films she had watched; CGI-designed bunkers with suits tailored to represent something about their wearers. *Had they already picked out a suit for their chosen one? I hope not.*

Marah didn't know much about alien clothes or their styles, but she couldn't believe that she was about to get *an actual real-life superhero suit.* Excitement churned in her blood as she gawked at the room in front of her.

I'm totally *fangirling.*

For starters, the room was much larger than Marah had originally anticipated. Glass cases stretched from the entrance all the way to the back of the room, each with a suit and weapons locked inside. Even though lights hung from the ceiling, each case had a light at the back of it, displaying suits on mannequins. Most of the mannequins wore the same suit, but others were more personalized, presumably tailored to accommodate different abilities. Almost all of the mannequins wore a simple black suit that was durable for fighting with holsters, arm and pant bands, and combat boots.

It's even better than I could have ever imagined.

"You like?"

Marah flickered her eyes to the source of the voice to see Leia, who smiled. She nodded slowly. "This is incredible."

"Yeah, it is," Natira tittered. "We wanted you to pick your suit. Most rebels have the regular suit, but some have more personalized ones, such as ourselves. Each panel has a nametag and only opens to a specific person's touch based on their DNA."

Marah nodded, focusing on the types of suits displayed. The first one that stood out to her was Leia's. Everything about Leia involved purple—her eyes, her hair, even her nails. If she was being honest, she'd have been surprised if the Novan didn't have purple in her apparel. The suit had a simple look to it: a purple tactical suit that had a collar for the sides of the neck and a belt buckled across the middle with patches of aubergine over the upper shoulders, mid-thighs, upper thighs under the belt, and two thin strips that followed the outline of her silhouette on the top piece. The suit was completed with a pair of boots.

Hazel eyes trailed to the case next to Leia's. From the time she had already spent with the trio of friends, she pegged Kiera as someone friendly and more colorful than the somewhat-dreary Natira.

Kiera's suit looked like Kiera. Instead of a two-piece tactical suit, there was a pastel pink top that had armbands across the elbow, curving from the base of the neck to run down the mannequin, ending at the start of dark gray pants that had bands across the knees.

As for Natira's suit, it was rather simple: a black suit consisting of a full-sleeved top, and a silver belt. The more Marah observed the suit, the more she noticed little extra things such as belts and straps across the front and back from which weapons poked out.

When she looked at the next case, she found it empty. Marah turned to the three, waiting for an explanation.

"If you're going to fight in a war, you're going to need something that will protect you. Each suit is tailored to different things and different needs. Some suits are bulletproof, like mine, while others keep you from getting blasted, like Natira's," Leia explained.

"Bullets, I can outrun. Blasters? Not my thing," Natira added gravely. "Like I mentioned before, they hurt. Besides, you need a suit that works to your strengths and your weaknesses. We have a few that you can choose from."

Kiera gestured to a small changing room that Marah had just noticed. "We thought of this for you."

Marah accepted the offer and headed inside. She gently shut the door behind her, taking off her bow and quiver, as she put on the suit.

The suit consisted of a few different pieces. There was a crimson leather jacket with sleeves that ended at her knuckles and a detachable cape that hung from the collar to the back of her knees. As if the suit was designed just for her, it sported a detachable arm guard for archery down the length of its right arm.

Under the jacket, which Marah was beginning to love, was a navy-blue one-piece. It wasn't tight-fitting or too loose; it fit her snug like her regular clothes and, judging by the material, was useful for combat. The piece was breathable and trailed to the bottoms of her ankles, where dark cherry boots were laced against her feet. To top it all off, there was a black belt at the waist with a small pouch that was strapped to a holster on her right calf.

Sick.

Once Marah's suit had been put into its case, she noticed a small scanner next to her name. "Put your hand over the pad. It's going to scan your handprint so only you can access it," explained Leia.

Marah nodded and did as Leia instructed her to. She watched as a light beam scanned her handprint and then made a humming sound.

"All done. C'mon. We'll show you around."

She followed the three out of the room and into the hallway. The human marveled at the facility's interior, mentally taking notes since she was going to be here for a while.

Kiera explained as she led the group. "Here we have the suits, training spaces, and bathrooms here. The bathrooms are all-inclusive, but we have ones for specific genders if you're more comfortable with that. There's also a break room where you can go if you feel overwhelmed. This section is the East Wing," she said as she approached the main area of the floor.

"If you continue down that hallway," Natira pointed, "you have the West Wing, with prayer rooms and a med bay. This area here is where everything happens."

Marah glanced at the open area, filled with a multitude of devices and even more rebels. At first glance, the area looked hectic and made her feel slightly overwhelmed, but the more she remained there, the less suffocating it felt. Everyone looked the same at first, wearing similar clothes and blurry faces, but as Marah took in her environment, she distinguished individual appearances.

What are they doing?

As if Leia had read her mind, the Novan spoke. "This is the North Wing. Here, we spend most of our time gathering information that others are tasked with getting, coming up with plans, and figuring out our next steps. Rebels are always working since information is always being processed and anything important can come at any hour. It's important to be ready whenever, wherever."

She became slightly uncomfortable as the others became aware of their presence. Specifically, her presence.

"And the South Wing?" she asked while lowering her gaze, feeling awkward with eyes glued to her face. Her cheeks reddened at the sound of whispering, and for a few moments, she felt like she was back in high school.

"That's where we stay, so we'll save that part for the end," the Novan replied.

Marah nodded, despite the lowness in her voice. "Alright. So, North Wing is here, West Wing is," she pointed behind her, "that way." She then gestured ahead of her. "And the East Wing is that way. That's not too complicated."

I think.

The Zonan gestured to the elevator in the far corner. "That's the main elevator. It takes you to the outside. There are three other elevators found in each of the other wings that take you between the different floors. We're on the third floor of the building; the rebels live on floors two and four. Floor one is deserted on purpose, should someone trespass and get curious."

"And the lowest floor is a network of underground tunnels that can be used to escape should the need arise," Natira concluded.

Well, that's creative.

The three girls started walking and Marah trailed a couple of steps behind them. She sighed softly, visibly relieved that she was no longer the center of attention.

Kiera paused and looked back at Marah. She must've sensed something from her since she spoke: "Don't worry about them. It's their first time seeing you and what you stand for. It won't be a daily thing."

Marah wore a tight-lipped smile, trying to show understanding instead of confusion and disbelief that aliens could look at her, a kid really, and see something far greater. *I hope so.*

Once Kiera was no longer looking at her, Marah let her lips droop downward into a frown.

They moved on from the "sorry for kidnapping you" stage pretty quickly. Could she blame them?

Marah was so absorbed in her thoughts that she hadn't realized the rebel leaders had stopped walking, causing her to bump into Kiera. "Oh, sorry about that."

Kiera dismissed the apology. "No worries. This is our cafe. It also doubles as a breakroom, since this line of work can be very tedious. The robots are friendly, I promise."

The room was about the same size as the North Wing, if not slightly smaller. There were a bunch of tables, chairs, and booths. It functioned more like a self-serve buffet, with small multi-colored robots. Some of them beeped or spoke in different dialects that her ears couldn't comprehend.

Marah couldn't help but smile at a pink and white robot that caught her attention. It wore a red apron that read "Kiss the cook" as it flipped what looked like pancakes.

She chuckled. "They're cute, do they have names?"

Leia smiled. "Yeah. They have ID collars. Some of them speak English, some speak other languages, and some don't speak at all. The pink one is Lizard, and the red one is Lucky- they speak English."

"Watch out for Toothy, the green one," Natira whispered. "He's a cleaner bot. He's always cleaning and gets upset when we walk over the freshly mopped areas."

Marah couldn't help but laugh at the idea of a two-foot-tall robot angrily beeping at Natira, who was the living embodiment of angst. *Now that's something I'd like to see.*

The room gave off comforting vibes despite its simplistic design. Running an entire underground operation meant that whatever money the rebels had was put towards fighting, not decorating.

"The robots stroll around, so if you ever get lost, they can direct you to where you need to go," the Zonan added.

Marah nodded, keeping quiet. This was a lot to take in, and she was sure that she would get lost a few times—minimum. She was okay with names, but this place twisted and turned in all sorts of directions, something that would take her a while to get familiar with. Her gut twisted, still feeling uncomfortable in her new environment.

"Any questions?"

How long will this operation take? How about why a supercomputer chose me to be the savior to a fight that doesn't even concern me? How about how the robots are programmed to do these things? Do you guys eat human food or something else? If my life is in danger, and I'm here, how long until The Committee dudes figure out that I'm here and try to kill me? What is the plan to take down The Committee?

Marah only voiced the last of her questions.

"That we can discuss later. For now, we could all use some rest after the day we've had," Natira answered, this time letting weariness slip into her tone.

They headed down the hallway a few more yards with Marah trailing behind, somewhat upset at the answer she had received.

"This room up ahead is our quarters. The rebels set up a room for you. It's not exactly perfect, but it should be enough to start with."

"Thanks," she mumbled, trying to conceal disappointment at the lack of an answer.

That's nice, I guess.

She watched curiously as Kiera placed her hand on a scanning pad that looked a lot like the one from the suit room. A voice - *Emme?* - chimed, "Welcome Kiera Dapolk, Natira Reyna, Leia Halim, and Marah Morana."

How does it know I'm here if I didn't scan my hand?

The doors parted from each other, and Marah joined the others in stepping inside. The room was nice, with sofas, chairs, tables, and the smallest bubbly-looking TV she had ever seen.

Aliens have TV? Can I watch Earth stuff?

The room looked like it was designed to be one but was split to accommodate the rebels' situation. Each "wall" had a door that Marah assumed was meant for each person. Now inside,

Marah couldn't help but feel like an alien herself as she looked around, trying to figure out which room was hers.

Do they even shower? She wrinkled her nose. *I hope so.*

Leia gestured to the door closest to Marah. "That's your room. Let any of us know if you need anything."

A low sigh slipped out of Marah's lips as her three kidnappers walked away to their own respective rooms.

She awkwardly opened the door, unsure of how to feel or what to make of the room or her situation. Since the first was easier to break down, Marah settled on the room that had now become her home away from home, literally.

It's not too bad, Marah thought as she settled inside. The room wasn't over the top, but she could tell that some effort had been put into it. Her apartment on Earth wasn't much, but it was enough space to keep her from feeling suffocated. Her new "apartment," was half the amount of space, but it consisted of the basic necessities. The bed wasn't exactly the fanciest, with a simple headboard at the corner adjacent to the door. She didn't like how close the bed was to the door, but she wasn't going to complain about it. *At least it was made. They didn't have to do all of this, let alone give her a room in their wing. Besides, how much can an underground rebellion group afford? Do they even have money?*

These were all questions for another time, though. Marah set her bow down on the freshly washed sheets and explored the room that was now hers. She first headed to the closet to find an entire wardrobe neatly organized for her with all types of clothing articles: oddly shaped vests, tops of various lengths, intricately patterned sweaters, pants with at least four pockets, and more.

She noticed a few empty hangers and hung her jacket and quiver on one of them, before turning to inspect the rest of the room. Adjacent to the foot of the bed rested a small dresser, with drawers that Marah discovered to be full of underwear and various sanitary products. A smaller room branched off deeper into the walls, which was found to be a bathroom.

After ensuring that everything was to her satisfaction, Marah sat on the bed, and only then did she realize how exhausted she was. It also didn't help that the mattress felt like a rock. Which, for a cheap-running secret organization that could probably be discovered at any time, made sense. *Or the fact that complete strangers from a different world want me dead.*

Marah yawned and moved her bow to the nightstand next to her. She got back up and rummaged through the closet for something suitable to sleep in; mesh cargo pants with a ridiculous number of zippers, a sleeveless sweater vest with a flower that she had never seen before, a dress that was half leather and half not by a glass box of jewelry, and the most comfortable looking was a pair of wool sweatpants with leather stripes and pockets.

Strange sense of design but looks comfy so I'll take it.

Marah exhaled slowly as she sunk into the spring of the mattress, casting her eyes toward the ceiling. As tired as she was, there was no certainty that she would be promised sleep. Sleep didn't come so easy to the supposed chosen one and tonight would probably be no different.

If anything, Marah thought as she rubbed her eyes, *my own thoughts will keep me awake as usual.* Her mind struggled to accept everything as reality, something that was evident across her scrunched-up features. The life that she thought was somewhat innocent and daringly normal, had her rendered clueless to whatever could come next. She lived her own little life the way she had wanted, finally free of control.

And now where am I?

Marah never expected that her life would bring her here, past the stars that freckled the Earth sky and to a whole other world. Another sigh slipped out of worn lips as the noirette folded her arms behind her head, propping herself up against the pillow. She knew she would have to fight for sleep, but the night was the best time to think, as it was always quieter.

Marah had never feared anything before. She had felt uncomfortable at home when she'd lived with her parents, but she had never been scared to be with them. Yesterday felt like an eternity ago, as the human tried to recall what she had done yesterday. She paused, unsure if she had even had dinner, let alone what she may or may not have eaten.

Everything will change now.

Change. Marah yawned, letting her eyes flutter shut.

Long gone was her simple life. Now, she would be dealing with things she couldn't even imagine. Unknowingly, Marah Morana would soon discover that she was about to become a criminal: a criminal for justice.

But for now, let's get some rest.

Marah sighed, her eyes sore and heavy. Her insomnia had gotten better over the past couple of years once she had taken back control of her life, and she felt worried that this sudden change would disrupt all of that.

For instance, her body was able to follow its circadian rhythm when she felt safe. She knew she was safe in this strange, foreign environment. However, her stomach churned, creating a pang of uncertainty in her body that crept through her veins and arteries. Her head felt imbalanced; one part of her felt safe, while another pumped out question after question and idea after idea.

What if the base gets raided tonight?

Marah groaned. *That would be impossible. The rebels are watching out for this stuff. You don't know that.*

Yes, you do. Relax. Just sleep.

Fine.

She huffed, turning on her right shoulder as another yawn escaped her lips. Her muscles felt weak, and her eyes hurt whenever she closed them.

I know we need to sleep, but what does all of this mean for you?

Marah exaggerated a sigh. *Shush! Figure that out in the morning!*

Nope. Answer that and then you can sleep. You don't need sleep, we need answers.

Conscience, I'm begging you. Please? I don't have a clue about what any of this means for me. All I know is that I'm not alone and that these strange people won't abandon me.

Why did—

Marah exaggerated another groan. *What now?*

Why did you say yes so easily?

I felt bad! I felt bad for them. They needed my help.

You said that you don't have anything fun back at home.

Marah frowned. She did say that.

She reasoned with herself. *Am I wrong? I'm alone back at home. I miss my stuff; that's the only thing that I have left. They said I could go back home when this was all done. Are you done now?*

She started chuckling, a sound that was drier than humored. *You're going insane. You met aliens, and now you're going insane.*

Maybe they'd let you go home now if they thought that.

Probably. Let's just get this over with one day at a time until we can go home.

Chapter 8

Location: Not California

Marah slept a dreamless sleep as she rolled around to the other side of the bed, pulling a blanket over her head. She sank deeper into the mattress and let out a low hum when someone gently shook her shoulder.

"Five more minutes," she mumbled, as she lazily threw her hand out from under the covers to swat the hand away. It missed.

The owner of the hand giggled quietly, tapping Marah's shoulder again. "Marah, c'mon."

Then, Marah remembered that she didn't live alone anymore. The sound of the voice speaking again prompted her to remember where she was and what she was doing there.

"I'm up, I'm up," the human said slowly, voice thick with sleep.

She blinked a few times and found Kiera standing in front of her. The blue-skinned Zonan greeted her with an amused smile. "Good, get dressed."

Marah grumbled groggily as she got out of bed and rummaged through the closet for an outfit. "What's happening?"

The Zonan chuckled at Marah's wild mop of black hair. "I'll let you know once you're fully awake. I'll wait outside the door." She then disappeared, which Marah assumed to be teleportation at work.

She quickly pulled on a pair of leather pants and a navy-blue t-shirt, brushing her hair so it didn't look like a total mess before meeting Kiera outside her room door.

She couldn't stop herself from asking the Zonan a question. "If you can teleport, why bother walking?" She snorted. "Can you use it to get back at Natira, assuming that scaring people is something she does often?"

Kiera snickered. "Well, there's only so many times that I can teleport without getting a headache. Also, I use energy, and I have to focus, so that'd be a real pain in the neck to do all the time."

"Fair point."

"But," she lamented, "to answer your other questions, yes and yes. Every first of the year, we celebrate the culture and traditions that we used to have in our home worlds. Leia, Natira, and I throw something small for everyone and it sometimes requires a bit of harmless pranking to get people to take a day off. We do something from all the worlds. It's a way of remembering and honoring where we came from."

"That's really sweet and creative," replied Marah softly, "it's sort of like what holidays are on Earth."

"Holidays?"

Marah did her best to explain, "Holidays are basically days that are designed to have fun. On Earth we have a holiday similar to pranking, it's called April Fool's Day. There's not much to it on Earth, but it's cool to see the different meanings here. I mean," she rushed to explain, "not that it's entirely great because of why you choose to do this, but it's cool because you choose to do this, if that makes sense."

Marah was put at ease by the empath's nod. She was surprised about the similarities between human and alien traditions, and was curious to know more, "So then I guess you guys must have some version of Valentine's Day? To celebrate love and give each other gifts?"

Kiera chuckled, "Yes, we have something like that. Here, if I'm using your language correctly," she paused, tilting her head to think before speaking, "the most popular holidays are when the cooking bots make too much breakfast. Which, speaking of, is a whole other holiday that all of Kosmir celebrates. The challenge is to eat as much breakfast as possible."

Marah couldn't help but ease into the conversation, not that she was complaining, "I don't think there's such a thing as too much breakfast." As they walked past the North Wing, her voice caught her by surprise, "If you don't mind me asking, is breakfast a different word in your language, or is it just breakfast?"

Kiera flashed Marah a strange look. "We're not that alien, y'know. Everyone's gotta eat. And before you ask, no, we cannot photosynthesize. That's a myth."

Marah raised her hands defensively, "I wasn't going to ask that!" *I totally was.*

"Did you sleep well last night?" Kiera sounded genuine, but Marah detected amusement in her question.

The human settled on replying with a nod since the pair just walked inside the cafe and saw Leia and Natira already helping themselves at the buffet. "You guys eat human food?" She stepped toward platters of some dishes she recognized—pancakes, waffles, cereal, juices—and others she didn't—cookies with some sort of icing, sandwiches with purple meat, and strangely, cubed fruits—confusion evident in her features.

Kiera nodded as if Marah was the alien and not the other way around, "Yeah, why wouldn't we? Food is food, isn't it? Most of the dishes you've seen before," she said while grabbing two square plates and handing one to Marah, "but if you want to try something new, go for it."

Marah nodded, taking the offered plate in her hands. *Perhaps they're more human-like than I thought.*

She looked down at all the dishes, trying to decide whether she was willing to try something alien or stick to what she already knew. The battle lasted for only a couple of moments before Marah picked up a pair of tongs and dove for pancakes that were decorated with syrup and whipped cream. She headed over to the juice section, filling a cup with orange juice while laughing to herself as the green robot that Natira had warned her about beeped angrily, getting rebels to move out of the way.

That is so cute.

She joined Leia, Kiera, and Natira at a table, where the latter two were arguing about which juice flavor was better.

Marah found herself chiming in as she set her plate on the table, "Kiera's right—if you don't like orange juice, then we can't be friends. It's just not possible."

Kiera pointed a four pronged-fork and her tongue towards Natira. "You know you're wrong when even the human disagrees with you." She and Marah high-fived, while Natira rolled her eyes and mumbled something in Nukum.

Leia spoke next. "While Marah makes a fair point, we can discuss this at another time. Now that we're all here, we can talk about today's agenda."

"Which is?" asked Marah as she cut a piece of square pancake and brought it to her mouth.

Leia swallowed a forkful of square red berries. "How we're going to take down The Committee," she responded.

Marah's ears perked up, eager to hear what the plan was. *The sooner we get this plan down, the sooner I can say hasta la vista.*

"Simple actually. We've been using spies to gather up as much intel about The Committee as possible. Their job is to report, and our job is to analyze and decide the necessary action for whatever news they can bring."

Natira took a sip of apple juice before replying. "The way to do that is to make sure you are ready for whatever may come. We'll train you every day to ensure you are prepared for the fight when it happens. Not only that, but we'll teach you about the war that we're fighting, and what it means to be a rebel."

That's it? Train all day waiting for something to happen?

"So, there's no super elaborate plan where we go undercover and ruin The Committee from the inside out? We're just going to sit here and train?" Marah prodded on the verge of impatience. *I'll be here forever.*

"Yes and no," answered Kiera. "We need you to be ready to fight. You're supposed to be the force that we need, which means that you need to be able to both fight and defend yourself, should the need arise. Especially if we're going to win. Things are bound to happen soon since The Committee will eventually figure out that you're here with us. They'll want to do things quickly and rashly, something that we can take advantage of."

I suppose that makes sense.

Swallowing sugary syrup, Marah wondered what things were expected to happen quickly.

Whoever was going to answer didn't get the chance to as one of the cafe droids rolled by, tittering, "Shall I take those plates for you, Miss Morana?"

"Sure," said Marah as she put her plate and cup on the tray the robot was holding. "Thank you," she said as the bot made its way around the table to collect all the dishes.

She got up and followed the three rebels towards the North Wing. Just as she had expected, the room was as lively as it had been yesterday. This time, everyone was so submerged in their own tasks and conversations that no one paid any heed to Marah, something the human was grateful for.

The Wing resembled a unified passionate force that was immensely dedicated to its cause. Marah couldn't help but feel inspired by what these people were doing, dedicating their entire lives to a cause that may or may not turn out for the better.

Leia gestured for the three to follow, so they did, with Marah trailing a few steps behind them into a side room. The aliens sat down at a circular table and Leia opened the chest that sat atop it, placing its contents—oval-shaped beacon-like devices—for all to see. The Novan tapped each one, causing projections of newspapers and images to appear.

The first was a projection of a thin purple beacon, a recording of Committee ships descended onto a planet with bomb-like devices humming to life before they smashed atop a world. The recording, dated years ago, glitched and a newspaper officiated by The Committee read: "Let the obliteration of Nantak be a warning to those that defy our order and peace. No Nantak remains unscathed from our wrath."

The words glitched and fast-forwarded clips of the bombs smashing homes, buildings, and people as they wept, bled, and struggled both atop and under the rubble. There was a call for someone to surrender in a phrase that Marah could not understand, but she cast her attention to a child with hair that Marah recognized almost immediately to be pushed against her will into a Committee ship. After seconds that played moments and hours of history, the ships lifted and then the planet broke.

Marah didn't need to ask the obvious question when the empath caught her eye as more projections appeared. "This is our history. Every one of these are news about a planet destroyed or surrendered."

"I don't understand," mused Marah as she glanced at the presentation of Natira's home world, "how can you break a planet?" She lifted her gaze to headlines of Nova and Zona welcoming The Committee. The Committee's description of rebuilding and peace paled in comparison to other projections describing the events with phrases such as "thousands killed," "bombings," and "shown no mercy or remorse." Her stomach churned as she sensed The Committee's determination.

Natira shrugged. "The Committee's entry was always the same: dropping bombs. Lethal bombs that first killed aliens and ruined cities. Eventually, bombs started to contain chemicals that, once released, could either rot a planet and anyone on it, or destroy it."

Marah held a sigh. It seemed that the more she learned about the enemy, the more she felt inadequate.

"Only one planet, Nantak, has ever been totally destroyed in our solar system of nine," pointed out Leia. "The only planets to not be entirely under The Committee's rule are Earth, Artemis, Stella with fifty percent dual-ownership."

A sour expression came over Marah's face as she counted that to be a grand sum of three. Two of which actually mattered. One and a half really.

"And the worlds didn't try to team up or something?"

"Nope," scoffed Natira, picking at dirt under her fingernails concomitantly, "some value political agendas and money over lives and liberties."

"And the worlds not taken over yet? Earth and…?"

Marah's question was answered by Kiera, with words gentler than Natira's. "Artemis. Because Artemis is a small planet too, with fewer than ten countries, and isn't as sophisticated as the other worlds. The people live in tribes, and because of their simplistic lives, The Committee hasn't taken an immense interest in them. Artemians aren't the most social beings across the galaxy."

"But if you guys know that Artemians," the word rolled off Marah's tongue strangely, "are in danger, why don't you just go and warn them before anyone gets hurt?"

"We did." Natira pushed a yellow beacon forward.

The projection dated back to two weeks ago.

It was written by *Keeping Up With the Times*, and had a rather interesting headline in big, bold lettering: "Rebel leaders arrested in attempt to harass planet Artemis." Underneath the headlines was a grainy photo of Leia and Natira, handcuffed and bloody.

Marah's hazel eyes looked up, fighting fear for an explanation. *Could this happen to me?*

"We need to do something bigger," stated Leia. "We showed up and got attacked by the Artemians. Somehow The Committee got involved and came, and you can probably figure out what happened from there."

Marah didn't understand but held her tongue.

As if Kiera could read the confusion that clouded Marah's head, she supplied, "In order to make the most effective stand we can, we need as much support as we can get. If The Committee takes Artemis, then they're only stronger. It's hard enough to resist an empire, but at least we know that the Artemians are old-fashioned and don't ally with other worlds. If we get there without an actual legitimate reason to convince them, they might set up another ambush. Because of this, our best bet is to go there right before The Committee strikes; that way they can see that we're on their side."

"Hopefully the Artemians won't be so barbaric when we try to save them again," Natira jeered.

Casting her eyes away from black and white pictures that displayed dead bodies with dark-colored liquid seeping out of lifeless, empty eyes, Marah contemplated aloud. "So how do we do all of that?"

The human resisted a shudder as the events she read about unfolded inside her mind, causing a sinking feeling to settle in the pit of her stomach. The disheartening shots of death and suffering on the front pages spoke volumes about what she was getting herself into; reinforced by images on the following pages of The Committee's ships. She could see that they had weapons capable of mass destruction, and what did the rebels have? Androids that could cook and clean. *Can they really pull this off?*

Marah bit her lip, sinking into the flesh hard enough to feel it but not to draw blood. *You can't think like that. We have to try at the very least.*

The Novan's answer pulled Marah away from her thoughts. "Yeah, that's the easy - well easy-ish - part. Hopefully, The Committee isn't in a rush to conquer Artemis, as far as we know. In the meantime, we can take advantage of that."

Marah nodded, unable to get the images in front of her out of her head. Empty eyes that were once full of life were branded into her mind, and she wasn't sure that this would be the only time she'd see death like this.

She wasn't the only one who was reliving the stories conveyed through words and photos, some dated back earlier than her birth. She pretended not to notice as Natira eyed the articles with a sour expression, long slender fingers curling slowly into fists. Kiera leaned over and placed a hand over one of the Nantak's, whispering softly, "Bono malum superate, bona fide." *Overcome evil with good in good faith.*

Marah couldn't help but blurt out, "You guys speak Latin? That's the super cool alien language, Latin?"

"Yeah," answered Leia, somewhat surprised. "Across the worlds are different languages, but on Kosmir the most popular ones are English and Latin. Latin was the first language of our kind, as our ancestors created it and carried it on to humans. Though we call it Kosna."

Natira stood sharply, setting the articles aside. "We need to train." She then rose from her seat and took off, a gesture that Marah took as an invitation to follow, who glanced at the Novan and the Zonan for reassurance.

Kiera wore a small smile that didn't match the pain in her eyes as she replied, "She'll be alright. She's sensitive about her planet, and seeing the articles was like a fresh cut to the heart."

Marah moved to catch up with Natira, not wanting to anger the rebel. She remained silent as she followed Natira to a large room, which she had a distinct memory of walking past yesterday.

"This is our arsenal," said Natira finally, walking through a door that didn't match the size of the area it concealed.

The arsenal was a large room that was similar to the suit room, Marah observed. Her eyes scoured over rows and rows of weapons hung up, stored in drawers, labeled in bins, or standing in lockers. They were displayed in sections that ranged from swords to blasters to blades.

"It's a dream come true." remarked Marah as she looked around the endless walls of various items, plasma blasters, neon-fused crossbows, and guns coated in gel, and a grip device that when she approached it illuminated into a sword. "Totally cool."

Natira shifted as she smoothed out her black t-shirt. "Alright, so we're going to do more weapon practice, but I wanted you to pick out a weapon that you want to work with. We're going to practice blasters more, but we can also try something else if you see something that you like. Take a look around."

Marah let herself walk around the room. Even though she would much rather stick to her bow and arrow, she didn't want to give Natira a hard time, especially since she was already not feeling her best.

Alright, so what's a cool weapon?

She walked past the swords and paused, marveling at one particular sword that looked like it belonged strapped to the back of a knight. It was about fifteen inches long, with a ruby stone smack in the center of its black leather hilt.

It looks nice, she mused, *but to carry that with my bow and arrow wouldn't be fun.*

She walked past the swords to a wall of shelves that held an array of blasters. Each blaster looked vastly different from the others, varying in height, weight, and even color scheme, making it hard for the human to pick one. She frowned, placing her hands on her hips as she scanned up and down for a weapon that resonated with her.

Think of the aesthetic! She held back a laugh. *If I was thinking of the aesthetic I would've gone for a dagger, duh.* Her thoughts trailed away as she eyed a ten-inch-long blaster just above her line of vision. She picked up the device, feeling how heavy it was. *It's not as comfortable as the bow, but it's not that bad,* she mulled as she held it up with one hand, poised to shoot.

"That's a nice blaster, one of my favorites actually. It's a plasma model 2k." Marah turned to find Natira flipping a sheathed dagger.

"Totally not stalkerish."

Natira shrugged coyly. "I like to see the weapon-choosing process. You don't choose the weapon; it chooses you. Each is inclined to their own. I see that while you're holding the blaster, you would much rather use your bow and arrow."

Marah half-laughed. "Can you blame me?"

The Nantak wryly shook her head. "Not at all. I'm the same way. I prefer sharp objects over these things. We can put it in your locker after we're done training."

Marah lowered the hand holding the blaster against her side. She shifted on her feet, waiting for Natira to further instruct. *Well, this is awkward.*

The two were silent until Natira raised a brow. "You don't have to."

Marah wore confusion like a well-fitted glove.

"You don't have to walk on eggshells is what I'm trying to say. You can still talk and make your," the Nantak scrunched up her face, "odd references. You don't have to be so quiet because of earlier."

Marah offered a wane smile. "Oh yeah, sure." A widening grin crept up her features. "I knew you liked my references."

Natira rolled gray eyes. "Oh, ha-ha. Now c'mon. We have to train if we're going to fight in a war."

Fast forward a few hours, a collection of black and blue bruises, and a whole lot of pointers from Natira, and the human still missed punches and had a form that had her tumbling to the ground.

Technically, Marah had already beaten Natira. At least, she had thought so when she had finally succeeded in pinning the alien to the ground. It came out of nowhere, surprising both girls. Before Marah could express some victory after three hours of constant defeat, the

Nantak pushed her knees at Marah's chest, who went skidding back and thumped to the floor.

Marah held back a sigh. She knew her self-worth and that there were things that she was good at and things that she wasn't. It was in her human nature, and she knew that this was always going to be the case. While the rebels had nothing on her archery skills, Marah didn't quite enjoy the struggle in attempting to overcome the inability of a skill that was seemingly demanded, required actually, of her.

It seemed that since she arrived on Kosmir, archery determined her worth—something that if her mother knew she'd scoff at.

To think that the one thing she hated is why I might be the key to stopping alien dictators.

Perhaps, the struggle of the idea that she would never do something good enough had driven her to run away from her parents' house and never look back. The words from the last comic she read rang through her head as she grunted from a punch from Natira: *The battle within often carries the most struggle.*

And as of right now, Marah was struggling to hold her own against Natira. The pestering dilemma encouraged feelings of frustration to pulse with every move.

She remained silent as she deflected a jab to the gut, focusing on how the hell she was supposed to take down Natira without accidentally unnerving her.

She already said that you were fine—why are you worried about upsetting her?

I want her to think that I'm worthy of helping their cause. I have to be good at something, remember what She always said?

Marah quietly sighed as Natira withdrew and circled her. "Again."

It's not all about her.

A sour taste filled her mouth as she refused to lose focus, looking ahead to Natira, who was much closer than she had remembered; trying to figure out what attack the alien would throw out. Natira was so hard yet so easy to read at the same time. The Nantak was tough, no doubt about it, with a rock-hard exterior at least in front of others. Somehow, there had been an earlier time, not too long ago, where she had seen Natira as someone who had been so scarred that she had become accustomed to the dark parts of life.

Marah just managed to throw her head back as the Nantak delivered two punches toward her chest, one right after the other. She caught the second fist and twisted it away from her chest, enough to create some tension in the alien's wrist but no harm.

But Marah could have sworn she saw Natira blink back tears, and it was then that she realized that under every tough shell was a human heart. It was just as Kiera had said—all hearts bled from reopened wounds.

She threw a kick towards Natira, creating some distance between the two. She kept her fists up, one protecting most of her face while the other was at her side ready to throw.

Just like you do.

Marah was still alien—pun fully intended—not only to the concepts of what she was doing and where, but also to whom she was doing all of this with. She knew names and faces, and yet still felt like an outsider. *After all, a supercomputer pulled my name out of a magic hard drive.* The so-called savior knew that she didn't belong with the rebels, and yet while her brain begged for her to go home, her heart urged her to stay and fight.

And what could be more superhero cliche than that?

"You go first. Defending without attacking is a decent strategy. But sometimes you have to be the attacker. You want to control the fight so you can win."

Marah hesitated, used to defending herself but never attacking. It wasn't in her nature to be the one to start something, and besides, she wouldn't know how to block Natira. She threw a cross punch towards Natira's head but her hand got knocked off course as Natira spun on her heel, roundhouse-kicking the hand out of orbit.

A grunt slipped out of Marah as Natira declared that they were going to take a break.

Annoyance was evident in Marah's features as Natira moved to a metal bench where robots tittered to and fro carrying various equipment. "Did you really have to do that? You couldn't have just let me win once out of how many times? We've been training for hours; the least you could do is let me win once."

Be careful where you bleed. Don't bleed accidentally.

Marah realizing what she had said, was about to apologize when Natira countered in a less chiding tone than her own. "On the battlefield, your opponent will do everything within their capability to take you down and will not," bitterness seeped into the rebel's tone, "let you win. You've never fought in a battle before. I have. It's not easy. As a child, I was forced to fight in arenas where my performance would win someone money or cause my death."

Marah looked away. At the white walls. At the black-tiled floor. At her bow.

"Other times, the fight needed to be fought. Either way, fighting isn't about winning or losing. It's about intention. If you fight for the wrong reasons, you're a lost fighter. If you're fighting for the right reasons, then you're a survivor. But that's not enough. If you don't know what you're doing then you will not succeed, intention be damned." She concluded with hard eyes, "The last thing we need is another person dead."

Great job. I thought you didn't want to upset her even more.

"I'm—"

As if right on cue, Leia burst through the door with worry etched all over her face. She didn't give either girl an opportunity to speak as she ordered, "You two need to come with me right now."

The conversation was put on hold as the two shared quizzical looks before following Leia into the North Wing. All the rebels were gathered there, including Kiera. A woman with frizzed and curly hair and a stone hanging from her neck stood in the center of attention, a timid expression donning her features.

The woman shrank under all of the attention as she waited for the leaders of the rebellion to gather.

As Marah walked through, the woman's eyes met hers and her hands fell slack by her sides. "It's you," she murmured, eyes lighting up.

Right, Marah remembered. *I'm the chosen one.*

Leia cleared her throat, and then the woman remembered what was at stake.

The rebel spoke plainly. "I've discovered that The Committee is planning on taking Artemis. Tonight."

The reaction to the woman's voice was immediate, sending a rippling effect through everyone who had heard the words. The sound of pens dropping collided against frenzied murmurs.

Marah watched worry and panic scrawl itself across faces while her gut churned, remembering the importance of planet Artemis to the rebellion's cause. She turned to the rebellion leaders, watching as something incomprehensible stirred inside the three of them.

Leia sprinted out of the Wing, not bothering to share where she was going. Kiera, meanwhile, addressed the crowd in a tone that suggested that she was forcing calmness. "Get the ships ready. We'll take four strike teams with us."

The Zonan then turned and followed Leia.

Natira was right behind Kiera when she turned around stiffly to see Marah still as she observed the effect the news had on the rebels. "Marah."

Marah looked about wildly, struggling to quicken her pace so as to keep up with the alien. "I'm sorry about earlier."

Natira dismissed her, and her voice sounded both like herself and not "Don't worry about it. Get ready, we're going to fight."

Marah looked at Natira incredulously. "We? I thought I wasn't ready to be in the field?"

The two entered the suit room, where Leia was already ready to go. "Well, you're going to have to be now," the rebel urged hastily. "C'mon, we've got to go, stat. There's a curtain on the top."

Marah nodded, scanning her hand to unlock her suit. The glass doors parted, and she stepped inside. Before she could pull down the curtain, Kiera appeared behind her, holding her quiver and bow. "Here." As quickly as she had come, she was gone.

Setting the weapons on the side, Marah pulled the curtain down and stared at the suit. *Her suit*, she remembered.

Putting the suit on, the human could only stare at the prophesied person that she was. The blue she was now wearing was the same color of the rebels' uniform, and it was hard for her to meet her own eyes in the mirror. She did not see the hero the rebels needed her to be. She was wearing a suit manufactured by people who had expectations and a vision of her that she wasn't quite sure she was ever going to fit, let alone surpass.

She eyed the plasma ray blaster she had picked out earlier today, chained to her side. *I'm not ready for any of this.*

She sucked in a breath while strapping her quiver across her back. It was now or never.

Chapter 9

Location: From the realm that fosters rebellion to the stars as constant as the skies above.

Marah Morana climbed onto *The Fortem* with aliens that she was only beginning to acquaint herself with. The aircraft that had brought her from Earth to Kosmir was relatively small from the outside and its steel bore a plethora of battle scars. She found it just her luck that the ship that she was boarding would bring her to the soils of another planet instead of the one that she called home. The craft was smaller than the ones carrying the fighter troops, and yet the human allowed herself to sit at the farthest seat from the others. She set her bow on her lap with her arms across her chest, not bothering to acknowledge what the beings around her were saying, instead choosing to think about what had become of her life.

Just last week, she had been living her quaint, normal life on Earth. Now, her life had spun some wonky one hundred and eighty degrees where aliens were undeniably real, and she was living alongside them.

She was going to fight in a war—an alien war —against aliens that wanted her dead.

What has my life even become?

She was so absorbed in her own little bubble that she failed to notice that *The Fortem* had begun to rise. Within a matter of minutes, Marah Morana had become the first human being to leave Kosmir's orbit.

She only realized this when she turned her head to and found the one view she never thought she'd see.

Twinkling stars that wore the appearance of dotted glitter were much larger than Marah could've ever fantasized. Giant hues of purple, blue and green sparkled amongst a vast inky black that was speckled with stardust.

It's almost poetic, Marah thought. *Spending countless hours staring up at the stars that looked like little lights that were out of reach, and now being on a ship seeing them up close, is so surreal.*

She had never felt so captivated, with her eyes trained to the visuals of space. All her life, she had been stuck on the ground with a universe as big as she wanted it to be. She had finally gained control of her life and wrote her own rules only for it all to be thrown out the window.

Here, to be a human on a spaceship soaring through the cosmos, it dawned on Marah that the universe was far bigger than she had ever anticipated.

She knew she shouldn't be freaking out so much, but because she was actually *in* space, she was. She had seen pictures of space before— computer-generated images pasted into National Geographic books, scientific textbooks, and sci-fi movies—but to physically be going to a planet no human ever has been to, was something that couldn't be put into words. Everything felt so real, with hidden traces of looming shadows that made the hair on the back of Marah's neck stand up.

This is real.

And it was majestic.

She didn't feel human anymore. She felt something else fill a void that she didn't even know had existed within her. Which was saying something, considering that she was in the presence of beings capable of the supernatural. All she had was herself, her bow, and a bunch of arrows.

She glanced toward the rebellion leaders conversing amongst themselves and considered sitting with them. But then she remembered Natira's words when she had let her emotions get the better of her while sparring and discarded the idea.

Marah knew that she shouldn't have said what she did, and yet she couldn't help but feel stung by the Nantak's words.

Natira was right. This wasn't some video game with do-overs. The chance that she could die hadn't become real until Natira had pointed it out, which of course only fueled the human's own ideas about what her role would be in this fight.

I'm not going to be a big help, but whatever.

You're supposed to be something more, something bigger and greater than just this.

Marah made a sour expression. *What even is this? They can do the impossible. What can I do?*

She missed her room, with novels, comics, and figurines strewn on shelves. She was just a seventeen-year-old kid who lived by herself.

And somehow, she was the one whom the universe was depending on.

When I said that I wanted to do good things in this life, I didn't mean one that could literally blow up on me.

She bit her lip, thinking about what Natira had mentioned during their sparring session. The rebels were mostly orphans, while the Committee were all much older with younger recruits. The Committee sat comfortably in their headquarters, thriving while the rebels barely had enough money to give everyone their own room while they planned for war.

The leftover children shouldn't be fighting battles.

Despite that, children were on their way to fighting a battle that may or may not be the conclusion of their existence.

"Are you nervous?"

The words took Marah by surprise as she turned her head away from the view out the window beside her and was met with Kiera in front of her.

Marah nodded, finding no reason to lie. *After all, it's not every day you're the only human fighting in an alien space war.*

Kiera wore a sympathetic expression as the oval-marking on her forehead glowed ever so slightly. "We're all nervous. Considering you just got here, I'm more than willing to bet that you're feeling all sorts of things."

"You could say that."

"The first time that I really fought," the Zonan looked down at her uniform with colors very bright for war attire, "I was wearing this, and I got arrested. I was supposed to carry the great legacy of the rebels before me and within my first week I had built a rather public criminal record. Don't be what we or others are expecting of you, be what you can be. So, take it from me, don't put pressure on yourself." She gestured to her forehead; I can feel it coming from you. I can sense that something happened between you and Natira."

Marah blushed. "I didn't mean to get all upset. How'd you know?"

Kiera smiled, but the smile only reached one of the corners of her lips. "Empath? It's alright. We've all been there. She's not upset, if you're wondering. Natira's not one to hold grudges over small things like that.

You two have more in common than either of you think. We're all made of stardust."

Marah nodded, unsure of where the Zonan was going with this.

"Anyway, I wanted to say that you'll be with us the whole time, something I hope helps your nerves." Kiera smiled, reaching out to pat Marah's knee with one hand while using the other to sweep hair from her eyes to capture a peek at the cosmos they were sailing through. "I know how hard this can be, and we're really grateful that you're here with us."

Marah couldn't help the slight sting in her words as she cast her eyes down, "Of course. I am the chosen one, after all."

Kiera nodded without comment. "You are," she added after a pause. Her words took Marah by surprise.

"Yes, you are," Kiera repeated when Marah looked up at her. "You have grit, I see it in your eyes. You are an able fighter. Having grit and confidence can make you superior to your opponents. Having those traits is admirable, especially when one encounters something they have never done, let alone dreamed of doing before. Most people fight with emotion. Justice, liberty, fear, anger. Find what resonates with you. What is motivating you to fight?"

Getting kidnapped and forced to be here. Marah was grateful that Kiera could only read emotions and not thoughts.

"If it's anger, you have to make sure that you manipulate anger for the right reasons. Use anger to make a strategic plan, so your victory is assured. Otherwise, you're throwing yourself out there to get hurt."

Marah shrugged, leaning her head against a window. "It's harder to do that with aliens. I don't really hunt, I practice shooting. I only hunt out of need. I took fighting classes for the same reason. Assuming that you saw me shoot that deer down, I know how to defend, but not attack." She hung her head low. "That's what Natira was trying to teach me."

"Same thing here. We realize that our plans, our actions, and our words might not make sense to you," The Zonan politely reminded. "This isn't something that you know a lot about, which is okay. When this first started, I promised myself I would never hurt anyone. I would let them hurt me, and then hurt back. To hurt without reason felt wrong. That's what The Committee does. But then I realized it's not the same."

Hazel eyes found brown. "How so?"

"The Committee hurts because they want control. They want power and greed. We want to end suffering. And sometimes, we have to sacrifice our morals if we want to do that. Or if we want to survive. I used to hate killing," Kiera winced, "but when I nearly had my life taken trying to save a planet, I realized that sometimes you have to do whatever it takes, as long as you know that you are doing it for the right reasons."

"That makes sense, I guess. History suggests Good always defends and Evil always attacks, but you're right. It's not always about what we do, but why."

Kiera smiled. "We're defending lives. Not just the lives of Artemians who probably have no clue what's coming their way, but other lives all across the universe. Every life saved here is one less life that has to suffer in the future. The Committee has been attacking planets and forcing their traditions and rules on everyone that survives their attacks. The ones that don't listen, whether on their planet or on Kosmir, are doomed to perish by their hands."

Marah paused, thinking about Kiera's words. "It's not only that," she confided. "What I'm doing and thinking is based on what I know and see, but it's all fiction. But that pales in comparison to what's coming."

Kiera hummed, listening intently.

Marah held her tongue to figure her wording out. "You guys have the experience, the etiquette, all of that. You know how to disarm someone and use your abilities to do amazing things. Apparently, I'm the chosen one, someone who is supposed to be all-powerful and capable of helping defeat The Committee. But I'm the one with the disadvantage compared to everyone else. I'm in unfamiliar territory, and I'm outpowered compared to my opponent. It's like bringing a hole-puncher to a gunfight, but all the people with guns were trained in the army." Marah sighed, looking at the bow in her hands. "What if this is all a mistake? What if I'm not the savior that you need? What if this is the tipping point in your battle, but because of me you'll lose it?"

Kiera was silent, and Marah considered the idea that Kiera would agree with her words. Instead, the alien tilted her head and pursed her lips, "So what?"

Marah blinked. "I'm sorry?"

"Bearing this title doesn't mean that you're facing this alone. The rebels are a team. We win together and we lose together. You might think you don't have the capability to do this," Kiera smiled, "but I do."

What are you seeing that I'm not?

"It's not because I spied on The Committee and found you. I'll admit, I had my doubts when I first heard that you were the key. Rather, the more I got to know you, the more I was convinced that you were right to be chosen."

"Why?"

"Because you're still here. You're trying. So, what if you've never fought like this before? We weren't born fighters. Think of it as like you're trying to hunt the enemy instead of…"

Marah finished with her arms lowered from across her chest, "A boar? Fair enough, I guess. I just don't want to get caught off-guard like a deer in headlights."

It was Kiera's turn to stare. "What's a deer?"

Marah laughed at the perplexion written over the alien's features, "I'll teach you later," she chuckled, "when we're not fighting evil dictators."

Kiera opened her mouth to speak when Leia interrupted. "We're landing in five minutes. Get ready. We don't know what we'll be facing out there."

Kiera turned back to Marah, a wan smile resting on her features as she tilted her head toward where Leia and Natira were discussing something amongst themselves. "Come on."

Holding back her hesitation, Marah stood up and followed Kiera, letting the words of the Zonan wash over her.

Maybe she's right, I can do this.

Chapter 10

Location: Planet 4 - Artemis, the realm of the "bloody barbarians"

Marah held onto Kiera's hope as she looked out the glass window while *The Fortem* descended onto the planet Artemis. Her eyes fell on sandstone terrain, which encouraged the girl to better observe the third planet she would venture to.

An infinite bank of haematic red sand was a heavy contrast from the milky atmosphere, standing proudly as color clouded against the black abyss of space. The planet resembled what Marah expected Mars to look like—if Mars had bare aspen trees, clans of tents, and low-leveled buildings.

And, of course, the evident living beings.

Despite the beauty of the realm, Marah couldn't help but fear what the planet had to offer. The Artemians were already painted a certain way in her head, which made her knees tremble and her fingers itch to hold her bow tighter.

Even worse, Marah had no idea what was coming. Nor did she want to know what would happen once The Committee came. It reminded her of whenever she'd go hunting and suspected that something was lurking about without being a hundred percent sure.

If this was a movie, she deduced, this would usually be the part where right as the rebels land, something out of nowhere would strike *The Fortem* and The Committee would try to blow the rebels to bits. Either they'd get wiped out then and there or somehow miraculously survive, only to die some point later that day.

Marah shuddered at the thought of her body being crushed under bomb debris, blood, and bodies. *Dying does not sound fun at all.*

Her allies must have shared the same thoughts as she looked over to them and noticed wary expressions creeping onto their faces. Kiera wore confliction, something that wasn't conveyed by her eyes or the frown on her lips, but rather by the light of her circular marking on her forehead pulsating between light and dim, mimicking the rumbling clouds overhead. Natira held the same dagger from earlier and was sharpening it against another blade, her eyes clouded with what Marah perceived as either determination or the past catching up with her. As for their leader, the girl had her arms crossed her chest with a stumped expression, which caught Marah by surprise since Leia was the one who gave orders and wore the title of leader fittingly. Marah could tell that Leia was dreading the fight that they were moments from entering, but she wasn't sure what it was about it that the Novan dreaded.

The Artemians? The Committee? The chance of death? What does she prefer to face?

Marah didn't have the chance to ask as the pilot spoke. "Strap in. We're landing."

She sat down and buckled her belt as the pilot had ordered. The landing was smoother than she had expected, and before she knew it, she was stepping down onto red sand. She crouched down and scooped a handful of sand, watching the grains trickle in between her fingers. The substance's color created an unsettling feeling in her chest, red reminding her of what lay ahead until a sparkle caught her eye.

A black opal was all that was left in her hand.

Curious, Marah scooped up another handful of sand and released it, this time not finding anything else. She closed the hand holding the stone tight as she lifted her head up and marveled at her surroundings, absorbing the world she had stepped on.

How can I breathe here?

She stood up and placed the opal in her suit pouch as she let herself walk away from the others to observe the foreign planet. The bank of sand stretched on for an infinity, which made her wonder if there was any water on the planet.

Marah didn't stray too far from the rebels as she continued to wander. Reminding herself of the woods and all the times she accidentally got lost, she knew that someone who was lost wasn't the same as someone who purposefully wandered unfamiliar territory.

She kept her distance minimal, fearing the planet that was soon to be a battleground.

Staring ahead, something collided right into her, knocking her to the ground. No longer in a state of reminiscence, Marah rolled over to find Kiera getting to her feet. A short distance away, where she had just been standing, was a small crater made by an exploding bomb, with a wake of smoke wafting upward.

Woah.

Marah locked eyes with the Zonan. "Thank you. Is it time?"

She followed the alien's eyes to see Leia's lips falling into a firm line. "Look for yourself."

Marah's eyes flickered upwards, and the color drained from her face. Replacing the once clear inky sky were large aircrafts with all sorts of weapons directed down toward the planet's surface.

Then came the fear, a swift dose of panic that thrummed in Marah's heart as she got to her feet, cape and hair flying. "What do we do?"

Leia's gaze was toward The Committee's aircrafts. "The two teams in the air are going to work on covering the airspace." By then, the rebel leaders and Marah were in a line, with two strike teams of thirty rebels behind them. The Novan cast her arms out to the side, fingers outstretched as purple bolts flickered to life. "We'll handle whatever decides to come down here," she concluded.

At that, Kiera braced herself, her marking glowing a blue somehow brighter than her as she moved her fists in front of her. Natira, next to Marah, was poised with a blaster in her right hand and wore a look as if she dared someone to start a fight with her.

As for Marah, she reached for an arrow from her quiver and nocked it, unsure of what she was supposed to do next except for stand in dreadful anticipation.

A robotic voice blared out of nowhere, and the lack of emotion sent chills rolling down Marah's spine, "Planet Artemis, we are The Committee. We intend to achieve universal peace. Surrender to us so we may unite and save the universe."

Do they not see us?

Marah looked left and then right, looking for someone to answer The Committee.

There was a moment of silence, and she was beginning to wonder if one of the rebels should answer when she heard the faint sound of an accented chant.

"Darci!"

"Darci!"

Then, one voice became two as another joined in on the chant. "Darci!"

"Darci!"

The two voices became three, until dozens of voices cried out into the fray.

"Darci!"

"Darci!"

"Darci!"

Marah turned to Leia, her face a question mark. "What are they saying?"

"I'm not sure. I think a battle cry? Hopefully, they get that we're on their side and we don't have a repeat of last time."

"Can't you just tell them? What happened last time?"

Leia winced. "Let's just say it didn't work out so well. None of us can speak their language."

You've got to be kidding me.

The protest against domination reverberated. Once Marah looked closely and found the Artemians ready to defend, emotion pooled in her chest.

Men were dressed in armor that Marah assumed to be their tribal colors as they raised their weapons - swords, spears, daggers, and axes - to the sky while descending the hill onto the battleground, a giant sweep of motion that was quite the spectacle.

Marah found women accompanying the men, some wearing headdresses while others wore intricate hairstyles as they donned violet-colored clothing and weapons, standing defiant against The Committee ships that swarmed over their homeland.

Natira made a pleased sound. "Would you look at that? They're on our side."

Marah looked at her. "But they don't know that. And the rest of the planet?" As hopeful as everyone had become, Marah couldn't rule out the fear that erupted in her heart.

Kiera explained in a hushed tone, as she too felt marveled by the unexpected support, "This is the capital of Artemis, Lonya. If the Committee conquers Lonya, they conquer the planet by default. The Minya tribe has ruled Lonya for centuries; they're the strongest tribe on the planet."

Marah gripped the handle of her bow tighter, worry foaming tenfold. "And what happens to the Artemians who don't know what's going on?"

No one replied.

By now, the Artemians' battle cry was deafening. Although Marah couldn't understand what the Artemians were saying, she couldn't help but steel herself, for war had arrived.

Marah had never thought of war like this. Not that she ever had the chance, given that this would be the first time the girl would be engaging in the sport. War was about power, money, territory. Though, war also had a habit of revealing the true colors of the characters that were to engage in its froth.

Earlier, Marah had been told the people of planet Artemis were barbaric. Looking into eyes that wore fury and determination like a golden crown, she knew the rebels had been wrong. This wasn't barbarism; this was an act of protection and unification, to stand together and defend morals, lives, rights, and honor.

The larger of The Committee's vessel opened, and smaller ships descended onto the sandstone soil, releasing troops of uniformed soldiers who brandished weapons of their own. They wore visors covering their eyes and Marah couldn't help but shrink back as they marched toward the rebels and Artemians.

In a voice thick with hesitancy, Marah drew an arrow back. "What is our plan, exactly?"

Natira began to advance toward the enemy as she cocked her blaster. "We fight." She pressed the blaster's trigger and started running toward the enemy soldiers.

Alrighty then. Here goes nothing.

Swallowing panic, Marah let go of an arrow, sending it toward a soldier's feet, stopping the alien in their tracks. She quickly drew another arrow and fired it in the same direction, watching it sail right into the arm of the masked soldier. With an anguished cry, the soldier released their weapon, and Marah knew she had to shoot the soldier, yet she couldn't bring herself to do so.

A blast from behind her shot the visored solider in the chest, who emitted an ear-splitting yell that pierced Marah's ears too loud for her comfort. He ungracefully sank onto Artemis's soil as his body went slack.

Taking her place was a blast sent by a rebel with antennas stemming from his forehead who came to her side. Each hand sporting a plasma blaster similar to the one Marah owned, he had no difficulty in shooting Committee soldiers. He looked at her while doing so, antennas humming a bright white as he asked, "Are you alright?"

Marah was slightly trembling, despite being nocked and loaded. She wondered if the rebel thought she was a fool to stand on the front lines in a suit that only made her stick out like a sore thumb—exactly what she was. "We do have to hit them. Don't we?"

"I'm afraid so. You don't have to kill them if that's what you're worried about. But I strongly suggest incapacitating them because—"

The rebel pulled Marah back to avoid a spray of energy from burning their faces. "This is pretty daunting," he said, "I get it. Take it one bad guy at a time, okay?"

He waited for her to somewhat nod before rolling to help out another rebel.

Facing the soldiers alone, Marah stood up. Shakily drawing her bow, she closed her eyes for a moment and let go. She winced as she tried to tune out the sound of a splintered yell as her arrowhead pierced a visored being's calf. Deciding that since the being was down, her damage was done, she forced herself to pluck another arrow and keep moving.

At the same time, the Artemian army had joined the rebels in the advancement towards The Committee. By then, the battlefield was a blur of colors and Marah had to move slowly on the offense and quickly on the defense because as fast as she tried to mimic the rebels' efforts in keeping Committee soldiers down, they were just as keen to do the same to them.

Marah inhaled sharply as she drew her bow once again, carefully pivoting on her heels as she scanned the crowd around her for a specific target. It was hard for her to figure out where she should aim the nocked arrow as rebels, Artemians, and Committee soldiers clashed all over; if her aim wasn't precise, she might hit the wrong person. She didn't get the chance to shoot as something hit her, sending her a few feet forward.

The impact took her by surprise, but she was able to stay on her feet. She whipped behind her and found a soldier advancing towards her with a scepter. Despite her stomach churning, she dismissed the painless attack and fired an arrow straight into the soldier's ankle.

The being, whom Marah assumed was a woman from the blonde ponytail protruding from the back of her visor, stumbled over, and writhed in pain.

Right as the arrow pierced flesh, the sound of a cocked gun grabbed Marah's attention, pulling her into a one-eighty turn. There, she found a trio of Committee soldiers making a beeline toward her, spacing themselves out so she wouldn't be able to outrun them with the blonde behind her.

She glanced wildly at each soldier and fought to hold back the thrumming fear and anticipation from getting to her as she shot three arrows, one right after the other toward some body part of the soldiers.

While Natira would chastise her for not shooting for the head, neck, or heart, two out of Marah's three efforts were successful as just when at the last minute, the blonde woman lunged at her.

Marah panicked and sloppily threw herself to the side, so all the woman did was kick up a cloud of dust as she got to her feet.

"Pathetic rebel," she hissed before throwing herself at Marah and tackling her to the ground. The soldier had more experience fighting, as she managed to pry the bow out of Marah's hands and grappled with the human, pinning her down effectively.

That really, really hurt. Ouch.

Marah winced as the breath was choked out of her. She lolled her head to the side and wriggled her chest so she could move, but the woman's hold on her was too strong. The blonde pushed her fist toward Marah's neck, but the latter did her best to hold it in place, let alone push back.

Uh-

Marah wheezed as more insults were hurled at her and felt the control of her breathing slip away when her hand, in an effort to reach her bow, grasped the holster of her blaster and smacked it against the woman's face.

The soldier immediately jerked back, and the sway of her weight gave Marah the opportunity to push her off with more effort than she thought it would take. She rolled, and with a groan, grasped her bow and slammed it into the woman's head hard enough to make her collapse to the ground with her eyes rolling to the back of her head.

"That was intense," she sighed when a flash of purple caused her to duck, curling in on herself. She quickly stood back up and turned away from the unconscious body that lay next to her, breathing loudly to calm herself down.

I'm okay. This is totally normal, everything is fine. It's not but I'm okay. I think.

She sucked in a breath, feeling her heartbeat thud against her chest as beads of sweat raced each other down her cheeks. She wiped her brow, letting oxygen fill her burning lungs, pausing, preparing to return to the battle ahead of her.

"Darci!"

Marah didn't get to prepare for long before, as usual, the battle came to her. Her ears pricked up at the sound of footsteps, and she quickly braced herself, slender fingers hardening over the middle piece of the bow. She raised it to shoulder level and nocked an arrow, waiting for the sound of footsteps to become louder. A couple of seconds later, she twisted behind herself and shot, puncturing her attacker right above the abdomen.

Marah, startled by her missed shot, apologized as more blood than she was comfortable with started to leak from the soldier's chest. It didn't matter though when a grenade hit the soldier's boots and pulsated, sending his limp body up and slamming back down onto the ground.

Mind spewing relief that the dead body that now lay mere feet from her was not her own, she could only stare as someone spoke over the comm that Leia had given her on *The Fortem*, "How do we know if we're winning or not?"

There was a loud crashing sound that came before a reply. "I'm pretty sure we're winning because I see more of us up and alive than The Committee."

Marah tilted her head, ponytail swinging as she reached gloved hands over her shoulder and pulled out another arrow. She was about to draw it when she noticed Kiera struggling with her opponent, who had thrown her onto the ground.

She made a beeline to the Zonan when a soldier threw himself into her path. He wielded a staff and jabbed it forward, speaking bluntly, "Halt or you will be terminated!"

Halt or you will be terminated? Who even says that?

Marah stared at the soldier. Unsure of how to respond to the face instead of the visor, she drew her bow as her fingers trembled in search of where she could shoot without hurting him too much. Despite trying to look as intimidating as possible, the face the man wore reminded Marah who the battle-hungry one was.

Marah bit her lip, remembering Kiera's earlier words about her grit. "I really don't want to be here or do any of this, so please get out of my way. Let's just not."

The soldier scoffed, his hand started glowing—illuminating blond features behind his visor as he shot energy at Marah, sending her flying a few feet backward and onto the ground. She stifled a groan as she wiped loose locks of hair off her face, lifting her head only to be met with a glowing hand a foot away from her eyes.

Tasting the cloud of dust kicked up, Marah let out a huff as she eyed the visor, wishing that she could see the faces of the people that were trying to kill her. She didn't know why she wanted to see the people who wanted her dead, but she preferred to present her humanity to someone who might understand.

If anything, those who wished to see attacked harder. Another blast was fired at Marah, who winced at the slight sting that came from it.

I thought the suit was supposed to be immune to all blasts?

Marah didn't get much time to argue the technicality of all blasts when the man in the mask's hand glowed and Marah twisted just in time. A rebel shot the soldier who made an odd irking sound and then collapsed onto the ground.

She stood up and looked around, unsure of what she should do next. Everyone was fighting, to the point where Marah couldn't match faces with affiliations. Her eyes couldn't tell friend from foe as her breathing became ragged and she eyed unconscious and fallen bodies strewn all over, accompanied by puddles of blood.

It also didn't help that her ears rang from the firing that took place above her. She glanced at the rebel ships that fired at Committee ships, unable to not think about how one blast in the wrong direction would hit her. Marah blinked, finding time and space stilling as sounds became fuzzy and all she could hear was grunts and the sound of blood being spilled.

The sound of a Committee pawn struggling to get up caught her attention. Knowing that she would be attacked soon, her fingers reacted before her mind could, nocking an arrow forward.

"Stay down!" she shouted as she pulled her bow into a half-draw.

"Or else what?" The soldier scoffed. "You're not like the others. They can do what's necessary, can you?"

Marah's throat tightened. She fought to maintain eye contact, "And you? What do you fight for?"

The soldier laughed. "Is that all you rebels have to say?" His left hand eased toward a pistol and Marah saw its progress. He eyed her carefully, "I've never seen you before, you're not in any database. It doesn't matter, though." He raised his pistol and shot straight for Marah's chest, but not before the noirette loosed, turned, and ducked.

The pistol dropped into blood-stained soil and Marah's arrow hit its mark perfectly. Too perfectly.

The arrow had pierced the man through and through. Scarlet drained out of him and so did his life, as indicated by his labored breathing.

Marah could only stand there, fingers and mind going numb. She could hear Kiera's voice reminding her that part of being a rebel was making the tough calls.

Adrenaline shot through her body in sprints, and Marah instinctively shook her head. *This is no time to crash. Keep going.*

What she didn't notice was the faint whizz from a Committee speedster running at her with a blaster in hand. Marah didn't see the blaster, nor the person holding it, rather her eyes followed a dagger flying through the air and sailed right past the skin on her cheek. It was so close that she could feel the metal caress her face as it sailed past her.

She blinked as her would-be attacker yelled in anguish and collapsed onto the ground. She turned in surprise, first to the dead body, then back to where Natira stood tall. "You good?"

Marah glanced at the dead body and again back at Natira, free hand moving to calm her racing heart. "Yeah," she breathed out airily. "Thanks."

"Stay on your toes. Toss me my dagger."

Marah nodded, gripping the blade's handle, and winced as she pulled it out of the woman's abdomen before tossing the bloody blade to the Nantak.

Natira caught the blade with ease, flesh curling around the handle as she scoured the battle, calculating her throws like it was a song she had mastered singing. Marah watched as Natira tapped the dagger's hilt over her heart before furiously flinging the steel forward, embracing combat like it was an old friend.

A foot kicked Marah's back and she stumbled but saw nothing when she turned around. She stood up again only for the same thing to happen, causing her to fall to her knees. She stood up slowly, predicting that her attacker would strike her from the back so when she was kicked down again, she used her fall to nock another arrow and fire it while ignoring the screaming protest that came from her knees slamming against the ground. She caught a glimpse of her attacker amidst a blur of blue and black and fired, then let her hand fall as the arrow sailed.

Please hit the enemy.

The arrow pierced through the dust-kicked atmosphere and into the abdomen of the soldier.

The archer panted as she ungracefully got to her feet, unable to see any of the Artemian army amongst the blur of standing troops and dead bodies. She knew that the fight wasn't over yet, not with the unified hollers and chants that she knew were from the Artemians.

She wasn't sure if they were truly winning, but it started to feel like it.

Trying to forget what she had just done, Kosmir's claimed savior nocked an arrow and stepped back into the fight. She shot where she needed to and determination conjoined with the high of everything that was going on prompted her limbs to move faster, bringing her into a state of mind where all she could do was look and shoot. There were no thoughts, just the routine that was practically muscle memory—pulling out an arrow, nocking, and then loosing. Marah's body easily kept up with her mind's pace and only came to a halt when lithe fingers reached back to her quiver and grabbed air.

She frowned, reaching further into her quiver only to feel nothing. It didn't help that two enemy soldiers were approaching her, pointing some form of weapon in her direction.

Shoot.

Marah would've laughed at her pun under very different circumstances. She held her bow protectively across her chest as the two Committee soldiers ganged up on Marah, firing bullets toward her.

She gulped, expecting to feel the alien bullets penetrate her skin and feel blood, but instead felt nothing. Confused and slightly delighted that she wasn't killed yet, she found the bullets deflected to the soldiers' feet by the suit she had donned.

A delighted expression overcame Marah as she realized that they couldn't hurt her.

Her opponents seemed confused as they continued to shoot only for their bullets to still be repelled. A risky idea came into Marah's head, but an idea was an idea all the same. She advanced toward the soldiers, eyes focused on how her suit was protecting her as she got close enough to one of the soldiers to kick him in the chest and try to yank the weapon out of his grip.

The soldier's grip was stronger, but when she threw a fist at Marah, she dodged it before it could bruise her forehead. She grabbed her hand and snapped it down harshly, causing the woman to let out a groan.

Before she could plan what to do next, the human paused at the sight of a freshly healed wrist.

It was the soldier's turn to smirk as she kicked her in the ribs, sending her sprawling to the ground.

Self-healing. Good for her.

Marah gulped, unsure of what she was supposed to do.

The soldier raised her leg to stomp on her, but Marah rolled, grabbing her bow and slamming it against the women's leg, swaying her off balance. From there, panic took over and she held the blaster Natira had given her inches from her face, switching their positions.

The woman wiped her bleeding nose, eyes mocking Marah. "Go on," she crooned, "I serve my planet and my Chairwoman."

Okay? Marah knew that if she didn't shoot the woman she was going to fight back, so with closed eyes Marah lowered the weapon slightly and fired. The sound blared against her ears, but she remained still in case the soldier was not ready for death yet.

She couldn't wait for too long.

"We're winning!" exclaimed someone over the comms, "they're retreating!"

Resting on one knee, she remained in the position as she caught her breath while staring at the bleeding soldier. "You know, I really think that I'm going to have a panic attack, puke, or maybe both."

No sooner had she spoken, than the older soldier scrambled to his feet. "Surrender." He veered closer, holding a ball of energy in a gloved hand.

Marah stood up slowly and fired her blaster at the soldier's jaw at the same time he launched the energy, with both landing on the ground.

Half-wincing, half-panting, Marah sat up while her opponent was rendered still, yet breathing.

That wasn't half-bad!

There were a few moments of silence before something crashed near her, the impact sending the girl flying off her feet. She winced as she slammed against a rock, breath stolen from her lungs.

Guess I jinxed that.

She didn't bother to stand up as another explosion unfolded in front of her eyes. A grim feeling overcame her as more bombs were pelted onto the planet. The feeling of dread intensified as Marah looked towards the sky where rebel ships fired at the smaller Committee ships as they continued to pummel the blood-stained planet.

"I thought we were winning?"

Another bomb crashed near Marah and released a rippling effect that sent her crashing back down to her knees. She groaned as she rolled on her back, seeing wakes of smoke rise and thicken the atmosphere.

The Committee's intercom spoke once more, "Planet Artemis, will you surrender?" The voice was emotionless, as if it was attempting to make a plea of sympathy but could not care enough to. Perhaps, deduced Marah, that was exactly the case.

She began to cough, looking about. What had once been a beautiful, infinite scarlet had become a realm of nothing but smoke, blood, and ash. Any Committee soldiers that she spotted were either dead or unconscious and she faltered at a rebel-uniformed body with drooped eyes and blood seeping out of a chest wound.

Natira's voice was dangerously soft as the Artemians howled in refusal. "Oh, no."

Natira was interrupted as Leia practically screamed, "Retreat! Everyone retreat to *The Fortem*!"

Marah got up to her knees, biting down on her lip as her knee buckled and a jolt of pain spread throughout her body. She looked around, wondering what had caused the call for retreat, when she heard a humming sound. She looked up once again, and this time ships overhead began to glow, creating an unsettling feeling in the pit of her stomach.

She turned on her heels, scouring for *The Fortem* amongst all the chaos around her. She caught sight of it where wounded rebels continued to fire as they backed into the ship.

Hearing the sounds of cocked weapons, Marah took off towards *The Fortem*, avoiding stepping over strewn bodies that were too drenched in blood and ash to tell if they were friend or foe. The impact of falling bombs and blasts cutting the air veered closer to Marah as she ran, threatening to throw her off her feet at any given moment, throwing up sand in her vision, but she spurred herself on despite the agonizing pain in her lungs and knees, wanting to be able to live to see tomorrow.

By the time Marah reached *The Fortem* she was high on adrenaline, drenched in sweat and blood that, for the most part, wasn't hers.

She wasted no time in collapsing onto a seat, allowing her eyes to flutter closed as they raced away. The ship bucked and felt like it was being pummeled as she breathed in jagged breaths, fighting for oxygen to flood her lungs. Once the color returned to her face, she opened her eyes to find The Fortem back in space and moving toward home with fewer people than Marah remembered coming with. Artemis was gone.

That's impossible. It was just there a second ago, she swore. She slowly stood up in disbelief, eyes following the floating pieces of the planet as *The Fortem* maneuvered around them. Marah's lip quivered and her words trickled out shakily, "That's not possible." She paused to catch another breath.

"Where'd the planet go?"

Her breath caught in her throat as she realized the answer but couldn't bring herself to accept it. And by "it," Marah couldn't believe that a whole planet, along with a whole civilization, had been blown to pieces. All because she and the rebels had failed. She hung her head as she unconsciously sat back down. As much as it pained her, it was the truth. She had failed. A part of her was beginning to rethink whether pretending to agree to all of this was really worth it. She was supposed to be something bold and powerful, capable of ending a decades-long war, and here she was sulking like a baby.

Marah fell silent, much like everyone else on the ship who couldn't help but think about all the blood that was on their hands. That and the fact that the rebels were no closer to stopping The Committee.

Looking away from worn faces and back at the empty abyss that was supposed to be Artemis, the chosen one's face remained stoic with the exception of dirt and water staining her cheeks as all she could do was replay the memory of Artemis over and over.

They came here for a reason, but all they had done was let The Committee get one step closer to their goal.

Chapter 11

Location: The home of The Committee, the greatest empire to exist among the universes

Chairwoman Kate, descendant of planet Nova, was seated in her office as light poured in behind her from a large window that displayed all the fruits of her labor.

Newly constructed cities had now flourished beyond belief, all thanks to the legacy she created.

Lights hung overhead, but they were dimmed halfway as the Kosmirian preferred natural light over artificial light. It was a thing about the Chairwoman; she was particular about everything. Because of that, everything had to be tailored to what she wanted.

Should that not be the case, she'd do what was needed to get there.

The sun had begun to set, and the woman couldn't help but sigh as she leaned back in her seat. She had spent the past month preparing for this very moment. Artemis was the last key piece to total domination, though it was a shame that it had to be extinguished.

Either way, I won.

There had once been nine planets in the universe. Eight really, to acquire what her predecessors wanted. Now, with Artemis out of the way, the Chairwoman of The Committee was free to finalize Kosmir being under her control. *As well as the rest of this galaxy.*

The Committee's kingpin moved her seat closer to her desk, pressing her spine against the plush back of her seat while doing so. Her brow furrowed as the sounds of a pen tip scratching against paper in tune to the melody that she had memorized since she was a child. "Buds blossom, blossom buds, buds die until they become a rose."

She was a bud that had been caught between perishing or becoming a rose. The worlds expected her to wither away, a seed buried in soil. What they didn't anticipate was that she'd blossom into the reddest rose they had ever seen.

Just as the hum had come to a close, she set the pen down and picked up the signed decree, reading it over to ensure that everything was to her liking. The decree that her hands held would be fundamental in the chain of organized attacks against the rebel society.

Before the decree, any captured rebels were imprisoned and then subject to questioning. This decree would change all of that.

Chairwoman Kate had learned very well that the rebels would neither betray their cause nor give up. She had learned that several dozen times from captured prisoners that were busted out or chose death rather than loosening sealed lips.

Those suspected of being affiliated with the rebel cause would be forcibly taken and interrogated. If proven to be a rebel, they were also to be killed immediately. No questioning or imprisonment would be necessary for them, as all they had proven to be useless. But not anymore. Now, no one could overpower her.

As Chairwoman, she had been lenient and impartial before, but those days were long gone. Her kindness was a mistake; one that had been killing her from the inside out. Though she had succeeded in destroying Artemis, for no planet should survive without their guidance and protection, her domain had suffered a plentiful number of casualties.

This was surprising to Chairwoman Kate. She was used to three-digit figures that were less than a hundred or two. But four hundred, not counting injured survivors. Impossible.

The white-haired Kosmirian had expected casualties; there always were. *Especially on a barbarian planet such as Artemis.* She wrinkled her nose. It didn't matter - there was a fight, and the blood of her pawn believers was spilled by the enemy. She had accounted for some of her own being caught in the crossfire when she had given the order to lay waste to that cursed world.

Not that Chairwoman Kate cared. All those lives were expendable. After all, the soldiers had taken an oath with a full conscience of what they were signing up for when they pledged allegiance to The Committee.

If anything, they died honorably. *What could be a better way to die? They died with the honor of success.* It was her job to execute the legacy of the Chairmen and Chairwomen before her.

Despite her anticipations, she couldn't find anything that explained such a high number of fatalities. *The rebels had been there, but how could they have killed so many people?* She had purposely outnumbered the rebel forces, and according to her Legionnaires, there had been less than five ships' worth of rebels.

Her Legionnaires had also made a rather intriguing claim - compared to previous rebel attacks, the attempted uprisings had never been this strong. *What changed?*

Suspicion would do the convener no good. Everything needed to be calculated to perfection so she could plan her next move of attack. The human, Marah Morana, was nowhere to be found, so it seemed that the slightest of errors could and would jeopardize everything.

Which still begged the question: How?

The Chairwoman's words were soft, and if anything, weary, as she broke the silence. "Iris, is the footage of Artemis available? If so, display that footage."

A robotic voice replied from the ceiling, "Of course, Chairwoman Kate."

Blue-lit pixels reflected in the Chairwoman's eyes. She raised her chin with her arms across her chest. "Proceed, Iris."

This time, Iris did not respond vocally as the video played.

Chairwoman Kate creased her brows, watching the hologram display the rebel ships descend onto Artemis, intrigue overlapping her features. The takeover of Artemis was a classified secret, kept between only her and the Legionnaires. She murmured softly, "How did they find out we were going to take Artemis? It appears," she proposed, resting a hand on her chin, "we have a spy or two in our ranks. Interesting."

Her voice died away as she watched the Artemians pour out of their homes and stand against her in unison. She rolled her eyes as she noticed three familiar people standing at the front of the army, the leaders of the organization hellbent on her ruin.

I have put countless death penalties on those pests, and they have the audacity to stand before me. How dare they!?

She tapped a finger to the hologram, causing it to still.

A soft sigh slipped out of glossed lips as she pressed the palms of her hands to her face. She moved her fingers to rub her eyes in annoyance, slightly smudging her mascara in the process.

Exhausting moments tended to come with sitting on the throne of eternal power.

She curled her fingers into fists and pressed them under her chin, supporting her head. *It is so goddamn annoying and unbelievably naive of these people to continue to interfere with me and The Committee.*

"Why can't you idiots see the good in this? Only with unison, we can withdraw from desolation. I'm trying to prevent another war, and here you are undoing just that. What could possibly be better than peace?"

Oh. I know. God finally getting rid of these damn pests.

The red-lipped woman shook her head to rid herself of her exhaustion. She straightened her spine as she moved to resume the video.

The head of The Committee frowned. "Iris, pause please."

The hologram stilled at her command. She placed her fingers over the left-hand side of the screen and zoomed in. Someone else was fighting alongside the three rebellion leaders.

Someone she had seen before, on a screen conjured by the Supreme Intelligence. Kate frowned. *So, the rebels did manage to recruit that damned human.*

She allowed the video to play for a few more minutes, focusing on the human that was supposedly the key to her destruction. She watched the human fight effectively against her soldiers, which took her by surprise. *A human able to fight our kind? Kill?*

Tension pulsated across her forehead as the footage continued.

Eventually, she stood up and straightened her skirt. "Iris, do let my Legionnaires know that we are having an emergency meeting in ten minutes," she said, adjusting her hair as she spoke.

There was a hum of approval from the artificial intelligence, letting the Chairwoman know that her request was being carried out. "My cousin is unbearably more persistent than I give her credit for," she muttered to herself as she exited her office.

Everyone wanted to rule the world. It was a common pursuit amongst the people who'd sat on the very same throne as her. But Kate had done more than that. She had done what they couldn't. While they conquered and reaped, she turned their reaping efforts into not only ruling this world, but the universe.

Mercy came at the expense of her word.

It was in the rebels' best interests to act on their best behavior because the Chairwoman's cup of mercy had finally run out.

Chapter 12

Location: From the stars to the home of fostered rebellion

Marah sat secluded from the rebels as *The Fortem* sailed through the regions of space with her lips pressed in a thin line. In an effort to calm the shaking of her shoulders, she fidgeted with her bow between calloused, blood-stained fingers as her mind continued to play the same sequence on repeat.

Blood and bodies everywhere. Life or death. Keep moving. Keep fighting.

It was like the memory was ingrained into the girl's head, refusing to leave. The taste of death took hold of her, and she closed her eyes.

Smoke clouding the path. The sound of bullets flying and bodies in pain.

Marah's eyes shot open. She turned her head to where the leaders of the rebellion were quietly articulating with some of the others. They didn't look like they wanted to be interrupted, nor did Marah make any attempt to see if that was true or not.

She frowned, looking down at her bow and wishing she had something to clean the blood off. All the stain did was reinforce the horrors that held her mind under lock and key.

She needed some time alone to process what she had just witnessed. From the looks of it, her kidnappers did too.

Their expressions were unreadable, but she didn't need to see facial expressions to know how they felt. It didn't matter if this was their umpteenth loss - a loss was still a loss. Lives were lost. A whole planet's worth of life, to be exact.

People who had witnessed their own destruction and people who had carried on with their day—completely unsuspecting of harm—had been reduced to nothing but stardust and ash. People who took up arms to fight and had to witness losing everything.

Evil.

Parents who watched fire rain down upon them, felt the ground tremble and break while their children who wouldn't get the chance to learn the life of being a parent whimpered. Children who had no part in a fight that was so much bigger than them, yet their lives were stolen anyway.

Was death better than being under oppression?

The human sighed softly as she blinked quickly to fight the prickling in her eyes, which became harder to hold back by the moment. She turned her head to the side, unable to avoid breathing the metallic stench from her hands as tears conjoined with her sweat.

She closed her eyes, trying to steady herself. As hard as she tried, the ache in her heart was stronger. A low sound that resembled a cry escaped from her quivering lips as her heart burned, simmering through tears that fell from her face and quietly plopped onto the floor.

Marah moved to rub her eyes, not wanting to appear like a baby in front of the others, lowering her hands to examine the blood under her nails. She tugged on a part of her cape, wiping away the evidence of what was burning in her heart. *Not here. Get to your room, then cry your heart out.*

She inhaled sharply once again. It was the only sound her ringing ears could pick up. She peeked back at the ship's other inhabitants, whose lips weren't moving either.

Silence had fallen on the ship like a plague, infecting everyone as they settled into the domains of their minds. Kiera wiped her nose; Natira flipped a butterfly knife open and closed; Leia appeared to be distant and dreaming.

Marah leaned back in her seat, mimicking Leia in the hopes that her tears would refrain from falling until she had privacy. The rebels were used to this. Fighting, blood, death, and all of that. Not her.

Every cloud has a silver lining, right? You just fought in a space battle and didn't die. At least the fight can still go on.

Marah paused. *Since when did you care about the rebels' fight? Since this.*

She cursed under her breath. *How could The Committee destroy the planet?*

Eventually, the pilot of *The Fortem*, whose name Marah hadn't bothered to pay attention to, announced that they were beginning to descend into Kosmir's atmosphere.

She frowned, anger churning through her chest. She hated how casual the alien sounded. *How could one be so calm after witnessing a planet blown to oblivion?* She shoved her anger away, knowing who deserved it more.

The only people to blame were those who spawned Artemis' demise.

The Committee.

Even thinking about them made Marah's blood boil like the flames that had consumed Artemis whole. She leaned her back against the seat as her lips stifled a yawn, indicating that *The Fortem* was getting closer to ground level. She decided to glance out of the window to see how long she'd have to pretend when her gaze fell upon lit homes and buildings.

Her frown increased tenfold.

How many of them were survivors of their worlds? How many of them had family or friends there and have no clue that they'll never be heard from again? How many dreams and intentions were snuffed by The Committee?

How many of them knew about Artemis and celebrated?

The Fortem progressively sank lower and lower into Kosmir's atmosphere until it swept through the open gates of the rebels' headquarters, arriving at the landing pad to be docked and unloaded of its passengers.

The transition ran smoothly. Too smoothly.

Marah contributed to the silence as she climbed out of the ship and jumped onto the floor. Her pulse thundered in her ears as she followed the leaders of the rebellion back to their wing, trailing a few feet behind. She could see from the looks on their faces that the three needed time together.

Together was an equation that Marah knew didn't include her.

Within five minutes, the trio plus Marah entered the South Wing and dispersed to their secluded rooms. She said a quiet goodnight to the trio before anyone else could say anything, needing to get away from the sinking of her heart; a feeling that she hadn't known before.

The first thing she did when she entered her room was wash her hands. She scrubbed and scrubbed over and over until the red blurred her vision. She kept running water in between the crevices and cracks on her skin until she was sure that there wasn't even a trace of the unwanted substance.

Her mask of innocence had shattered.

She exhaled slowly as she wrung her hands on a towel, allowing a heavy sigh to slip from her dry lips. Her eyes hurt, and when she moved to rub them, she let out a yawn.

She walked back to her room and shrugged her quiver off, placing it and her bow on the dresser. Having peeled herself out of her suit, she put the stained garment on a hanger and closed the closet.

She knew she should put her suit back with the other suits, but - with the headache and heartache she had - the only thing she wanted to do was lie down.

She pulled on the same pair of clothes that she had slept in previously, welcoming the warmth and comfort with open arms.

As tired as she was, she had things to think about.

For one, she felt like she could pass out at any given moment. Not only were her muscles and limbs exhausted from fighting, but her head had begun to take on the mental toll of the battle.

It's sad. Artemis was a beautiful world, and now it's gone.

Marah froze at the sight of the black opal poking out of her suit. Instantly she was transported back to Artemis.

This isn't about leisure but saving Kosmir.

Guilt crept through her veins as her heart fluttered, thinking of what the Artemians must've felt when Artemis cracked, licked up in flames and frothing with fury. *They said that I was chosen to end the suffering, but this type of suffering can't be stopped. I'm only one person. What power do I have to stop them compared to what they can do?*

Marah sniffled and a tear fell from her eyes. She quickly wiped the tear away, despite another falling in its place. She knew sadness, but she had never experienced emotion like this. Sadness was an emotion that she could control. It was something that she kept closed off, memories existent but buried in deep waters.

Growing up, she had never been a part of something. She had dreamed of joining book clubs and doing teenager stuff with friends, but with her mother's adamance for her to get into the best university possible, she wasn't in the position to argue otherwise.

And yet, here she was, needed by these people, only to feel hopelessly alone once again. She blinked and shuddered, finding herself back on the battleground.

Bodies littered everywhere. Were they scared? I was.

A whole planet and its civilization had crumbled out of existence, and Marah couldn't help but hope that Kiera, Leia, or Natira would talk to her and free her from the drowning feeling in her heart.

Was it so awful of her that she thought by joining their cause she might have finally become a part of something? She bit down on her lip, letting blood fill her mouth. She winced. It appeared that everywhere she looked she saw the red substance.

Maybe they've gone to sleep. It's late and they're probably tired.

The thought was discarded at the sound of quiet chatter outside her bedroom door.

She hung her head low as she shifted on the bed, unable not to think bitterly that maybe it was never in her cards to fit in. Not here, at least, where she had more differences than similarities with the people around her.

Leia, Natira, and Kiera had been through so much together, and with all of their strengths and abilities, Marah didn't see herself fitting in. She was only there because she was needed, and then they'd get rid of her. Only that and nothing more.

The rebellion leaders had built everything. They knew how to fight and to be leaders without doubting themselves. During the fight, she had done the opposite, diving into panic mode and hoping that whatever she did would work.

Now, with the fight over, the shadows of darkness furthered their veils. Marah couldn't help but feel bad - guilty, even.

She glanced down at her hands, and for a split-second she saw the same blood and ash drenched hands from when she had escaped death.

I killed someone.

Many people, actually.

Marah blinked and looked back down at her palms. She hadn't processed that the blood on her hands was blood that she had spilled. A bitter flavor filled her mouth as she realized that she played a part in creating sorrow and loss; all of those feelings of grief that were so hard to endure. *Do they mourn for their losses?*

During battle, it hadn't dawned on the her that she had stolen lives like a grim reaper. In a way, she had become one.

The idea shocked her. Marah could be molded into judge and jury, but she was no executioner.

So, what does that make me?

A killer for the right reasons?

Killer felt too harsh for the weary girl's mind. There was no glossing over the fact that she had killed people, but that didn't make her a killer. A killer was someone who wouldn't hesitate to end lives because they wanted to.

Marah killed because she wanted to survive. She killed because she wanted to protect and defend. She didn't kill to attack. She rubbed eyes that yearned for sleep, trying to focus on the part of the fight where she hadn't had to kill anyone. It wasn't much better, but it was some.

She exhaled slowly, trying to sort out the mess in her head. Everything had changed all of a sudden: her purpose, her morals, and what it meant to live in the world.

Artemis had changed her, yes, in a way where she no longer felt like herself. A piece of her felt different in a way that she couldn't describe, for better or for worse.

What she did know, however, was that she'd come to terms with it. *I have to, otherwise I won't get to go home.*

This was a rebellion group. The call for freedom and justice was always high, and sometimes the best way to raise justice was the messiest.

The call to Artemis was a call to defend against The Committee - Marah understood that much. But to actually fight and kill people who were both innocent and guilty made her feel conflicted.

How does one define innocence?

There was no innocence in this fight, Marah realized. She had seen it from the start, but she had never embraced it. Neither side was innocent, not if they were going to use any means necessary to force their hand and win. Two wrongs never made a right.

Marah leaned her head against the bed's headboard and raised her gaze to the ceiling.

This is insane. They were willing to do all of that - what if the rebels hadn't escaped in time? The Committee will get stronger. It's not about going home anymore. It's about ending The Committee.

Suddenly, the idea of going home wasn't all that important.

What matters is the fight. Then I can go home. What home?

And those were the thoughts that plagued Marah's mind as her head hit her pillow. She curled under the warmth of the blanket, unsure if sleep would take hold of her. Falling asleep felt too easy, and Marah knew better than most that sleep had a habit of leaving her frustrated and with questions.

Maybe you were always meant to be alone. That's why the others haven't said anything to you. A disappointment, maybe, since you're supposed to help the rebels - not take them backwards. Maybe you were always in over your head, just like Mother always said. She always said it would cost you everything.

At that thought, the gears in her brain stopped churning and she fell into darkness.

Marah walked down the street, earbuds bumping against her coat as she turned toward the path that led to her house. She hummed along to the tune that filled her ears while unlocking the door, shutting it behind her absentmindedly as she entered. The shrill voice of her mother made her cringe, and she yanked her earbuds out of her ears and thrust them into her pocket.

Her mother's pupils were blown with rage as she stood up from the table, practically shrieking, "I cannot believe you! You were supposed to be at tryouts. This club is the gateway to the college that we've been dreaming of!"

Marah looked at her mother and then at her father, who had a red face and puffy eyes. She eyed the bottle on the floor and immediately moved her gaze. "There will be other tryouts. And other clubs."

Her mother exaggerated a groan as she folded her arms across her chest. "Can you believe her! 'There will be other tryouts and clubs." She scoffed. "You are a junior - this is your year to make your college application look your best. What are you doing sitting here and wasting your life?"

Marah looked away as her mother's rage ensued.

"I have done my best to keep this family together, and quite frankly I'm done with you! You seem to have no care about your place in this world, and the answer to that isn't in those damn comics and books you read! You're not one of those fake heroes, so quit thinking that one day you'll sprout wings and take off. With the way you are now," her tone oozed with disappointment, "I wouldn't be surprised if even the most basic of colleges doesn't accept you. Remember that you live in my house, so get with the program."

College. Marah mentally groaned. Was that the only way to gain some love and respect?

The sound of her father, someone she hadn't seen nor heard from in years, slamming his hand on the table caused Marah to jolt. His voice was exactly how she had remembered it; empty and unforgiving.

"This is why," he stood up and walked past Marah, "I'm getting a divorce." From the way he was walking, Marah could tell that he had a few drinks at minimum. "I'm tired of this. You," he swiveled and jabbed a finger to a rather annoyed mother, "and you," the jabbed finger now pointed at Marah, "are so exhausting and I cannot put up with this anymore!" He staggered towards Marah and slapped his hand across her face, causing shock to race across her skin. "I'm done!"

He walked away, leaving Marah blinking back tears with a hand to her cheek. She watched as he cracked open another glass bottle, chugging it down before aimlessly tossing it to the side.

Marah's eyes shot open, strangely relieved to find herself back on Kosmir. The rest of the nightmare continued to unfold in front of her conflicted eyes. She was no stranger to this memory, but after everything that had happened today, she didn't have the strength to shake it off with her mind. *And when in doubt, punch a way out.*

She kicked the blanket off and sat up, placing her feet onto cold wood. She breathed in slowly and then exhaled, trying to calm herself down.

"Emme?" She felt strange speaking to a robot. *AI?*

If Emme detected the rapid beating of Marah's heart, she didn't say anything. "What can I get for you?"

"Are the others awake?"

"Kiera and Leia are asleep. Natira is not. She is in her room and does not show any sign of coming out, if that is what you are wondering. Shall I request for her?"

Marah shook her head, her eyes finding her bow. "I was just wondering. Thank you."

She stood up and crept out of the Wing, heading toward the training room. The hallway lights were dimmed, which was a relief to Marah as she looked for the room, uneager to make conversation with anyone. However, with the lack of light and rebels, she had no clue where she was going.

"Where the hell am I?" She looked forward and then behind her, poking her head through dark doors.

Beep beep.

Marah turned behind her and looked down at a pink android. "Oh, um, hi."

The android beeped again, tittering, "Good evening, Marah Morana. My name is Lizard. Are you alright?"

Marah looked down at its green eyes, "I'm alright," her tone was humorous as she addressed the robot, "Lizard. You don't have to call me by my full name." *This isn't awkward at all.*

"I am programmed to address you respectfully," replied Lizard. "Unless you prefer I call you by something else? Natira Reyna has informed me that I should store names so that I may address you properly."

"Marah is okay." She chuckled as she bent down to get eye-to-eye level with Lizard, "Marah Morana makes me sound old."

The android made a sound. "I do not understand the meaning of old."

Marah faintly smiled at the android. "Getting old is like when you're here for too long. We are born for a purpose, and once we tire from it and the years go by, our purpose ends." Lizard made an intrigued expression. "Then what?"

"We go to sleep for a long time."

Lizard raised a digital brow. "Like for a week?" Marah looked down. "Forever."

"Ah," said Lizard, with a sense of pride airing its tone. "Like when Bubbles's wheels broke. I haven't seen Bubbles since, but Lucky tells me Bubbles's time has popped."

Was that a goddamn pun?

Marah nodded. "Yeah, I guess so. Where is the training room? The one where Natira trains me?"

Lizard made a few beeping sounds as it rolled forward and then backward. "This way, Marah."

"Here it is," chimed Lizard.

Marah felt awkward as she followed the droid through the parted doors, feeling alien in an alien world. The white-walled room was empty, and the absence of light gave it a ghost-like aura.

"I have to help the others clean up," said Lizard after a few moments. "Emme will help you with anything else you may need. Goodbye, Marah."

"Goodnight, Lizard."

Marah chuckled as the green-eyed robot wheeled away. She turned back to the empty room, unsure of how she was supposed to activate it. There were no switches, buttons, or anything to press. "Where's the light switch around here?"

As soon as she spoke, the lights lit up halfway. "Is this alright, Marah?" asked Emme.

Marah stood there awkwardly. *Lizard did say to ask Emme.* "Yeah, that's good. Is there a punching bag around here?"

A punching bag materialized out of thin air a couple of feet in front of her. At first, the human thought that the punching bag was another hologram, but the swinging of the sack that hung from the ceiling was so realistic that she knew otherwise.

She approached the bag, tying her hair back. She sucked in a breath as she adjusted her posture, dipping her head downwards and moving her left foot in front of her right. She inhaled, thrusting her right fist out hard against the sand-filled bag. The impact of her punch was loud, and only encouraged Marah to continue as the bag flew backward before swinging back toward her face.

Before it could hit her, Marah swung her fist out again and again, blending breathing and punching into one act. She couldn't stop the rhythm that she had worked up, nor did she want to. The now-breathable feeling was intoxicating, a high that worked out all of the problems occupying her mind.

Confusion. Punch. Frustration. Punch. Disappointment. Punch.

It was pure bliss and sweat until the stiff sound of a voice pulled Marah away from her assault on the sandbag. "Your form needs improvement."

Marah stopped to catch the punching bag before it could swing back and hit her like a pendulum. She turned to face Natira, who ran a hand down her clothed arms.

"Why are you up?" she asked, joining her.

"I could ask you the same question," Marah replied, as a punching bag appeared in front of the Nantak.

"Asked you first," chimed the alien. She tsked. "Straighten your arm when you punch. It will land better."

Marah flashed Natira an irritated look as she remained in her posture.

Natira raised an eyebrow. "Also, both of your feet should be pointing straight," she got into a punching position, "like this."

Marah looked at Natira's feet, which had tattoos similar to the ones on her arms. "Where are your shoes?"

"Where are yours?" returned Natira as she threw a punch.

"I'm wearing socks. Won't your feet get dirty?"

Natira paused and looked at Marah strangely. "Socks?"

"Do you not have socks on this planet? They're like gloves for your feet, but for everyday use."

"Gloves?" Natira waited before bursting into laughter at Marah's dumbfounded expression. "I was kidding!" She continued her assault on the punching bag, "So why are you up?"

"Couldn't sleep. You?"

The war-made orphan made a sympathetic face. "Likewise. Nightmares or anxiety? I find it hard to sleep after battles. It reminds me of all the bad things that happened in my life. But, if there's one thing I learned from my unfortunate experiences, life is a deity, and we are its remnants."

Marah paused her assault on the bag. "That's actually really beautiful. The second part, I mean."

"I suspect you're overworked on everything that happened today?"

"Where do I even begin?" answered Marah. "I understand that we had to fight and kill, I do, but we were fighting because we wanted to protect others and they wanted to hurt us. It was survival." Her face fell as her lips parted and gave voice. "What The Committee did to Artemis was downright evil. I can't help but feel so upset and the urge to just—"

"Clobber them?" interjected Natira. "Yeah. But it's more than that."

"What do you mean?"

The noirette kicked the punching bag. "This. Me. Failure. All my life, I was told that I was a disappointment and that I would never be something great. I never wanted to be great," she paused to crack her wrist, the memory fresh in her head. "I just want to be good enough. For someone else. I'm good enough for myself, at least, I think I am, but what's the point when no one sees that? I thought that here, because I'm needed, I can finally be good enough for something greater." She punched the bag, and it made a thumping sound. "But I can't. I'm not like you all."

She shrugged. "I mean, it's not important anyway. We're here to save Kosmir. I don't know why I'm wallowing over something as little as this." She punched the bag harder, and collided her other fist with sand before it could swing back. "I'm sorry."

Natira shook her head, and her loose locks of hair followed suit. "You have nothing to be sorry for. You're supposed to talk about things that bother you-especially when you're in another world, trying to help out a cause like this. That, itself, takes a lot of work. I feel that guilt."

Marah wondered what guilt Natira felt because she was sure it wasn't the same. While Natira was mourning Artemians or herself, Marah believed her feelings of guilt to be due to the lame excuse she had been telling herself why she was still on Kosmir.

She had only agreed to help the rebels because she had to. She didn't bother fighting them, she wasn't one then, but now, she wasn't sure how she felt.

Then came the casualness: "It happens. Like I said, there's worse things than Hell."

Should there be worse things than Hell?

Marah noticed the dark circles that rested under the orphan's eyes.

Natira, continuing her assault on the sand-filled sack, probed, "Why do you think you feared us at first?"

Marah looked at Natira, the layers of the firm soldier cracking with grief.

"It's nothing to be ashamed of. We failed, but we can't put blame on ourselves right now."

"Like you, I'm not okay," the Nantak continued as a loud bang rattled the room, "but, you didn't fail. You weren't alone. We all went, and we all lost. There's a difference, believe it or not in these painful worlds. You can't blame yourself, otherwise you'll spend the rest of your life doing so. We haven't known each other for a long time, but I do know for a fact that you have some strengths. You being here is more than good enough for me. Even if," she jested, "you say weird things sometimes. It's hard, and it's going to feel hard, but I want you to know that I admire your strength."

Marah looked down at the praise. "How do you keep it all in so neatly? At least, on the outside."

"You think you're okay and you'll get over it, but the next thing you know you're crying on the bathroom floor," Natira lamented dispassionately. "If someone walks in, they're going to ask you questions; make you reveal everything about yourself, down to the nitty-gritty core. It's easier to store everything in boxes - boxes that can be opened at any second but are under your control. Artemis reminded me of losing Nantak, and all the other planets. I was a survivor then," she glanced down at thin lines that cut across her forearms, "and I'm a survivor now."

"Do you think we will be able to take down The Committee?" Marah let go of the question all of a sudden. It had been on the verge of keeping her up all night.

"It's up to the deity of life, but I know us remnants have the potential to succeed."

Chapter 13

Location: The battlefield before the battle

Marah didn't go back to sleep. She lay in bed for the rest of the early morning, unable to think about what the fight had meant for her. Before, she hadn't cared about the rebels nor their goals. This was their fight, not hers.

The Committee wanted nothing from her planet. *What if one day they did?*

Marah knew Earth had hundreds of sovereign leaders who wouldn't be able to tackle a threat like this. Not with the ambition, greed, and plotting politics that controlled and clouded their minds, ears, and eyes. She had no doubt that if The Committee paraded down on her home world, Earth's fate would be a lot like that of Artemis.

How could Natira be so optimistic about this? She thinks that we'll succeed, but we're outnumbered and outpowered. The way I see it, the odds are definitely not in our favor.

This was something that bugged Marah more than she cared to admit. Wandering around the rebel facilities after undergoing hours of training that left her head hurting with physical and mental fighting tactics, she was exhausted and in need of a break.

The feeling of failure had inspired her volition to find more arrows, since she had used most of them up on Artemis. That, and she wanted to see if she could enhance the arrows to make fighting a bit more fair.

She didn't know who she'd face in her next fight, whenever that would be. Judging by what her three kidnappers—*not to be bitter about it, since I already forgave them, but I have no clue what else to call them*—said, the rebels were beginning to prepare for what they had described as *all of us against all of them.*

Personally, I don't understand how they can be so ready to dive into the next fight. Fighting is exhausting, but as long as they know what we're doing, I'm good.

Speaking of knowing what we're doing, I am once again lost. Marah sighed, turning around, and heading in the opposite direction. "Kiera said that the arsenal was in this Wing. Somewhere."

She stepped into the closest room only for the doors to part and reveal the interior of a storage closet.

"Huh. That's a lot of storage."

She walked out and continued walking down the hall in the hope that one of the rooms was the arsenal. She spotted a room with a familiar door and headed inside, only to stumble into a room that was definitely not the arsenal.

Replacing spacious displays of weapons was a carpeted room divided into smaller sections through the use of colored partitions. Each section had its own vibe, as practitioners of different religions engaged with the space.

Women with thick braided hair had colorful cloths draped over their bodies as their painted fingernails curled over the edges of ancient texts. Nearby, Stellans donned loose cotton clothing that resembled both a robe and a dress. The garments consisted of an embroidered top, of green, red, pink, or blue, complemented by baggy black bottoms that rested just above the ankle. Some wore intricate jewelry, while others concealed their hair. Some delicately sipped drinks that resembled chai, setting cups down only to turn pages. In another corner, bold colored cloths painted with various symbols caught Marah's attention, as beings lit oil candles atop bookshelves filled with books and prayer mats. Nearby rested chests with beaded strings poking out. On the opposite corner, Marah found pillows where rebels were seated conversing amongst each other, reading books, while others did what Marah assumed to be praying.

Oh.

She quickly walked out of the room, and in doing so bumped into an unsuspecting rebel. "Oh, I'm sorry," she apologized. "I thought that this was the arsenal area."

The rebel, who looked to be the same age as her, waved off the apology, "No worries. You were close." He pointed at the room across the hall, "That's the room that you're looking for. I was about to go there too, so I'll let you in."

Marah nodded as she walked alongside the rebel, remembering him from the previous day's battle.

She entered the arsenal and set her bow and quiver down on a small table.

She walked past walls of weapons to a chest marked with a scripture she didn't know how to read. She reached to open the drawer.

"I wouldn't do that if I were you. That's where we keep our explosives."

She turned. "Do you have any spare pieces of weapons that aren't going to be used? Like bomb fragments or remote detonators? And arrows?"

The brown-skinned rebel nodded. "I'll go check the back. If you need anything just holler for Emme or Joven - that's me."

She nodded and sat on a chair, pulling out the few arrows that were inside her quiver. She examined them as she waited for Joven to come back. *Let's see, with the right wiring or a different material the impact could be better.*

"What are your arrows made of?" she asked, turning to find Joven back with a tray in his hands and two more hovering beside him. He set the tray down on the table, and the other two followed suit. "Unless Emme tells me that I'm needed elsewhere, would you like some help?"

"If you want to," said Marah. "Mine are made of aluminum. I'm thinking if I can do something with the arrowheads then they'll be more efficient."

"That could work. I brought some carbon arrows - they are much stronger and won't break. They also work well long-distance." Joven moved a chair behind himself. "If you don't mind me asking, are you alright? You don't have to answer."

"I'm alright. Recovering from the shock."

"I get that," said Joven softly. He didn't say anything more.

Did people become so used to this that many weren't willing to fight back?

Right before Marah could ask the question, Emme interrupted diligently: "Joven, Captain Tessa requires your assistance in the docking."

The rebel threw an apology over his shoulder as he dashed off.

The noirette placed a hand in one of the bins, rummaging through its contents until she found a piece that caught her interest. She pressed the only button on it and winced immediately as a jolt of electricity crackled against her fingertips. The sting caused her to drop the remote device onto the table as she moved one hand to rub her other.

Marah blew on her stung hand and picked the device back up. The gesture caused her to wince again, provoking her to check if there was a mark on her hand. There wasn't one that she could see - the only trace of injury was the stinging sensation beneath her skin.

Not that it mattered. It'd be another wound to add to the growing collection.

She sat back down and noticed a screwdriver in the same bin. She pulled it out and used the edge to pry open the back of the remote, revealing a bunch of colored wires.

I never thought I would be grateful for that engineering class.

She carefully pulled the wires out of the remote and wrapped them around the arrowhead, realizing that even without the device the wires still stung to touch. She fit them around the edges and point of the arrowhead, lifting the arrow to ensure that the wires would stay in place.

Marah smiled. If this worked, it might tip their fight toward slightly more even.

All that was left to find out was whether the wires would actually work if she shot the arrow. *Electric arrows. That sounds lame, I've got to come up with a better name for them.*

She repeated the process again, finding another remote and this time wiring the arrows that Joven had brought. Sliding them back in her quiver, she hung it across her neck and grabbed her bow, heading for the training room.

This time, she got there with ease, spotting a couple of rebels entering inside. She joined them and settled herself in a corner away from them as she called out, "Emme, can I get a few targets?"

At the wall in front of her, a couple of targets formed. "Thanks."

Marah moved her fingers across the riser of her bow, raising the device to her shoulder level, letting the blood in her fingers pump just enough to get them ready.

Not that she needed much time to warm up. Archery was a sport that became easier with time and practice.

She plucked out an arrow from her quiver and twirled it in her hand. "Emme, I'm going to need a few more targets than that."

Targets instantly scattered all over the white-walled room.

She nocked the arrow and drew back until the muscles in her shoulders screamed. She released it, flicking her hand upward as the arrow hit the bullseye perfectly in the center.

She reached her hand behind her head and pulled out another arrow by the fletching, aligning the electric arrowhead to nock it once again.

Breathe in. Think about what you're going to do.

She pulled the arrow back further on the drawstring, ready to let it soar.

Don't grip the bow too hard. Otherwise, the arrow won't be as strong.

She inhaled slowly, squinting at the center of the target.

Ready.

Her fingers bumped against curved metal while tugging on her bowstring a centimeter more.

Set.

She dipped the arrow a fraction of an inch down, tilting it to get a more accurate shot when-

"Marah!"

Go!

Marah's arrow soared through the air and penetrated the red and white circle. It hit exactly where she wanted it to, leaving electricity crackling on the singed target.

It works. Sick.

"Sorry," apologized Leia. "I didn't mean to scare you. C'mon, we have to talk about our next steps after Artemis."

"Sure thing," said Marah as she picked up the arrows. "Where are we going?" "North Wing. Our spies have new information."

Marah faced the alien. "What kind of information?" "Let's find out."

Marah walked a step behind Leia into a small room where a few rebels were seated around a table. She took the seat adjacent to Leia, and was offered the alien equivalent of a cookie by a Litnickian, as implied by their neon features and tails. She thanked them before accepting the gesture, only realizing a moment after that she didn't remember knowing the woman's name.

The woman across the table cleared her throat. Under her coiled lock of hair darker than ink, were clothes that resembled the ones that The Committee wore on Artemis. "The Committee is surprised by the fleeting moment of success we had on Artemis; they plan to import newer technology and increase regiment training."

Leia took in the first order of business. "We'll have to compensate. They rely less on natural power, and that's what we're going to focus on. If you can do anything about these shipments, names, delaying, information, anything."

The rebel didn't need the rest of the order to be said for her to confirm. "I'll do what I can."

Captain Tessa was next to speak. "We need to do better with our aircrafts. *The Fortem* used to be just rusty, but it took a few hits. It can go on for a little longer, but if another Artemis happens, I don't see us able to go."

Marah observed the last bit of information reflect Tessa's audience. Some rebels wore a look of withering at the idea of another Artemis, while others took offense at the idea of not being able to save another world.

"What do you think we should do?" Leia paused, "Is there anything we can do to support the spies better as well?"

Tessa leaned back in her seat, shrugging. "I don't know what we can do. We can't just rummage in a junkyard for parts, that's why they're in the junkyard. Even if we did, they'd figure out why anyone's there."

"Speaking of," a rebel with scarlet irises gently interrupted, "the Chairwoman plans to pass a new decree. Anyone suspected of rebel behavior is to be immediately arrested. Minimal trial efforts."

The ring-nosed alien next to her elaborated, "The Chairwoman had an emergency meeting with the Legionnaires last night. Rumor has it she believes there's a spy or two. She plans to run deep profile checks, random interrogations, and even use some secret tech to root out the spies."

A collective sigh was cast upon the room. Marah watched each rebel react to decide her response. None of this made any sense to her nor did she know what any of this meant to the fight, and that's why she was there.

She turned to Leia whose eyes dilated in rumination before declaring, "We keep going. We need to keep taking risks and getting information. Make use of the tunnels in the basement. If anyone is caught or detained, I want to know. We can change meeting points throughout the city to avoid suspicion, but we cannot afford to lay low. Laying low means, we could suffer an even worse defeat than Artemis. Protect each other and keep taking risks. The information you bring in helps us know what we need to do."

Marah observed the words take effect on the rebels. She didn't know what alien jail was like, but couldn't imagine it was anything pleasant, and it gave her an idea of what it meant to be a rebel. At least, she thought it did.

The rebel who shared the information chimed in, "Is there such a technology possible? To root out spies simply on DNA?"

The rebels' head of technology pursued his lips together. "Well, it's no secret that The Committee has the most advanced technology in the galaxy. Their inventory catalogs show an overwhelming number of finger-print scanners. Ideally, the fingerprints are run through the Kosmir databases to match the genomes to the being. As much as we can protect us from interacted with them, I have no solutions for those captured."

A collective silence fell over the group.

"But," he then started with a hint of optimism that Marah didn't see coming, "perhaps we should ask the solution no one saw coming." His eyes found Marah. Then, so did everyone else.

Marah wished that she had the power to disappear. Of course, it was fitting to get the answer that no one was thinking from the answer no one had seen coming.

To be fair, she had one idea.

Still, she was hesitant to share what felt feeble. "Well, one thing that might work is to overproduce the electrical current in those devices? Like, maybe," she was looking down without trying to, "you could use the same chips that I used with the arrows? It could be done with fingerprints, I uh, saw it on a show once and it worked."

"Do you have the chips?"

"Yeah, they're back in the training room." She hadn't expected her idea to be met with praise. She knew she was only some good on the battlefield, and she felt no different here.

And yet, her words seemed to conclude the meeting, even if she hadn't meant to. The head of technology stated a time and place to drop off the chips and headed off, followed by everyone else little by little. Joven wore a slight smile and flashed a thumbs-up to Marah as he was leaving. Before it could be too awkward with just her and Leia—who looked like she wanted to say something to her, perhaps about Artemis—Marah pretended that someone was calling her and moved to leave the room.

"Marah?"

She had almost reached the sliding glass doors, when the weight of Leia's pained voice had her turning around.

The way the Novan sat in the chair that represented her power and control of the entire organization and rebellion gave Marah an inkling toward understanding what it was like to live the life of a rebel.

"I'll walk with you back to our rooms."

Despite being next to each other, there was still space between the two.

Leia started walking down the corridor, indicating Marah to follow, holding her hands behind her back like a Captain would. "I wanted to check in with you after last night. You hadn't been in a fight before, and this wasn't a good fight. I wanted to make sure that you were okay. Natira mentioned earlier after training that you couldn't sleep last night."

Marah avoided the question. "I understand what you guys have been going through. I wish we could've won somehow." Her hands were in her pockets and her gaze on her feet.

"Me too," admitted the Novan. "Defending Artemis would have prevented The Committee from getting stronger." She wiped her cheeks despite no tears being present, at least from what Marah could see. "I wish no one had to die. A whole planet is gone. Shown no mercy. We couldn't even bury the dead. At least there weren't too many."

How many isn't too many?

Marah's tone was unintentionally emotional as her words spilled. "We have to end this. I now understand better that my help is needed." *It's not even that. After Artemis, how can I not put my heart and soul into this fight?*

Leia looked at the noirette with a half-smile, "We're going to stop The Committee. We couldn't before, but now we have help. We have you, and new ideas to take them down." She raised a brow as they followed the hall's turn. "That was a great idea about the rebels, coming up with special technology to keep their fingerprints from getting recorded. That's genius. With you, we're stronger now."

Marah shrugged her shoulders. "I hope so."

"Hey," offered Leia as she wore a reassuring smile, "here, we believe that everything happens for a reason. We lost Artemis, but maybe this will help us win in the long run."

The human only nodded as she forced herself to meet Leia's lilac eyes, finding that the look there didn't match the smile that the alien wore. Marah could sense that Leia wanted to promote hope, but it didn't meet her eyes. The Novan's watery purple eyes harbored only specks of hope amid loss and confliction, and Marah couldn't help but try to hold onto that hope.

Leia refused to falter and give in to the tears. Not in front of Marah anyway. Marah did the same.

As they entered their Wing, the Novan sparked another conversation as Marah opened her room's door, "Do you need anything for yourself or your room?"

Leia broke eye contact to survey Marah's room. Marah followed the alien's gaze.

It was clean. Too clean for someone that lived inside. Even the closet was neatly arranged, with shirts hung up and pants folded in a manner to combat wrinkles. Even on the small dresser, everything was stowed away neatly, except for her quiver. One would think that no one even occupied the space.

Marah was unsure if she should enter the room or not. She didn't know what to say that wouldn't make the atmosphere more awkward, or worse, give Leia the wrong impression. Or the right impression. Marah wasn't sure which one she'd prefer Leia to take.

This room wasn't like hers back on Earth. Her room was messy, with comic books, posters, a closet with coats poking out, and an unmade bed. Evidence of life.

Marah held her emotions in her throat, adjusting where whoever had found her bow had left it, the one important thing she had with her from Earth. She wiped her face quickly as tears that she hadn't felt before fell, coursing down the smoothness of her face.

Just the memory of home and all of her things were enough to make Marah long to be back immediately. She missed her home, with its smell and her things. They made her feel content and happy. They made her feel normal—unlike here, where she was anything but that.

Leia spoke up finally. "You know, we can change your room up, if you'd like. Like posters and decorations. If you miss some of your old clothes, books, or anything really, our robots can do that. Ever heard of four-dimensional printing?"

And remind myself even more that I'm not home? No thanks.

Not wanting to sour the mood, Marah replied, "Sure, maybe I'll do that later."

She wouldn't. She couldn't be messy here. She had to be perfect because even the slightest mistake could compromise not only her own life but countless others. Artemis had already proved that. The rebels weren't strong enough and an entire civilization paid the price for that.

A whole planet gone as if it were as simple as snapping my fingers.

If Marah was being honest, it scared her how easily The Committee had obliterated Artemis. If the Committee ever set their sights on Earth, every single human, living or buried six feet under, would be reduced to stardust, and that terrified her.

Not just that, but the fall of Artemis put into perspective what everyone inside the rebel facility lived with.

What else will I have to live with? What else will I have to endure that no one should?

Everyone here was a kid. Teenagers, sure, but technically kids. Kids shouldn't have to live like this. Kids shouldn't have to fight wars like this.

The human yawned. *And yet here we are.*

She moved her hands to rub her eyes. She'd much rather focus on feeling tired and upset than guilty and homesick.

Leia broke the silence, eyeing her with concern. "You sure you're okay?"

Just because I've kept quiet doesn't mean that I'm okay. I never explicitly said that I was okay. Silence isn't acceptance, but it can mean defeat.

Sincerity was scrawled across Leia's light features as she continued, "It's normal to be shaken up about stuff like this."

There it was again—that casualness about all of this that rubbed Marah the wrong way.

Stuff like this? Fire crackling, embers as red as blood. Bodies strewn everywhere, and friend indistinguishable from foe. The ocean of sand, gone, replaced with layers of chaos and death. People fought for their beliefs and died while living a life that some consider to be nothing. People only wanted a home and to live freely and they were rewarded with death. A planet blown to pieces, and all of this is normal to you?

She looked past Leia and at the dresser where the black opal from Artemis rested; the only physical piece of Artemis still left. She couldn't bring herself to get rid of the stone, and wanted to hold onto it to remember why she was truly here.

"It shouldn't be."

The rebels didn't deserve to live like this. No one did. Perhaps, one day everyone would be able to wake up in a universe where tyrants had finally stopped killing the oppressed. Perhaps, one day the rebels would wake up and feel happy instead of guilty for being alive.

And according to the whole universe, that would only become possible with her help. For better or for worse.

Leia tilted her head, as if she had this conversation a dozen or more times. "But it is. There's no use fighting injustice that can't be undone, only the one that can be controlled." She looked down only for a moment before training her irises at Marah's, "We're not fighting because we shouldn't have to. There are more wrong reasons for a fight or rebellion than right. I watched past rebels fight to not have to, or to end the fight," she shrugged, "or for vengeance. The art of rebellion is justice. Maybe we can't avenge the kids that we are, or the kids that we were, or even all of who we lost on this path, but we owe it to ourselves, all of us—past, present, and future to give ourselves the things that we know we deserve."

Marah nodded, smoothening the yellow covers she found in a spare closet. "You're right. Still sucks though."

Leia sadly chuckled. "It sure does. That's why we have hope."

"You know," started Marah, "for people who don't know what superheroes are, you sure do embody them really well. You got the whole hope thing nailed down. I'll have to teach you guys about them."

The Novan laughed. "I'm sure Natira would love that." The laugh conformed into a knowing look. "I know you probably want to be alone right now, and I respect that completely. But," she stood, "if you're up to not be a total teenager, Kiera is making ice cream for dinner. Care to join?"

On the one hand, Leia was absolutely right. But, on the other hand, Marah knew that if she stayed alone, she'd drown in anxiety and guilt, which sounded utterly exhausting. It was already enough that her heart hurt with the concept of messy justice and how she was supposed to accomplish that. She didn't need a headache on top of that. Surprising herself, she accepted Leia's offer.

"You know, you're a teenager too."

"Yeah," Leia wore a sly smile, "but I'm older than you, so you're practically a child."

"If Kiera is going to make ice cream, which is a spectacle in itself, you guys better have vanilla and sprinkles."

Chapter 14

Location: Where legends befriend a fight

"Today," started Natira as she circled Marah, "we're going to try different types of training."

Marah looked at the Nantak and then at the Novan and Zonan behind, confusion evident on her face. "Define different types of training."

Natira wore a sly smile as she met hazel eyes. "Sure." She threw a fist toward Marah, who twisted it before the alien's knuckles could make contact with her skin.

"Still doesn't answer the question."

Natira swept her leg under Marah's, bringing the latter down to the ground. She leaned closer to Marah as she explained simply, "Combat practice with powers. Every single being on this planet has powers, some you have seen and others not. It's important to know how to handle those."

Marah nodded and moved to stand up, but Natira didn't relent. The girl watched as the alien reached to her side and pulled out a blaster. She looked up at Natira, waiting for some sort of explanation.

"What would you do if I was about to shoot you?" Natira said. "Do you want me to answer that?"

"Is that what you're going to say before I shoot you?"

Marah attempted to pry the blaster out of Natira's grip. While Natira focused on maintaining her hold on the weapon, Marah found her other hand reaching to throw a punch and when Natira jerked back, Marah snatched the weapon and aimed at Natira. "That's what I would do if you were about to shoot me."

Natira smiled. "Good. Your suit can handle most weapons. However, suits and skin are not immune to sharp objects or to the effects of all powers."

Natira gestured for Marah to return the weapon, strapping it back to its holster and placed her hands on her hips. "On the field, you have to be ready to take hits, avoid hits, and deliver surprise hits. Just because someone is using a weapon doesn't mean that they don't have tricks up their sleeves. Like Kiera. Her touch is powerful and weakens one immediately."

"But I'd have a weapon so I could take someone like that down, right?" Marah inquired, putting her hands in her suit pant pockets.

"Hopefully," said Natira as she took a few steps away from Marah, now standing next to Leia and Kiera. "What's that Earth saying?"

"Perfection makes practice?" Kiera piped up.

Marah winced. "Practice makes perfect. Is that why we're wearing our suits?"

"Yep," answered Leia this time. "You need to get used to fighting and moving around in it. Don't forget, your suit is a weapon of its own. Ready?"

Before she could ask for what, something rammed into her, knocking her down and having her rolling on the cape of her suit. The noirette whipped back and forth to see everyone still in their places. The only difference was a faint streak of orange dotting her vision.

The human stood up, unsure of what had knocked her down. "What was that?"

"That, was Miko."

A girl who looked in her early teens whizzed back into the room, the same slight orange streak following behind her.

"That is so cool."

Miko blushed.

Leia tossed Marah a quiver filled with foam-tipped arrows.

Marah plucked one out and drew back on her bow. "Whenever you're ready?"

Miko disappeared within the blink of an eye. Marah couldn't see her at all and turned on her heel, unsure of where to angle the drawn arrow. She turned to the right and then to the left, looking to catch Miko still for even a moment, but the Kosmirian didn't relent.

Marah inhaled, taking a bet and shooting. The arrow sailed past her vision and bumped into the wall, thudding to the ground.

She redrew her bow, squinting for the streak of orange that she used to look for Miko. This time, she noticed the color whizzing by her, and an idea sprang into her mind. She altered the direction of the arrow so that this time the arrow would go in front of the alien.

She released her hand, and the arrow bumped the speedster's arm. "Draw?"

Marah winced as she got back up to her feet despite the scream of protest in her legs. "I'm taking five."

Kiera chuckled as she rose from the floor. "You did good, Mar. We can go take a lunch break." She paused, taking a swing from a bottle, and wrinkled her nose. "Besides, Natira smells."

"I do not!" Natira protested while trying to surreptitiously sneak a sniff.

"Yeah, you do. After Natira takes a shower," the Zonan rolled her eyes at Natira, who poked her tongue out, "what are we doing?"

"Checking in with the others and seeing what they have to tell, and then training again," Leia answered. "This is really the only thing we've got to keep working on. Preparing for the fight." She stood up and began to head out. "I'm starving - let's go eat."

Marah followed the Novan, hiding a snicker as Natira sniffed her arms. "It's not as bad as Kiera makes it sound."

Kiera snickered while Natira grumbled as she crossed her arms over her chest. "I hate you all."

Marah couldn't help the twitch in her lips as Kiera bumped elbows with the Nantak. She looked down, feeling a pang in her chest. *I didn't come here to make friends, but it would be nice not to feel so lonely.*

She opened her mouth to speak but decided against it. *They have their own cliques. I could never fit in with them.*

Marah's stomach growled. Before she could ask what was for lunch, an android greeted the four: "Spaghetti a la tosta?"

"Spaghetti?" asked Marah. "I'm down for that." She made her way toward the table stands and piled up spaghetti with colored sauces onto a plate, forgetting that she was with company.

She only remembered when she heard Leia chuckling as she did the same. "What?"

Leia raised her hands defensively. "I didn't say anything. Pass me those breadsticks, I love this stuff." The Novan stuffed her face with a breadstick, causing Marah to laugh as she piled a couple of breadsticks onto her own plate.

She set her plate down where Kiera was sitting and was about to walk over to the drink bar when Natira stopped her. "I'm choosing drinks. You need to try this."

Marah had taken no more than a couple of bites when Natira returned, hands filled with cups of sparkling pink liquid.

"Raspberry cherry cola."

Marah turned to the Nantak. "No way. That's a thing here?" She took a sip of the beverage and then set the cup down, letting the flavor fill her mouth. "This is awesome. I have so much respect for you now. Even though you hate orange juice."

Natira rolled her eyes. "Can't please everyone all the time."

Leia joined them. "No, you can't, which is why while you get yourself all cleaned up, the three of us will run check-ins with the others at the North Wing. A couple of the agents have already reported that more Committee soldiers are out on the street, meaning that we need to be more careful coming and going. Everyone should have an alibi and only go outside if they absolutely must. A lot of our contacts on the streets are getting detained."

Marah frowned. "But don't they need a trial or evidence before they can get detained?"

Leia shook her head. "Not anymore." She took a swig of mizka, a beverage made of grapefruit syrup and water. "Since Artemis, the Chairwoman has gotten pissed. She's probably wondering how we knew and taking out anyone that has the potential to harm her or her cause. Now, if someone says that you're a rebel then you're pretty much dead."

Natira shook her head, hatred thick in her tone. "Bastards, the lot of them. I'm glad we pissed the Chairwoman off. Serves her right."

Kiera nodded. "I believe there's an Earth phrase for that. I believe it's called 'amen'?" She turned to Marah for clarification.

Marah made a thoughtful expression before shrugging. "Sure. Amen to that."

Leia downed the rest of the cola in a single gulp. "We're going to be training for the rest of the day, so eat."

Marah groaned, deflating against her seat. "Again?"

Natira laughed as she picked up another can of cherry cola. "I think you'll need this more than I will."

Chapter 15

Location: Where the living prepare for death

ONE WEEK LATER

Marah stood in the center of the training room with three rebels surrounding her in a circle. She held her bow in one hand, calling out to three rebellion leaders, "Is all of this really necessary?"

The first two rounds were her facing off with heat vision, electrical volt manipulation, and freeze-breath. Round three were some of the rebels' best with, with abilities such as super- speed, energy and elemental manipulation, along with enhanced strength, and one of the coolest abilities that Marah had encountered—a Litnickian girl who could predict the move of her attacker and thus use that to her advantage.

"Begin!" prompted Natira.

The human eyed her surroundings carefully.

None of the rebels moved.

Marah didn't ease. She heard the faint sound of a whoosh and then an orange streak bolting quickly for her. She used her heel to pivot her body just out of the reach of a swinging punch, causing Miko to skid past her.

Like her speed, the rebel acted quickly and instead of moving to fight her as Natira would've, all she did was push Marah back. Stumbling, someone pulled her backward.

She didn't have to look to see that it was Joven who had pulled her, instead focusing on staying upright. The two had gotten close over the past week when she asked about alien pop culture and had binge-watched a show where aliens had worse fighting skills than she did.

Marah raised her heel to send a kick to Joven's ankle, using him dodging her to turn and face him. He mock punched her, and she was grateful for that because she got swept up in Miko's orange streak running around that she hadn't noticed.

Then, her left hand reached for the opportunity that she was waiting for, slipping a model of her electric arrows into her hand and she waved it teasingly in front of Joven's face.

Knowing the damage since he helped her create it, he raised his hands, signaling his defeat.

Or so she thought.

Joven flipped his hand upward and made a quick circle with his hand, and somehow something invisible collided into Marah, knocking her over backward.

Being that this was only a spar, she barely felt any pain. She threw herself to the side, dodging another blast of energy, and winced as her knee scraped against the rough tiles but stood up anyway.

Lesson number ten in fighting: you get hurt, suck it up. Focus on it and you'll end up with double the injuries. Lesson number eleven: adrenaline is not your friend, so keep moving.

Joven backed off, leaving Marah's favorite Litnickian ready for her with open arms.

Marah stood, knowing she had to choose her approach carefully as she wasn't sure how much of her mind the alien was reading. She moved closer to attack only for a white barrier to push her back.

That is beyond awesome! Imagine getting shot at and then you can make your own shield? I swear, Litnickians have the most interesting abilities.

She pulled out her blaster and cranked its settings to stun before shooting the barrier, causing it to flicker before thickening. Her electric arrow was still in her other hand, so Marah placed the blaster back in its holster and lined up the arrow.

The shock was unforeseen as the arrow latched onto it and waves of electricity crackled around it. The rebel accepted it and took down her shield. Marah expected it to be back up, but instead the pink-haired rebel decided to lunge toward Marah with a raised fist composed of four fingers.

The punch hit Marah, causing her to sway off-balance. Her opponent used that time to stomp on her cape, causing Marah to trip over her feet.

With her back pressed to the floor, Marah kicked her legs up and out toward the hand that was about to hit her, sending her opponent backward.

She huffed as she got to her feet, only to nearly fall over as another energy blast was absorbed by her suit. Friction made her skid to a halt as she dug her heeled boots into the ground from the impact. Despite her foot slipping, she used her left arm to hold herself upright.

From there, she plucked an electric arrow from her quiver and released it.

The arrow bounced against the rebel's protective gear. If it was a real fight, it would've pierced through and maybe killed. True to battle, the rebel took the hit as if it were a real one and retreated.

Marah turned at the sound of crackling electricity, remembering that the fight wasn't finished. She leaped over a whip of electricity and rolled while using her blaster to deflect another. A further blast bounced off her cape as Marah wracked her mind for ideas on how to take the rebel down.

"Okay, I got nothing."

Natira broke up the spar. "Draw." She helped Marah up, "We've got to talk."

Marah fanned the sweat on her face. "What's up?"

The Nantak didn't reveal much. "Leia will tell you. Good form," she turned to face her, "even though your posture could've been a little bit better."

Marah laughed. "I'll take that compliment, thank you very much. Besides," she met Natira's eyes, "that was awesome. I feel like a badass."

Natira chuckled. "Beat me and then you can call yourself one."

Beep. "Hello, Natira Reyna and Marah. Leia requests your presence in the North Wing." "Thanks, Lizard," acknowledged Natira as she petted the top of his head. "Let's go."

The two walked past the android, seeing rebels entering and exiting rooms. Some of them were training in smaller spaces practicing hand-to-hand combat. Others were using blasters, rays, and their own abilities against each other. They all looked focused on their activities, and Marah couldn't help but wonder how much pain drove that determination.

"Did you get the joke?"

She raised a brow. "You told a joke? Like something funny, and I didn't hear? How awful." She burst into snickers.

"Oh, ha ha," retorted the Nantak. "Lizard's pink, like a lizard," she paused to continue, "c'mon, it's funny."

"Lizards are green. Not pink."

"Told you so," chimed Kiera as the two took seats in a private room. She opened a bag and pointed it towards the two. "Prezla?"

Marah accepted the offer, plucking one and tossing it into her mouth. It was as salty and soft as a classic New York pretzel. "So, what's today's plan? Checking in with the other undercover rebels? Seeing what lost ground we still need to make up?"

"Actually," spoke Keia through a mouthful of prezla, "there's been a change in the plan."

Before Marah could ask what, Leia continued. "Because of these changes, we've decided that we're going to send you to The Committee."

What?!

Hazel eyes shot open as Marah nearly choked. "Did I hear you right? You're going to send me, public enemy number one, to the people who want to kill me? Are you crazy?" She turned to face Natira and Kiera, who looked as serious as the Novan in front of her. "We could jeopardize this entire fight! They know who I am—they'll kill me, and then what?"

Crossing her arms, she leaned back in her seat, gaze trained on Leia as she waited for the alien to say that she was kidding.

Leia wore confidence as she tightened her ponytail. "Relax, we're not that crazy. You'll be a spy. We believe that The Committee has a power source called the Poten, if we can take it from them, they're powerless, or at least it'll even the fighting field a little bit."

Marah's tone was pitched with disbelief. "Me? A spy?"

"The Committee already knows who we are and that we were on Artemis," Leia explained. "However, I'm willing to bet good money that they don't know about you being here. That is something we can use against them. The minute we step inside they'll know it's us, but they won't know you.

"You won't be alone either," Natira added. "There are already other spies there who'll be helping you. We'll give you a comm so we can stay in touch."

"You won't be attacking anyone," averred Kiera. "The idea is that you find and extract the Poten."

Marah sighed as she shrugged her braid off her shoulder. "I still don't think this is a good idea. You said that I won't be going as myself, what does that mean?"

"Means you'll have a cover."

"Define cover? And when do I leave?"

"Today," Leia declared. "As a matter of fact, one of our spies was able to pull something together." She reached a hand into a pocket on her pants and slid a card on the table.

"That's your ID card."

Marah looked down at the card unsurely. Red lettering read "Member of The Committee" with a picture of her face, that she wondered when was taken, along with her ID and her date of birth.

"You're now Nima Adver, born on Kosmir." Leia then handed Marah a resume that belonged to Nima Adver.

"I don't remember writing a cover letter."

Leia was quick to reply, "The Committee hires for multipurpose. Any set of skills on your resume you already know. Let's get you ready—you should be reporting for work soon." She stood, a gesture for everyone to follow.

Marah stood, holding the ID and resume, and followed, despite feeling unsure. *I'm not a spy. I just learned how to beat people up and now I'm going to have to pretend to be someone and infiltrate the enemy? Should I say that I have no idea how to be a spy and only worked retail for less than a year?*

Kiera bumped Marah's elbow gently. "Your worry is very loud. You'll be fine," she eased. "You aren't expected to know what to do. Just keep a low profile." She offered a smile. "Don't worry. Like Natira said, you won't be alone."

Marah returned the smile, even though it didn't reach her eyes, as she followed the rebels back to their Wing. Inside rested a Committee uniform atop a table: a white blouse, blue dress pants, a blazer that matched the pants, and black heels.

Sucking in a breath, she looked at the three in hopes that this wasn't the armor that was supposed to protect her. She opened her mouth to voice that, but decided against it since her words were useless and weightless compared to the spies whose hands she was putting her life in. She took the clothes and dragged herself to her room and shut the door.

This is insane. She eyed the mannequin. *This is like Jaws. Right into the shark's waters.* She sighed as she slipped into the outfit, making a sour expression as she looked at herself in the mirror, cringing at the sight of a wispy sun insignia over her left shoulder.

The more she stared at the symbol, the sicker she felt. This was the symbol of the beings who wanted her dead, killed the rebels, and destroyed Artemis. Looking in the mirror, she nearly saw the soldiers she had fought and wished for nothing more than to take the blazer off.

She stepped outside. "Not that I doubt your knowledge or expertise, but are you absolutely one hundred percent sure about this? Cause I'm not. I really don't think this is going to work."

Leia dismissed Marah's worry. "You'll be fine. You're Nima Adver, new to The Committee. Just pretend that this is your first day on the job."

"This *is* my first day on the job," stressed Marah.

"You know, the whole comic book thing that you love so much. Lizard's been showing us some of the stuff that you've been talking about," Natira snickered, "and they're hilarious."

Marah flashed her an irritated look.

Kiera added, "It's not like they're going to run your genome or anything like that. Sector five in the Articles of Kosmir Employment states that it's illegal. And that was created by The Committee."

"Or," suggested Marah thoughtfully, "let them, and then we can arrest them. Problem solved."

Kiera's lips turned a fraction of an inch upward. "I wish it were that easy. If they make the rules, they can bend them too." She flashed a warm smile that was the opposite of the frown on Marah's face. "Trust us, you'll be fine. All we need to do is give you a disguise."

"Here!" Natira exclaimed, handing the human a pair of glasses, "put these on."

Marah accepted the frames from the Nantak's outstretched hand and slid them onto her face. "And these will…?"

Kiera wore a toothy smile as she answered, "Disguise. Makes you look less like you. Without them, you're blind. Makes you a whole lot less likely to be you or a spy if you can't see a thing without these. It was Natira's idea."

Natira had the audacity to wink. "I got the idea from one of the comics Lizard told me you like."

"Oh well, thank you," sassed Marah dryly. "What's the actual disguise?"

"These are part of your disguise," replied Natira, "but I was thinking we could do something with your hair?"

Marah shook her head. "You will not touch my hair, thank you very much." Natira shrugged, "It won't be permanent, you can even choose!"

"And what exactly am I supposed to do with this?" Marah tucked a lock of hair behind her ear, not totally minding what Natira had done to it. Her natural black hair now had large streaks of red standing boldly and was considerably shorter, sitting just above her shoulders.

"Simple," answered Leia. "Walk in there, scan your ID and follow the crowd."

Easier said than done.

"When the best opportunity presents itself for us to take them down, we'll take it," said Natira. "Oh, and you'll need this." She handed Marah a small circular piece and gestured to a matching piece in her ear, "It's a comm, we'll be able to stay in touch the whole time, should anything happen."

What's that supposed to mean?

Marah didn't get much time to debate the question as Leia said. "If you don't leave now, you're going to be late to your first day of work. Go." The Novan handed her a map.

"Here's your directions."

"You don't have GPS?" groaned the human. "So much for super-advanced technology."

Chapter 16

Marah couldn't believe what she was about to do as she stepped out of the smallest elevator she had ever been in and onto cracked concrete. She inhaled slowly, blinking as what she assumed to be the sun hit her eyes. The sun had never felt so close. She looked around her, hesitant and almost scared to step out onto Kosmir's streets.

I'm going to work with the people who want to kill me. Not terrifying at all.

She stepped outside, and then understood why Kiera had said that she wouldn't have to worry about cameras on the street. The road was dirty with debris and littered with junk, and the sidewalk was in no better shape with cracked and unleveled concrete. Dingy shops and sheds were the only facilities around, and the stench of what Marah could only describe as cigarette smoke filled her lungs.

She wrinkled her nose. Now it made sense that the rebels had picked this place as their location for their headquarters. "No one would suspect anything in this dump."

There were barely any people on the street, and Marah made no attempt to converse with the ones she saw. Not with their knuckles encased in brass and fingers curled around thin slivers of metal.

She started walking on the cracked sidewalk, keeping her gaze on the map in her hands, away from the souls harmed by the people associated with the insignia on her shoulder.

She moved a hand to a strap of her backpack, filled with clothes and basic necessities. Another bombshell thrown by the rebels was that those who worked at The Committee's headquarters lived there. *Which was just great!*

She stepped to the side, allowing a brisk walker to go by. She heard him huff angrily and speak words that she didn't understand. He looked back at her and his fingers tightened into fists. Marah pretended not to notice, looking down at the wispy sun insignia on her left shoulder.

Never would I have ever thought I'd breathe air on three worlds.

Now that the human was thinking about it, if she went back in time and told her younger self—*wait, how does time travel even work? I'm sure the aliens have figured that out too.*

She didn't believe in time travel. She wouldn't, despite everything else that had turned out to be real. Not until she saw it with her own eyes. *Besides, if they had time travel the Committee would probably use that to prevent the rebels from becoming rebels, unless—*

"Let go of me!"

Marah came to an abrupt halt.

Keep a low profile and you'll be fine.

She turned to see a man with a massive amount of neat, peppery blonde curls stacked on top of his head grab a smaller woman by the arm and slam her back against a wall of an abandoned shack. Noticing the sun emblem on the man's shirt, she made a face of disgust. She had only seen that logo twice before: on Artemis and on the clothes that she was wearing.

Marah was about to turn and walk the other way when she saw a knife move to the woman's throat. The idea of keeping a low profile was immediately discarded as she strode over to the pair and mustered as much of an intimidating tone as she could. "Leave her alone." She raised her chin, meeting the girl's eyes and then the officer's. "Now."

He looked at her before scoffing, "I'm an officer in the patrolling section. Don't tell me what to do. Now," he matched Marah's tone, "if you'll excuse me—"

She followed the officer's gaze and glimpsed Joven crossing the street. He looked at her and then toward the officer, his face a question mark. As he got closer, his fingers curled into a fist.

The officer noticed this as well and sneered at Joven. "You take one more step toward me and I'll cut your throat after I cut up hers," he spat, venom rolling off his tongue like a viper's poison. "You and your kind."

Marah stared at the officer. *You and your kind? What the hell is that supposed to mean?* "What are you talking about? Leave him alone." She flashed a pleading look to Joven, asking the rebel to let her handle the situation.

Joven unclenched his hand but stayed put.

"Oh," snarled the officer, "you don't know what the hell I'm talking about?" He pointed a slim, knuckle-bruised finger at Joven. "They live in our land while their," he cursed a string of words before assigning them, "Queen refuses to allow the Chairwoman full power. They're not like us, with their violent ways and refusal to comply." He pressed on the blade and the girl let out a low whimper.

Joven raised his hands and walked away, looking back at Marah every few seconds.

"Stellan scum!" The officer turned back to the girl, whose wide eyebrows were scrunched together as if she wanted nothing more than to flip the blade and switch her and the officer's positions.

The Stellan was much smaller than the officer, with ragged clothes and untamed, thick curly hair. She was quiet, eyes darting from the man who held a knife to her neck to Marah and then back to the officer.

The officer's voice grated as he spoke. "I'm not letting you go so quick," he drawled as he got in her face. "Little girl thinks she can get away with stealing and trash-talking us. I ought to teach the filthy Stellan here a lesson." He flicked the blade as he turned his head toward Marah as if they were two members of an exclusive club—technically, they were. "Wouldn't we have to teach her a lesson?"

We. Dammit. Not even five minutes in this disguise and look at this.

The girl spat at the officer right in the face, causing him to cringe and cough. "I didn't steal anything," she said roughly, curls bouncing with every word, "but because I'm Stellan, God forbid you Committee morons can't mind your damn business. You make sure to give Stellans hell whenever you've got something to whine about."

The officer glared daggers, spitting on the woman. "You'll get your liberties once you fall in line with the Committee." The hand holding the knife trembled, and Marah began to worry that he might kill the girl right there.

Before she could interject, the officer exhaled slowly, eyes flickering to the Stellan. "If I killed you right now, I'd have to deal with your body. I'd rather leave bruises and scars. I find those more memorable."

Marah opened her mouth, but the officer turned to her and huffed, "Mind your business, I'm handling the situation. Anyone asks, it's standard protocol." His eyes wandered the girl's body.

Knowing she had to intervene, Marah spoke again, seriousness thick in her tone. "Stealing isn't a life offense. Neither is this the standard protocol, according to subsection 10A." It was a fib, but she didn't care.

The girl spoke up, amused by the situation as she eyed Marah and then the officer. "Look at the two of you, acting so high and mighty. You think that hurting and killing us will keep us in line." Her gaze fell on Marah before staring the officer down. "At least one of you is decent." Her tone intensified as words spilled stories. "You don't know what you have put me and my family through. But you will when you go to hell!"

The officer raised his hand to slap the Stellan. "You little—"

He was cut off by Marah, who grabbed his hand midair before he could hit the girl. The Stellan blinked, confused. She wasn't the only one.

"What's wrong with you?" barked the officer.

Irritation seeped into Marah's voice as she met the man's eyes. "We don't touch anyone. We especially don't hit anyone. Get the knife away from her neck or I'll do it myself."

"Yeah? Try it."

Fine. This was not in my cover letter, resume, or job description!

Marah kicked her leg at the man's wrist, causing the blade to shoot out into the air.

She spoke firmly to the girl as the knife plunged into the ground. "Go. Don't do anything stupid. You won't be so lucky next time."

The Stellan nodded fervently and ran.

The officer jostled Marah as he tried to free his hand from her grasp. "What the hell was that for?"

"I'll be reporting you for that," was all Marah replied. She didn't know if that was actually possible, but she was almost certain that the officer wasn't aware of the answer.

He rubbed his hand while Marah eyed his wrist, which was beginning to turn black and blue. "Are we done here?"

The officer only grumbled something vulgar.

Marah raised a brow, somewhat amused. "Let's do a count, shall we? So far you held a knife to a girl's throat for stealing, which by the way, you've yet to prove. Two, you were about to do something highly inappropriate, abusing your power. And now, you're badmouthing your fellow worker?" She concluded as he opened his mouth to argue, "This will make a fine report."

"Alright, alright, I got it," sighed the officer as he backed away from Marah and retrieved his weapon.

"Good," said Marah as she turned on her heel and headed back to the main road. Once there, she pulled out the map and glanced down. She lowered her hand, deciding to observe her surroundings as a full-fledged Kosmirian.

These streets weren't as dirty, and the sidewalks had fewer cracks. Buildings looked decent and cleaner, and Marah could see people living inside houses and storefronts.

The further she walked the more her surroundings began to contrast. More people roamed the streets talking on devices, carrying bags, and wearing smiling faces. As she approached the beginning of Kosmir's capital, she turned right, as indicated by the purple marking that depicted the route from the rebels' guild to The Committee's.

Marah couldn't help but laugh at the fact that Leia, who always wore purple in some form, also happened to possess purple pens.

Then again, Novans really do like their colors.

She passed children with antennas kicking a ball. Then she saw older beings behind them with solemn faces, as if they wished to have memories such as those.

All because of The Committee, probably.

She softened, and then looked away, training her gaze back on the map. She folded it and put it in her pocket, realizing that if she continued to walk in a straight line she'd end up at her destination.

Walking felt odd to the human. For one, Kosmir wasn't her planet. Each block had three trees which intrigued her, one at each corner and then one in the middle of the pavement.

Vehicles of every color imaginable hovered above streets, waiting for glowing streetlights to flicker from red to green. *There are no wheels, that's so cool!*

Small creatures that looked like blobs picked at scraps on the street as they tittered their stories to each other. Bold buildings stretched from the ground to the tips of clouds, basking in the glow of the shining sun. People of every possible age, shape, color, and type roamed the streets. It was incredible and enticing all at once, and Marah couldn't help but yearn to learn more about this strange world and its strange people.

Everyone was immersed in their own routine. That was—until they noticed her.

The effect of her presence was immediate. Children immediately scrambled away from her, abandoning their games of running around in circles with balls and sticks. Hooded teens spray-painting graffiti on walls took one look at her and darted into the shadows. Parents eyed her warily with brows creased in disappointment and tight jaws as they moved past the symbol of what was, in their eyes, a monster.

Tension thickened the atmosphere as everything around the human came to a pause. Regular pedestrians looked at her with disdain and anger, seeing her as an outlet for blame for all of the pain that they had endured.

She looked away, glancing at abandoned graffiti on a wall. Bubbly lettering read: *Down with The Committee and their tyranny!*

A winged girl who was probably a couple of years older than Marah, shoved past her, most likely blaming Marah for what The Committee had done to her.

Marah bit her lip as she looked past the girl, guilt hammering in her chest despite the fact that she hadn't done anything to these people. Rather, these people were depending on her to be liberated from The Committee and to have their suffering avenged. They just didn't know it.

Still, she couldn't help but let her heart fill with blame. She bit down on her lip as she continued walking, ignoring the urge to rip off *this goddamn uniform* and tell them all that she didn't hurt them.

In their eyes, she was one of the countless names and faces who had destroyed ancestors, cultures, homes, pieces of souls, and history. In their eyes, she was only a soldier who brought death and destruction.

At the same time, she couldn't help but notice the slight minority of beings who looked at the logo and didn't wish her ill but acknowledged her with lips tilted upward and heads dipped down to a complete a salute, signs of respect and approval that she didn't want. *How can one respect someone who stands for conquest and death?*

She hated how the world had suddenly split into two sides: wary glances and salutes.

She trudged on, though, pretending not to notice. *If I play my part perfectly, I'll be able to prevent their suffering from increasing.*

This division continued as Marah crossed the streets of Kosmir. She diverted her attention to Kosmir's details - twinkling stars that were more than dotting, teenagers determining who had the cooler ability, and graffiti scrawled on the backs of floating trucks and the sides of buildings.

One particular graffiti caught Marah's attention. A shoe store had a drawing of a woman with horns on her head, eyes that were as sharp as knives, and teeth that were crowded upon a flaming tongue. Underneath the face were words in a dialect that was foreign to Marah, but she didn't need to know what the words meant to know that they weren't something nice, since men dressed like her were pressing soap and water to the paint.

Before she could wonder more about the construction of Kosmir, she caught a glimpse of The Committee's headquarters. The Citadel was a large building that easily rivaled the Empire State Building, but three times the height, as it stretched up and past the clouds. The outside was decorated with large glass panes that revealed the bustling life inside.

If that's the outside, then the inside is definitely going to be something else.

She reached for the door and then paused, realizing that she was about to walk into enemy territory. Hesitancy swept over the girl, and she debated whether or not she should turn back to the rebels' base. After all, once she went in, there wouldn't be any turning back.

So, she opened the door and walked in before her feet could take her in any other direction.

I was right, this is definitely something else.

As soon as she walked through the glass doors, she was hit with numerous stairwells and escalators. The main floor was huge with dusty gray-black pillars that stretched from floor to ceiling. Right at the front of her line of vision were help desks, but with all of the people roaming about, all she could see were colors of white, blue, and black.

From the ground floor, she glanced upward at mezzanines that went from the second floor all the way to a glass ceiling that filtered in light. Each mezzanine had at least a hundred people heading to and fro.

That's a lot of people.

She moved her teeth over her bottom lip, beginning to feel small and overwhelmed in comparison to her surroundings. *Like a really big fish out of water.*

She couldn't even crack that joke because apparently animals weren't a thing in space, which to be honest, really sucked.

Kiera's voice brought the human back to reality. "Hello? Marah, are you inside? What's happening?"

Utterly mesmerized, Marah's reply was a faint nod. *How could a ceiling be so high?*

"Marah?"

Marah snapped out of her daze. "Yes, what do I do again?"

"Check-in," replied the Zonan. "Our spies say there should be a help desk where new employees sign in."

"Found one."

Marah approached a worker behind one of the help desks in hopes that she could be of assistance. "Hi, I'm new here. My name is," she paused and glanced down at her clipped ID badge, "Nima Adver?" The name rolled off her tongue strangely, and she cringed at her pronunciation. "I'm new here." *You're new here? Who even says that?*

The worker at the desk with hair that resembled a red velvet cupcake wore a friendly smile. "Welcome to the greatest place in the galaxy, Nima. You'll need to scan your ID here, and then I'll make you your backups. It's important that you always have your ID clipped per Chairwoman Kate's orders. It's been mandated after Artemis." She laughed. "You'll learn what happened there later. There's a lot of working and double the talking here."

Marah forced a laugh through gritted teeth as she unclipped the card that Leia had given to her and handed it to the worker, anxiety flooding her chest. She fidgeted with her glasses, hoping that her cover wouldn't be blown already as the worker typed on a computer screen.

"You're all good here, Nima."

Marah looked at her a second too late, remembering what her name here was.

"Now for your backup ID." The worker, whose tag read Sonia, handed Marah the plastic card back. "A beam is going to scan your face to take your photo. I've been told it looks scary, but it's not going to do anything."

Marah nodded, resisting the urge to bite her lips for the umpteenth time.

Sonia clapped her hands together as she stood up and clicked a button on a panel. "Great! Just stand still and look directly at the black circle on the wall behind me."

Marah followed as instructed, stiffening as a green beam began to scan her face. Dread pooled in her stomach as she waited for the scanner to reveal who she really was. Her heartbeat thundered as she began to wonder how long until someone came to arrest her.

Maybe the beam is a sniper that's going to take you out at any second.

Finally, the beam disappeared. "You're all done!"

Marah exhaled, relieved.

"Do me a favor and clip your badge, then you're all good to go. Keep your ID though, I stamped your username and password on the back. You're going to head down the hall on the right, where your main working station is. Your mentor left a little surprise on your desk, so you'll know which one's yours."

"Mentor?"

Sonia flashed a very white smile. "Of course, every new member gets a mentor for their first year here. Anything else?"

Marah shook her head, thanking the woman before walking away. She set out to the right hall and couldn't help but marvel at the scene in front of her. The hall was filled with numerous rooms and doors. An overwhelming sea of color bombarded her eyes. She blinked, letting her eyes adjust to the hues, and once she could see clearly, she was met with *so many people.*

Aliens with so many colors and features spoke over each other in so many disparate languages that pulled her attention in all sorts of directions.

Her lungs clenched, but the feeling was nothing in comparison to the wonder that filled her heart. She spotted a woman with pale skin and bold pink hair talking on what looked like a phone, walking with a sense of urgency that drew attention toward her.

Behind were two men engaged in a frivolous conversation, with exaggerated expressions that reminded Marah of a typical high school hallway. The one who had rolled their eyes and looked forward saw her and, apparently sensing that she was new, waved.

She returned the gesture.

Marah walked past a large glass window that revealed a training room where two identical women were sparring with batons. The women were exact mirrors of each other, with the only difference being their hair. One had their hair in a braid that reminded her of Leia, who always had her hair up, while the other's hair was loose in short, choppy locks like Natira.

The human watched in awe as the two exchanged jabs, ducked, and swiveled. Their exchanges were precise and sharp, which only captivated her even more. In fact, she hadn't realized that she was still walking, let alone right into someone.

She only registered that she had done so when a silky voice spoke up, pulling her from her thoughts. She immediately panicked and apologized. "Oh, I just bumped into you. I'm sorry, I really should look where I walk."

Okay, don't panic. She doesn't know who you really are.

The owner of the silky voice waved her apology off. "It's fine." The woman grinned, revealing white teeth, as she glanced around the premises. "This place is so cool. Trust me," she met Marah's eyes, "you can't help but wander about. I still do and I've been here for a while." The blonde looked at Marah intently, who was unable not to ruminate if the woman was going to put two and two together.

"I haven't seen you around here before. First day on the job?" She then gasped with excitement, startling Marah, "Nima, right?"

Marah nodded rather quickly. Her shoulders sagged slightly out of relief.

The girl extended a hand and Marah shook it. "I'm Beth, your mentor! Nice to meet you!" She continued, "Come with me."

All three of her alien comrades spoke over the comms at once. Unable to answer their questions, Marah managed a loose smile as she glanced around before focusing on Beth who winked, "We can start the exclusive tour first and we'll end at our workstation." She led Marah down the bustling hall, which branched off into several different areas while explaining the overwhelming ins and outs of the place.

Marah did her best to take notes mentally, but there was so much to the place that there was no way she'd remember even a fraction of what Beth said, or at least she thought.

"And this is the main section where we work," said Beth finally, as they approached a space that resembled the North Wing but had everything that the rebel base didn't have. Smiling faces. Large, flashy touchscreen computers and tablets. A coffee machine. Space. Sunlight.

The two strode past rows of computer monitors and paperwork on desks to a section all the way on the right-hand side. Beth gestured toward the first seat on one of the rows, marked with pink and blue confetti decorations that were oddly cute for The Committee, "And this is your very own seat." She smiled brightly and clasped her hands together as if she was nominating Marah for some sort of prestigious honor, "Welcome to The Committee! You're now at the best place to work ever, so of course, I had to go all out!"

Marah's smile was eccedentesiast—as fake as her ID badge. "Thank you so much." *This is totally not awkward.*

"Say that you love it or something," Natira suggested.

Marah met Beth's cerulean blue eyes, unable to believe how easily she could accept what the people did here, destroying planets and killing innocents. It was disgusting.

And yet, her voice somehow managed to say, "I can't wait to get started." *Sooner we start, the sooner this is all over and then we can all return to our happy little lives.*

"Great!" exclaimed Beth, voice still chipper, "Let's get right into it." She pulled her chair from the station directly in front of Marah to next to her. "We can start with how to use your workstation and what it means to work here."

Marah nodded, already knowing what it meant to work at The Committee but held her tongue for obvious reasons. Beth had spoken nonstop during the tour of all the places that she had clearance to, which was around half of the Citadel, and Marah wondered if that was a superpower within itself.

"First you're going to log in," said Beth, laughing, "big shocker, I know." Marah looked at the monitor in front of her that was missing a keyboard.

Beth tapped under the screen twice, and a holographic keyboard materialized in front of her.

Oh.

She typed in her login and was greeted with a homepage interface.

"At The Committee, we value efficiency, so the device works to fit you. If you ever get stuck or lost, simply tap the question mark on your keyboard and say whatever you're looking for. That way, no time is wasted getting what needs to be done." Beth then tapped the question mark to demonstrate and then used her voice to inquire, "What is the mission and purpose of The Committee?"

A pleasant robotic voice chimed, "To keep the worlds and streets safe and as one."

Beth smiled, "Yep! As an officer, your number one duty is to make sure that the streets reflect the peace we have worked to bring. There's not a lot of that, but some areas are more," she strained to find the right word, "resistant to us."

Marah considered asking why that might be as she thought of the interaction she had not too long ago with an officer.

"But, don't worry about that, you'll be perfect for the job!" Beth waved off Marah's feigned confusion. "Most of the time newbies do the boring work and then once they complete three years, they're assigned to the streets, so you won't have to worry about that. There are some videos that you'll have to watch about managing your station, basic protocols, and all of that stuff. Oh, another thing," piped the blonde with the same enthusiasm as every other word, "we take any and all things rebel-like very seriously, so make sure to file it if you ever see or suspect anything."

Marah nodded, "Of course." She hated to imagine spending three years in this place, let alone undercover. It hadn't dawned on her how long this ruse may take her in the worst-case scenario.

"Just so you know, we get paid by salary. You can always try to negotiate for higher pay if you or your family needs it, but shift hours are just rough guidelines. We are to serve and embody the Chairwoman's greatness so feel free to spend as much time as you need to ensure that everything is perfect!" She beamed once again, flashing her pearly white teeth, "Which, I'm sure you'll have no problem fitting in with!"

She finally stood up, blonde curls bouncing with every move, "I have to go collect and review this week's police reports. Which, by the way," she laughed, "would you believe that crime has gone down to three percent in the past three years all because of the Chairwoman?"

Marah opened her mouth to string some form of answer that would match the alien's energy when Beth answered for her, "I know, it's insane! Not even the rebels themselves would believe it. Anyways, I'll leave you to get comfortable and settled with those videos. If you need anything, don't hesitate to come find me or page me with the question mark. I'm also the desk in front of you so that'll be great for our buddy system!"

"I'm sorry?" Marah wasn't sure if her predicament was getting worse or better with every word.

"Duh," exclaimed Beth as if Marah was an alien. "What kind of mentor would I be if I wasn't with you all the time?"

Marah smiled, "Of course, yeah. Thank you, Beth, for everything already." "Of course!" called Beth over her shoulder with a fluttery wave.

The human lowered her gaze as Beth walked away. Once she was sure that Beth was out of earshot, she visibly relaxed. She moved a finger to her comm. "She's gone."

"Thank God," sighed Natira. "She spoke so much." She made her voice shrill as she mimicked, "Over here is this, over here is that, but don't worry, we often use the buddy system for newbies. If you'd like, you can be my buddy." She broke off into snickers. "That by far is the cheesiest thing I've ever heard in my life."

"I can't believe The Committee uses the buddy system," joined Kiera. "But then again, Natira's treasured dagger has a pink handle."

Natira hissed. "Kiera!"

The Zonan laughed, "I could've told her about your—" "Don't you dare!"

"—pink dress!"

Marah snickered. "Kiera, you should have led with that. Please tell me you got a picture."

"Try it and I'll test out your bow again."

Marah's laughter was cut short. "You nearly broke the bowstring last time. Don't even *look* at my bow, let alone *touch* it!"

"I was drunk!"

"So, imagine what you'll do sober."

A Committee worker sitting across from Marah looked at her strangely. "Who are you talking to?"

Natira and Kiera immediately went silent.

Thanks a lot, guys.

Marah was positive she was blushing as she gestured to her ear. "Bluetooth." Right as she realized what she had said, she nearly facepalmed herself. *Great job, Bluetooth is only on Earth!*

The worker nodded and resumed working

Kiera was the first to speak. "How'd you know about Bluetooth? Humans took that too, huh?"

There's Bluetooth in space?

"Well, it's as Beth said," Natira offered, speaking in a shrill voice, "oh Nima, you're going to fit in here perfectly, just you watch."

Leia interrupted, "Can we get back to the actual mission, please?"

"Yes ma'am." Marah typed her username and password into her computer as she inquired, "I guess I start?"

She opened first a manual of where all the files and information were stored, trying to get a sense of what information existed and how much she was supposed to know. She found a tab labeled restricted and decided to scroll through lists of files and came across one of interest: prophecy. It piqued her interest, as she hadn't pegged dictators or aliens to believe in something as mystical as a prophecy.

"Should I be aware of a prophecy?"

Natira questioned, "A prophecy? The Committee has a religion?" She mused, "And here I thought they did whatever they wanted for their own selfish reasons. Can you send it?"

"I don't have access to it."

Natira dismissed her worry, "The drive that we gave you, can you put it anywhere?"

The question-mark button directed her to it.

A chat box message came up that was small enough for only Marah to see.

"Did you get that?" Natira.

"**Yes**", she typed out and sent, grateful for the dividers between each workstation.

Good, this will be our means of communication when it's better to not speak on comms. We'll hang out here, so it doesn't look like you're talking to yourself. Focus on learning your job for now and then use whatever free time you have to look for the Poten.

Marah: **Any hints on where to start?**

Nope.

Marah: **Great.**

She sighed.

"Or you could ask Beth," Natira quipped. "I'm sure she'd love to help you."

Marah shook her head as she clicked on a file about beginners and began to read the plans, notes, and agenda.

What if you get caught right now?

Now is not the time for this! You have a job to do! Can you do it, though?

Finding the quiet that had fallen too uncomfortable, the voice inside her mind piped up: *Hopefully, the cut on my face from last week's training isn't showing. Otherwise, someone could ask and blow my cover.*

She held her lips together from possibly incriminating herself, instead, she found her fingers commanding her to type those words out to the rebels.

You'll be fine. Worst comes to worst if you go down, it'll be as a superhero.

Any other time, she'd roll her eyes. Instead, Marah found Natira's quip comforting.

So, you do think that superheroes are cool. That's a win for me.

Shifting uncomfortably on a chair that she couldn't sink into just right, she crossed one leg over the other; trying to shake off the nerves that struck at every movement.

She instantly became super aware of her surroundings as she glanced at a sea of faces that seemed to be all looking at her, a bug under a very large microscope.

You're supposed to be a hero. A spy. This is not the time to panic.

Give me one reason not to panic.

She held her breath as someone walked past her. Self-consciousness and the speculation of how stupid she looked provoked the human to nearly blurt that she couldn't do this. Her fingers trembled as she typed out: There are too many things that can go wrong. If something goes wrong…

…the consequences are worse than being yelled at or hit.

I forgot to mention, she stressed as she typed out, I know I may sound good at lying, but I'm really just panicking underneath. How am I supposed to do this? This was a bad idea.

For a moment, she thought that she had turned her comm or the window off, or that the rebels didn't care or want to deal with her. Her pulse was a thunderstorm lurching over unknown waters.

Committee workers at the other end of the workstation were laughing about something.

All these people are bad guys, and I don't know how to be one of them. I don't want to be like them.

Her vision became too clear for her liking, everything precise and large. She needed to get out of that damned building. She couldn't look at the screen in front of her, let alone think about what she was doing. There was too much of a risk being at the Citadel.

What was I thinking when I let the rebels talk me into this?

Regret for her decision panged in her body but was quickly replaced with a bitter jittery sensation as she realized that she was stuck where she was.

Leaving was impossible. She had signed in. The rebels were counting on her. Leaving would make her another disappointment, and the frustration of her dilemma was more than enough to keep her chest hurting. The uniform she wore felt uncomfortable and if Marah continued to press her lips against each other, they'd soon hurt.

Breathing was hard. She was grateful to not have asthma, because she would never get used to the pain that inhaling brought her when she was in a state like this. Exhaling seemed impossible as her teeth ground themselves against each other, keeping her entire body stiff.

She hadn't felt this way in a long time, and she fought to keep herself in check. A battle that she was losing quickly.

That was until Leia spoke softly over the comms, "Marah, you need to breathe. We're here with you every step of the way. Our spies are protecting you as we speak - no one can hurt you."

How do you know?

Marah couldn't understand why Leia was so confident in her reply. "Because I do. You're letting that small voice in your head cloud your heart. Nobody knows who you are. Our spies are ensuring that. This disguise can be whoever you want it to be. Have fun with it. Use this to your advantage."

Kiera chimed in, "Remember that movie we watched the other day? You're playing a game. One space forward at a time."

There was a sense of innocence and almost understanding, as if Kiera's empath abilities stretched from the streets to the desk where her elbows were resting.

She rubbed the stress-induced rough patches on her forehead, trying not to pick at them. *One step at a time, c'mon. First day on the job, right? Just don't get caught, I mean, how hard can it really be? Remember that time in ninth grade when mother found your diary and asked about the codes? You used the Arabic number system to cipher the English alphabet and lied about it being a writing assignment and not your plan for when you figured out, she was going to kick you out?*

Determination furrowed her brow. She needed to do this for the rebels. For her friends who were counting on her now more than ever.

Friends. That does sound better than saying Leia, Kiera, and Natira. Or my kidnappers.

Even though Marah expected to feel the most alienated among the rebels who were literal aliens, they were the first people to worm their way into her heart and stay there.

Sure, the whole kidnapping and expecting me to help them wasn't the best. But here I still am. I can't let others fall the way Artemis did.

Besides, the rebels aren't too bad, thought Marah with a smile. The more she thought about it, the more she realized that she wasn't angry anymore at the rebels for kidnapping her.

They care about you. They're counting on you. They won't give up on you. They're like a family that you're now part of. Maybe the family that you need. Maybe it's destiny.

Whatever it is, she decided conclusively, *it's worth a shot to find out.* She started the next set of videos explaining the year-long training that it took to become an officer.

Eventually, a pop-up on the screen broke the silence as it spoke: "There's going to be a conference today where they will set up the final steps to take over Kosmir. Those steps include new laws passed and raiding all facilities to find rebels or rebel-like activity. The Committee will enforce their laws on all business retails, offices, complexes, as well as in all schools worldwide and elsewhere."

Someone tapped her shoulder, causing her to panic and close the browser. She turned around to find Beth standing behind her.

She feebly opened her mouth, but Beth beat her to it. "As invested as you are in your work, I was wondering if you wanted to join me during lunch break? Our break hours run from twelve to one, and at one we have a conference with the Chairwoman."

"Oh, yeah, sure." A smile that didn't match Marah's eyes formed on her face. "That sounds great, let me just log out first." She spoke slowly as if she was trying to convince herself that Beth's proposition really did sound great.

If Beth noticed, she didn't comment.

Marah's lower lip twitched. "So, what do you have in mind?"

"Well, there's this new place, Conspersio et Vade, that just opened up," the girl replied enthusiastically. "I heard they have the best coffee on the planet. At least in the social world—check GramChat often?"

Marah shook her head.

"You should get one, we have a Committee Officer group chat. Anyway, Gema was talking about it so yeah. Besides," she faced Marah and chuckled, "you'll need the caffeine to keep you going."

A Committee group chat? I don't even have a phone.

Marah forced a chuckle and moved a lock of hair over her ear to cover her comm. She replied at the bare minimum, "Nothing like caffeine to keep me going."

She nearly face-palmed herself.

The walk was approximately ten minutes from the building. During that time, the human couldn't help but wear a mask of curiosity as she explored the streets of Kosmir once again.

"Cute."

Marah whipped her head to face Beth, who looked like she was holding herself back from laughing. She donned an expression of confusion as she waited for Beth to elaborate.

"The way you're looking at everything." Eyes the color of the sky met hazel eyes buried in a similar hue. "I take it you're not from the urban parts of Kosmir?"

Marah blinked. "Oh, yeah no. I'm not from here." She then realized her mistake, panic throbbing in her chest as she corrected herself. "There, I mean." She played it off with a smile as she forced herself to speak steadily. "This is all new and exciting."

Beth grinned. "Yeah, it is. These parts of Kosmir can be intimidating at first, but once you get used to it, you'll be fine. It's the best place in the universe."

She nodded as she moved her gaze away from Beth and the tingling of her legs to streets that reverberated with stories that she wanted to know, from the cracks to the sidewalks to what made the cars move to the glum expression on the face of a teenager.

"We're here." Beth said as she gestured toward a door, pulling Marah away from her thoughts. "So, what do you want?" asked Beth. "I'll pay. I always try to help the newbies out, because I sure could have used some when I was one."

"Oh, that's really nice of you. I'll just have a small coffee," replied Marah as she opened the door and followed Beth inside. *I wasn't aware the Committee could be nice.*

Then again, they don't know who I am.

As polite as she was pretending to be, the human couldn't help but wonder if the same girl who was offering to cover the tab might be someone who had participated in the manslaughter on Artemis.

She didn't argue with the alien for that reason, and because she had no clue how to use the money that the rebels had only given her a little of.

"If we end up not liking Conspersio et Vade, we can always try some other place. Where do you usually go for takeout?"

The sudden question took Marah by surprise.

"I don't eat out too much," she fibbed, hating the sour feeling lying left on her tongue as the two entered the cafe.

Right from the first step inside, her senses were hit with such a scent, that it had her immediately craving *whatever this is.*

The sweet aroma of sugar and bread wavered through the human's nostrils, adding to her relief as she found herself standing in a short line.

While Beth took her time to think about what she wanted, Marah surveyed the restaurant.

It was so unbelievably normal. People at tables sipped beverages in tall white cups and stuffed pastries neatly into their mouths, dabbing the corners with a napkin. Teenagers were huddled around tables engaging in conversations as they talked through chewed donuts, cake, and technology. Parents took sips from large steaming mugs of caffeinated beverages, caffeine no doubt being the ultimate arsenal to combat the thrills of parenthood. A trove of children littered the premises with faces smudged against glass, fantasizing sugary goodies and delectables that they may or may not gain access to. Brown-colored walls and low chorused chatter contributed to the serene cacophony that pleased Marah's ears.

Beth pulled out her phone and snapped a pic, the flash startling Marah.

"Sorry, for the Gram."

Marah watched the blonde post and used an overwhelming number of hashtags as she pushed her hands deeper into her pockets. Though her uniform wasn't ideal, she was grateful for the pockets. *Alien clothing is way better though. I can't believe people make jeans with fake pockets. I don't know what else to do with my hands.*

"Next!"

The barista, a light-brown-skinned woman with a veil over her hair and face, delivered a standard greeting as she asked, "So, what can I get you two today?"

Beth answered before Marah could. "Hi, we'll have two small coffees and two chocolate cake slices."

The barista clicked buttons on a screen before announcing, "That'll be twenty liros and six pecas."

Beth pulled a small pouch out of her blazer pocket and handed the woman a blue-colored bill among purple and pinks.

That's probably the twenty-dollar bill?

"One kelc and five neps, here you go."

One nickel and five pennies?

While Beth dealt with the rest of the transaction, Marah took the time to observe the woman. It was a force of habit, but it was also a way for her to keep track of everything in this world.

Beth, she realized, wasn't much taller than her. She herself was five foot three, almost five foot four, while Beth stood at about five foot six. The girl's face was as smooth as cream and the same color, with blonde hair perfectly tied into a ponytail. Her eyes flickered blue and her oval nails, a contrast from Marah's squares and rectangles, were coated with sky-colored paint.

"Like I said, my treat," explained Beth as the barista returned with their order.

"Try and see what she knows about the Poten," said Natira in her ear. "Smalltalk her first though."

I don't think I'll be doing most of the talking, Marah wanted to say as Beth had already begun to speak.

"These smell so good," exclaimed Beth as she took a seat at a booth by a glass wall. She brought the beverage to her lips and smiled dreamily.

Marah followed, letting sugar and milk fizzle in her mouth. She found herself speaking before she even realized, "Whoever told you this place has the best coffee is definitely right. This is, by far, the best coffee I've ever had. So, I wanted to ask…"

"Definitely!" interrupted Beth. She nibbled on her pastry. "Oh, this is delicious. I think this is my new favorite place now."

Marah took a bite from her pastry. She held her breath for a moment, hoping that her attempt at small talk wouldn't blow up in her face. "Mhm. So, I actually heard about this power source and I was curious about…"

"I know it might be a little awkward to work at the Citadel," started Beth as she swallowed.

Does she not hear me?

"July will be my third year officially," resumed Beth as if Marah had never spoken, "At first it was overwhelming because, well, as you know, after high school you get to work in the major that you're studying. But I've been interning since before I turned fifteen. Chairwoman Kate saw my dedication and let me drop my classes so I could work here full time."

Marah was confused, unsure of how any of what Beth said related to what she was trying to work at. Beth was looking at her as if it were her turn to speak. "I think I'm okay. My high school was small and I'm the only one from there. I used to work hard." She attempted to divert the conversation back to where she wanted, "So…"

"Can you tell me about your high school?"

The only lies that Marah could think of slipped through her teeth, "I didn't grow up in the best parts of here. My parents were poor, so they couldn't afford the best school in the area." Truth be told, she had no idea if schools here did cost anything, but she assumed that she was on the right track when Beth gave her a pitiful look.

She continued her pitch of an origin story. "Yeah. They didn't have enough to support both me and my brother, so I had to work small jobs." At this point, she said whatever she could think of. "I didn't get into the best high school per se, but I went to school full time, to the point where my mother would joke that I should live there."

"That's really sad," remarked Beth as she popped open a sugar packet into her drink. "At least here you have a friend."

Maybe flattery?

"So, you probably know everything there is to know about The Committee and the Citadel..."

Beth sighed as she scarfed down her pastry, bits and crumbs sprinkling down her face. "I love it here so much. Being a part of such a great organization makes me feel really good. Some people don't like what we do here," she spat, "like the rebels." Her tone turned chipper as she continued, "but I feel that we're on the path to greatness."

She paused before admitting, "My grandparents weren't supportive of me joining, neither were my parents. I'm no longer welcome at home, so I stay where I feel at home. But it doesn't matter," the Kosmirian smiled, "the things we do here are great, you obviously know that."

"Yeah," echoed Marah, close to giving up. "The Committee does such great things." *Like universal domination and killing people. Totally great things.* She sipped the rest of her beverage as her tongue soured at her words.

Beth was still smiling at her, to the point where she began to wonder if the alien's face had frozen. Tension thickening, she glanced at a clock behind Beth. "Look at the time. We should get going to the conference, right?"

Beth scrambled to stand. "You're totally right! We shouldn't be late, especially on your first day here. Let's go."

Chapter 17

Location: The heart of the enemy

"Thank you again," said Marah as she brought coffee to her lips, the contact of the liquid supplying her with warmth to combat the breeze that blew past her suddenly.

"Don't sweat it," grinned Beth. "I wonder what the meeting is going to be about. We're so close to finding the rebels' location. We're bound to find it soon. With the background checks on everyone and everything, one mistake on their part will be their demise."

I hope they heard that.

"Copy," replied Kiera as if she had read Marah's mind.

"Or," suggested Beth as she cracked her knuckles and reapplied lipstick, "they'll talk about what the next steps are for Marah Morana."

Marah came to a halt. She turned to face Beth and inquired urgently, "What about Marah Morana? Not that I know her, but what do you know about her?"

Right after the words left her lips she stiffened, realizing how she sounded.

Beth either didn't notice the wavering panic in the human's voice or didn't comment on it. "Apparently, she's working with the rebels. That's the rumor I've heard going around since Artemis. I was dealing with the Kazna tribe, so I have no clue. The Chairwoman hasn't confirmed if she was there. Not yet." She shrugged as if she didn't believe the words she uttered. "No one knows who she is, where she's from, or what she looks like except the Chairwoman. Apparently, she's dangerous."

As they neared the Citadel, Marah couldn't help but wonder if The Committee knew the answer she'd pay to know. "What makes her so dangerous? She's just a human, no?"

She mentally face-palmed herself. *It really is so awkward to talk about myself in the third person.*

Beth chuckled darkly. "The Chairwoman says that she's dangerous. But I only know that because of the gossip. All I know for certain, is that Chairwoman Kate wants the human dead."

Well, that's a nice way to put it, Marah bitterly thought as they entered the Citadel.

They had just walked past the helpdesks when Beth came to a stop. "I'll be right back. I have to use the restroom. You go on ahead. The conference hall is on the right hall, first door on the left. Follow the crowd, you won't miss it."

And before she knew it, Beth had disappeared into the swarm of people, leaving behind a faint blue steak that disappeared as quickly as she saw it.

She let out a sigh of relief that she had been holding in her chest for a while. She looked around at the crowd of people and felt her lungs begin to constrict. They were all engaged in their own conversations and were being awfully loud about it.

She moved a finger to her ear and spoke just loud enough for the comm to pick up her voice. "You guys heard all of that?"

Leia mimicked a sound of confirmation. "Yep, all loud and clear. So, your next move is to go to the conference and find out what's happening. We'll figure out our next move from there."

"Copy."

Marah eyed the tightly packed crowd uneasily before following, doing her best not to bump into anyone. *How can so many people fit in a building?* She increased her walking pace to avoid getting stepped on as suffocation followed her into the conference hall.

The hall was practically an indoor stadium, with rows and rows of seats each higher than the one in front. In the center of the hall was a platform with a long rectangular desk and seven seats.

Workers continued to trickle into the hall, all making themselves heard with loud clashing voices that made Marah struggle to see clearly. It didn't help that someone was flickering with lights that refused to go anywhere except for her eyes, as she took a few steps to soothe her burning eyelids. Breathing became a conscious effort as oxygen slithered down an unusually narrow passage, and her tongue felt like sour candy as it rested uncomfortably in her mouth. Her ears began to hurt from the constant shuffling of feet and chatter of people. Her palms felt like they had been licked with sweat and her knees began to tremble slightly.

She headed toward the upper decks, eager to get away from the bright lights and constant chatter. As she hiked up the walkway, she noticed a blonde-haired girl wave at her and gesture toward an empty seat next to her.

She squinted, trying to get a better look at the person to realize that the girl was Beth.

She hastily forced the faintest of grins as she raced up the stairs to Beth. She slid into the seat next to the Kosmirian, wondering how Beth could've gotten here so quickly if she had to use the restroom.

She trained her eyes toward the empty desk ahead of her. The seat in the middle stood out from the others, with a higher back and decorated arms. If Marah had to guess, she presumed that seat belonged to the Chairwoman. *But what about the other seats?*

She was about to ask Beth when a clicking sound silenced all the chatter carried by her "colleagues."

She watched as the space behind the desk pulled apart, revealing something beneath it. Seven figures emerged, standing on a platform that rose onto the floor and clicked in place. The figures wore power on their sleeves along with contrasting looks of tattoos, wild hair colors, and features such as tails and scars. Besides their unique distinctions, Marah noticed that these people weren't dressed like the people she was seated amongst. Instead of the navy-blue uniform, they wore all black intricate outfits and had weapons sheathed to their thighs, except for a hilt of a sword that poked out from behind an armored neck.

Marah assumed this was done to show the hierarchy amongst the Committee. She ruminated if the weapons were really necessary. *What do they have to fear? Me? The idea of me?*

The figures brought an airy presence to the table, one that Marah definitely didn't like. She followed their gaze as they inspected each and every member of their audience as if they were expendable subjects.

She resisted a shudder.

Beth nudged Marah with her elbow, whispering, "You see the woman in the center with the white hair? That's the Chairwoman. She's been here for seven years, and she has all of the power here."

"So, who are the others?"

"Those are the Legionnaires," whispered Beth patiently. "They're the Chairwoman's closest and most trusted associates. They're powerful too, as you can tell from the clothes that they're wearing."

Marah opened her mouth but quickly clamped it shut as the Chairwoman, who for some strange reason vaguely resembled someone, but she couldn't place who, rose, indicating that she was to speak.

Marah immediately discarded the thought because *what were the chances of that?*

The Chairwoman cleared her throat and silence fell over her audience. Her tone was smoky as she spoke, pinning all attention toward her. "Wake up and smell the coffee." She lifted her chin upward as her eyes twinkled darkly. "Is the cup half full or half empty? We've been seeing the rebellion situation as an empty cup. However, in reality, that cup is filling to the brim.

Members of the audience looked at each other in confusion. Marah looked at Beth, who only shrugged.

"We are being drained from the inside and if we do not act quickly, our regime of universal peace will be all over. By that," she said, her enunciation strong and clear as day, "I mean that the rebellion group has become, and continues to grow, stronger."

The head of Kosmir's regiment paused for a reaction and got exactly that.

Wearing disbelief like a well-fitted mask, Marah blended in as murmurs spiraled from all corners of the hall as sounds of absurdity rang against her ears.

The Chairwoman curled her slender fingers into a fist as she raised a hand just above her neck.

The audience immediately fell to a silence as members leaned forward, eager to hear what else their leader would have to say; Marah included.

Chairwoman Kate's voice increased in volume. "My Legionnaires have informed me about rumors circulating that the rebels have recruited someone powerful enough to stop this very organization. I am here to address these rumors. These rumors are correct. The rebels are equipped with Marah Morana, a human decoded by our very own Poten, and are set on destroying us."

The audience reacted immediately as protests and sounds of disbelief erupted in Marah's ears all over again.

At the mention of her name, she cast her eyes down. Remembering who and where she was, more importantly, who she wasn't here, she raised her gaze back up to avoid drawing suspicion.

"As you all know," the Chairwoman continued, voice trilling with anger threatening to bubble over, "the rebels were on Artemis, a pathetic attempt to prevent our success."

"I'm not sure if you've heard, but the rebels were doomed to fail from the start," whispered Beth, leaning close. "We have more people, weapons, and devices than they could ever dream of. They do all of this work and yet always miss us coming. It's quite sad, honestly. Especially Artemis. They didn't even have ten ships. We had a cloaking device that they never picked up." She smiled, crossing her arms as she leaned back against her seat. "They didn't stand a chance."

Marah gritted her teeth at Beth's remark. The girl seemed proud of the fact that she had been a part of the ruin of a planet, and Marah didn't feel so bad about Beth paying for her lunch. She couldn't afford to look at Beth in fear that she would ruin her facade immediately.

"And the whole Marah Morana thing?" Beth laughed. "Baloney, if you ask me. Sure, she can supposedly fight, but we all can." Beth's assertive tone only encouraged her words to worm right into Marah's head. "There's nothing heroic about her. She's just a human, after all. Nothing fancy about that."

Marah looked at her hands. Beth's words stung the human, and she couldn't help but agree. She was supposed to be the savior of Kosmir, the weapon to defeat The Committee once and for all, and yet the girl struggled to understand why she out of all people was that person.

Beth had a point: she was only human.

There isn't anything special about me, yet for some reason I'm here.

Marah didn't say anything as Beth continued to speak proudly, "We have the upper advantage, I mean, just look at us. We stand tall and proud. We don't cower. A mere human cannot end a war or start a riot just like that."

Irritated, Marah bit her lip. Beth really had no idea about how many people, both fictional and real, were perceived as powerless and still managed to do exactly as Beth suggested.

She believed that there was someone capable of ending this war. *Just not me.*

Then again, I'd love to see Beth's face when she finds out who I really am.

She'd love to know why she was the solution to this problem. She wondered if the prophecy was the answer she needed and if Beth knew anything about it.

Even if she did, whether or not she would say, is another question.

But Marah remembered who she was supposed to be, a pawn on a chessboard for Kosmir. She needed to act the part, as much as she hated it with every fiber in her being. The spy forced herself to nod with gritted teeth as she listened to what else the Queen of the chessboard had to say.

"Needless to say, new decrees have been passed. The Fugitive Decree states that anyone on the streets suspected of being a rebel, or is one, is to be immediately imprisoned without delay. Internally, everything will remain as is. I don't intend on wasting my workers for allegations. However, anyone imprisoned must be brought before me before they can be accounted for treason."

One pawn had the guts to interrupt her. "No trial or evidence?"

Chairwoman Kate shook her head as malice and the same fire that Marah saw in the graffiti surged through the woman's eyes. "There is no need for a trial," she spoke frankly. "I am the judge, jury, and executioner. Anyone who is proven to be collaborating with the rebels will comply with the standard processes and provide information or will refuse to do so. Either way," she promised, "they will meet death."

Marah felt her fingers curl into fists. *Who did the Chairwoman think she was?* The woman looked at her audience as if they were nothing but little pawns in a grand scheme, which was more than enough to boil Marah's blood. Not even on her behalf, but on behalf of her disguise. *How could these people be so dedicated to someone who only needs them for their own success and bidding?*

Not only that, but to have the audacity to think that captured or imprisoned rebels would just willingly tell you what you want to hear, knowing they would be killed anyway? That was outrageous. And yet, much to Marah's disgust, the people around her only looked more dedicated to this malicious cause.

"Additionally," the leader of The Committee recommended, "if anyone is to sight Marah Morana, they are to report her to me, and only me, immediately. Should any of you run into her, it is preferable that you bring her to me alive than dead." She took a breath while raising her chin, reveling in her position of power, "In fact, whoever does manage to alert me of the human's or any other rebel leaders' whereabouts, should they come to your awareness of course, will be rewarded immensely."

Marah opened her mouth only to quickly clamp it shut. She knew her life was in danger since she arrived on Kosmir, but a bounty on her head was completely different. The noirette couldn't help but feel terror as her pulse thrummed in her ears at how easily the Chairwoman could announce that she was starting a manhunt.

"On occasion," the red-lipped woman drawled as her gaze hovered across the room before settling at Marah's eyes for a moment and then across the hall, "checks will be done for everyone to ensure that they are who they say they are."

The only thing that kept Marah from panicking was that her glasses, while comically useless, placed a filter over her eyes that allowed her eyes to look icy blue. That, and the wave of comfort she had felt when she confided in the rebels, and they didn't insult her.

Marah held the woman's gaze as the latter continued, "It's time to end the rebellion once and for all."

"Everyone will resume their current posts and work for maximum efficiency," concluded the Chairwoman. "All training will be shortened, and mentors will take recruits along with them. Do what is needed to establish our reign on the galaxy. The only way we can do that is by eliminating the rebel force once and for all. She paused, surveying the sea of employees that hearkened to her every word, "After all, life is an arena, and we are it's slayers."

The audience burst into a round of applause as Chairwoman Kate returned to her seat. For what, Marah was uncertain.

The noirette frowned as she leaned back in her seat and clapped her hands together. While she did so, her friends were asking her question after question, but the archer made no attempt to answer any of them.

Her chances of being caught had just skyrocketed through the building's roof. *I'm screwed. One test and I'd be out just like that.*

Beth whispered not so quietly to combat the roar of the crowd, "This means you'll get to help capture and kill rebels now, isn't that great!"

If only she knew.

Marah blurted out the first excuse that came to her mind, "Yeah. I'll be right back. I have to use the restroom."

The rebel spy didn't wait for Beth to reply as she speed-walked away. She didn't know where she was going but hoped that no one would stop and ask her anything. She ducked into the first room she saw, and, ironically, it was the women's restroom.

Marah first made sure that no one was in the room before throwing open the farthest stall door and locking it behind her. She hesitated before moving a finger to her comm, looking under the stalls to see no one there.

After waiting to see if anyone would enter the bathroom, Marah whispered, "One question at a time, please."

Kiera was the first to speak. "It got fuzzy once the Chairwoman started to speak. What did she say?"

"A bunch of stuff," answered Marah. "First, they know that I'm with the rebels. They're looking for the base and I'm pretty sure they know that there are spies here. They're issuing new decrees to imprison anyone outside who they think is a rebel." She breathed out shakily as she added, "And there's a bounty on my head." *Even though I don't really know why.*

Leia was quick to console, "Don't worry about that, we're going to make sure that they don't find out about you. Our spies are already onto that. We'll protect the base; we heard about the cloaking device so we'll get Joven to run stats on that. Anything else?"

"They're going to be running checks on everyone. I might be able to skip some of them."

"How exactly?" probed Natira.

Marah shrugged, "I'll figure something out. Maybe Beth will come in handy. Or the other spies."

Leia offered, "We'll talk to the other spies. Still, stay low. We don't intend on keeping you there for a long time. Just enough for you to find and take the Poten."

"Only question is," asked Natira, "do you think you can give us that window?"

Marah shrugged. "Yeah. No. Ish? I tried to talk about that with Beth, but you all heard how that went. I'll try and ask around." She peeked through the slit of the stall door to make sure that she was still alone. "What's my next move? Also, how do I use money? If I'm going to build a friendship with Beth, I'll need to be able to return the favor."

"Alright. One of our spies, Elena, is going to give you the stuff you need since you might be staying there for a while. She'll tell you where you need to go, stuff like that. Just remember this code: *et aeterni.*"

Marah breathed out, "Got it. Oh, one more thing. I forgot to ask before, if someone asks me what abilities I have, what should I say? What abilities do people here have?"

Kiera listed, "There's a power for anything. Phasing, energy manipulation, hypermotility." She added helpfully, "Power has no limits, though."

She groaned, "If someone asks me for a demonstration, what am I supposed to do then?"

The human could tell that Natira was smirking as the Nantak offered, "Just pick something from those comic books and movies that you love so much."

Marah rolled her eyes, "Natira, you're such a—" Her words died away at the sound of Beth calling her name a few feet outside the bathroom. "Got to go," she said quickly, exiting the stall and started to wash her hands.

Beth smiled cheerily as she approached Marah. "Oh good. You left so quickly; I was worried that you were going to get lost."

Marah wore a fake smile, "Oh, I followed the signs. Sorry about bursting out so quickly." She attempted to joke, "All that caffeine, y'know?"

Beth chuckled, "We've all been there. It's not like anyone noticed anyways. C'mon," she said while grabbing a paper towel, "We'll be ramping up the officer regiments. Unfortunately, we're not on street patrol."

Marah mimicked a look of disappointment as water and soap trickled down her fingers. "Bummer. So then, what did we get?"

Beth's facial features brightened as she answered, "We're the behind-the-scenes people, it's not as fun as being outside and patrolling, but it's still something." She smiled, "I'm so happy we have the same post," she playfully bumped elbows with Marah, "me and you are going to be great friends, Nima, I just know it."

Marah beamed with gritted teeth as she wrung her hands to dry them, "Definitely." *She's not going to leave me alone, is she?*

The corners of Beth's lips tugged upwards as she started to ramble, "Not to seem clingy or whatever, but you're the first friend I've made here in a long time. Not that I'm odd or anything, the others have such bold and loud personalities. A little quiet wouldn't do any harm, you're friendly. Not overkill, like them."

"Thanks." *I guess?*

"I'm pretty sure I'm going to start rambling," continued the blonde, "so please, say the word and I'll stop."

Marah wore assurance like a well-fitted mask, "No worries. I'd love that."

Beth let out a sigh of relief, baby blue eyes sparkling as she led the two back to their workstations, leaving Marah to wonder what else she would have to face on only her first day here.

Chapter 18

Location: The battle before the battle

Marah followed Beth back to their workstations as the Kosmirian explained the basics of the system that she was going to be dealing with. "Basically, we'll have one of four jobs. We'll be reviewing and setting up the cameras inside the Citadel, doing training regiments, reviewing camera footage for documenting and approving police reports, or interrogating suspected rebels."

If I work on the cameras, I can probably find or get some hints as to where the Poten actually is. I'm sure they have a lot of cameras watching their valuable power source.

She started to form her question aloud, but was shot down before she could utter a single word.

"But don't worry, you'll have me sticking by your side." Beth's tone was as ardent as her smile as she glanced at a watch on her wrist, "That will be in about fifteen minutes, though. I have to meet up with Legionnaire Zafre right now."

Marah nodded, taking a seat as Beth walked away. She sighed, looking back at the alien. "This may be harder than I thought."

"Right?" snickered Natira in her ear, "It's like a superpower. You know, I've seen this before in that Earth movie I watched the other day."

"How do you even have the time to watch movies?" retorted Marah. "Also, how many have you watched? You must really like them."

The Nantak swiftly replied, "Plenty enough to know that this is classic. You're literally the new girl trying to prove her self-worth and you meet someone who will quickly become your best friend."

Marah grumbled, "There's a lot of missing things in your story."

The alien was unconvinced, "I'm just saying. You say that something is impossible, but life has a way of proving otherwise. Didn't you say that aliens were impossible?" Marah was certain that if she could see the Nantak's face she'd be winking, "I'm very much real if I do say so myself."

Marah groaned as she buried her face against the smoothness of her palms, "What are you implying?"

Natira spoke in a humorous tone, "I could be wrong, but to a degree that I haven't figured out yet, I'm sure the two of you will become best friends."

"Don't you dare jinx me!"

Kiera chimed, "Natira, just because that was the plot of the newest episode of *Improfi* doesn't mean that it's happening now. You said the same thing when you saw me with—"

"First of all, that episode was a personal attack against my heart! The fanfics aren't making it any better. Secondly, raise your hand if you've been on a movie-binge since I don't have to train anyone."

There was a brief pause before Natira declared smugly, "Exactly."

Marah sighed as she logged into her computer to find a new set of training videos and documents to review for her first set of cases that would come tomorrow. "I hope you're wrong, so I can rub it in your face. Though, it would be pretty funny considering how she sees the real me as pathetic."

"If and until you prove me wrong, I will gladly enjoy this," replied Natira gleefully. "In fact, don't turn your comm off at all. This is so entertaining. Kiera's taking notes on everything that you hear, and Leia is in charge of responding to their moves and I've been training the rebels. We found a copy of one of the movies you always talk about."

"You're going to watch an Earth movie while I have to worry about literally anything and everything?" said Marah incredulously. "What movie are you even watching?"

The noirette heard the sound of snapping fingers, "The one with the big green lizard. Yogurt was his name?"

Marah nearly choked on her spit. "What is up with you and lizards?"

"I feel like lizards are my spirit animal," said Natira thoughtfully. "Small and deadly."

Leia interjected, "As weird as Natira is, Marah, maintaining a friendship with Beth could be useful. She might be able to assist your mission."

"And how do you suggest I do that?"

The Novan didn't get the chance to answer as Beth returned, opting to sit first and then speak, "Legionnaire Zafre was busy. Anyways, I forgot to show you the other basics to your workstation." She smiled as she brought her chair toward Marah, much to the girl's pleasure, "Since today is your first day you can get familiar with the systems but starting tomorrow, we'll be doing the assigned tasks and proper training."

"We? But don't you have to do your job since you're not new?" *Please leave so I can figure out how the hell I'm going to mess this up.*

Beth replied as her lips stretched wider and Marah wondered how she wasn't feeling any pain at all, "I'm your mentor, so I have full permission to spend the day helping you, so you'll be perfect tomorrow.

Marah bit down on her smile and couldn't afford to look at the alien as Natira all but cackled in her ear. "So, what do I do?"

Let's get this over with.

"I don't know if you already know, but all of our monitors are touchscreens. It's the perk of having the best tech out of all the worlds." Beth laughed for some reason, which only irritated Marah.

"But we have the keyboards too because some have disabilities, so the choice makes it easier for them to work and whatnot. Not everyone's a fan of touching the glass screens, which is why they're see-through and larger than regular monitors. So anyway, you're going to click on the pop-up in the corner. That's where all important notices such as meetings, updates, and more are."

While Beth explained more and Marah clicked absentmindedly, her thoughts returned to all the ways she could use her role as an officer to not only find the Poten, but maybe support the rebel cause too. She had been meaning to ask her rebel friends the inquiry, but Beth hadn't given the noirette an opportunity to do so, which only irked her even more as the blonde droned on about software, finally having a friend, and some other stuff that Marah didn't feel like paying attention to.

Marah bit her lip, resisting the urge to roll her eyes and tell Beth to *shut up for God's sake!* But, to not put herself in an uncomfortable position, she kept her mouth shut. *Hopefully, I'll only have to put up with her for a little longer.*

Beth spoke matter-of-factly, "I don't know why Chairwoman Kate is so adamant about the rebels, but whatever." She shrugged, "It's not like I was alive during the time of The Great War."

Marah raised a brow. It was probably common knowledge, but never once had anyone spoken of a war.

The blonde mimicked a shudder, "The Great War is barely talked about, and for good reason. All I know is that the war involved horrible, gruesome deaths. That's probably why the Legion formed."

"The Legion? Who are they?"

Beth chuckled darkly, "The Committee before they became The Committee. I know it's hard to believe, but before all of this," she looked up at the ceiling, "they were just ordinary people like you and me who wanted to make a change."

Marah raised dark brows. "What do you mean?"

Beth tsked, "There's a saying. When there is no control, then there is chaos. Chaos is known to unfold to catastrophe." She spoke as if she were reciting, "And catastrophe breeds war."

Beth lowered her gaze and Marah began to wonder if the Kosmirian had lost someone from the war. The alien spoke wistfully, "War is a universal language. It speaks of conflict, power, and greed, but it also speaks of blood and death." She continued, "The Great War left all the main eight realms in shambles. It took all of the universe's soldiers, resources, and power to reach a standstill."

"What do you mean?" Both assignments were put on pause. Marah was surprised that no one was telling them off for not working, but in the building that was full of sounds, lights, and colors, she supposed a conversation here and there didn't actually matter.

Beth answered, "Eventually all the leaders of the worlds got tired of killing each other. The war was fought for decades and took countless lives in the process. Once the war was over, it took several years for recovery. The war began forty years ago and ended two decades ago thanks to The Committee."

"What happened?" *If The Committee was that strong, will we be able to beat them?*

"During the second war, Chairwoman Kate lost her entire family and was relocated into a new one at nine years old. The trauma must have been so bad," Beth sniffed, "and that encouraged her to make things right. To prevent war, so we wouldn't have to endure the pain that she did. She found The Committee who had been recruiting, and the rest, as they say, is history."

That's awful, but suffering isn't an excuse to create more war. How can Beth be so blind to the pains that exist solely because of the Chairwoman? What about the people like the rebels and the children who looked at her with fear and disgust? Was that not suffering to them?

"That's horrible," breathed Marah. "Did anyone try to stop her? Obsession isn't healthy."

Beth shrugged her shoulders, "Maybe. Maybe not. I personally agree with her views. If I had lost everything, I'd do anything to ensure that no one else would suffer the same as I had ever again. My extended family died in the Great War, so I think I get it."

"I'm so sorry to hear that."

Beth didn't get the chance to reply when a hoarse voice barked, "Everybody in a line! Now! Checking IDs and interrogations!"

The officer next to the owner of the hoarse voice—a tall, slender man who was much calmer than his partner—spoke, "There's nothing to worry about, we're only here to make sure that everyone is supposed to be here. You have nothing to be afraid of as long as you comply."

Officer number one, short and stout grumbled, "Or aren't one of those damn spies. Already caught one of 'em this morning."

I thought the rebels had taken measures? I'm going to get caught and then we're all going to die.

Marah froze, biting her lip to avoid displaying the panic that quickened her heartbeat. She hadn't gotten the chance to prepare for something like this. And judging by the officer's implications, they knew how to find spies like herself.

Marah would've pressed her comm to get advice from the rebels, but with Beth standing so close to her it was impossible to do so. Even worse, Beth had to be such a goody-two shoes and started to head to the line, dragging Marah with her.

Marah was working on how she was going to get herself out of this, someone grabbed her by the arm that Beth wasn't holding. Right before Marah could think that she was caught, a slip of paper was thrust into her hand.

She looked at the paper and relaxed. *Et aeterni.*

Marah let out a sigh of relief as the woman led her to a secluded place concealed in the shadows.

Marah was pushed deeper into the darkness by her mysterious savior who glanced over her shoulder to ensure that the two were safe before thrusting a small package into Marah's arms. "I assume you're Elena?"

Elena nodded minimally. She handed Marah a backpack that looked a bit worn.

Marah rattled the box, quiet sounds of metal clinking against her ears. "What's inside?" Elena brought a hand to her ear and used the other to open and close it.

"A phone?"

She nodded, then held her hand out and mimicked giving Marah something. Noting Marah's confusion, she repeated the gesture, this time with more emphasis.

Marah frowned. "I'm sorry but I don't understand? Can you tell me what you mean?"

Elena winced before moving closer so the human could get a better view of who she was talking to. Marah was able to make out cinnamon blonde hair behind ears along with a thick slash laid across bleeding lips and mouth.

Marah dipped her head down. "I'm sorry. Who did that to you?"

Elena tilted her head in the direction of the officers that were supposed to be interrogating them. If Marah had to guess which one, she assumed that the more aggressive officer was behind Elena's would-be scar as he remarked about catching "more rebel scum."

Marah inquired softly as she flickered her eyes back to the alien, "Did they just find out that you're here?" She refused to show pity toward the girl. There was no room for pity in fights that had worse consequences than damaged limbs.

Elena nodded. She held her hand out once again, waving bruised fingers. "Something you can give?"

Elena nodded and then made a circle with her index finger and thumb.

Marah guessed, "Money?"

Elena nodded. She then reached into her pocket and handed Marah a slip of paper that read: *I don't have much time before they realize I escaped. I wish you the best of luck in your mission. I will return to the others back home and let them know that I gave you the package. The money instructions are there. Be safe.*

Marah tucked the slip into the fold of her pant pocket, "Thank you." The noirette couldn't help but wonder if Elena had been caught on her way to help her, "Not only for the stuff but for back there. Thanks."

Elena smiled and then darted out of the corner, leaving Marah alone in the darkness. "That was easy," she muttered lowly as she lingered in the shadows, "and unexpected."

She sucked in a breath, resting the package against her hip and arm. "Now what am I going to say if Beth asks where I went?"

The sound of shuffling feet gained Marah's attention as officers one and two headed off. Once she was absolutely sure that they were gone, she strode out to find Beth at their workstations looking around for someone, presumably her. She walked up to Beth from behind and tapped her on the shoulder.

Beth exclaimed while making a one eighty turn, "There you are! What happened? Where were you?"

"One of the officers wanted to interrogate me since she hadn't seen me before," answered Marah, lowering the backpack to her side so as to not make it obvious. "I showed her my badge and told her that I was new. That was all." *Yep. Totally. Please don't ask any questions.*

Beth nodded with a frown, "Did you catch her name by any chance? Because from the way she grabbed you, you'd think she was going to hurt you." She seemed ready to file a report at any second.

Why is she so worried about me?

Marah waved Beth's worry off, "I didn't, but she didn't hurt me." *Even if someone did, I think I can take care of myself.*

Beth inquired hesitantly as she raised her brows, "Are you sure?"

"Positive." She quickly changed the topic away from her, "So when does our shift end?" "At five," said Beth as she checked her watch, "which happens to be right now. Did you get your room number and key?"

Marah nodded. "I got the number, not the key. What's yours?"

Beth answered with a smile as she shut off her computer and led the two to the elevators, "I'm on the fifth floor, room fifty-eight. You?"

Oh, come on!

"Me too!" Marah forced a smile as they entered an elevator, ignoring the pain in her cheeks because of it.

Beth's eyes lit up, "No way!" She actually giggled as she ecstatically slung an arm around Marah, "Just you wait, Nima, we're going to have so much fun together as roomies! I cannot wait! I was nervous when I applied for a roommate, but I know you and me are going to be perfect together!"

She strained to match Beth's enthusiasm, "Definitely!" *I cannot believe this is happening, I'm never going to get any peace and quiet at this rate.* She looked away from the alien, unsure if she could handle being around Beth for every single second of the day while Beth wore a smile, displaying her excitement.

She couldn't tear her mind away from Elena. Marah didn't know what the girl had gone through, but she was certain that the scar over her lips and the bloody fingers wasn't even half of her story.

Though the alien seemed okay, it still bothered Marah. *How could someone just do that to another person?*

Then, she remembered where she was. There was no trial, no chance for Elena to prove or feign her innocence. Just brute, punishing force to maul someone and strip their voice away because they used it.

Maybe that was why Beth was so worried about me? ruminated Marah as the elevator chimed softly and the two stepped off of metal onto carpet.

Marah grimaced at the sight of a room door with the number that matched her room number. Disappointment creased her features as Beth led them to their room. Marah hadn't expected that she would have to pass every second as a spy. She had hoped for some privacy. Then again, there were no luxuries when the stakes for others included damaged limbs and children unable to attend their parents' funerals.

Beth's voice pulled Marah away from her thoughts as the blonde opened the door to their room in a tone that was way too cheerily, "Welcome to your home away from home, roomie!"

What did she just call me?

This room was everything that her room back at the rebels' guild wasn't. The room was at least ten times the size of the room she had been living in, with two polished nightstands against the center of the wall. Adjacent to each nightstand were massive beds with fluffy pillows and thick covers. Pressed against the opposite wall rested vanities with stools. Each side of the wall opened to a doorless closet, with Beth's next to a balcony and Marah's filled with clothes that she had no clue how they got there. Another door that Marah presumed to be the restroom was on her side of the space.

It's so plain. Why is everything either blue, black, or white?

She bit back a frown. Home was her messy old room with its poster-covered walls, knickknacks strewn everywhere, and felt like home. Or the room back at the rebels' facilities that had begun to grow on her. *Not this.*

It didn't feel like home as Beth had joyously claimed. It felt strange and cold, a large contrast that didn't settle right in her gut. Like the furniture was watching her every move with secret cameras, mocking and belittling her.

Beth took her silence as awe, "You do realize that you're not speaking, right? Starstruck? We've all been there."

She forced a lie through her teeth, "I love it!"

Beth spoke dreamily, "How can you not?" She plopped onto her bed, "So, what do you want to do now?"

For some reason, the question took the human by surprise, "What do you mean?"

Beth let out a sigh as she tucked her forearms under her head to support herself, "Well, we're here and we've got nothing to do. So, bestie," she tried the nickname on for size, "what would you like to do now? Oh, I forgot to ask you earlier, what are your abilities? Mine's super speed."

Hence how she got to the meeting so fast. That is so cool!

Marah chewed on her lip for the umpteenth time of the day, unsure how to answer the question. It didn't help that her comm was radio silent. "That's pretty cool." *People compliment others' abilities, right?*

"You think so? Thanks," gushed Beth, "not many agree. Others have these fancy abilities like energy manipulation, flight, or telekinesis, but I don't mind the simpler powers. All powers are unique. What's yours?"

Marah fell silent, trying to figure out what she could say. She moved to rub her eyes but hit her hand with her glasses.

Aha.

"I, um, have enhanced senses. Hence the glasses." She traced the length of the frames down the bridge of her nose, the added weight to her face still bore discomfort. *That's a thing, right?*

Marah sounded like she was trying to convince herself rather than Beth as she elaborated, "Yeah, I have enhanced senses. When I take these off, I can hear and see practically anything and everything. The sight, um, doubles as enhanced vision, which is why I need the glasses so I can see normally." She slipped some truth into her explanation, "I prefer to look at the real world with all its colors and sounds. I don't need much to be happy. It's grounding," she added, hoping that she made sense.

She shifted her gaze to Beth who was silent. Marah began to think that Beth didn't buy any of what she said only to be proven wrong.

Beth chose her words carefully, "If I had your abilities, I don't think I would wear the glasses. Though the glasses would make me feel normal, I don't think that would work well for me. I mean," Beth's eyes met hazel ones that were peering over the top of the glasses, then she tilted her face to meet the blue ones visible through the lenses, "I respect your choice completely, but in worlds like this, you can't hide from yourself. You just can't. If you do, you'll be stuck forever in a bubble."

"What do you mean?" *Here she goes again.*

"I mean, we're all here because we have a purpose. If we hide what makes us special and don't appreciate it, then how can we find our purpose? No one will recognize you," passion filled the aliens' tone, "for your true potential. We all have goals, but if we shrink away in hiding or think that we're not important, then aren't we giving up? Sure, we serve others, but we're not puppets bound to strings. We can express ourselves for who we are freely."

Marah offered, "Well when you put it like that, in a way, yes. Though, it depends. Not everyone dreams of ambition. Some are more down to Earth." *Literally.* She resisted a snort, "It's a phrase."

She looked around the room, realizing that she was trapped with Beth. *What do I do now?*

Beth pushed herself off the bed while shrugging off her blazer, "So what else?" She turned to face Marah, "Not that I don't enjoy talking to you, I do." She peered closely at the spy who held her breath, waiting for Beth to recognize who she really was.

"What mascara are you using? Your eyelashes look flawless."

Her shoulders slumped, relieved. "Oh, um, I'm not wearing any?"

If Beth found it strange how the reply was a question, she didn't show it. If anything, she found herself stumbling to reply. The light pale skin that made up her cheeks tinted rosy, "Oh, sorry. Not that I'm disappointed," she corrected, "cause makeup doesn't define your

beauty, but you can obviously choose to wear what makes you happy —
"

Marah nodded slowly.

Beth paused to fix her wording. "What I'm trying to say is," she threw a hand out, "you look nice." She added lamely, "I'm sorry, I get anxious around people sometimes and I start rambling."

Marah blushed awkwardly, a creeping blush darkening at the sound of Natira's snickering, "Oh, no worries. Thanks, though."

"So, roomie," lamented Beth, forgetting the awkwardness that had lingered in the first place, "we ought to get to know each other. I'll go first. My favorite colors are pink and blue and I'm really bad at cooking." She chuckled, "I hope you know how to work your way with the outdated TI-90 stoves, because I sure don't."

Marah shook her head as she took off her blazer and shoes so she could sit comfortably on the bed, "I like to say yes, though others would disagree. And my favorite color is yellow."

The pretending of favorite foods, movie types, and personalities began to overwhelm Marah, so she said something about being right back and walked to the bathroom, gently closing the door shut. She exhaled slowly as she pressed her back against the wooden door and set her glasses on the sink countertop adjacent to her.

She brought her hands to her temples and rubbed, feeling exhausted, a feeling that increased tenfold as she rubbed her eyes, reflecting on everything that had happened so far. The day was long no doubt, but the nights had a tendency to last longer.

And then there's Beth.

Marah frowned into the mirror as she couldn't quite see herself. While seeing herself in this uniform would take some time to get used to, she realized that the Kosmirian had put her in yet another predicament. It was already a challenge that she had to be undercover and find the Poten, but her ruse was about to become a whole lot more complicated if Beth planned on being glued to Marah the whole time.

And if Natira's right about Beth and I becoming best friends?

Though the idea of it seemed unfathomable to her, crazier things have happened. "You can't be too friendly," muttered Marah softly, uncertain of how thin the walls were, "she's bad." She groaned, changing into the pajamas that came in Elena's package, "When I totally didn't sign up to meet aliens, I didn't think that one of them would want to be my best friend, or like me or whatever. Then again, Natira plays matchmaker as much as she trains. I mean, how can Beth justify murder? It's murder!"

But, just in case, interact with her as little as possible. Let's not make things even more complicated. I don't want to break anyone's heart.

"Not that I even know how to."

She stifled a yawn, eyelids nearly drooping as she splashed some water on her face before drying it with a towel that hung from a clear magnetic tile. *Just thinking about Beth is tiring enough.* She decided to check in with the rebels before calling it a night.

She pressed a finger to her comm, "Anyone on?"

"How are things going?"

Marah smiled, registering the voice that replied as her favorite Zonan. "Aside from the fact that I'm living with Beth, not too shabby. I'm going to be working on in-house police reports for rebels and security cameras, so I think I can do something there. The only thing I was able to get from Beth is that she's a hopeless romantic and The Great War. Basically, how The Committee is the Chairwoman's personal murder group. And Beth, bless her soul, loves that." She sighed, shaking her head as she glanced at the two sets of pink and blue slippers that had to belong to Beth. "How's the base?"

"As operational as you left it," answered Kiera with a slight chuckle. "We're getting it one hundred percent concealed and Natira is looking for someone who can help you use your tasks against The Committee, if it overlaps."

Marah hummed, "That's good." Her spine straightened as she ran a hand through her hair, "Kiera, do the spies have hidden exits in the Committee?"

"Not that I know of, why?"

Marah explained as she loosened her hair, "The Committee just declared war on the rebels. They're gearing up troops and officers. Beth said that we might be interrogating suspects and more likely than not, they'll find rebels. There has to be something I can do without compromising myself."

"Yeah, that could be something," theorized Kiera. Marah heard the sound of a pen clicking. "I'll run that with the others. Anything else?"

Marah glanced downward at her feet as another question grew in her heart. She longed to ask it but feared the answer that she'd get. She rested her head against the door and toward the side, looking at herself in the mirror.

She slackened, lowering her shoulders for the first time that day. Her malachite-spotted eyes had seen many things, but fear was not one to usually be speckled in the human's eyes. *Is this fear for myself or fear for the future?*

She hesitated before letting the words roll off her tongue and heart, "Do you think I'm going to make things better?"

Kiera spoke candidly, "Of course. It's only your first day there, but you've done a lot. You fought on Artemis, learned to fight physically and with weapons, and most importantly, you're doing your best. You are making a difference, and it's going to save us.'"

"Even though I don't have powers?"

"Marah," said Kiera softly, "having powers doesn't make you great. It's what one chooses to do with them that makes the difference. You were chosen out of every single being in this universe, the Poten has its name for a reason."

"Doesn't mean that it can't make a mistake," replied Marah loosely. She ran water down her face, using the gesture as an attempt toward cleaning the mess in her mind out of her.

"I've seen you. We all have. Both the rebels and the Chairwoman. There's always going to be people who won't believe in us, but for every one of those people, there are ten of those who do. Like us."

I hope you're right because I'm having a hard time believing that.

Instead, she half-smiled. "Thank you."

Kiera didn't get the chance to respond as the concerned voice of Beth called out, "Nima, are you okay in there?"

Marah rolled her eyes as she half-yelled, "Yeah. I'm fine."

"Beth again," sighed Marah at the other end of the comm. "By the way, whose idea was it to put me and her together?"

"Natira's actually."

"Of course, it was."

Chapter 19

Location: Where the supreme reign

The next morning, Marah woke up to a voice that was way too chipper for the early hours of waking up. She grumbled as she pulled the covers further over messy hair, "Ugh, too early. Gimme five more minutes."

Beth's voice was as cheery as ever, much to Marah's displeasure, as she persisted, "Nima, it really is time to get ready for work." She pulled the covers off Marah, urging, "C'mon, up, up, up!"

Marah bit her tongue as she reluctantly got out of bed. She headed to the bathroom before the alien could toss a nickname at her. Not that she minded the friendship she was building with Beth, but there was an irking to the fact that Beth was the enemy.

Locked in the privacy of the bathroom, Marah slipped on her glasses after fluffing her hair up by her shoulders.

When she exited the bathroom to grab her ID and backpack—filled with her new phone, wallet, and things that were inside that she didn't feel should be laying around—she was immediately greeted with scented spritzes of far too strong perfume that smelled like milkshakes and candy. She wrinkled her nose, the scent too sweet for her liking.

Like Beth.

"You like it?" asked Beth, placing the bottle back on her vanity, "It's cotton candy. I can order one for you, if you'd like?"

Marah politely declined the offer as she readied her bag with what she deemed necessary, unknowingly wearing a pout as she found out that there was still an hour until their shift started.

"Oh stop," chuckled Beth. "After all, the early bird gets the worm." She even had the audacity to wink as she joked, "As inferior as Earth is, I am quite fond of that particular saying."

Don't you dare use my own culture against me, Marah thought bitterly. *Do aliens even know Earth phrases? I swear, full respect to every spy in existence because this is so hard.*

She sauntered out of the room she shared and headed down the elevator to "work," hoping Kiera had any answers for her.

She had to remind herself to relax her face as the pair stepped into the elevator. She couldn't quite match the faces of the others and Beth, who was ever the radiant ball of energy for something that involved murder for hundreds, if not thousands of people, and spoke with so much excitement, "We'll be starting at our workstations for a quick debrief then we'll be working on updating the surveillance systems inside the Citadel. Did you hear the rumor?"

Brows raised; Marah was definitely paying attention now.

Beth whispered, "There are rebel spies here! In the Citadel! Can you believe it? I don't think it's true, but if it is…"

Marah merely shrugged, thinking of all the things that would happen to her if she was caught…the former noirette shuddered at the thought of that.

Before she knew it, they had arrived at their workstation. This time, the area was bustling with people starting their work even though their shifts started later. It confused Marah, but she assumed that it didn't have to do with wages, but dedication to stopping her and the cause she was now a part of.

As much as she didn't want to, she plopped into her seat and got to work, thankful for the dividers between her and her neighbor. She couldn't help but notice that she was surrounded by a few dozen individuals with all sorts of characteristics that ranged from wings attached to backs to eyes that changed color. More interestingly, each person had an ID with a higher level than her, leaving the human to wonder what they thought of her. She turned, expecting someone to lead the process of what was to be done, but to her surprise, found no one.

Instead, a set of interactive instructions on her computer screen listed what she was supposed to do, making her job much easier than she had anticipated since she didn't have to worry about someone looking over her shoulder at any given moment.

She moved forward in her chair and reviewed the pages outlining the sectors she was assigned to look at. She scrolled past her duties to collect the old chips and replace them with new ones, searching for the Poten but found nothing. She didn't get much time to think about where the Poten could be on the five-page map of the Citadel as Beth stood, an indication that Marah was to follow.

"So," Marah started, "how many cameras are we going to be working with today?" "We're going to be covering the entire third floor today. We're going to handle the arsenal and the storage." Beth made a sharp turn down the hallway and just avoided bumping into what Marah assumed to be the alien equivalent of coffee or tea. "Then we'll be sorting the police files later."

Marah decided to just ask instead of beating around the bushes, "What about the Poten? Chairwoman Kate mentioned it before, I'm curious about it. What is it exactly? Are there cameras for it, too?"

By then, they had reached the office and got the chips that they needed to put into the cameras. Beth had stacked up her trays before answering, "Oh, it's this thing that powers everything. The Chairwoman doesn't really talk about it," she said as if it where the most casual thing Marah could ever ask, "only the Head Officers can change the cameras there."

"Oh." Marah held herself from deflating as they entered an elevator, glass doors phasing out of existence as they stepped in, then phasing back into place once it was filled.

"Third floor!" chimed Beth while Marah held her awe.

They stepped out, Marah more carefully than Beth, and had to walk quickly so as to not lose Beth from all of the hustle and bustle that occupied the third floor. She overheard workers engaging with people from their seats, drawing up specs for weapons, and discussing the best way to catch a rebel.

"The arsenal's right here," said Beth as they entered a room that resembled the interior of a factory more than the most advanced building on the planet. It was nothing in comparison to what Natira showed her. As traditional and factory-like as the room appeared to be, it was modern and futuristic in ways that the human couldn't put a word to.

Members of The Committee were already at work; they took weapons from bins, inspected them, and did what they needed to before sending them off on a conveyor belt to be used. She shuffled quietly behind Beth, taking account of the higher badge numbers and the same expression on very different types of faces.

Beth stood by the door, tapping a polished nail on a small silver diamond-shape that unless Marah looked twice and hard, she would've completely missed. "After seven days the cameras turn silver, so you know which ones need to be changed. To take them off, show your ID in front of it and then it will come off. They go in the same cases. When you want to put a new one on, push it into the slot and then scan your ID again to activate it."

"Sounds easy. I'll start on that side," Marah offered, "and we can meet in the middle."

Marah was surprised that Beth had agreed, and twice as much so as for the first time since Marah had met the girl, Beth was silent as she worked. Which was why she couldn't help but let out a soft sigh of relief as she got to work.

Finally, some peace and quiet.

Starting at the opposite end of Beth, Marah scanned her ID with the camera and the device fell into the palm of her hand. She bent down, putting the silver camera into a slot before opening the first case of new ones. She was hit with a strong metallic scent as she gingerly lifted the first one up and placed it into its slot as Beth had demonstrated. She then put her ID in front of the camera, and it hummed to life once it had registered her.

It amazed her how such little devices were so powerful. It reminded the human of who she was supposed to be. She wondered if the Chairwoman or anyone would speak of her and lead her to some fulfilling answer about her role in all of this.

As if she were performing archery drills, Marah moved in tune to the sounds of beeping and cocking. She only stopped once she had reached the halfway point of her first wall, which had been fifteen cameras of various heights. She decided to pause for a minute to glance around at her co- workers since she had covered more ground than Beth.

Someone was refusing to stop yawning.

Marah held back a laugh at how human these aliens were.

A familiar face from her time with the rebels caught her eye. She watched the undercover rebel avert her eyes, making sure that no one was peeking in her direction through the barriers. She caught Marah's gaze, who quickly looked away and unlocked the next case set of cameras.

The rebel slid her fingers down to the trigger and pressed the button under it. Two batteries slid into the spaces between her fingers and were then placed into a pocket in her purse as the gun was placed on the conveyor belt, on to some unlucky soldier.

Marah repeated the process as it became rhythmic and she didn't realize how many cameras she had swapped when Beth suddenly spoke over her shoulder, "Dang, girl! Tone it down a bit!" She whisper-laughed, "Kidding, kidding." She playfully bumped elbows with Marah, "Told you you'd fit right in."

Marah had just finished with the last of the cameras for the storage, the size of her high school's top floor when Beth exaggerated a yawn. "I don't know how you did all of that so quickly. "You'll have to teach me. Not now, though, it's break time."

Marah wore gratitude like a well-tied mask.

"So, what's our plan for today?"

Beth stood and Marah followed suit, the former spoke as she thumbed words on her phone, "Vade?"

The human had her own phone in her pocket, one of the many things Elena gave her. The cell phone was encrypted so only she could open it with her fingerprint. How that was obtained, the girl had no clue. "Sounds good to me."

"Great," said Beth as she led the way to the exit, rain dripping over them as they stepped outside, "You have your card for the speedbus, right?"

Marah nodded, the speedbus card was among a bunch of other cards, passes, and money that Elena had given her. She had managed to hide the package from Beth in her nightstand until the alien had fallen asleep. Once the rebel spy was sure that Beth was sound asleep, she opened the package to find guides on how to use the contents of the package.

She engaged in light chatter with Beth as they got on the bus, the blonde rambling about a text from her brother and how unfair it was being the middle child and *blah blah blah.*

When the speedbus came to halt, she followed Beth off, quickly walking to avoid getting drenched in the downpour of rain. She clenched her blazer across her chest as Beth shook her mop of hair, "Some weather, huh?" She smirked while looking into Marah's eyes, "One would say it's raining nuts and bolts even."

Are you kidding me? She forced a chuckle, "True." She rolled her eyes when Beth wasn't looking as they got in line.

Beth started as the two walked into Conspersio et Vade, "So, I was thinking that this could be something we do every day, you and me hanging out." She blushed, baby blue eyes meeting darker, hesitant ones, "I really like having company."

The only response Marah could afford to lend was a nod since her ears were filled with the sound of Natira snickering. Though she couldn't fathom what was so funny, she tucked a wisp of dyed red hair behind her ear and grit her teeth while speaking when Beth was called over by someone, "I swear I'll tell you what happens in *Improfi*, Beth loves that show and we get early access content."

She was answered with silence.

She pretended to pay attention to Beth's ramblings once the alien returned, instead choosing to focus on the cafe.

The cafe was no different to what it was yesterday, playing a soft tune that was similar to the one from yesterday and had that delicious aroma that made her want to spend all of her money at once. While the two waited to give their orders, Leia's voice filtered through the comm.

Marah told Beth that she needed to use the bathroom. The human didn't need to ask where it was as she remembered the cafe's layout from yesterday. She made eye contact with no one as she politely excused herself and shut the door behind her.

She pressed her back against the door, trying to figure out what to do with the excess electrical weight. Before she could give the rebels the clear to speak, a familiar gold diamond caught her eye from the mirror's reflection.

"Gross." *How many people have done their business unaware that they were being watched? Which then begs the next question: where else are people being watched? Or listened to?*

Fearful that there was a hidden mic also in the bathroom, Marah pressed her lips together, unsure of what she should do. Saying so would only give herself away. In a situation like this, Marah had no clue on Earth—*full pun intended*—what to do.

Out of habit, Marah folded her arms across her chest, fingerprints trailing over litters of bruises from the rebels' headquarters. Marah found herself considering that for the first time the bruises weren't from home.

Home. A place that didn't always feel like home.

"This is not the time to think about the past," said Marah lowly, "we need to figure out what we're going to do. Think! What would the…" she refrained from using the word rebel, should the camera pick up on that, "what would they do?"

No darn clue.

Spies don't want to be seen, so I need to get rid of that camera by turning it off…somehow.

She frowned, moving her hands off of her arms and to her hips to where her ID was clipped, and then realized the obvious solution. *This is one camera feed sent to The Committee. One camera wouldn't make a difference to some creepy Committee workers.*

She stood under the camera, trying to reach for it. Her frown deepened as she was unable to reach the camera with just her height.

"So that leaves only one option then," concluded the rebel spy distastefully as she eyed the toilet. She unraveled a sliver of toilet paper and lowered the seat. She immediately threw the toilet paper in the trash can and washed her hands before returning to the seat. She sighed with a cringe; *never did I think that I'd be in a situation like this.*

She grimaced as she stood atop the toilet seat, the camera now within the grasp of her fingers.

It would be so awkward if someone walked in right now.

Marah shook her head, quietly scanning her ID in front of the camera and a hologram of options was projected in front of her. She tapped on the temporary pause all recording and then jumped down.

"Hey."

"Kiera told me about your question," started Leia, "and the answer is yes. You mentioned that later you'll be sorting the police reports, so as long as you reject anything that relates to the rebellion, that'll keep us in safer waters for more time."

Marah followed up, "But, won't it be suspicious? Like what if it's about the leaders or anyone that I actually know."

"You're the first one to see those cases. You'll also be the last. Remember your number one focus though, finding the Poten."

"About that," said Marah, "I tried to see if I could do my cameras post there, but I don't have the clearance for it. Not even Beth has it. No one really talks about it."

There was a knock on the bathroom door. "We'll have to talk about this later."

She quickly washed her hands and found Beth by a booth.

She spoke as she slid in, "Sorry about that, long line."

Beth waved the apology off, "No biggie. I wasn't sure what you wanted so I ordered the same thing as yesterday."

"Thanks." Marah's cheeks tinted pink as she realized, "Now that's two days I have to pay you back for."

Beth giggled as she took a sip of coffee, "Nima, c'mon, we're friends. You don't have to pay me back for being a nice person. So," she added as she dug into her pastry, "how did you enjoy your first day on the job?"

Marah replied with false cheeriness as she brought a plastic fork to her mouth, "It was normal, I guess."

Beth grinned as she slurped from her cup, "How did you get through all of those cameras so quickly? Only someone who's really experienced can do that so fast. Was this your first time working with our tech?"

Leia hissed in Marah's ear, "Say yes. Otherwise, she'll probably ask where and when and then things will get complicated."

Marah brushed a strand of hair over her ear, conscious of the comm, "Actually, this was my first time. I guess, I just get into things pretty fast."

Someone exhaled on the comms, but Marah couldn't tell who.

Beth hummed, "Still, you're pretty fast compared to someone who has literal super speed. So," she asked, fiddling with a fork, "do you miss your home?"

The voices from her comm went silent.

Nice one guys.

Marah sighed, allowing herself to tell the truth to Beth for the first time, "I do. I mean, growing up where I did and here, it's practically two different worlds," she confessed, "I can't bring myself to move on and believe that I'm really here. But, at the same time, I can't keep looking back if I want to move forward and accomplish great things. I suppose this is my normal now, but I can't help but miss what used to be my normal." She didn't know why water suddenly began to prick the back of her eyes but rubbed her eyes anyway. "You?"

Beth pondered the matter as she downed another forkful of chocolate. She shrugged, cutting a piece of chocolate, "I don't know. I don't really miss my adoptive parents. They never really supported me or my decisions."

"How so?" *Who knows, maybe I can appeal to Beth's heart and make her realize how bad The Committee is.*

The thought was random, it would have taken Marah by surprise were it not for Beth sitting in front of her. She couldn't help but hear the voice of her mother echo: *"Stop trying to play a hero, you're not!"*

"Well, my mother doesn't support me being at The Committee." The Kosmirian paused to swallow, "She grew up on Romana, so for her, she only sees the supposed harm The Committee has done. She doesn't understand that sometimes sacrifices have to be made for the greater good."

There goes appealing to her heart.

"And your father?"

"Kosmirian. That and he doesn't support my pursuits in love. He's never liked the people I've brought home." She chuckled wanly, "The first time I brought a boy home, he kicked him out because he thought that I wasn't ready for a relationship."

Marah frowned. "That's awful. I would say that I'm sorry but that's not something that I can apologize for."

Beth smiled appreciatively, "Thank you. Sometimes saying sorry isn't the best thing that you can do."

"Yeah," echoed Marah, empathy reflecting across ocean irises, "sometimes it isn't."

Beth sighed, setting her fork down, "That's the story of my life pretty much. Didn't get so lucky in the parent department, you?"

We're not so different after all.

Marah shook her head.

Beth sighed, "My older brother is the golden child. And my younger is tolerable at best. Siblings, y'know?"

The human nodded sympathetically, something that she could personally relate to, "Yeah, siblings." She shuddered, "They're the worst. But they have their moments when they're not bothering you."

"Right?" laughed Beth. "We could have a dozen charges at home and my brothers would still take mine."

Marah gave herself time to laugh before diverting the topic, "What time do we have to get back to HQ?"

So, I can look for what makes The Committee so strong.

Beth casually glanced at her watch, "Around one, but we have time." She suddenly stiffened as her gaze lifted past Marah.

Marah noticed the shift of the blonde's attention and turned to find a woman and a man walking hand in hand. She remembered seeing the pink-haired woman from yesterday. Today, her hair looked more like cotton candy with streaks of white instead of bold fuchsia. Her partner also wore The Committee uniform with loose unruly hair and stacks of gold rings on all of his tattooed fingers. He sneaked a kiss onto his girlfriend's neck and Marah swiveled back to face a rather pissed Beth.

Before Marah could ask Beth what had made her upset, the blonde huffed with a disparaging smirk, "It appears that my ex has even worse taste than I thought." She shifted her position, leaning back in the booth and folding her arms across her chest, happy mood snuffed out like a spark.

Marah inquired, "Who?"

Beth gestured, "Him."

She took another glance at the dark-haired, tattooed man who had his cotton-candy-haired girlfriend leaning on his shoulder, the two exchanging silent whispers and loudly kissing. She wrinkled her nose, finding it hard to believe that the two had dated since they were so different. *Then again, it's not like you know them well enough.*

Abruptly, the Kosmirian asked, "What is she saying?" Marah tilted her head, "Hmm?"

Beth's irises flickered at her ex, "What is she saying? With your abilities, you can hear what she's saying, right?"

Dammit.

Marah slowly nodded. "Totally. Yep."

"Well," said Beth as she leaned forward toward Marah, mischief written all over her cream-colored face, "what is she saying?"

She looked back at Beth's ex as she bit her lip and fumbled with her hands, two signs of anxious ticks. She exhaled loosely, pretending that everything was fine and that she was listening in as she replied, "She's um, talking about going out for dinner." She adjusted her frames nervously, "That's what she said."

No sooner had Marah uttered the last syllable, than her front teeth found their way to the flesh of her lower lip. She anticipated Beth to disprove her, only for the blonde to lean back, a glower seeping through sea-hued irises that were coated with unwelcome sentimentality. "Funny. She said the same to me and then never showed up."

Beth shook her head, changing the topic, "So, is there anything I can do to help you feel more at home? Just because I don't miss my home doesn't mean that I'm going to let my bestie feel sad at the best place that she could possibly be working. If you ever need anything I'm always free."

Marah paused to think about how she should answer. She settled on saying, "I really appreciate that. If there is, I'll be sure to let you know."

Rule number one of being a spy: never consort with the enemy unless absolutely necessary.

Beth beamed.

Natira's voice filled Marah's eardrums, "You should ask if she knows anything about the Poten or knows someone who can direct you to it. It'd make everyone's' lives easier."

That's not a bad idea.

"Actually, there is one thing I've been wondering."

Of course, Beth was too busy glaring daggers at her ex.

Marah took the initiative to head back to their home— definitely, away from home. She started to stand up, "Why don't we go back," she offered, "and leave your—" Marah paused, struggling to find an appropriate word, and then gave up, "and head back so we can get started on defeating rebel scum?" The forced enthusiasm felt wrong in her mouth, but the human steeled her composure.

Beth instantly smiled as she followed Marah out the door into the rain, "Yeah, let's go. Whatever did I do to deserve a friend like you, Nima?"

Here she goes again. Before she could reply, the speedbus appeared in front of them. The two rushed on board to avoid getting drenched, but still were soaked despite only moments of exposure.

The ride back was quieter than the trip there. While Beth oversaw the notifications on her phone, Marah wrung water from her hair.

Seeing no harm in trying again, she spoke, "What do you know about the Poten?" She groaned mentally, *that sounded too random.* She blurted, "It's really fascinating that it could decode Marah Morana, which speaking of, is incredible."

Beth lowered the device from her face. "The Poten is the power source of the Citadel. It stores all the energy and power to run the place, support the weapons and troops, and it figured out Marah as you said. Without it, we are as weak as the rebels."

Marah nodded; interest captured, but held her tongue so as to not draw suspicion from poking Beth.

"It was my research entry project. I was going to go to the Archives, but Chairwoman Kate protects it so well that no one really knows where it is or how to get there. Pretty disappointing, huh? I can use my clearance to try and help you out, just between the two of us."

"That would be great," she smiled. "There is actually another thing you could help me out with. Is there anything on Marah Morana that isn't classified?"

It was Beth's turn to wince, "I highly doubt it."

Back at her station, Marah sighed softly as she adjusted her fake glasses. Putting up with Beth was beginning to exhaust her, and yet, a part of her felt sympathetic to the woman underneath the cheery exterior. Something that was pissing off the human herself. "To hell with The Committee," she muttered under her breath, hating that here she had to deal with Beth and things that prevented her from doing what she needed to do—find the Poten and then get out of there.

She didn't plan on sticking around much longer. She supposed the rebels wouldn't need her after that, in truth, she had no idea why she was the one being needed. There wasn't anything remarkable about her. The only reason she had was what Leia had told her days ago that her choosing to stay was merely enough. It didn't feel that way, though. It also didn't help that The Committee kept anything about her hidden, she wanted to know what this powerful organization had to fear, but it seemed that there were no answers to give.

The worker next to her twitched their lip and she instantly realized her mistake. She mimicked an eye roll and gestured to her comm as she spoke, "That's what she said? She's always complaining about them. Yeah, I know, can I call you back?"

That was close, she thought as her co-worker shared a knowing look. "My grandma's the same way."

Marah wore a loose smile, "What can you do?"

Once the worker resumed his work, she followed. For the second half of her day, she was to examine reports to see if they needed to be investigated by officers or not. It was an easy assignment, after reviewing the case she was to press red to send it to the officers for further inspection, or green and it would be deleted permanently.

Her first ten cases were based on little to no concrete evidence, even in her amateur opinion, so she pressed the green button for those. The next case she recognized all too well.

It was the Stellan she had saved yesterday. The filer claimed that she was a thief and badmouthed The Committee, therefore she had to be a rebel. The report also stated that she was found in a public area where previously identified rebels had a tendency to lurk. She opened the mini browser that portaled her to the rebels and let them know. She pressed green. She was then asked for her password and typed the code in.

The next case almost startled her. The filer claimed to have seen Marah Morana walking in broad daylight. *Because that's the best thing to do when you're in an alien world and wanted by an evil government.* The only comfort Marah had was that the woman in the photo was not actually her—with icy blue eyes and half her black hair streaked a burgundy red.

She pressed green, not bothering to read any of the written comments.

I just committed another alien crime. Oh, if Natira was here, all the superhero puns I could make. Not superheroes, she said!

She proceeded to her next case, the first one that she knew to be actually true. The report consisted of the finest quality photo Marah had ever seen of Kiera Dapolk, her favorite Zonan who also happened to be, according to the report, "one of the rebellious trinity." The photo was dated as her last day on Earth with her hood just off her head to confirm who exactly she was as she held a wanted poster with her face on it in disdain. There were no comments on the file, so Marah glanced at the mouse where blemished nails were curled over and clicked to delete.

An abrupt shout startled the human

"Just what do you think you're doing?"

Marah jolted, nearly choking on her spit. She lifted her gaze to see the aggressive officer from yesterday. She blinked, confused as blush crept up her cheeks.

Everyone's looking at me, shoot, shoot, shoot. "I'm sorry?"

She recognized the officer to be the short, stout, and loud one that had slashed Elena's lips. He was even more menacing up close with bruised fingers on wide hips and piercing eyes that stared her up and down. "Don't play stupid with me." His words were defiant, sharp, and loud, making Marah shrink back in her seat. Within a mere moment, her heart's beat thumped loudly, reminding her of how tight her throat had become all of a sudden. She blinked, trying to instill the memories of a place on Earth that wasn't associated with kindness.

He jabbed a finger in her face and Marah's hand twitched. "Don't ya know how to do your job? Or are you trying to mess this entire operation up?"

"I don't understand," she spoke quickly.

"Don't you know who Kiera Dapolk is?"

Marah shook her head quickly, eyes darting around so fast she wasn't sure what was making her feel dizzy.

"She's one of the leaders of the damn rebellion." He pulled the cigar from his mouth, scratching a prickly beard that matched his authoritative tone, "You are supposed to press red, not green! Are you trying to let the rebels win?" He huffed as he stared directly into Marah's eyes, "Don't make that mistake again," he retorted, "if that even *was* a mistake. I don't care who you are, but if you are trying to sabotage us," he held up a meaty fist, "I will gladly take care of you. Just like that other girl."

With that, he walked away.

Marah's expression of confusion lingered as the officer walked away. *How had I missed him?* She blinked, her processing abilities running slower than usual.

What is wrong with you? Don't you care about this? This right here determines the rest of your life! And of course, you manage to mess up here, because what else would you do? Do you even care?

Marah's mouth ran dry as her mother's words echoed in the back of her head.

You're lucky your father doesn't give a shit about either of us, otherwise, imagine the things he'd do to you. Can't you be like me? How will you carry a great legacy when you can't even be great now?

Beth had noticed Marah's blank expression and moved toward the spy. Waving a hand in front of the spy's face she asked, "Nima, are you alright?"

Her mom's voice continued to drone on in her head: *Everyone's watching you now! This is your junior year! This is the time when everything counts!*

"Nima?"

Everyone's watching me. I messed up.

Marah inhaled sharply as her fingers curled over the edges of her seat. *This is not the time to freak out, now with everyone watching.* The human nodded, answering Beth's question while thinking about how this could've gotten a thousand times worse. *Such as getting caught and dooming the entire mission as well as the rebels' last chance to end the tyranny rooted here. You could've gotten captured and probably killed because you weren't careful!*

I need to be more careful. Take more precautions. Not panic, something that Marah was close to doing, the human could practically feel it.

"What happened?" One of her friends was speaking through the comm and were it not for the slight swaying of Beth in front of her, the rebel would have recognized who was speaking.

Marah spoke slowly to relieve all the attention of her, "I'm fine." Her eyes fluttered shut for a couple of moments, striving to drown the panic inside of her. Her words were still slow and spacey as she continued, "I'm fine, really. That startled me, that's all."

Beth's voice was laced with concern as she spoke, "You sure? That guy's a pain to everyone."

Marah shook her head as she steeled her composure. "I'm good," she forced a smile, "I swear. As I said, he just startled me." She turned back to the screen in front of her, voice wobbly as she continued, "Let's get back to work."

Leia spoke as Beth returned to her seat and Marah detected a smidge of concern—something that she couldn't help but appreciate; Leia cared about her, "Mar?"

Marah didn't trust herself to speak. Instead, she opened the browser: I'll be fine. That just brought me back to some stuff from before. I'm good, just a little shaken up. Sorry about that, I'll do better. I promise.

Leia's voice thickened with concern and slight confusion, "There's no need to apologize, it's okay." The Novan sensed something was wrong with her friend so she offered, "Would you like to talk about it later?"

"**Sure**," typed Marah to not make Leia worry more. *That was too close*, she thought warily.

Chapter 20

Location: Home not sweet home

Marah was asleep, or at least she was supposed to be given the hour of night. Instead, the spy tossed and turned in her bed while loose strings of incoherent phrases spilled from her lips.

Despite closed eyes, Marah's vision was blurry and began to spin as unwelcome voices she hadn't heard in years other than her nightmares demanded to be heard.

Her mother's annoyed voice had the same degree of coldness and was exactly how she last remembered it. The human shook her head as she rolled on the bed, mumbling words over her tongue. Despite being asleep, she flinched, jerking her face the other way. A single tear rolled down the length of her face.

A voice called out to her, "Nima?"

Marah's groggy yet slurred voice made a hum-like sound in reply.

257

"Wake up," were some of the words that she was able to register from the person who was talking to her. Then it hit Marah: the only person that could be talking to her right now was Beth.

Her eyes shot open and she bolted upright to find Beth standing next to her, concern evident in the furrow of her blonde brows. She tore her gaze from the Kosmirian's eyes to the glass of glowing neon liquid in one of her hands.

Beth offered the beverage, "Here, this should help you feel a little better."

Marah accepted the glass and let the cold liquid fizz down her throat. As much as the rebel didn't want to admit it, Beth's offering did make her feel a little better. And the fact that it was Beth standing here looking at her with genuine care about her wellbeing, despite the obsessive part, made it all a thousand times worse.

Curse her never-ending kindness, she thought bitterly

Beth leaned closer to Marah, who in turn couldn't help but lean a little back as the former asked, "You okay?"

Marah nodded slowly as she took another sip of water, "Yeah, I'm fine. Thanks." The noirette sighed slowly, using the cold water running inside of her to calm her nerves. *Just a day or two to shake this off.* She strained to sound as okay as possible, not wanting to invite Beth closer and potentially complicate her life even more. *Because life is already complicated enough.*

Beth frowned, not buying Marah's words, "C'mon. We're friends, remember? We tell each other when something is bothering us." Her lips curled upward as she moved closer.

Marah made a face, resting her head on the smooth headboard, "I'm fine. I swear."

The Kosmirian moved closer to Marah, taking her hands in her own. Beth's warm touch dulled the cold tingle inside the human's hands as she persisted sincerely, "You don't have to beat yourself up about feeling like this or pretend that you're fine when you're not. You did the same earlier with that officer."

Marah cast her gaze away from Beth's flickering eyes as she opened her mouth to protest, but Beth raised her chin and she fell silent.

"And your eyes have this spacey look. That's how I know that despite how calm you sound, I don't think you really are."

Marah bit her lip. She didn't want to indulge in Beth, but with those damn baby blues that practically held her hostage, the rebel didn't have the will to tell Beth to leave her alone and call it a night. *Or morning.*

There it was again—friendship. Marah wished she could turn off the ability with Beth, who persisted against her insistence that she was fine three times. As much as she didn't want to admit it, it was clear that Beth, who she had only known for a day, cared about her the same way the rebels did. And a selfish part in her heart was somewhat relieved.

Dammit, fumed Marah, *I have one nightmare and my entire mood is ruined. Ugh, I need to focus on finding the Poten and defeating The Committee and none of this is helping.*

Marah sucked in a sharp breath before finding herself admitting, "My parents weren't the best. My mother had such high expectations of me, and I didn't meet those. I wasn't able to, nor did I want to. So, I would get yelled at all the time. There were times where she would, um..." Marah's voice trailed away as she blinked, seeing her mother instead of Beth in front of her. "Actually, never mind."

You'll never be something great unless you change!

But I don't want to!

Too bad!

Beth softened, squeezing Marah's hands, "If something's bothering you, you shouldn't keep it in. I'm here and I'm listening. If it was something to never mind, then it wouldn't be bothering you right now."

The human wanted to say no. She wanted to tell Beth that she was fine and go back to sleep. But she wasn't. She remembered all the times her lip quivered after her cheeks burnt furiously. She remembered wishing to be saved—the very reason she loved heroes so much. They were the beacon of hope that she yearned to have. Someone who could leave the demons of the past where they belonged.

But when did life ever go Marah's way?

She wanted to run away from Beth and from the reminders of the life she had left behind and back to the life she had just before Kosmir, rebels, and The Committee.

And yet, Marah found herself opening up to Beth. "Hit me. So, getting yelled at like that back there brought all of that back." She exhaled softly, moving her hands from Beth's hold slowly to rub her eyes, Beth's warm touch still lingering on the rebel's hands.

Beth hummed as she offered a smile, "Tragic backstories, huh? I understand," her gaze fell to Marah's hands that were slack by her sides atop the smoothened covers, "that's awful. But just because someone's telling you forcefully that you're not good enough, doesn't mean that you aren't."

Then why would they be saying it?

"I mean it," said Beth. "We all have a story. Don't let someone else dictate yours. Also, who is anyone to tell you who you are?"

Who is she to tell me that I'll never do anything great in my life unless it's her way? Who is my father to make me feel at fault for the late-night fights because it was only him, my mother, and I? Who's The Committee, the rebels, and the Poten to claim that I, Marah Morana, am the key to ending an interplanetary regime?

Marah obviously couldn't vocalize these points to Beth, nor did she want to get any more comfortable with the girl, her roommate—someone who, despite her best efforts, was dangerously close to becoming her friend. She quickly pulled herself together after a minute more of pondering all the ways she disagreed with Beth before saying, "You're right, thank you. Not just for your words. Although, we should go back to sleep so we're not zombies during work." She knew aliens had some version of zombies in *Improfi*, though their version was far more terrifying.

Beth chuckled, tapping Marah's hand once more before returning to her own bed. "Goodnight then, or good morning, if you want to look at it like that."

Marah smiled as she moved her head back to her pillow, "Mornin'."

Beth added with hints of hesitation thick in her tone, "Nima?"

"Hmm?"

"I know we just met, so I hope I didn't make you uncomfortable or anything. I just really like caring about the people around me. If there's anything, anything at all that you need, don't hesitate to ask. Alright?"

Then came the embarrassment of confiding in Beth. "Thank you, I really appreciate that."

Beth grinned, eyes twinkling, "Anytime." She smiled softly. "Like I said, it's okay to not always be okay. I don't know your past, but I see the you that you are now." Her cheeks became a rosy red before admitting, "We all have our demons. We all feel bad about ourselves and think that we're not worth what we have."

She inhaled sharply, and Marah swore she saw water gather in Beth's eyes. "That's why we have friends who will always be there to pick you up," vouched Beth. "No one deserves to feel like this, and neither did you deserve what that officer said."

She blinked. She wasn't upset about what was said, rather because it happened. The ambience of the room has shifted, and though Marah appreciated how much Beth cared for her wellbeing, she was more grateful that her comm was secured safely in her bag.

She only wished that Beth would just go to sleep. The quicker she could sleep the quicker she could forget about all of this.

However, the Kosmirian wasn't finished.

"It's no fun being lonely," confessed Beth with such emotion that Marah couldn't help but soften for the Kosmirian. "It's really not," she sighed, "I grew up without any lasting friendships. The only type of relationships I have had are romantic flings. They only wanted the cheap thrills of love, but I wanted the thrill of friendship." She remarked, explaining, "I'm tired of romance, but what's life worth living lonely?"

"Yeah," said Marah for the sake of saying something.

"Making authentic friends is hard. But, once I met you," Beth said benevolently "something in my heart changed, in a good way of course." Her gaze dropped to her hands as she elaborated, "I get anxious a lot, especially when I'm alone, but now, I feel like I can finally have a friend. Maybe it was destiny, or just a coincidence, but I'm glad that we're roomies." She sighed. "I just want you to be comfortable too."

Beth suddenly shut down, perhaps realizing that she said probably too much all at once, "I wish I could fully explain what I mean. I just," she sighed, "I don't know."

"I understand," buzzed Marah, interrupting Beth.

Marah understood Beth's words in a way that resonated deep within her heart. Beth's pouring of words was definitely sincere. Laced beneath the cards of confusion, Marah realized, was raw, earnest emotion.

Dubious of how to possibly respond, Marah blinked. Beth had confessed her own demons; an earnest desire for true friendship, and the human didn't have the faintest clue how to react. She didn't want to crush Beth's heart with even the least brutal version of the truth.

At least not yet.

So, instead of sliding another lie through her teeth, the noirette settled on the truth as she rolled her head to face Beth, "That really means a lot to me. Thank you so much." It was true, Beth's words made Marah's heart swell, making it hard to maintain the casualness that her tone was laced with. Because, before Kosmir and the rebels, that was exactly what Marah had wanted.

Marah continued after swallowing thickly, trying to find the best wording to let Beth down gently without making it sound like she was trying to, "You're right. That's what friends do for each other." Then came the acquitted lie, "The same goes for you. I'm here for you if you need me." *Please leave me alone, I need to focus on saving the universe before Chairwoman Kate burns it all.*

She waited with a smile as Beth beamed once more before letting her eyes fall shut. Marah quietly faced away from the alien, unable to not feel a little bit bad that she was crushing Beth's feelings.

Maybe Beth isn't all that bad, Marah thought while pulling the covers toward her, *I mean, she did stick up for you. She didn't have to do that. She doesn't have to be so nice, hell, why is she so nice? I can't help but see her as a friend when she's the enemy!*

Her thoughts continued to unravel, *maybe all of this isn't worth it. I mean look at Beth for instance, she's sweet and nice, maybe there are more like her, gullible and if they just saw the truth they would choose against The Committee. Only the Chairwoman would have to die.*

Maybe there's some good in them too, and some in Beth?

Marah shook her head, sending locks of hair flying across a pillow. She hissed to herself, "Snap out of it!" *Remember when we walked here, those kids and parents who looked at you with such terror? That's why you're here. To help them and prevent more people from suffering what they've endured. What about Artemis? Beth was proud of that, can there be redemption for that? You cannot and will not just abandon all of this. The rebels are counting on you! How many more orphans must there be? How many more people will have to suffer?*

Marah exhaled softly, ignoring Beth's snores. She suddenly felt extremely uncomfortable and too close to Beth. She contemplated getting up but decided against it, having nowhere to go where she could punch her feelings out. "She's one of them," she muttered, "the enemy. Thank God the comms are off, otherwise whoever's on would probably think that I'm losing my mind. You can't trust her," she continued, "you just can't. We need to take them down as quickly as possible."

She mused dryly, "Sometimes you have to break someone's heart and not one of their bones. No matter how many they have."

Chapter 21

Location: The force of the flame

Marah knew this was a dream.

Which was odd because most of her dreams were about the memories behind colored bruises, and brought tears. She found herself standing in pitch-black darkness, and her first thoughts recalled her time at the rebels' guild.

During her beginning days there, she had met a Litnickian rebel that many would go to when they had questions about their dreams. He had the ability to not only channel and weaponize dream energy but was able to interpret deeper meanings of dreams than one would usually care for. According to Litnickian mythology, often, dreams would resonate deep within one's soul as a means to communicate, which they perceived as their God relaying dreams as the answers to their cries.

"They could be foreshadowing a fight to come," he had said, "or they could be the answers to the questions that keep you up at night.

Dreams are powerful things, a sense of poison to some, while to others, a sip of wine."

At first, she thought that was baloney. Sure, dreams could do stuff like that, but what was the probability that one night you dream of yourself getting beat up and then the next morning it happens?

Turns out, the probability was far higher than Marah had originally anticipated.

Though Marah didn't know what to expect from this dream, she couldn't swallow away the feeling that this dream wasn't just an ordinary tale pulled out of her head.

Dream-Marah looked down at herself amongst the darkness. She was dressed in her suit, a welcome relief compared to the loathed, itchy Committee uniform. She frowned as she looked around her empty surroundings, wondering aloud, "Where am I?"

Instantly, she found herself standing on sandstone. A candle stood in front of her, and she picked it up, loose grains of red slipping through her fingers as she did so. The glittering bank of vermillion red appeared to stretch on for an infinity, reminding Marah of Artemis.

Marah looked around the planet that no longer existed in the real world, finding all evidence of life was gone. No buildings, no trees, no people, nothing. The vacancy compelled the human to wonder if she was the only living thing on the planet.

The dream felt like it was trying to reach deep within Marah's soul and delineate something that she needed to know. Something that was related to what she was looking for to tip the odds in the rebels' favor or some other problem she had, Marah would gladly take whatever help she could get.

Unsure of what was happening, the noirette decided to wander the ventures of her dream.

Why Artemis? And...a candle?

She took a step forward on the blood-stained planet, curious to see what would happen next.

A howl pierced the silence, and a strong gust of wind whipped Marah's hair in front of her face. "Marah!"

The voice bellowed her name again, even louder, and she felt the ground that she was standing on tremble and quiver.

Then silence.

Suddenly, a booming voice rattled against her eardrums. "You must find it!"

Startled by the foreign voice, she dropped the candle. The wax sank into the sand, and the candle's flame raced in a straight line that ran north of her.

The flame danced as it reached past Marah's vision, something that the human took as a sign to follow the burning path, wherever it led.

Marah ran alongside the flame. Her boots pressed against loose erosion as her cape fluttered lightly on her back, spurring her on faster. She followed the flame till it curved and surrounded her, trapping her. Marah skidded to halt to avoid being burned by the flames that threatened to engulf her whole.

Just as Marah was about to open her mouth and ask what was going on, the voice thundered once again, "If you want to prevent the doom of other worlds, you must find it!"

She looked around, unsure of who was talking to her. Her fingers curled into fists as she itched to hold something, preferably her bow. Here, she was defenseless to whatever her dream planned for her.

Without knowing who she was talking to, Marah probed, "What do I have to find? I'll find anything, just tell me what to do!" Her reply was earnest and truthful as she couldn't help but replay the horrors of Artemis in her head.

"Who *are* you?"

The foreign voice merely stated, "It doesn't matter who I am. What matters is you, Marah Morana, finding the Archives before it's too late."

"Too late?" solicited Marah. "What do you mean by too late?"

The voice only responded with a roar, "You must find the Archives!"

"Okay," said Marah, raising her hands to ease the voice, "but how do I do that?"

Silence.

"Well?"

Still silence.

Frustrated with the sudden disappearance, she shouted even louder, "How am I supposed to find the Archives? If they're so important, the least you could do is give me a hint! And you never answered the question of who the hell you are! Too late for what?" She implored, desperation thick in her tone, "You can't just disappear after you've said your piece, I have questions!"

The only response Marah received was the flame rising higher and higher, until that became all that Marah could see.

Right after, Marah fell back into the darkness. When she opened her eyes, she found herself back in her bed with Beth inches from her face.

Well, this is awkward.

Beth immediately retracted, flustered, "I've been trying to get you to wake up for ten minutes. We have to get ready for work, remember?"

Marah groaned as she pulled the covers back over her head, "Can't we just not go? Can't we take a day off and do literally anything else?" *That way I can try and find out where the Archives are and never see this awful place again. Whether that meant waiting with the rebels or being able to go home, she was uncertain but that didn't quite matter to her at the moment.*

Beth shook her head, blonde coils of hair bouncing at the gesture. "I know you're still anxious because of the officer, but you've got nothing to worry about. I'm going to be right by your side the whole time. Now c'mon, up and at it."

Who even says "up and at it" anymore? Besides, that's not what I'm worried about. I'm wary of him, not scared. There's a difference.

Marah forced herself to get out of bed, much to her great and infinite pleasure. *Yeah. Right. Here we go again.*

She was going to use the opportunity of privacy in the bathroom, but with Beth keeping her on her toes all morning while chiding herself for tardiness, she never got the chance to.

Marah was irritated as she stepped into an elevator. *Why can't she just leave me alone?*

Unfortunately, that was a mystery to crack another time since Marah needed to focus on the Archives and the Poten.

As she begrudgingly walked with Beth out of the elevator to their workstation, the human couldn't help but feel self-conscious as she arrived at her desk. After yesterday's incident, she felt all eyes were on her. The noirette knew it was unreasonable for her to think that everyone was gossiping about her and the officer, but Marah couldn't help but think otherwise.

Though she tried to display a confident exterior, she couldn't help but shift her gaze amongst her colleagues and every crevice in her clothing, trying to occupy her hands with something. That way, her mind would focus on that instead of the tension that snaked through her lungs, rendering her trapped in paranoia.

You have bigger issues than your insecurities! If the people here find out who you are, they'll arrest you. If you die, that means that everything could fall into the flames of injustice. If you're arrested, that means you failed. If you die solely because you got arrested, that means that you fought for nothing.

Marah fumbled with her ID, convincing herself that she could do this. She promised herself that she'd do everything within her power to avoid getting caught. No matter what consequences would come. *If I have to burn for the process of messy justice, then so be it.* The liberties of justice and freedom always came with a price, and Marah was by no means exempt from that. No one was. After all, there were reasons why fights for justice birthed vengeance, power, glory, and legends. Fights birthed survivors who were willing to pursue any challenge to better the livelihoods of the people around them. To avenge the ones who perished on the journey. They didn't care about their own lives or how much time their fights took until the objective was reached.

And Marah would too. It was a yearning that sparked within her heart after Artemis, a force that would simmer until the flames of freedom were quenched deep within the rebel's heart. How easily The Committee destroyed Artemis terrified the girl, but it also served as motivation to do everything within her human power to end the tyranny that existed before her eyes once and for all.

Beth, who was very much aware that Marah felt self-conscious but not for the right reasons, spoke up in an attempt to make the human feel better, "Remember what we talked about?" She smiled while placing a hand on Marah's arm, "There's nothing to worry about."

You see, I have everything to worry about. That's basically my superpower at this point. And yours is sticking to my side twenty-four seven. Ugh, I know I've only been here for three days, but it feels like it's been forever.

Gratitude sweeping over her features, she struggled to piece together an appropriate reply, "Yeah. I know, thanks."

Today, they were assigned to the arsenal on the fourth floor, because, of course, The Committee had more than one arsenal.

While entering the arsenal with the cameras, Marah planned what she was going to do. She was forced to depart from her thoughts suddenly as Beth bumped her elbow with a grin, "Maybe that rude officer will see how fast you work; that'll put him to shame."

Marah returned the expression while her stomach dropped. As she got to work, she anticipated for someone to remark about how she had sabotaged "their totally amazing cause"—Beth's words—but to the human's surprise, no one seemed remotely interested in her.

Whether that was a good thing or a bad thing, she couldn't help the sigh of relief that slipped through her lips. She shut the first tray of old cameras and opened the next one, flashing her ID to collect the silver camera in hand.

Out of the corner of her eye, Marah glanced around to see if anyone was looking in her direction and found none, to her relief. Though she wasn't doing anything wrong, the idea of being caught had come to the front of her worries.

Like yesterday, Marah's pace was much quicker than Beth's. She worked in silence while the gears in her mind churned, thinking about the dream she had. *What did the voice mean before it's too late?* Marah immediately thought of the rebels. *Maybe The Committee is getting close to finding the rebels' location and if I don't act as quickly as possible, they're all going to die?*

Or, she contemplated, *something bad was coming their way and the only way to prevent that was through the Poten and the Archives?*

One thing was certain: Marah needed to find the Archives and get the Poten.

She had just replaced another camera when someone walked past her. The woman dropped an orange nep beside Marah and as she bent down to retrieve the coin, she whispered, "*Et aeterni.*"

Marah froze, remembering those words from somewhere. She looked at the woman with thick brown hair with pink tips and the darkest brows she had ever seen. The woman, who couldn't have been more than a couple years older than her, winked, slipping Marah a piece of paper before walking away.

And then Marah remembered hearing that phrase once before, the code that Elena whispered to her days ago.

She looked back at the rebel with raised eyebrows, confused as to why the girl had revealed her presence to her.

The girl only looked down at Marah's hand, where the slip of paper was concealed and winked once again.

Marah nodded, understanding the message. She flashed a glance at Beth to ensure that the Kosmirian hadn't watched their exchange before unfolding the slip of paper. The message detailed in cursive: *My name is Clyna. Don't leave the Citadel. We need to talk. We, meaning the base.*

Marah crumpled the slip into a paper ball and slipped it into her pocket. She locked eyes with Clyna and nodded before getting back to work.

While Marah continued to scan and replace cameras, she couldn't help but wonder what Clyna wanted to talk about. Certainly nothing too terrible happened otherwise the rebels would have contacted her through comms otherwise. *Unless the comms aren't working.*

That turned out to not be the case as Marah's thoughts were interrupted by the voice of her favorite Zonan—Kiera. "Whenever you're free from Beth, we need to talk. After you speak to Clyna."

A certain Nantak interrupted: "How's Beth? Last night really gave me the feels." She broke into fits of laughter.

"The comm was still on?" Marah fought embarrassment. She whispered, "You're so creepy, don't you sleep?"

Natira chortled. "And miss out on this?"

"Which is what exactly?"

"An adorable friendship," answered Natira, voice dripping in humor. "Wouldn't you agree, *Nima*?"

Marah teased, "Just say the word, I'd be happy to introduce you to her."

Kiera sounded like she was trying not to laugh as she spoke over Natira's grumbling, "We think we found out something important about the Archives and the Poten. Clyna is going to give you that information. She'll also help get Beth away from you so you can work."

Speaking of—Beth had now come to her side, speaking blithely, "That went by quick! I wish the officer would've come and see how much you've done." She gushed, "There's no way he'd be able to say those things literally ever again. C'mon, let's go."

I'm glad he didn't.

Marah followed Beth out of the arsenal, assuming that Clyna would come and find her to discuss whatever the rebel spy needed to discuss. She headed back to her station and took a seat, while Beth took her seat in front of the human, getting to work on the suspected rebel case files.

Beth's snow-white fingers make click-clacking sounds as she typed on her keyboard, sounds that only made Marah's blood boil because *Beth couldn't just be quiet for a single damn second.*

And of course, the Kosmirian decided to speak, contributing to the chosen one's irritation, "So since today's Friday, our shift ends early. Usually, we work from nine to five, but on Friday's we end at three. So, I was thinking we could have a movie night tonight. Or, like, every Friday," she paused, "or something else that's fun on Fridays, if you're not into movies?"

Marah didn't need to lift her eyes from the screen to see pink lips faintly smiling, "Definitely!"

Beth beamed.

Right as Marah was about to examine her next case, an arm was slung around the back of her neck. A voice that she had never heard before chimed pleasantly, "Sorry I couldn't greet you on your first days here, but you know what my mother says, 'better late than never,' huh?"

Marah turned to see Clyna with a pointed expression scribbled all over her features.

"Yep," replied Marah as Beth's face became masked with what could only be deduced as confusion. She stammered as she caught on to what the spy was doing, "How are you? I haven't seen you since the summer." Despite talking to Clyna, Marah couldn't help but observe Beth, who had her lips pressed together as if she was reading between lines that Marah wasn't sure even existed.

It was impossible for Marah to miss the sliver of panic in the Kosmirian's baby blue eyes as they flickered between herself and Clyna, sourness dotting the specks of light in her irises. Confusion was evident on the alien's face, reflecting what Marah thought resembled disappointment.

If Clyna noticed, she didn't say anything. The rebel beamed as she looked at her with such an easy-going expression, as if she had known the human all her life. "I'm doing great, I've missed you so much. You know how your aunt is when one of us catches a cold."

Marah nodded, looking at Beth out of the corner of her eyes.

Clyna then turned to face Beth, who looked like a fish out of water, "Beth, right? Legionnaire Azim needs you to run badges with him on floor five. He also said that he needs your help cataloging weapons from this week."

Beth got up and thanked Clyna with a smile that didn't match the somberness in her eyes.

Once Beth was out of earshot, Clyna retracted from Marah who spoke, "Is everything alright? What's going on? Also, how many of us are there in here?"

"Not enough," Clyna replied, as she turned on her heels, with Marah getting up from her desk to follow her. "Everything's alright back at home, but I've been trying to find out information to help with your mission."

"Where are we going?" Marah couldn't help but ask as she quickened her pace to match the spy's. If you don't mind me asking, what's your actual mission? And, if you know the answer, is Elena okay?"

The brown-skinned woman answered, "My sister's okay. As for me, I usually deal with training regiments. And we're going to the café. I'm starving."

The two got to the cafe quickly, a large space that resembled a food court at a mall rather than a cafeteria at a workplace. The two sat at the farthest table from everyone else on the balcony for as much privacy as possible. "Let's get right to it. It took me a while, but I've been getting close to one of the Chairwoman's goons, those Legionnaires." She rolled fuchsia irises, "I heard them talking about the Archives being on campus and that there's a map."

"A map?"

"Two problems: finding the map and finding the Archives. It has to be you. I guess it is the prophecy," she shrugged.

"Prophecy?" Marah's ears pricked, "What do you mean?" Hope glimmered in her words, "So there's a reason for all of this and why it is me, and not anyone else in the galaxy?"

Clyna took a sip out of her straw. "Yeah, the prophecy that the Poten warned of." She chose her words carefully as aliens moved around them, "That's how the rebels knew that there was someone they needed to look for." She picked at her nose ring as a smirk overcame her features, "So, how's Beth?"

Marah groaned as she leaned back in her seat, "What? Has Natira told *everyone*?"

Clyna laughed. "Yep. Between the two of us, I never expected Natira to be so invested in friendship. She's usually so brooding."

"Tell me about it," replied Marah. "So," smirked Clyna, "how is it?"

"Never a quiet moment," grumbled Marah. *Plenty of dull ones though.*

As she finished the last of her mustard fries, Clyna offered sympathetically, "Beth will be busy for at least an hour, Legionnaire Azim tends to keep talking. You might want to check in with the base, I have to go now."

Marah headed back to her workstation to find Beth back. "Did you get lunch?"

"Yep." She wondered why Beth cared if she ate or not. Then Marah remembered that the two were considered friends and friends cared about each other's well-being.

"That's good," said Beth, relieved. "You didn't have anything for breakfast, and I was worried that you'd skip out on lunch too. I have to get lunch; Legionnaire Azim talks so much. Want to come with?"

"Actually, I need to get some work done so—"

"No biggie," reassured Beth, "I'll grab lunch and eat here. I'll bring you something to make up for those lost calories."

Marah suppressed a frown as she watched the blonde walk away. She had received a message from Clyna regarding the map under the guise of an assignment and glanced over the map's intricacy.

She could've opened comms with the rebels, but she wanted to do this on her own. Clyna's mention of her being a prophecy sparked some ideas in her, though she would've liked to have seen the prophecy. It gave her a sense of something, what, though was unknown.

All Marah could see were the problems: getting to the marked spot, getting there without getting caught, and some other third thing she knew would hit her.

She spotted the officer who she had been avoiding all day long, bark at another officer, and then turn in her direction. She looked away, focusing on the screen in front of her. "Feels easy enough."

A too happy voice chirped in her ear, "What are you doing while we await your bestie's return?"

"She's not my bestie!" defended Marah. "She's the one—" She immediately shut herself up remembering that she had made a bet with Natira about this exact matter.

"Go on," inquired Natira cheekily.

"Nothing," answered Marah lamely. The human couldn't help but reel in the irony of Beth hating Marah Morana while desperately wanting to be friends with Nima Adver. *If only she knew that the two were one and the same.* "You should hear the things she says about me, and then says the opposite about me. It's a borderline identity crisis."

"I can imagine," humored Natira, "actually I don't have to since I'm getting a front row seat. I'm deeply invested, where is she now?"

The way that I can imagine Natira hunched over laughing at my predicament says a lot about our friendship.

"If I tell you," groaned Marah, "you'll make fun of me."

"Actually," Natira corrected as if she were Marah's big sister and caught her doing something that she wasn't supposed to, "I'll make fun of you either way."

There was a beat of silence before she sighed and confessed, "She insisted on getting me lunch. Again. Even though I already ate."

Natira burst into cackles. "For real? That's the third time since you've been here!"

"I've only been here for three days." The human felt blush creep back on her cheeks as she replayed memories from last night. *Or was it earlier today? Honestly, what is time even?*

Natira *actually hooted,* "That makes it even better!"

"You're so mean."

"But you love it," singsonged Natira.

As if right on cue, Beth returned with two plates of food. She smiled through her teeth as she set the plate down by Marah and then plopped onto her plush seat. The blonde popped open a plastic fork from a plastic bag and dipped it into her lunch while asking, "Is it alright if I ask you something?"

"Sure," replied Marah nonchalantly, having an idea about what Beth wanted to ask about.

Beth started with hesitation thick in her tone, "You don't have to answer, but um, who was that girl?"

And it's a perfect bullseye!

Marah waited before answering, realizing that envy could be a weapon to use should she need Beth to ease off.

"Just a friend."

Beth then followed up, "What are you working on? You've been really working on it for a while. Would you like some help?"

A gruff voice served as an answer, "Whatever it is, she's going to have to stop."

Marah turned to see the Officer Kentar—whose name she learned by reading his badge, and whom she had been avoiding—standing next to her, alongside a man too tall for her to look at.

He spoke roughly, as if he had just been smoking. "Miss Adver and Miss Liluana, I need you two on regiments."

Marah raised a brow, trying to look past his yellow-stained teeth. "We have to do our next shift." She looked at Beth who returned the glance with equal confusion.

Officer Kentar didn't seem to care much as he continued curtly, "Chairwoman Kate wants all officers actively preparing to fight the rebels. Sorting their cases will not help you kill them." He crossed his thick arms across his chest as if he was challenging Marah, "After all, you two do work here."

She nodded, "Yes—"

"Yes, *sir*," spat Officer Kentar.

"Yes, sir," corrected Marah. "But isn't our other work just as important?"

Her teeth returned to the flesh that made up her lip as the officer glowered at her. The human resisted shrinking back in her seat, an action that was as much muscle memory as shooting an arrow.

Officer Kentar spoke flatly, "You work here, no?"

Marah nodded. "Yes." She quickly added, "sir."

"A real Committee worker," stated Officer Kentar tensely, "wouldn't hesitate to do anything to defeat the rebels. Am I wrong?"

Marah shook her head.

"Good," said the officer stiffly. "To make sure that there's no funny business, London here will personally escort you two there." With that, he left.

You've got to be kidding me.

"You again?" exclaimed Marah before realizing that she had opened her mouth.

London raised a brow as thick and bushy as a hedgerow. "How the tables turn. You really thought you could report me? Don't you know who my father is?"

Marah and Beth looked at each other and shrugged.

London smirked. "You were just looking at him."

Guess the saying is true—ugly looks, ugly personality.

Beth raised a brow, "This is really weird, let's just go.

Marah nodded, following Beth. She sighed at the footsteps of London; *I couldn't even get anything done.*

Beth looked past him and sighed, "He's such a jerk. I never knew that the two were related, looks like nastiness, being a rude jerk, and even egocentricity runs in the family."

She sighed as he followed them inside, announcing that he would be leading their regiment training. She took a slot stall next to Beth and accepted one of the clear circle discs London gave to each worker.

Out of the corner of her eye, she spotted the others bringing it to the space between their eyes and then tapped it, so she did the same. As she picked up her weapon, a holographic visor surrounded her face. Before she could process the tech, she was instructed to begin shooting.

Confusion rolled through Marah's body as a conundrum of thoughts filled her brain. She cocked the gun and re-loaded, waiting for London's signal before releasing a spray of blasts.

Chapter 22

Location: Where embers burn

TWO DAYS LATER

"We reviewed your proposed plan for the final takedown of The Committee, and it sounds good."

There was a reason why Kiera was Marah's favorite Zonan. She sat up straighter, "Really? That's great!"

Marah could tell that Kiera was smiling as she voiced, "We can finally stop them." *And get away from Beth. And working on Sundays. With aliens who want to kill me.*

"Where did you want to meet after, again?" Kiera's trill was drowned out by the sound of someone dropping a lot of something, a cacophony of *clangs* nearly drowned out the Zonan's question.

"Bring *it* to the alleyway with the graffiti of the Chairwoman. At least, I think it's of her." She paused and assumed Kiera was confirming her statement.

"There you'll meet with Joven, and since the Poten should disable The Committee's power, we can use the vents to get in and take over."

Marah's smile didn't last long as she realized, "But we have to find the Archives and the Poten for all of those things to happen."

"Right," grimaced Kiera. "Any plans to find it today?"

"Not yet." Marah explained with a slight frown as she logged her work for the cameras as per Officer Kentar's request. "Officers Kentar and London keep me and Beth busy because we're apparently suspicious. I have to say," she lowered her tone as she spotted London nearby, "I really hate the work ethic here. You make one mistake and it's like you're being watched twenty-four seven."

Kiera sighed and Marah could detect emotion behind her words. "Another reason to hate The Committee."

Marah watched London glance at her strangely before darting off. "Something wrong?"

"It's just that we're so close and we have this big obstacle ahead of us." Kiera sighed. "I know I'm always saying not to worry and be optimistic, but sometimes it's hard."

The human confessed, "As someone who's been feeling that way for a while, I get that. We'll find the Archives, that's what we're here for, right?" *I'm here for*, she corrected herself.

As if Kiera could sense her pang of emotion, the Zonan chimed, "You'll do it, Marah. Don't worry. You gave us a great plan which I would love to commend you on if Natira wasn't drunk and about to do something she shouldn't."

She was about to transition to her next task when a pop-up appeared on the screen.

She rolled her eyes as she read the pop-up aloud, "More captured rebels on the streets and we're closer than ever to total control over

Kosmir and the rest of the galaxy!" She sighed as she closed the pop-up while mocking enthusiasm, "Woo! Can't wait!"

We need to work faster or else we'll lose. We need to get past Beth and these officers so we can finally end this.

Speaking of the blonde-haired speedster, Beth was nowhere to be found. She knew that Beth had been looking into the Archives for her, but some of the information was above Marah's clearance so she was only able to get so much out of it.

But, Beth had left her ID and the disc containing all of her information at her workstation in a rush as Officer London had her run another errand.

Seizing the opportunity, she reached forward for the ID and copied the Kosmirian's username and password but then hesitated, moving the paper back down to her lap before grabbing the disc and plugging it into her computer. She glanced left and right, making sure that no one was watching her before quickly typing the contents of the paper onto the screen.

She logged out of her account and entered Beth's information and was greeted with hundreds of more files, which encouraged her to grin as she leaned closer to the screen.

"Which one of you has what I need?" she whispered softly. She stumbled upon a file marking Poten and clicked on it. "I might've done something," she said softly as her other co- workers weren't at their stations. "Might've solved the clearance issue."

She got an answer from Natira who sounded like she was doing her best to not slur her words, "Oh? Is little miss bestie not around?" Her voice was thick with amusement and Marah felt her cheeks redden when someone, presumably Kiera, giggled.

Despite the blush, the noirette couldn't help but smile as she copied files, "Nope, which I am beyond grateful for." She poked, "And if I recall, Natira, this was your idea. If I have to suffer, then so do you, besides, you've only heard what's said when the comms are on."

Marah began to count off her fingers, "You haven't heard the sleep-talking, her rants, and more. As a matter of fact, do you know what she made me watch yesterday? A friggin' documentary about The Committee!

Kiera chimed in, "t's cute though, this whole secret enemies thing."

"It was the logical play," laughed Natira. "I don't like hearing her talk any more than you like to hear it."

"Aww," said Marah as her cheeks began to hurt from all the smiling, real and fake, "you do care. I'm touched." She copied everything on Beth's disc into her computer, using Beth's login to override clearance, knowing that she wouldn't have much time before the blonde returned.

Natira mimicked a scoff, but her tone indicated that she was fibbing, "Oh you wish. Find anything yet? Kiera, I don't think adding sugar to burnt cookies will make them taste any better."

Before Marah could ask what this meant for her mission, Beth's ever so chipper voice popped out of nowhere, "Whatcha reading? I brought food!"

"Gotta go," hissed Marah, "Beth."

Marah quickly minimized the tab and slid the disc to where Beth had left it.

Beth piped up, "I heard that the Chairwoman has an announcement to make and that we all have to be here to hear it."

Marah's heart skipped a beat. "Like a good announcement or a bad announcement?"

"Dunno," shrugged the Kosmirian. "Maybe it's about that Marah person? I heard that Chairwoman Kate is still looking for her, but I personally don't see the value. I mean," she spoke over a swallow, "if she was supposedly the fall of us and she's with the rebels, then why hasn't she done anything yet?"

Marah bit her lip to prevent her face from falling. *Beth has a point. You're supposed to be this great thing, where's the greatness?* She didn't want to give Beth all the satisfaction of lowering her self-esteem, so she countered, "Who said that silence equals compliance?"

Beth shrugged, using her sleeve to wipe crumbs on the corner of her lips, "You make a fair point. What do you think the rebels have been doing all this time?"

Marah didn't get the chance to answer before Beth steered the conversation elsewhere, "You know what I *do* wonder about the human; how do all of these people get picked?"

Marah's ears perked, "What do you mean by these people? Are there more people like Marah?" Her name rolled off her tongue weirdly.

"Well," the Kosmirian began to type again and Marah bit her lip as the sound of nails clacking against a keyboard drummed in her ears, "when The Committee first started, they needed a central piece of technology to guide them, for success to be assured. The very first Chairwoman recruited the greatest scientists of her time to create something that would do just that. With the right algorithm, the Poten would rattle off all the beings in the universes that would be able to stop their success. People like kings and queens, like the King of Nova."

Must she type so loudly?

"What happened to him?"

Beth paused typing to crack her knuckles, "He was the first out of all the realms to declare that they were against what The Committee stood for. So, he was the first to be put in line. The Committee exploited his weakness, seeing the empire that his bloodline built on the verge of annihilation because of him."

That struck Marah. "Who else is on the list?" *If there are others like me, then maybe I'm not the one that the rebels need. What if Chairwoman Kate got the wrong name? Are one of those people the eternity the prophecy is talking about?*

"Was on the list," corrected Beth.

Marah paused her own typing and brought her hand to her comm using the cover of scratching her ear, "What do you mean?"

Beth sighed, resting her hand on her chin as she looked up to think. "Well, from my conversations with the Legionnaires, the only people still on the list today are the rebel leaders, her, and some ruler in a different galaxy. The Committee doesn't like to talk much about their targets."

"And Marah?"

Beth clipped her ID to her blazer and Marah was grateful that she had saved the files to her computer. Her lips pursed as she read the case file on the screen and submitted. "It's interesting, I suppose. She's the first target to be a human. Not only that, but she doesn't come from a very political background. You'd think someone who knows a thing or two about government would be keen on taking one down."

Marah forced a nod. "So," she hoped she sounded as casual as she intended, "then why focus on her? I get why the rebel leaders are on the list, but why focus on Marah when she's a human?"

Beth leaned in closer, almost hesitating for a moment. "She's at the top of the rank."

Marah was deep in thought. Her eyes shone, "What do you mean?" *Where do I fit in then?*

Beth submitted another case, making a soft remark about how another report of a rebel leader's sighting had to be true simply because The Committee needed every chance to investigate and take down the rebels. "Ranks are a list." She moved her fingers from the holographic mouse to type in her login information. "The more dangerous the Poten deems you, the higher your rank is. The higher the rank, the quicker Chairwoman Kate deals with them." She shrugged casually. "Sometimes the targets disappear off the list, and the ones that accelerate up the list are discarded off the list and marked as dead."

Marah wore a dumbfounded expression. *Is she really seeing nothing wrong with this?* She brought her cursor to the red button and clicked on it. *And that's another alien crime!*

She bit her lip, "And the human?" The comm link wasn't static, which meant that every word that Beth uttered was being received at the rebel base.

Beth glanced around warily before leaning close to Marah, "She's at the highest rank. No clue why or how. She's been on the list since 2003, and only now she's a problem."

That's the year I was born! Marah would have completely freaked out but knew she couldn't.

Beth's tone was too casual for Marah's liking as she tapped on her screen, nails making clicking sounds, "I think that the Poten is broken, cause there's no way a mere human could ruin us. It's practically impossible."

Marah nodded, getting back to work while her thoughts ran at hundreds of miles per minute. She was a human, with no powers or fancy assassin skills. *So, what does all of this mean?* She moved to prop her head on her hand as all of this thinking began to make her head hurt.

"Then again," said a snide voice that irritated Marah's headache tenfold, "anything's possible."

London smirked, resting a hand on the corner of the table that Marah and Beth shared. "I couldn't help but overhear your conversation. Why do you ask?"

Marah shot back, "Why do *you* ask?"

"Uh," said London as if it was the most obvious question in the world, "because I can." He sighed, directing his citrus orange eyes to Beth.

Beth rolled her eyes, "You never have been good at minding your own business, but I'll say it again, mind your own business."

Marah looked at Beth strangely, not understanding the alien's implications. Beth blushed, casting her gaze to the floor.

Then it hit her.

"If you're thinking that we were a thing," London chuckled dryly, "you would be correct."

Well now, this is awkward.

Marah decided to resume "working" while London focused his attention back on Beth. "My father is the head of security here and I report to him. Your business is my business."

Beth didn't get the chance to say anything when a crackling sound pierced the atmosphere, causing a hushed silence to sweep over the floor.

"As we all know, tomorrow is the 150th anniversary of The Committee's original formation," announced the Chairwoman pleased, "and in honor of another year of success, we will be hosting a gala."

That would be a perfect opportunity to get inside the Archives and get the Poten.

"Everyone's attendance will be checked by the Legionnaires, as it is mandatory."

Oh, come on!

The Chairwoman spoke in a silky tone, "In addition to hosting our usual festivities, we will continue our preparations against the anarchists that are set on ruining our lives. That is all."

Marah couldn't help but frown at the intercom. *Anarchists? They are children, orphans, who have had their homes and families stripped from them by force. And they are the violent ones? You are the ones flowing the anger, you are the ones feeding the flame and then blaming the spark for catching fire so quickly. You are the ones wanting to play with fire!*

London stood up, "Beth, if you happen to be up for a date, call me."

Marah looked at London strangely as he strutted away. She turned to face Beth who was looking everywhere but at her, "Well, that was something."

Beth grimaced, as if the encounter was a stinging slap to the face that she was recovering from.

Marah leaned forward, "Are you going to go with him?"

Beth returned to defeating "rebel scum" by hitting the red button again, as she laughed hollowly. "Definitely not."

The human couldn't help but laugh. She re-opened the browser with the files she had copied from Beth and with a bit of scrolling, she stumbled upon the file that she was looking for, at least, she hoped it was what she was looking for.

She clicked on the file and hummed, waiting for it to load.

The file had just opened when London's father strutted toward the two merely to state, "Beth Liluana, you're scheduled for interrogations," and walked away.

Beth followed the officer away, leaving Marah to her devices.

Only time I'll ever say this but thank you. Sir.

Marah opened the file and scrolled down, pausing in shock as the pen that she was twirling in her hand fell out and clinked upon falling to the floor. Her eyes fell over a red circle around the structure labelled "Archives."

Would you look at that?

"I think I just found the Archives."

Chapter 23

Location: The bearings of knowledge

"Hold up," said Leia in a tone that was dangerously close to disbelief, "what do you mean you found the Archives?"

Marah confirmed while looking over her shoulder for anyone who was attempting to listen in, "I found some blueprints that show me exactly where the Archives are."

"Which means," inferred Natira, "we know where the Poten is."

"We win," breathed out Marah. *We just might actually win.*

Kiera chimed in, "Which means that our plan can move forward then, this is great!"

"Kiera's right," Leia added, words filled with passion and excitement because this revelation would change the entire cause of the rebels drastically, "we'll begin to prepare the necessary resources for when you find the Poten. The minute everything goes dark there, we'll storm The Citadel first and then supply the troops."

A surge of adrenaline pumped through Marah's veins. For the first time the rebels had what they needed.

If I can get the Poten, we'll be able to take down The Committee. Wouldn't that be great?

I wouldn't have to be here anymore, I could...go home.

Marah soured at the thought of home. She had been able to put her homesickness on a back burner, but now that it had come up again, there was a lackluster attitude toward the idea, an absence of enthusiasm, one that the human was thriving off of some number of days ago.

"What?" Natira was the first to interrupt Marah's train of thought, "No pop culture reference?" The Nantak laughed, "That's a first."

Marah clapped her hands together giddy, "No way!"

The worker sitting three seats away from her looked at Marah curiously and then shrugged, returning to what he was doing.

Natira shot back in a tone that was preposterous, "No way what?"

"I knew it!" exclaimed Marah quietly, remembering where she was before continuing in a singsong voice, "Natira loves my pop culture references, Natira loves my pop culture references, ha!"

Kiera interrupted with a giggle, "Natira's blushing! I had no idea that she could do that."

Marah spoke seriously as she straightened her back and moved closer to her screen, trying to figure out how to get to the Archives now that she knew they were somewhere near her, "Kiera, snap a picture. If I was there, I'd do it and give you a high five, but," she sighed, "I have to deal with Beth."

Natira grumbled something incoherently.

Leia concluded in a tone that suggested that she was holding in a chuckle of her own, "Alright children, time to—"

Marah opened her mouth, the perfect reply ready on her tongue.

Natira must've gained the superpower of telepathy since she before Marah could speak, she shrilly interjected, "If you make a pop culture reference, I will strangle you the next time I see you!"

Marah rolled her eyes, "How do you know what I was going to say? Have you been watching movies or has Lizard just been telling you this? Besides," she added, "I'll only take death from you with your pink knife."

The sound of metal clashing that could only be from Natira caused Marah to hold herself from doubling over in laughter *because oh, how the tables turn!*

"Children," toyed Leia, "time to get back to work."

Marah's tone was still thick with amusement as she imagined Natira, of all people, throwing a stoic fit. Her smile widened at the warmth behind Natira's grumbles, not realizing just how much she had warmed up to her friends. "Tomorrow's the gala. I'll need something to wear, but not for long, if you're thinking what I'm thinking. I'll need to see it first before we can do what we need to. Just in case."

The familiar sound of clicking heels had become ingrained in Marah's mind, causing muscle memory to take over as she opened a browser. "Which leaves one more problem," finished Marah, "how do I get there without a certain someone pestering me?"

Right on cue, Beth's cheery voice echoed against her eardrums, "This is literally the third time this week I've had to go to interrogations," she took her seat and began to type, much to the human's displeasure. "At this point, I'm beginning to think that London is doing this just so he can annoy me even more. You'd think for a guy who wants to go out with me, I'd be there a lot longer."

"Did they catch any other spies?"

Beth shook her head, blonde locks falling out of place, "Surprisingly not."

Marah breathed out a sigh of relief. "That's good." She added quickly, "Right?"

The blonde affirmed, "I hope so since those pesky rebels are apparently everywhere." She sighed, shaking her head with furrowed brows. "I can't believe everything that has been going on without anyone knowing." The blonde scoffed, "Makes you wonder who's who around here."

"Yeah," echoed Marah, clicking the red button for the umpteenth time. "It does." She didn't dare elaborate anything further, even if she wanted to. She kept her mouth shut as an officer that she had been keen on avoiding strolled down toward the two.

Take two, shall we?

"Well, well, well," the officer started as he placed two chubby fists on his hips, one hand pressed against the holster of a weapon, "Lookie here what the rookie is doin' today." He leaned closer to Marah, who resisted leaning back from stale breath, "I presume, actual work?"

Has he ever heard of brushing his teeth?

"Yes, sir," answered Marah while biting her tongue to remain professional. She resisted rolling her eyes as Officer Kentar moved closer toward her to see her screen, keen on disbelief.

"Funny," spoke the officer sourly while resting a hand on top of Marah's monitor, causing the human to bite back a cringe as hot breath tickled the rims of her glasses. "I haven't seen you in any interrogations all week. And I know you're on my list because I made sure that you were on it."

She retorted as she raised her gaze to meet the officer's sharp eyes, "Dare I ask why?"

Officer Kentar danced around her inquiry. "You know exactly why." He pointed one of the fingers curled around her monitor at her while the other reached inside his pocket and brought another alien-version-of-a-cigarette to his lips, "I'm onto you, rookie, there's something' fishy about you." He removed the cigarette while nodding to himself as if he were convincing himself of his words, "And sooner or later, I'm going to figure out exactly what that is."

Marah just looked at Kentar as if he had gone mad, "I have nothing to hide, but you can see for yourself."

"I'm sure you don't," grunted Officer Kentar before turning on his heels.

Marah raised a black brow as the stout man disappeared amongst the sea of Committee workers and turned to face Beth who wore an equally annoyed expression, "I seriously cannot deal with him! He's trying to catch me, has he never heard of making a mistake?"

Beth replied wanly, "Looks like being toxic runs in the family."

"He's so creepy," whispered Beth as she glanced at Kentar over Marah's shoulder, "the way he just stands there and watches, it's like he's watching you and only you." She moved closer toward Marah while mimicking a shudder, "Just ignore him, he'll realize soon just how great you are and get over it."

"I await that day eagerly," Marah huffed as she signed out of her computer and stood after what felt like forever. "Let's get out of here before he decides to come back again."

Beth followed Marah as the two headed toward the elevators near the entry of The Citadel, "I cannot wait to get some sleep, today has been exhausting. Thank Kosmir for the gala tomorrow because with all this extra work," the blonde yawned, "I can't keep up."

Leaning against the transparent wall, the speedster yawned again, this time bringing the cuff of her cardigan to her face. As if it wasn't already enough that The Committee had them working every day including Sundays, but the idea of one last attack against the rebels had

The Committee demanding two hundred percent from their workers. The pay matched the hours, not that she knew what to do with the money.

Their usual shift was a standard sixteen to eight—because *of course* aliens were so sophisticated that their numeric time wasn't based on how much time passed, but how much time was left. Basically, it translated to the ratio of sixteen hours off to eight hours on—*or sixteen on and eight off?* That was something Marah was still getting used to.

So, she didn't blame Beth for yawning through her words. "During the interrogation, one of the officers mentioned that we'll be going to every home and building to try and get the location of the rebel base. That means we're only going to get more work. Who knew there was so much preparation and training for an invasion?"

Marah knew her friends back at the base heard what the Kosmirian had said as she opened her mouth to speak when Beth beat her to it, "but for now, let's leave the destroying of evil to another day. I'm exhausted."

Drained, the rebel spy placed her bags by her bedside before exclaiming, "I don't know about you, but I'm going to hit the hay." It was almost two, so Beth wouldn't question her after spending nearly four hours at the mall. In truth, she wasn't actually that tired, but the human didn't want to put up with Beth when the only thing her mind could focus on was the Archives.

There was something strange about it. *Them?*

Beth decided to have another meal so while she strung together ingredients that Marah couldn't pronounce, she rummaged her closet for clothes that she brought from the rebels' base. She pulled out a pair of sweatpants and a yellow t-shirt and headed to the bathroom to change.

Inside, the first thing Marah did was remove her glasses with a sigh. She pressed her head against the wooden door, trying to calm down the sea of thoughts that was beginning to rise with every intention of drowning Marah in it. "I know there's a lot going on but you know yourself. You need rest."

Who needs sleep when we can get answers?

Marah huffed as she bunched up the material of her sweatpants, "Fair point. Still."

Fine, huffed the voice in her head. *One thought at a time, then.*

Marah whispered as she changed into the colored shirt, "It doesn't make sense. It was right there; it was too easy. Nothing here is easy," mumbled the girl with dismay.

Why can't we take the win when we have it? offered the voice in Marah's head as she slipped out of the bathroom and placed her uniform on a hanger and her glasses on her nightstand. *You found the Archives and you helped pitch a plan to get the Poten. Makes all of this with Beth and the officers worth it.*

She wrinkled her nose, muttering to herself as Beth entered the bathroom, shutting the door behind her, "Let's not think about that."

Marah yawned as she moved to rest her head on a pillow as she heard the lights in the bathroom flicker off.

"Goodnight, Nima."

"Night."

Marah tucked her arms under her head, focusing her gaze on the ceiling. Despite her yawns, the human knew she wasn't going to fall asleep right away. Her lips were at rest, but the gears in her head were anything but.

Marah felt strange. Odd. Peculiar. Different. Discombobulated. A castaway. Ever since she woke up on Kosmir, her life has been a never-ending blur. At first, that blur was something that she loathed and wanted to lock up and throw away the key. The hatred she had for Kosmir and the rebels for dragging her into the mess had long since disappeared compared to today. *And today, they're my friends. Who would've thought when I wanted to make friends, they'd be aliens?*

Marah glanced over at Beth who was gracefully covered in the sheets while her phone quietly pinged.

And one of them thinks that I'm the friend that won't break her heart.

When I walked into those doors, never would I have thought that things would go the way they did. At first, Beth was nothing more than a tool to get what she needed: information. That tool began to double as an obstacle, always clinging to her side and being a friend. But still, valuable. *You know, if Beth wasn't the enemy, I think I'd like her a whole lot more.*

But Beth was the enemy. So, such feelings of friendship needed to be buried.

She wasn't angry at Beth. *How can I be? Just like how I couldn't stay angry at the rebels after Artemis, who am I to deny them a better life?*

Marah exhaled, relinquishing the rare moment of silence that had fallen on her. Everything prior was all hustle and bustle: find intel, wear a disguise, and try to save the world without losing herself in the messy process. *Following what I've been told in a world where the lines between spies and soldiers are too blurred to tell which is which.*

Up until now, Marah hadn't gotten the chance to be herself instead of what others wanted her to be. The human was still grasping how to be the apparent chosen one and the only help she had was everyone insistently telling she possessed the capability.

Her old thoughts came to her: *I'm not like them. The rebels are soldiers, I'm just a human. They can conjure power, walk through walls, and put people to sleep on sheer command. And I'm just me.*

That was where she was at today.

Outside, she'd been Nima Adver, a character she may or may not truly understand as she's been wearing pretenses for as long as she can remember since she walked out of the rebel's guild. *It's nice*, she thought with a smile, *to just be me for a while and think.*

The off feeling within the pit of the claimed paragon's stomach encouraged Marah to put all of her weight on the right side of her body as she moved to find a better position to sleep in. She rubbed at her arms where bruises used to lay regularly. Marah began to wonder how her life brought her from her past to here. *Do you think they miss you?*

Not that her parents would know where she was, here or back on Earth, since the teenager was kicked out of her house not that long ago.

It was ironic to the girl that she had gotten kicked out for not wanting to go to college and yet bore the title of "the chosen one" amongst the stars.

Marah exhaled with a sigh, rolling flat onto her back, and rubbed at the acne that called her forehead home and frowned. There was a lot more acne than the human remembered, dozens more small bumps felt rough against her fingers. Only then did the girl realize that she hadn't used any scrub, cream, or product on her face in what she assumed to be months.

Do aliens even have acne cleansers?

Marah shook her head, black and red locks of hair falling onto her face. It was almost laughable, *here I am trying to save the universe and I'm stressing about forehead acne. As if that's the biggest of my problems.*

Though she had given the rebels the impression that she could, she had no idea how to get to the Archives, and the Poten itself was a whole other mystery. The gala was her best bet, but sensibly she knew not to get her hopes up. If she failed then, the spy had no clue how she'd pull this off in broad daylight. There were too many risks without another opportunity like the gala.

There was also Officer Kentar and his son, who would surely work to prevent her from doing what she needed to. It was quite annoying, to be honest, since the officer claimed that her panic was from a guilty conscience. *Or he's never heard of childhood trauma,* Marah thought bitterly.

She frowned, never having associated the word trauma with herself. *Do I have trauma?* The human didn't think so. She had—well—*abusive parents? Non-supporting caregivers? Not that they didn't care about me, but they didn't necessarily traumatize me.* Even if using the word felt appropriate.

Marah's eyes found the clock atop her nightstand read half past twenty-two in bright red numbers. She exhaled softly, letting the thoughts in her head pour out into the air around her.

Marah was no stranger to nights like these where she was held captive, sometimes willingly throughout the hours of late and early. Usually, she'd plug in her headphones and listen to whatever until her mind caved in to her body's need for slumber.

Or she'd go for a walk.

Since option one wasn't possible, she settled on option two.

The girl quietly got dressed into more outside-acceptable clothes, a light sweater, and jeans, grabbing her frames and ID before shutting the door behind her.

Both hands in her pockets, Marah wore a slight smile for the officers patrolling the halls as she entered an elevator with the doors softly closing in front of her.

The lights were still on at the first floor, so she didn't feel worried as she slipped out of the glass doors and into crisp oxygen. That was one of the things she liked about Kosmir, the air was actually clean, how, Marah had no idea.

She walked on the streets with no sense of purpose, not bothering to bring the map with her, deciding to go wherever her feet would take her.

Eventually, it became too quiet in Marah's head alone with just her thoughts. The human hated silence. It was unnerving, a deafening ringing that refused to settle inside of her hence why she always kept her comm on, so she'd have some background noise to help her focus. She brought a hand to the comm resting against the curve of her ear, "Hello?"

Marah wasn't sure if anyone was awake but hoped that someone was.

She expected Natira who usually stayed up past midnight, but instead heard Leia's voice who greeted, "Hey yourself. What's up?"

"Nothing much." Marah waited for the floating traffic lights overhead to turn red so she could cross the street. "I wanted to clear my head. Have someone to talk to."

"I'm all ears."

Marah paused, searching, and organizing her thoughts before voicing them. "I don't know where to begin actually. Everything has been happening so quickly." She curled her fingers into loose fists as she crossed the street, gazing past automobiles that floated above pavement, "I'm still having a hard time adjusting to all of this. With the Archives and the Poten right in our grasp, I don't know. I never thought that any of this would happen in my life and it's all happening so fast. Especially for someone like me."

"What do you mean? You're doing great." Leia spoke proudly, not in a manner that suggested that she hadn't believed Marah was capable or competent, rather like an older sister. It felt nice to be cared for occasionally. At least, by someone who actually knew who she was.

"Because it's me," answered Marah lamely, burying her hands deeper into her pockets. "Because of who I am. I don't have any cool powers or abilities. I'm just a girl with a semi-bad past. I can't do any of these great things on my own, unlike the rebels. Not everyone is destined for greatness, and the ones that are, aren't like me."

Leia stated emphatically, "So what if you had a bad past or you're just a girl? For the record, we're awesome. Sucky childhoods don't determine our future. We choose to let it. For you, that showed you good from bad. That, right there, defines a small part of you. You know, just because you don't have powers in a world that lives off of power doesn't make you powerless."

"Yeah," echoed Marah as she held out her ID to an officer walking past her. She didn't want any unnecessary interactions.

"You know, when I first came to Kosmir, I felt alone. My father died back on Nova, and everyone that worked in both the government and the monarchy were killed immediately, so most of my family died that night. It was just me, my mother, and my cousin who had become an orphan. My grandparents fell ill due to the radiation from bombs falling onto their houses. My mother was so drunk with grief and anger," the Novan paused and sniffed, "she killed herself six months later."

Marah wanted to offer condolences but decided against it. She hated how useless the phrase was. Saying that she was sorry didn't change the past nor would it have any impact on Leia's life. She didn't hurt Leia, The Committee did. But she could acknowledge the pain in the alien's life, "That's awful."

Leia continued, "It's fine, but thank you. It was just me and my cousin then. We disagreed a lot, so she abandoned me. I was eight years old, an orphan who was homeless on a planet that she didn't even know. I was so angry at my mother and my cousin for leaving me, and even angrier at the people who were at fault for that. I lived in my past, skipping classes, getting myself in trouble, until I met Kiera and Natira. They helped open my eyes to the fact that change was needed."

"The rebels?"

"Exactly." The Novan admitted, "Even though we had powers, that didn't mean that we felt powerful. No one was willing to help orphans like us, so we had to be the ones to make things better. And over the past eight years, we've become powerful. And so have you. Being great doesn't mean being powerful. Heroes aren't born with powers, it's what they do with what they have that makes them a hero."

Marah sighed softly, looking both ways before crossing a street, "It doesn't make sense though. I mean, you can make magic out of your freaking hands! You can lift cars with your thoughts. I'm sure if you tried hard enough, you could probably set the Citadel on fire! Natira can walk through walls and Kiera can put anyone to sleep with her mind. But why have I been on the Poten's list since I was born?"

Leia mused thoughtfully, "That's something I can't answer. What I can say is that not having powers is your greatest strength. Perhaps it's as your Earth movies say, saviors need to be someone who knows what humanity is. This world is alien, we don't think of being different. You are someone who knows what it's like to not be like everyone else. We're aliens, we were born with these abilities and this cause, but not you. You're here, fighting a war that doesn't even concern you. Your world isn't in danger and yet, here you are, a regular human being. But at the end of the day, isn't that we all are? We are born out of nothing, and we become nothing again when we die. I believe that is the moral of the story. Take it from experience, having the capacity to do great, doesn't mean that great things will be done for the benefit of the people."

Like Chairwoman Kate.

"But, what if we can't?" countered Marah. Her voice was urgent and flooded with desperation, "If I can't do this, then what?"

Leia's voice was too calm for Marah's liking, and yet it calmed the flames in her heart, "Then we don't. Except, I know we won't. As scary as all of this may be, I take refuge knowing that we're a team, we do everything together, for better or for worse. We all have our strengths and weaknesses. You're focusing on what you think is a weakness."

"It's not?"

"It's not." Leia's confident tone reminded Marah of her role in all of this. "I would not be able to survive like you are. I'm not used to following orders, usually I'm the one giving them. No doubt, Natira is an able fighter, but she often lets survival rule her heart. That isn't necessarily a weakness, is it?"

"And Kiera is uncomfortable with killing. That's not a weakness, but we make ourselves feel like it. And if we lose, it's okay

"How?" aid Marah, feeling the weight of the worlds on her shoulders. She spotted a bench and sat down, lifting her head to look at the white twinkle that was smaller than all of the other twinkling lights in the sky.

"Because," answered Leia in a manner that suggested she had to teach herself the very same lesson several times, "we're trying. We fight to live as long as we can. That's the only way to live with the world and with yourself."

Marah was quiet, taking in the Novan's words. She was not entirely convinced yet. "I don't know how you do it. All of you. I have this urge to focus entirely on this, but," she confessed, "at the same time, the things that I want to know I can't find. I wish I knew why all of this is happening the way it is. Maybe when we finish this, it'll make sense."

"It will."

Marah turned on the phone that Elena had given her and found the time close to twenty-one. She wanted to explore Kosmir's streets with its cacophony of dialects, some she knew, and others she didn't, but what she *did* know was that she needed sleep if she was to optimize her success the next day.

So, she decided to head back to the Citadel, walking past cobblestone walkways, glass doors and windows that were the shelter of the generations that called Kosmir home. *How many of them were content with Kosmir being home?*

The spy mumbled to no one, "You just have to get this done, for your friends and all of the people like them." She walked past the people's lives who would soon change, her heart beating differently—a tune for ripening war. *She's right, the time for war is coming. And that time is in my hands.*

"I can do this," Marah whispered in a tone that suggested justice would prevail over suffering as she headed back inside The Citadel, "We can do this."

She had just walked past the security desks when a gruff voice stopped her right in her tracks, "Well, well, well, lookie who we've got here."

I got ninety-nine problems, and you are definitely one of them.

Marah rolled her eyes, choosing to stay quiet as she walked past Officer Kentar.

"Oh no, ya don't," grunted the officer that seemed to be everywhere she was. He waddled in front of her and crossed his arms, blocking her from going anywhere else. "Tell me, what are you doing at this hour?" He narrowed his eyes as he drank in Marah's clothes, "Some secret spy business, I bet."

Marah sighed, rubbing the bridge of her frames. "I went for a walk. Must you always assume the worst in people?"

The officer raised a brow, "I am an officer to you, Adver. You will address me as you would to all officers, as sir."

Marah resisted rolling her eyes again. "I went for a walk, sir."

Officer Kentar nodded as he huffed, bringing his crossed arms up his chest. "And why were you out for a walk?"

"Because I couldn't sleep," answered the girl flatly. She quickly added, "Sir." "And why's that?"

Must you continue to pester me? "Because," sighed Marah as she stretched her enunciation, allowing annoyance to fill her tone, "I couldn't sleep. Now, if you'll excuse me, I need to get back to my room. Sir." She walked past him toward the elevators.

Officer Kentar didn't seem convinced. "Alright, go then, Miss Adver. I wouldn't want you to mess up tomorrow."

Marah froze and bit down the urge to curl her fingers into fists as she turned around to face Officer Kentar who wore a smirk that she wanted to wipe clean off.

Kentar continued slowly yet steadily, as if he were a detective trying to outsmart a culprit, "I haven't seen you in any interrogations, let's fix that shall we? In fact, I'll be speaking to Chairwoman Kate about doing so personally, after tomorrow's gala of course."

She smiled tightly, irked, which was what the officer wanted as he turned on his heel and left.

Chapter 24

Location: The residence of the dead and the Anticipated's celebration

Marah didn't know much about galas, so she was surprised to be woken up at the equivalent of eight in the morning by Beth. She groaned, but due to her voice being thick with sleep the sound barely came out. She turned away from the Kosmirian, "Isn't the gala at like three? You're worrying over nothing."

Just as she expected, Beth didn't relent. She stood by the bed, fingers propped on her sides as she explained as if it was common knowledge, "That's the gala. We have the celebratory breakfast and rebels to be interrogated. We only have the first shift until twelve, then we get ready for the gala."

"Interrogate rebels?" echoed Marah, lifting her head out of confusion. She rubbed her eyes yearning for nothing more than throwing the covers back over her head and returning to a comfy black abyss.

Beth clasped her hands together to exhort, "Looks like we're pretty trustworthy in the stale, lifeless eyes of Officer Kentar."

Marah was up now, wearing a smile that didn't quite match her eyes, not that Beth noticed. She remembered Kentar's words to her last night and wondered if this was a trick. The rebels kept on moving her off the lists to avoid unnecessary interactions, and she wondered what type of luck this was.

"And there's the celebratory breakfast," Beth repeated as if it was the most obvious statement in the world. She had a bounce in her step as Marah plucked her uniform off triangle hangers with far less energy, and fewer hand gestures, "It's a buffet, too. Hopefully, London can see what great officers we are when we interrogate rebels."

Marah softly laughed, recollecting her first encounter with Officer Kentar's son.

Beth was already dressed, so Marah worked to quickly tear herself from sleepiness and dreams as she got changed, deciding to try something new with her look. Glancing at her reflection, she picked at her forehead, frowning at the stubbly acne, and rummaged through the cabinets for some sort of product. *With Beth's clear skin, she's got to be using something.*

Unfortunately, Marah did not find anything. After picking at the mulish bumps for several minutes, she decided to give up for the sake of her fingernails, washing them before slipping on her glasses and finding Beth waiting for her.

Beth had planned their time smartly because, for the first time, the hallways and elevators were full. Marah and Beth were only two of dozens waiting to catch an elevator. Just as they got to the front of the line, the barrier dissolved, letting them enter. The elevator was almost full, and she couldn't help but wonder how the elevator's platform was expanding to fit everyone comfortably.

Marah could sense the excitement surrounding the buffet, especially since Beth snapped selfie after selfie, soaking up the glory of the cause they supposedly stood for.

Marah looked away, replacing the flames of anticipation and power in her heart with flames of patience.

The cafeteria, it turned out, was closed off, and food was served on buffet tables. Marah assumed this was part of the tradition since she was the only one who looked confused as more people spilled onto the main floor.

Marah scanned the hovering tables, not recognizing most of the dishes there: A label that read "kisfur" in the loopiest handwriting Marah had ever seen had plates and plates of flaky circles that were full of cream inside, and the flaky shell was peppered with some substance that Marah couldn't guess. Next to it was a tray of perfectly cut jelly-like cubes that looked like rubber. She watched people bite into them and liquid dribble off their lips the color of rose petals. She decided to add one to her plate and headed down the table with Beth practically at her hip, suggesting what Marah should get.

She was impressed by the elegance of all the trays and couldn't help herself from snatching a few cisfran flowers—pentagon-leaved flowers that came in the palest of yellows, lilacs, rose, and brown—that were peppered in a powder that Marah had seen stocked in Kiera's kitchen cabinets but had never nailed the pronunciation for.

She took a bite out of the cube first and didn't know any words in the English or any alien language to describe the pleasant taste that was so good that it warmed her mouth. She ate the sky-colored cube in three bites, savoring each bite.

Her eyes lit at the sight of the alien equivalent of an ice cream machine and knew what would make up the rest of her meal as she chewed on each flower.

"I can't wait to start interrogations!" exclaimed Beth as she chewed on the same cube that Marah had fallen in love with. "It's one of the most prestigious honors one can have, sending a rebel to their doom. There is just something about seeing the light of the world that they've ruined that compels them to beg for mercy."

Marah willed anger out of her voice. "I'm sure."

For someone who is all sunshine and rainbows she sure does enjoy death a lot.

Marah walked alongside Beth to their workstations, dread filling in her stomach as she contemplated Beth's words. There was no doubt that Beth would carelessly send the rebel to the Legionnaires or the Chairwoman, and her agenda was the exact opposite. She wasn't sure what she was hoping for more: someone she knew or someone who she had no connection to.

She took another bite of ice cream as Beth directed them to turn down a corridor she hadn't been down before. The human then understood why, as Beth held up her ID in front of thick steel doors and Marah did the same.

She was half-way done with the cone while Beth droned on about the prestigious experience they were about to embark on.

They were then greeted by a Legionnaire.

Marah stopped in her tracks. She resisted the urge to shrink away under the woman's gaze, which was sharper than the sword she wore. It was a reaction that time had gifted her, along with collections of colored marks across her arms.

"Yep, let that feeling sink in," chimed Beth, helpfully. "So much power has been attained here."

Legionnaire Mizra stared at them flatly, eyebrows dipping down slightly. "Adver, you will read the results and pitch in when you deem necessary. Liluana, you will lead. Make sure you log the results of the interrogation."

"You won't be listening?" Marah had not realized she had questioned the Legionnaire until it was too late. She looked down, cheeks rosy with what was either embarrassment or fear.

The woman looked at Marah with a smidge of scorn. "I don't waste my time interrogating. I know they are all guilty." She wore a silky smile, "My time is better suited to our Chairwoman's commands, such as slaying our criminals. Room three."

"Of course," said Marah meekly, leading the way down the hall to their room, not wanting to maintain a presence with the Legionnaire longer than she needed to.

The door dissolved as she stepped inside, and she fought to control her facial features at the sight of a very familiar face. Thick metal cuffs held Joven's wrists together and thinner chains were strewn along his brown fingers. As if that were not already enough, there was another chain holding him to the side of the table.

The room contained two other things: a folder and a device. The device displayed two sets of bars, one with blue and one with yellow. Marah took to stand behind the device while Beth picked up the wires connected to the device and wrapped it tightly around each of the rebel's thumbs.

The whole time Marah couldn't break eye contact with Joven. She obviously needed to do something to help him, but she was unable to understand the message that he was trying to communicate with his oval eyes.

Beth took a seat in front of Joven.

He wore an amused expression. "What game will we play today?"

Beth shrugged, opening his folder to see his past interactions with The Committee. "You tell me. You have been accounted for three acts of suspicion already. Is that true?"

Joven nodded.

The small blue bar inched to the right a few millimeters.

Both turned to Marah, who quickly looked down to confirm. "Blue."

Beth folded her legs neatly under each other. "Not bad, starting with the truth. Why don't we cut straight to the chase?"

Marah couldn't help but frown at how weird the Earth saying sounded as it rolled off Beth's lips. She remained quiet, thinking about what she could do to help Joven.

"Did you commit a crime?"

Well, that was to the point.

Joven took his time. Marah assumed he was panicking but held her tongue. Beth turned to her, "Readings?"

She tapped the screen and fibbed, "Calm."

"I don't know if I would consider it a crime. I will say, he had it coming."

With Joven's first sentence, the yellow bar inched. With the second, the blue bar.

"Blue," was all Marah chose to say.

"What do you mean?"

Joven smiled, leaning back in his seat. "You have my file. You know the report and I know that your mind is already made up. Are you just giving me a common courtesy because of your friend there or because you have nothing better to do?"

Beth frowned and for the first time since they had met, anger glimmered in the baby blue of the Kosmirian's irises. "You have nothing to prove to me. Whether you are just a nobody with either terrible luck to be arrested three times, or incredibly lucky to somehow be released each time, you are the only powerless one here. Clearly, there's something about you since this is now your fourth time here. I'll assume that you know what that means, right?" Beth lifted her chin and Marah was beginning to see a different side to the girl. "What were you doing when you were arrested?"

"Buying flowers."

Marah raised an eyebrow. She expected him to have engaged in a fight or something. This was so simple, but it suggested the differences between her and who she worked for.

Joven's tone held a hint of sarcasm that made Marah's job a smidge easier. "Officer Kentar recognized me from a previous arrest. Guess he did not get the memo that I was out."

Blue inched forward.

Beth picked up a sheet of paper and read aloud triumphantly, "Because you escaped before your trial with the Chairwoman. Reading?"

Joven shook his head.

Obviously, the yellow bar stretched across the screen. Saying blue would be as obvious of a lie as the truth was. "It's mixed."

"Your file says that you assaulted an officer."

"He threw the first punch."

Blue took a step forward.

"A punch is still a punch. Why have you been arrested so many times? Your cases and mannerism match those of who we have found to be rebels."

"You tell me, you decide who gets arrested."

Both blue and yellow took a step forward.

Beth began to get frustrated. "And your location for buying flowers happens to be in the same location as an exceedingly popular rebel hangout. The only girl you could be buying flowers for is also arrested, so either you moved along very quickly," Beth tilted her hair, blonde coils mimicking snakes, "or flowers is a euphemism for something else."

Joven was quiet for a moment. "If you've hurt her..."

Beth leaned forward, "Answer my questions."

"I killed two birds in one stone. After buying flowers, I sought out the officer who targeted my heartmate because of all of my arrests."

Marah did not expect the brutal honesty. She quickly covered for him. "Yellow."

Joven was staring at her. "He came to start something. Mentioned my heartmate since I am very suspicious."

"Yel—"

Joven shook his head ever so slightly.

"—blue?"

Joven nodded.

Beth narrowed her eyes. "Is that a confession? You are a rebel?"

Joven smiled. "If being a rebel means stopping The Committee, then I'll gladly take the title." He turned, facing Marah head-on, "Go on, confirm it."

Marah looked at Beth and nodded.

At the face of disgust Beth made, Joven laughed. "Keep living in your picture-perfect world, you have no idea about the real one."

Beth stood up sharply and Marah held her breath, wondering what the rage that filled her eyes would compel her to do. Instead, she marked him as a confirmed rebel and threw his file on the table. "Marah, you get to do the honor of escorting him to prison. Put him in an isolated cell."

Marah nodded, taking the key to all of Joven's cuffs in her hands and slid it in her pocket after Beth freed Joven from being held to the table. She placed a hand on his shoulder and led him down the hall, but it was more of him leading her since he knew a moment before she did when to turn along the way.

After the third turn down the hall, Joven came to a stop. "I can take it from here."

Marah handed him the key and he quickly discarded his cuffs. "How are you going to get out of here?"

Joven smiled, wiggling his freed fingers. "Technically, you got me out." Marah didn't bother hiding her confusion.

"As far as Beth knows, I'm in a cell and so is my heartmate. By the time we escape, it'll be too late. Go, I'll be careful." He saw her face, "I won't hang out near flower shops, I swear."

In truth, Marah preferred to hold a bow and arrow than a brush or palette, while Beth delicately expressed herself on the canvas that was her face, with smooth penmanship. The only effort Marah put into her appearance was a concealer she decided to buy at the mall the night before for the stubborn bumps on her face—rubbing the minimum amount that would serve its purpose before closing the drawer.

She wasted no time heading to her nightstand and reached for her phone, which hadn't lost any battery since she received it.

Now that I think about it, the rebels never gave me a charger.

Marah: **Are we all set for tonight?**

L: **Yep. Joven will be leaving soon to meet you at the point. Whenever you get your first chance, take it.**

Marah: **Understood.**

"I wanted to ask," started Beth out of nowhere, "what did you think of the rebel?" Marah quickly shut her phone off. "What do you mean?"

"He had been arrested three times and was never detained as a rebel. I thought it would take more to make him confess. The rebels are a growing problem. Was there anything off on his readings?"

Beth sighed, rubbing glitter over her lips. Glitter covered her all over, from being sprinkled on her blonde coils to the blue and pink puffy gown that entailed princess-like sleeves and mesh-like material that collected evenly around the knees in a perfect ratio of shimmery pink and blue that clung from the knees and upward.

Marah held back a frown. "It was even. What did you expect?" She had already given Beth the truth, for the most part, but it frustrated her to have this conversation. Hopefully, it would be one of their last ones, she was beginning to tire herself from playing both sides of this fight.

"Some rebels lie their whole case, so a tower of yellow. Or a tower of blue. He must have known the system and what he was doing. Why admit to being a rebel if there was no concrete evidence as per the readings?"

Marah shrugged. "We'll find out soon, I guess. They are determined to fight for their cause," she found herself adding, "like us." Her gown was simple in style: a sequined ruby gown with an open back and a slit that rode up the lower thigh.

"Even when they stand against you?" Beth challenged as she slid her feet into heels.

There was that question of moral ambiguity again. She had killed for the same reason the invaders of Artemis had. But there was a difference between the rebels and the people that she was infiltrating—one killed because they wanted to, while the other killed to avenge and save lives. Maybe the rebels were the lesser of two evils, Marah considered, *and if they are, then so be it.*

Truthfully, Marah sighed. "I don't know."

She wasn't sure if she was more surprised at her honesty or Beth's hum of agreement. She wondered how much messier the rebels' fight would need to be and if she would follow the same path. She had become a much more tangled, looser version of herself, yet she had not had to compromise much of herself. Though, she had only spent a few months here and lived mostly through second-hand experiences.

Once she was satisfied with her hair, her gaze returned to her eyes in the mirror and for a minute she wished she could take off her glasses just so she could see herself while pondering her words.

It was one of the things that reminded Marah how little she had truly done for herself on Kosmir. She fought aliens, saved some, and was able to live among them. She grabbed her bag as Beth did the same, signaling that they were ready.

It was much farther than she ever thought she'd get, she reminded herself as she stepped into the cooled hallway. If all went well and Marah gave the rebels the Poten, she'd end it all.

Right?

She noticed Beth's fingers reach into her pocket before the alien's camera crossed her vision. She slipped into a smile too easily or at least, easily enough.

Beth gushed after snapping a few photos and uploading them on her social media, "This is going to be great! One party before we finish the rebels off," she winked, "then the real celebrating will begin."

It took Marah a decent amount of strength to pretend to share the blonde's enthusiasm about a gala that celebrated mass murder. The two joined the elevator brimming with those who were dressed to all numbers.

Marah had to bite her lip so she wouldn't make a snide comment about *all celebrating the deaths of how many innocents?* "How long does the gala last?" She needed to know how much time she'd have to execute the plan.

Beth laughed, "Probably after midnight, but not too late since we have work tomorrow." She waved at the crowds of people on the streets who saluted them.

Marah arched an eyebrow. "What's with the audience?"

Beth was glowing as she took in all of the attention, much like everyone else to a degree, "This is the biggest event ever!"

Marah nodded, watching beings from all realms pool inside the same joint, chattering amongst themselves as they took in the banners and flyers of The Committee and Chairwoman Kate. The sight before her was a whole other world compared to the one she saw upon her first steps on Kosmir. She expected that there were supporters of The Committee, but to actually see large masses rather than a divided crowd sent chills racing down her spine.

"I should tell you," Beth had her camera out to touch up lipstick, "there's a lot of alcohol at these parties, more alcohol than not so if you're not into that you might want to be careful."

"Noted. I'm afraid to ask, but what are we supposed to do there?"

"Sit back, relax, and have fun!"

"Right," appeased Marah. *Have fun at a booze-fest with the people who want to kill me.*

What could go wrong?

A booze-fest is an understatement. As Marah walked past doors coated with shimmering gold, the smell of champagne and cocktails wafted around her, a reminder of what her old life was like. The clinking of wine glasses and a well-played piano blended together like planned music, pondered the human as she walked alongside Beth, unsure of where they were supposed to go.

Though the alcohol made Marah uneasy, she was grateful for how large the hall was so she wouldn't have to worry about her lungs caving in on her.

The lights were dimmed, a cue Marah took to reveal that the Chairwoman was bound to enter. Despite this, Marah could still see perfectly in the hall that was as big as an airport terminal, especially the thrones in the center, with the one in the center being the grandest one.

A throne? A bit overkill.

In fact, everything about this is overkill.

Marah watched as members of The Committee moved around proudly, inflating their egos to the applause and declarations of praise and love.

She rolled her eyes, unable to believe how The Committee flaunted its prestige while the rebels had bare necessities.

Beth took a seat and Marah followed suit, uncertain of what else she was supposed to do. The sounds of her "coworkers" pressing their lips and bodies against each other caused the human's cheeks to flush as she skimmed the menu on the table.

She didn't get far as Beth sighed dreamily, resting her knuckles under her chin. "I'm really going to enjoy this, it's great to have a night off from worrying about rebel spies and just focus on the good things in life, y'know?"

Marah nodded. *Wouldn't you like to know?*

"So, roomie," enunciated Beth, "what do you want to do? There's a photobooth, a dance floor," she chuckled, "or we can stuff so much food in our faces that we can't work tomorrow."

Before Marah could think of a reply, the door was thrown open and everyone fell silent as a woman with high cheekbones decked to the nines entered the hall. Dressed in a black satin gown with a deep V-neckline that ended near the navel, flaunting a display of nicely rounded cleavage, all attention fell onto the woman. Satin also hugged shoulders and wrists, extending into an evening gown-like skirt that slit at the upper thigh. A sun-kissed jewel hung around Chairwoman Kate's rather thin neck and golden raindrops clung to cream ears. A glittering belt was wrapped around Chairwoman Kate's torso as she strutted inside with a dominating presence. More interesting to the human than the dagger strapped to her leg, was the fury that creased between her eyebrows and emanated from her every step.

Marah quickly averted her eyes away from the woman who reaped nothing but death and destruction. Behind her entered the Legionnaires, wearing suits and gowns of their own. They all took their seats and Marah forced her lips to remain flat as Chairwoman Kate reclined into her throne.

She rested her hands on the armrests as she surveyed the pawns of her success. "Good evening, all," her voice was smoother than silk, "I am delight to see all of you here."

Murmurs of greetings danced around Marah's ears.

"Organizations of power rarely last long amongst the cosmos," she paused to adore her audience and Marah noted how the woman relished in how every person staring at her face clung to every sound she uttered.

I wonder why, grumbled Marah as she recalled how empires had been slain by the very woman who acted as if she were royalty.

"So, it is truly an accomplishment to be here among you all. "Today," she accepted a glass from a waiter and held it out to make a toast, "we celebrate the fruits of our success. Today," she surveyed the entire crowd with curved lips the color of blood, "we celebrate you."

The crowd erupted in cheers and applause, why was something Marah would've paid good money to know.

Chairwoman Kate's eyes glistened as she placed a raised fist over her heart, which the audience took as a sign to ease off. She smiled, but Marah saw the smile was more for her than anyone else, "Let the festivities begin!"

Waiters and servers emerged from the shadows with long, slender glasses filled with sparkling liquid.

Marah half-smiled as a glass was placed in front of her. She didn't bother bringing the beverage to her lips like everyone around her, not because of the legality but because she needed to be focused. It did not help that the smell of the liquor was strong enough to drift her senses back to Earth and to her father. *He couldn't live a day without this damn stuff.*

Keep your composure, the voice in her head hissed while brushing a lock of hair over her ear to ensure that her comm was hidden. *Don't look suspicious, pretend that you're enjoying this.*

Beth stood up from her seat and dragged Marah with her, "C'mon, let's take some photos."

Marah begrudgingly followed, flashing a few smiles as a photographer snapped a dozen photos. She was about to come up with an excuse while they waited for the pictures to be ready, but to her surprise found Beth already holding two photosticks.

She slipped the stick Beth handed her in her pocket when Leia's voice crackled in her ear, "Take your chance."

She blurted to Beth who was humming along to the piano, "I just remembered, I forgot my phone back in our room. I'll be right back," she took a step quickly.

Beth was immediately at her side. "I'll go with you."

Marah eased the blonde back towards the festivities. "It's alright, I won't take long."

She didn't give Beth a chance to protest as she darted outside and pulled her phone out of her pocket. She unlocked it as she sped-walked and opened the file of the map.

Within minutes she entered The Citadel, seeing the Archives' location marked on the first floor.

"Which way is it?" she murmured as she headed past the elevators and security desks. "Where is what?"

Marah came to a halt, shoving her phone in her pocket and locking it. She raised a brow as she lifted her head to see London. "Sorry?"

London crossed his arms across his chest. "You said and I quote, which way is it?"

"Oh yes," replied Marah bashfully, "I'm looking for the restrooms."

London didn't relent as he squinted. "You don't know where the restrooms are by now? Why not use the restrooms at the hall?"

"Crowded," supplied Marah, hoping she didn't answer too quickly. "I needed to get away from the smell of alcohol there too. Now, if you don't mind, I'll be on my way."

"No," stiffened London, "I do mind."

Marah's brows furrowed. "And why's that?" The human felt her fingers curl into fists, something she felt would have to be used soon if this conversation headed the way she thought it would.

"Because," answered London as he took a step toward her, "there's something about you that isn't like the rest of us. You've been asking plenty of questions, and the more I look at you, the more you remind me of someone who Chairwoman Kate wants dead."

Marah's mind went numb, blood rushing to her fingers.

"At first, I thought it was just my mind playing tricks on me. Though, the more I look at you, the more I know that you're not one of us." He moved his hands from behind his back, revealing a pair of handcuffs, "Quite a coincidence, isn't it?" His voice made it clear it was anything but as he towered over her, "This time, *I'm* going to be the one reporting *you*," he spoke dangerously, "Marah Morana."

Marah shook her head. "I have no idea what you're talking about." She snatched her wrist away before London could grab it and swung it into his jaw, knocking him out.

She breathed out a shaky sigh of relief and walked away from London only to stop in her tracks as none other than Officer Kentar spoke in a clipped tone, "Well, what do we have here?"

Marah felt her blood rush through her body. *Does he also know who I am?*

"Care to turn around and explain yourself?"

The human exhaled softly, racking her brain as to how she was supposed to explain this while complying with the officer's orders. "You see, sir," she started, "I was on my way to use the restrooms, and I found him on the floor."

Officer Kentar raised a brow. "You found my son just lying on the floor?"

Marah nodded, "Yes, sir. I was about to get help, but I was nervous that something would happen to him if I left," she quickly added with a breath of relief, "but you're here now so…"

"Yes," spoke Officer Kentar, "I am here now. And that interrogation is going to happen the second I get security to analyze the camera feed."

Dammit!

Officer Kentar moved to grab her, but Marah stepped back, "I don't think so, sir."

"And what's that supposed to mean?"

Just at that moment, Beth stumbled through the glass doors, looking at Marah, then at an unconscious London sprawled on the floor behind her, and then at Officer Kentar. Right behind her came Clyna.

Because this cannot get any worse.

Beth's eyes widened. "What happened?"

Clyna remained separate from everyone else, and Marah wished she knew how to answer Beth's question when a voice spoke in her head: *What happened?*

Marah's brows as she matched the voice to Clyna and stared. *How are you in my head?*

Officer Kentar smiled, thick mustache making him look even more manic. "Yes, Adver, do tell."

She decided to answer Clyna first: *Was making my chance to grab the Poten. London stopped me, he knows who I am. Kentar wants to check the cameras to see what happened since I told him that I just found him on the floor.*

Clyna's face remained stoic except for the furrowing of black brows. *I'll handle it.*

Officer Kentar directed impatiently, "Miss Adver," he all but spat, "would you care to explain what I walked in on? If I have to wait another ten seconds, I won't bother with interrogations and arrest you myself."

Suddenly, all eyes were on Marah. She cleared her throat to speak, "Of course, sir, you see, I was on my way to use the restroom when I found London on the floor. I was going to get help but then I feared something would happen to him if I left."

Beth's sigh of relief gave Marah some hope.

"You're lying!" snarled Officer Kentar. He flexed a chubby finger toward Marah, "You're coming with me. Miss Bal, see to it that video footage is sent to my desk within ten minutes.

Clyna brought her right fist over her heart and headed past Marah.

Beth remained put, looking ready to whisk Marah away the moment Officer Kentar took another step toward her.

Officer Kentar noticed this and spoke in a clipped tone with rage threatening to loom, "Unless you're going to do something helpful, Liluana, leave. Adver, with me."

Marah sighed, "Can I at least use the restroom first?"

"Now."

Chapter 25

Location: The bruises that fade into the future

Marah couldn't sit comfortably, glancing around the grey-walled room she was going to be interrogated in. The room was the same as depicted in the movies when they detained prisoners, enforcing the idea of where she would end up if she did not play her part well. Pressing her weight into her heels, she sat straight while doing her best to get comfortable with the wiring on her fingers that would distinguish if reality or fiction spilled from her lips.

As if the itch from the wires on her thumbs wasn't enough to compel Marah to not do anything out of nervousness, the only barrier from the officer who eyed her like a fox about to devour its prey was a flimsy, rickety table. Not wanting to give Officer Kentar even more of a reason to interrogate her, nor the satisfaction, she cultivated poise despite the itch in her lungs that came from all the things that could go wrong.

The last time she had ever felt this trapped was a couple of years ago. It had been the last parent-teacher conference of her sophomore year. She had managed to evade the topic of college with all her teachers only to bump into her grade's guidance counselor, who, of course, had to bring it up with her parents. *Well, mother really.*

He had asked what colleges she was thinking of applying to.

Her mother had answered before Marah could realize that she had no clue, "We're actually thinking of early admissions to Stanford."

"Good for you!" The counselor even had the audacity to drawl, "What are you looking to major in?"

"Film studies?"

"Medicine," said her mother, much louder.

That had been so long ago. It felt even longer.

Officer Kentar stood in front of Marah; palms pressed against the smoothness of the table. "Name?"

"Nima Adver." The name had rolled off so easily that she knew the blue inched up the screen.

"Age?"

"Seventeen."

"Birthday?"

Marah contemplated a lie, but considered the chance that her birthday could incriminate her. "On the Kosmirian calendar, sixth day of the sixth week."

"What made you want to join The Committee?"

Marah willed her teeth and lips to move freely as she answered, "My friends wanted me to."

It was the truth, as unlikely as it sounded. Plus, if alien polygraphs worked like human ones, the only thing determining what color would inch up the screen would be based off how nervous she was.

Kentar continued with a smidge of disbelief, "Really? Not anything else? No sort of selfish or personal gain?"

"Nope." *Is that why you are here?*

Kentar looked over at the polygraph machine, "So you aren't lying. Yet."

Since there was no use in arguing, Marah merely spoke, "Next question, please?"

Kentar frowned, leaning closer to Marah before asking, "What's your hurry? You got someplace to be?" He raised a brow, "Or, are you trying to cause more problems?"

"The restroom," Marah reminded as if it were the most obvious question Kentar could have asked her. "Is this about when you startled me, and I pressed the green button by mistake? Are mistakes something you don't believe in?"

Kentar moved his hands off the table and began to pace around her as he articulated in a calculated manner, "I watched you that day. You read the manuals and continued to press the wrong button. That tells me you know what you were doing, therefore, not a mistake."

Marah frowned. She remained silent as she conjured up a feasible answer when a voice in her head inquired: *why was he watching me in the first place?*

Officer Kentar leaned closer to the human, who, despite feeling uncomfortable, didn't budge backward, "That's right." He sneered with flared nostrils, deeming Marah's silence as guilt. "You may just be a mere footnote in my life within The Committee, but a very suspicious one."

Marah raised her chin, forcing her light blue eyes to meet the officer's. "You can think that, but that is your only evidence of any wrongdoing despite everything else that I have done here." She spoke coolly while maintaining respect.

Kentar scoffed, pulling out a seat. "Tell me about yourself."

Marah tilted her head, eyeing the camera in the farthest corner from her. "Well, you and your son have been stalking me, how about you tell me?"

Kentar raised a brow. "I don't owe you that."

"Whatever, what do you want to know?"

"What planet are you from?"

Marah paused. Her heart began to beat faster as she tried to remember if she had ever discussed her ruse's origins before.

The omen of avenging perished souls steeled her resolve. "I'm Kosmirian." She practically was. She breathed its air, talked, and lived among its people, and was fighting for it. Her true nature was always in the back of her head, attached to her new, temporary nature.

She caught a glimpse of both blue and yellow moving up.

Confusion betrayed the officer's face. "How do you plan to maintain a universe without war?"

What about the war brewing right under your feet?

"I'm not sure it's possible. Not until the rebels' fight is over."

Marah didn't need to see the blue rise on the screen to know it did. "What do your parents do?"

Within an instant, Marah was in her old home. She could see the dust that filled her mother's office and the filing cabinets that documented dozens, if not hundreds of legal cases. As much as she hated the room because it mirrored the vision her mother had of her, it was the only other room besides hers that never faintly smelled of alcohol. She saw the room where she grew up in and could taste bitterness on her tongue.

In a flash, she was back.

So used to lying on the spot, Marah didn't even realize that what she was saying wasn't a complete lie. "My mother was a lawyer. My father was a mechanic. Most of the time."

Kentar frowned, "Most of the time? You don't know your father's career?"

"No, I don't," Marah defended. "You're here to interrogate me, not ask about my parents." She itched to remain still, yet she was eager to get out of here and find the Archives.

Kentar glowered at her. "I'm the boss here, so you're going to answer as I tell you. You never answered what happened."

"I already told you," said Marah exasperated. "You can watch the footage and see for yourself."

Again, both colors rose on the screen.

"Fine," sighed Kentar, "you're done. I'm keeping my eyes on you, though. Now, get out."

Marah spared not even a second in peeling the wires off and shutting the door behind her, where she was surprised to see Beth standing, waiting for her.

She seemed to have listened to the whole interrogation, which struck her as a little odd.

Had she seen the readings?

The blonde popped a gumball bubble as she bumped elbows with Marah. "Such a jerk! I hope you're okay, I was worried he was going to hurt you. Now that that's over, let's go have some fun!"

Chapter 26

Location: Living for the living legend

Marah resisted a yawn as she pressed her face into her hands. True to Beth's word, the gala had lasted well into the morning and there wasn't enough time for the human to get much sleep.

Carrying cases of cameras, she observed two kinds of workers: those like Beth who were able to carry on as if they had a perfect rest and those who, like her, had no clue how such a thing was possible.

She also did not get the chance to explain her absence to the rebels or the lack of obtaining the Poten.

Which left them with another problem; they now had to plan their heist in broad daylight with Beth, still as clingy as ever, and Officer Kentar, still as wary as ever.

Clyna must have caught the rebels up to speed since Natira asked over the comms, "How did the interrogation go?"

After handing the old cameras to an officer, she pulled out her phone and quickly typed: Well, I think. But, he's still a pain in the neck.

I'm thinking of looking for the Archives during lunch, all I have to do is be free. At least, London's in the infirmary with no recollection of last night.

Thankfully.

When Natira spoke, Marah could tell that the Nantak's irritations were just as much as hers, "You're right. Beth and Kentar are two key obstacles. You know," she added with a snicker, "the whole secret rivals plus the roommates cliche would make a great fanfic. I have to give you humans some credit; it's cute how you try to rewrite destiny."

Marah replied in a voice dripping with irritation, "Roommates, thanks to you." She dodged an elbow to the chest, remarking, "These hallways remind me of high school." Approaching her seat, she was surprised to see that for the first time Beth looked *upset?*

Beth's features were contorted in a way that was different than usual, in ways that Marah wouldn't have picked up without spending so much time with the girl. Her painted lips were set in a firm line and her perfectly smooth cheeks and forehead had creases in them. It also appeared the eyes that were normally filled with light, had their flames extinguished, and she wore an unreadable expression.

Concern laced Marah's voice as she asked, "Beth?"

"Yeah? What's up?"

Marah met the girl's eyes, though Beth didn't return the gesture, "Is something wrong?"

Beth sighed softly, "Have you ever had a fake friend before?"

The human hoped her cheeks weren't as pink as she felt they were. "Not really, you?"

Beth wore a sheepish smile. "Plenty. Usually, they were pranks to be the girl who was head over heels for someone to call a friend, or small flings like my exes, but ever since I met this person, all I wanted was to have a true friendship."

Marah could only pray that Natira still wasn't on comms, "Who's this person? Do they work here?"

Beth nodded, baby blue eyes finally sparkling as she confided, "Yeah, she does. I'm so grateful to have her as a friend. She's dorky," her lips curved upward, "she makes me feel like there's someone who I can relate to, y'know?"

Natira was doubling over in laughter as she managed to speak through cackles, "She's not wrong about you being dorky."

God, save me please.

"Thing is," said Beth, "I'm scared that I'm not a good enough friend. I know it's childish and stupid, but after trying to be friends with so many people and ending up with awful relationships, I just don't want to get hurt again."

If only she knew.

Natira cackled as Beth continued, "I really like her as a friend. She's great." The blonde sighed and blue eyes found blue. "I can tell she's been through some stuff, and I want to support her and show her she's worth more than she thinks."

That's actually so sweet.

It pained Marah to pretend to be oblivious. "I'm sensing a but?" Unable to digest the irony of her situation, she logged into her computer and opened a file to work out so her hands would have something to do.

Beth pouted, "I had a dream about a not so good relationship. It just has me wondering if this is all I'm meant for. I've suffered so much alone for so long; I'd hate to be burned again." She lamented, voice somber, "But, she's different," the Kosmirian fidgeted with her fingers, cracking knuckles decorated in slim gold rings, "she's a really good person and we're good friends, but there's this voice in my head reminding me how scared I am to lose our friendship."

Torn, Marah could only offer, "If she's as great of a friend as she sounds, I think you should just take things one day at a time. Not everyone is out to get you," she smiled, "and all types of relationships can be scary, so you just have to have patience with yourself.

I don't want to break your heart any more than I already have to.

Beth smiled, but the noirette could tell that the woman did not feel like smiling as she spoke coolly, "Yeah, you're right. Thanks."

Marah moved a hand to her forehead, frowning at the little bumps that grazed against her fingertips. She began to feel awkward and a twinge of guilt for how she had treated Beth since she arrived at the Citadel. She hadn't meant to become friends with Beth; she couldn't consort with the enemy—let alone become best friends with them!

Why is life so hard? Said everyone ever.

Marah exhaled softly as she tried to find something to distract herself from Beth but was unsuccessful as Beth sneaked occasional glances at her.

"Sounds like you're in a bit of a pickle," chuckled a voice Marah hadn't heard in a while.

She refrained from saying his name with Beth right in front of her. She tapped her comm as if she had picked up a call and talking to an old friend, which—technically, she was. "How are you?"

"Doing good, the others are busy so I'm running the comms. Since I'm very wanted," Joven snickered, "just not in the way I'd like. Plus," Marah imagined him leaning back and twirling something in his fingers as he normally did when he paused, "Natira said there's drama and as a heartmate, I couldn't not listen. She's getting more *pizka* and what you insist on calling soda if you're curious."

Marah chuckled at how amused Joven sounded. "I'm glad the two of you are enjoying this. Heartmate?"

"It's the equivalent of what you would call a soulmate. By the way, I've been meaning to thank you the other day for saving Pasca." Joven's voice was thick with gratitude and Marah theorized that the girl she had saved was Joven's heartmate.

"You're very welcome," the rebel smiled, "I couldn't not help her."

"I hope you didn't get in too much trouble for that," the rebel spoke sincerely. "We revised the plan."

"Do tell." Marah could not help but feel a rush of adrenaline at the idea of fulfilling the yearning in her heart to take this place down.

"By taking the Poten, the Citadel loses power, except for the Chairwoman's private elevator. That's because it works based off her powers, which is its own prestigious thing. While the original plan was for you to go straight to the Archives, we hadn't accounted for the Citadel's AI stopping you."

"I didn't know there was one." Marah was more than a smidge grateful that London had been the one to catch her and not the Chairwoman's personal AI system, which would probably scan her face and ruin everything.

"Good thing for London, then," mused Joven as if he had read her mind. "You take the elevator back down, get the Poten, and then we'll attack."

"That sounds perfect." All that was missing was the execution of said plan. *Cue getting to the Archives.*

"See you then," she added to make her conversation more fluid, pulse thrumming with her impatience of waiting for the opportunity to present itself, eager for all of this to be over.

What would you do then?

Marah would go home, at least that's what her old self would declare. The minute she was done as a crusader it'd be "See ya!

Sayonara!" and then she'd go back to living her boring life as if nothing had ever happened.

But now?

The human wasn't so sure. She had a whole world to explore with people who enjoyed her for who she was. People who could see the worth she had, that she didn't. *I never had that before, and it's something really nice to have.*

The rebels, all of them, even with their bold personalities, were her friends. Marah couldn't, wouldn't, leave them and Kosmir as if none of this had ever happened.

Just as she decided upon that, she realized that her break had started. Before Beth could propose a lunch plan despite them both eating a late breakfast of tacsa, a traditional Zonan dish with what Marah could only describe as a form of rice, sprinkled with potatoes and a cheese sauce, Marah stood and moved toward the place that the Archives was hidden. She needed to make sure she could get there in any way that she needed and once she could confirm that she knew where exactly she needed to go, she and the rebels would be in the clear.

She pulled out her phone to take a quick glance, making sure that she was heading in the right direction. She walked past the workstations and toward an area of the building that she hadn't been to before, with less people and more fountains, statues, and plaques.

Then she realized that she was in one of the housing areas as she noticed people walking among the floors above. She walked further, zooming in on the map and found a bright red mark beside a statue that she was approaching.

The statue of Chairwoman Kate was massive. It was easily fifteen feet tall composed of smooth white marble, and if Marah had wrinkled her face to cringe at the sight, she would've missed the slight tint of color directly behind the statue compared to the general wall.

"I found it," she said softly, realizing the power of her words.

"Tomorrow, we move," was her only reply. At least, the only words that Marah could pay attention to as her attention drifted off in rumination of what tomorrow would entail for her as both Marah Morana and a rebel; tomorrow would bring her the end of false smiles and the close of Nima Adver's story. Tomorrow would bring a new era for Marah Morana, and if all went well, would be the start of a new universal order.

Chapter 27

Location: Where the deceivers reign

Marah adjusted her supposedly element-lined frames as she walked alongside Beth, mind and mouth in polar opposite realms. While the rebel spy's mouth spewed lines of how she couldn't wait for the incomparable glory of defeating the rebels once and for all, all her conscience could think about was when she would get the signal to begin the end of The Committee.

All Marah could do was hope that nothing would go wrong as she swapped cases of old cameras and new cameras. She couldn't help but think about what would happen, unconsciously picking at her fingernails, and her feet refused to stop bouncing, reinforcing the dryness in her throat.

Marah exhaled softly, letting her eyes flutter closed to steady herself.

"What are you nervous about?"

Marah's teeth missed her nail and instead sunk into soft flesh, accidentally tearing it as warm liquid filled in the spy's mouth.

She turned to see a familiar young woman with golden-brown skin cock a plasma ray, slipping the fluid-filled batteries into her pocket before placing it on the conveyor belt where it'd end up in an unfortunate soldier's hands.

Clyna patiently repeated curiously, "You look nervous. Usually you're chill with Beth, what's up? Where is she?"

Marah dismissed her co-worker's concern. "It's nothing. I'm alright. She's at interrogations again." She remembered that Clyna could read her thoughts, so she resumed working.

"Again?" Clyna shrugged, "Oh, Azni and Jana brought donuts for the party later today. I wasn't sure if you knew or not, but Sonia from check-ins said that they had something big to announce."

Marah spared the alien a glance, faking intrigue, "What do you think the announcement is?"

Clyna spoke as if it was a secret that she had told everyone, "Between you and me, I think they're having a kid. Cher was mentioning that there's something off about them and couples don't really celebrate much in public aside from birthdays, anniversaries, or pregnancies, so…"

Marah hummed absentmindedly as they were dismissed. "Maybe. They've been together for a while, huh?" *Good thing Beth's always rambling about Committee gossip.*

"Definitely," continued Clyna, walking with Marah back to their workstation. "They've been dating since their first years here, and Azni proposed three years ago." She smiled softly, "In time, they'll make great parents."

Marah then understood the point of Clyna's words.

My timing has to be perfect, no Kentar, London, or Beth.

Marah couldn't help but groan under her breath as a familiar woman approached her.

Beth took her seat with a wide smile on her face as she exclaimed with her hands, "I got it all figured out!"

Marah raised a brow as she prepared for Beth's answer, "Figured what out?"

Marah noticed Kentar out of the corner of her eye amongst the sea of people who roamed through the halls. He was standing perfectly straight with his arms crossed over his chest as he wore a pointed look that Marah was sure was meant for her. She rolled her eyes before fixating her gaze to Beth who revealed excitedly, "I spent all night thinking; I'm going to have a proper conversation with her so we're on the same page."

Marah smiled, logging into her computer for what would be the last time. "That's great!" she congratulated, "what's your idea?"

Beth was practically vibrating and spoke animatedly, throwing her hands around so much that Marah couldn't keep track of what she was doing, "I'll ask her to go out to dinner together, my cousin works at a restaurant and her *noozles* are the best. We'll talk about the things holding us back."

Marah averted her eyes as she raised her lips on one end, "I can't wait to hear if she says yes."

Beth faltered, and Marah assumed the Kosmirian must have remembered her dilemma.

Clyna suddenly spoke up, "Good for you, Beth! I just remembered that Officer Kentar needs you to run down the reports for all the weapons at your earliest convenience." Once the blonde was well out of earshot, Clyna hissed quietly, "You need to get into the Chairwoman's office per the plan. Now."

Marah blinked. "Now? No one said anything—"

Clyna interrupted patiently, "I'm your signal. Go in an elevator by yourself. One hundredth floor. Two guards, take them out. The code for her office is 3664. Once you get inside, put this drive in her computer, it'll disable Iris."

Marah frowned as she slipped the drive into her pocket, "Now?"

"Go! urged Clyna, already briskly walking away, "I'll handle the Chairwoman."

Marah stood up abruptly, taken aback from how sudden all of this was. Clyna shooed her away as Marah nearly tripped on her way to the elevators. She slipped into the first open one and announced the floor she intended to go to, all while pretending to miss someone shouting at her to hold the door.

She put her glasses in her pocket and rolled up her sleeves before turning on her comm, "I'm going up."

"Good luck," said someone over the comms just as the doors pulled apart.

Marah was greeted with two officers who didn't look happy to see her. She brought up a hand awkwardly, "How's it going?"

The officer on the left stiffened at the sight of her, "You're not supposed to be here."

"And The Committee shouldn't be killing people, but here we are."

With Marah's allegiance revealed, the officer lunged for her, an attack the human easily dodged.

The female officer held up a gun. "Stand down. I'll shoot."

Marah raised her hands, causing the officer to relax a little. Just as the woman lowered the gun, she smashed her foot onto the woman's hand, causing the weapon to skitter away.

Before the officer could move, Marah's other foot crashed against the officer's nose. There was a sharp snapping sound, which Marah assumed to be the woman's nose breaking. The officer stumbled against a wall from the impact, rendered unconscious.

A rough pair of hands grabbed her from behind and pushed her against a wall, an arm grabbing both of Marah's wrists to keep the rebel in place. He alerted over his comm while trying to restrain Marah's hands, "We got a rebel trying to break in. Floor 100, I repeat—"

Marah stomped her foot on top of the officer's, causing him to jerk backward. She then used his pain as an opportunity to get him off her and yanked his comm, "False alarm. Just a wrong floor resident." She dropped the device to the floor before crushing it with her heel.

Just as the officer stood back up, Marah punched him right in the jaw and watched as his eyes rolled back, body following. She didn't bother hiding the bodies as she raced toward the Chairwoman's office.

She hastily punched in the four-digit code before throwing the door open.

A robotic voice blared upon her entry. "You are not authorized to be here. You have exactly thirty seconds before I remove you."

Ignoring Iris, Marah inserted the drive into the first slot she saw. "The drive's in, what do I do?"

The rebels' head on technology spoke, twinged with urgency and excitement, "Sit tight, once the screen turns black, you'll be in the clear of her."

"Remove yourself or I will have you removed."

A faint laser illuminated over her chest and Marah looked around the room wildly for the invisible weapon.

"Twenty seconds to surrender yourself before I alert Chairwoman Kate." The laser brightened in color, alluding to the AI's threat as Marah stepped to the side only for the AI to be a step ahead of her.

"Fifteen seconds. Running facial scan."

Marah jerked her head back, but it was too late. "How much longer?" Panic thrummed in her veins, "Time's running a bit short."

"Ten seconds. The rebels are about to descend on the Citadel."

"Ten seconds to surrender," Iris gleefully aired, "Marah Morana. In that case, you must surrender now." The small laser dot expanded in size and just as it was about to shoot at her, it disappeared altogether, and the AI was rendered silent.

Blood thrumming in her ears, Marah bolted toward the Chairwoman's elevator, not bothering to wait for the doors to fully open before throwing herself inside, which Marah had to admit was rather exquisite with a pearl and charcoal interior. Bouncing on her toes, Marah declared her intended floor and waited in painstaking silence as she began to descend downward, knots in her stomach tying together.

Marah was out of the elevator before the doors were fully open, revealing what had become of the Citadel.

The Citadel had become utter chaos. Everyone was screaming and running around as rebels, and rebel spies, launched their attacks. Tables were flipped and panicked workers turned to officers—who were just as confused—for some form of instruction. Marah detected the faint sound of crying near her as everyone and everything was nothing but a blur of bodies.

Marah sucked in a breath, focusing her vision before darting between herds of people to where the Archives lay hidden. She pushed past people, not caring about staying undercover as she bolted past a table with donuts and a sign that read: *We're pregnant with twin boys!*

How nice.

Marah yelped as she all but flung herself at the wall behind the statue of the Chairwoman, frantically rubbing her hands over the off-colored paint as she searched for the right spot. "Please open, secret door, please!" she grunted impatiently while banging on the wall.

Suddenly, she heard a snapping sound and her vision blurred before she could even realize that it had. Her eyes fell shut as the floor spun beneath her, only opening once she had come to a halt. She knew she had hit the right spot because when she opened her eyes, she found herself long gone from the chatter and bustle on the Citadel's main floor.

Taking in the quietness, Marah breathed out, "I think I'm inside the Archives?"

Kiera, Leia, and Natira all shouted at the same time, "You *think?*"

Marah walked further down the secret tunnel as she replied, "I'm pretty sure I am." She paused, realizing what she confirmed, and then trekked further into the unknown territory, jogging to a sunlit tunnel-like opening that beckoned her forth.

Marah complied with the inaudible demand as she walked through the opening, only for the breath to be stolen from her mouth as she became victim to her surroundings.

"Woah," she exhaled in a manner that was soft and measured as if she was just revealed the greatest secret of the universe. She may as well have been as she marveled at the living legend that was the Archives.

Glittering columns and obelisks stretched from floor to the top of the glass ceiling, demonstrating just how tall the building was, both inside and out. The pillars were decorated with sparkling stone and ivory-like material as they depicted faces and bodies of many. Mosaics stretched from the floor all the way, surrounded by bookshelves holding holy artifacts amongst thick leather-bound books.

Marah couldn't believe that she was standing in the place many powerful figures had.

She pondered the matter as she finally regained control of her limbs, taking a couple of steps as her eyes glazed by hundreds, if not, thousands of ancient texts covered in rusted spines and glossy pages that protruded out of soft, worn covers.

Marah remarked quietly, unable to fathom how something so beautiful could be so hidden from everyone, "This is incredible."

"Marah?"

Light reflected from above, and when Marah looked up, the noirette was star-struck with a grand chandelier that lit the room with such a sense of strength one would think its sheer light was a weapon forged of the brightest flames.

A trail of orange swam past her vision, beckoning her forth, so she followed the light all the way to a glowing sphere standing on a pillar cased in glass, preventing its content from leaking.

The Poten was much smaller than she had expected, it was about the size of a toaster, and yet there was something about the sphere that captivated Marah in a way she couldn't describe.

"Woah." The word slipped out before the girl could even realize that she had said something as she stared ahead at raw power.

Someone urged on the comms, "Woah, what? What's happening?"

Marah's voice was detached and clinical, and her eyes began to sparkle with the reflection of the Poten, "The Poten. It's right here." Utterly captivated by what the Poten had to offer, the noirette moved closer to it. It was almost as if the human was in a trance with the Poten calling her forth, and she indulged in what the invite would have to offer.

Someone was speaking on the comms, but whoever it was sounded fuzzy to Marah who merely ignored the voice as she grazed a hand over the Poten's cover and lifted it. Her hands fell slack as the case slipped through her fingers, causing glass to shatter to pieces as it ricocheted off the floor.

"What was that?" someone shouted frantically. They sounded scared. "Take the Poten and get the hell to the meeting point!"

Another voice echoed against Marah's eardrums, calmer than the previous speaker, "Do you have the Poten?"

Marah remained silent, watching the device pulse, emitting jets of orangish energy. Before the human could register it, the sphere became all she could think about.

What's your hurry? soothed a foreign voice in her head. *The power? Going home? Tell me.*

All Marah could do was breathily reply, "You know me?"

"Of course I do," prompted the hypnotic voice softly, making Marah focus solely on the voice and not anything else, "You're Marah Morana. You love archery, your favorite color is yellow, and you display symptoms of insomnia and childhood trauma."

That's not creepy.

Marah's voice was trance-like as she slurred, "How do you know all of that?"

That's totally creepy. Take the Poten and run. Don't run. Sit and chat.

"There's a lot of them!"

"I know everything about everyone," hummed the Poten's silky voice. Orange brightened in color, as if a fire kindled. "Even your mission to end The Committee, the very beings I am designed to protect."

Huh?

Marah jolted back to reality at the sound of someone speaking, "Well, well, well. If it isn't the rookie who claimed to be oh so innocent. I always knew you were a bad apple. Now, I'm going to do what I should've done the second I laid eyes on ya. Turn around with your hands up. Now."

Did I just get psyched?!

Marah's mind produced no voice and her heart hammered in her chest as all she could think about was how on Earth, *Kosmir actually*, she was supposed to bring the Poten to Joven now. Not wanting to worsen her situation, she complied with the officer's orders, taking a slight step back as she faced Officer Kentar and six others.

Officer Kentar crossed his arms over his chest, fingertips just out of reach of a gun as he came toward Marah and reached for her. Before he could succeed, Marah reacted by shoving an elbow to his chest, causing the officer to bend over in pain.

Officer Kentar moved to rise, but Marah kicked the officer in the chest, keeping him down. "What?" she retorted as she faced the remaining officers that were all poised to attack, "is no one going to read me my rights or is that not a thing here?"

"Don't just stand there! Seize her!" snarled Kentar, fumbling for his weapon.

The first officer to approach her was Kentar's timid patrol buddy. He fired from his blaster. The rebel easily dodged the attack, prompting the officer to swing a fist at her. The noirette caught said fist and returned the favor with a sharp jab to the nose. The officer stumbled back only for Kentar to take his place instead.

Marah stepped back at the pointed weapons, only to end up in Kentar's hands as he yanked her to the ground. Her face slammed on the ground hard and before she could register the pain, there was a humming sound of electricity and the next thing the human knew, it was lighting her on fire.

She held back an anguished shout as electricity waves flashed around her, stinging every part of her that it could touch. Her face contorted in pain, more so when she realized how she had fallen. Straining, she moved her foot, touching Officer Kentar so he, too, could share her pain.

With the first of his screams, the assault evaporated altogether.

Despite the lingering shaking, the officers moved to shoot plasma weapons at her. Some shots she would've been able to miss were it not for her hitched breathing and recovery from being electrocuted. The blasts hit her shoulders and knees, drawing bruises and blood down her uniform.

Just like sparring with the rebels, she thought as plasma rays blurred past her vision too many times for her to count. During the chaos, one of the officers got close enough to yank her up and aimed to punch her in the head.

Marah threw her head back at the same time as she brought her feet to the officer's chest and pushed hard, forcing them apart. Marah landed back on the ground, her wince deepening.

There were still plenty of officers left, and Marah had a feeling more were on their way.

Every second I spend here is one more that the rebels are fighting, and I don't have the Poten.

The officers showed no signs of stopping and neither did Officer Kentar, who took the liberty to fire as much as he possibly could at her, so she rolled toward the nearest pillar and ducked, pressing her fingers against the cool marble as she attempted to think of how to remedy her problem.

"All slight problems," she muttered, feeling her shoulder, and staining her fingers with blood, "emphasis on slight."

Out of the corner of her eye, Marah noticed a tube looped to the belt of the officer she rendered unconscious. She peered forward, trying to figure out what it was, but jerked backward as a bullet flew past her, chipping off a piece of marble that was too close to Marah for her liking.

She crouched low and reached for the weapon, flinching every time she heard ricocheting bullets and fizzing blasts. Once she unsnagged the tube, she threw herself backward and missed a bullet to her cheek by a fraction of an inch.

"Alright," mused Marah as she pressed the only button on the tube and it expanded into a crossbow that wasn't entirely a crossbow, "this can't be too hard. Just like shooting a regular arrow." She looked over her shoulder and positioned the gun in the direction of the officers. The weapon was small, so the rebel struggled to find a clear shot but fired anyway.

Marah didn't know where she had shot, nor had she realized that her eyes were closed until she opened them to see no difference than before. She grumbled and resumed shooting in all directions, causing some officers to retreat or shield themselves behind various obelisks.

Marah pressed on the trigger once again, and this time nothing fired.

Come on!

Officer Kentar must've been on the same page as Marah as he threw his gun down in frustration. "This is going nowhere! Stand down, she's mine! Come out, rebel scum!"

Marah obliged, practically leaping to her feet with a hand still fastened around the gun. Anything could be a weapon, something she knew well. After all, she was one herself.

"Nowhere else to run," drawled Kentar as he stood in front of the line of officers, towering in front of both Marah and the Poten, "It's just you and me. I've been itching to get rid of you for a while, so I must say," he smirked as his fingers clenched into fists, "bring it on."

Everyone has their own fighting technique, Natira had told her once during a sparring session. *Find it. Learn it. Exploit it.*

Marah opened herself up for attack as she clenched the handle of the crossbow tighter. "After you."

Kentar strutted toward the human and threw a punch that Marah caught with ease. However, he summoned more strength into his punch, guiding both of their hands in a slam into her chest. She was then met with the officer's other fist, that collided into Marah's abdomen, causing the girl to fall backwards onto the ground.

Marah's teeth sunk into the pink flesh of her lips as a wince overcame her face, back pressed against the waxed, now-slippery floor, with Kentar hovering above her. Her chest stung and Marah could feel bruises begin to form atop her ribs that felt fractured where everything beneath the skin hurt a little more than a typical punch would.

What is his power, Marah yearned to scoff, *super strength?*

Kentar laughed hoarsely as he kicked Marah's wrist, causing the crossbow in her hand to skid across the floor. Despite the throb in her bones, Marah moved but collapsed from the impact of Kentar's heavy boots.

He didn't need to apply much pressure to render her stuck. Amused with his success, Kentar left Marah to writhe in pain before kicking her away, and she rolled against the pillar the Poten sat atop. "Well, that was easy. Give up and Chairwoman Kate might let you live, traitor."

Oh, it is definitely bad breath.

Marah burst into snickers as she ran a hand over her bleeding lip. "I wonder though, will Chairwoman Kate let you live knowing that you let Marah Morana slip through your fingers several times?"

Officer Kentar's head whirled so quickly Marah thought his neck might snap. He staggered, voice dangerously thin, "What. Did. You. Just. Say?"

"I said," repeated Marah, who fought her muscles to stand upright, "I wonder what Chairwoman Kate will do to you once she finds out that you let Marah Morana slip right past you undetected." She reached for the Poten behind her and pressed it against Kentar's chest, where orange pulses of energy smacked into the officer, rendering him unconscious.

Woah.

The sound of cocked weapons reminded Marah of her dilemma, provoking her to raise the Poten, ready to wield the device if necessary. Unfortunately, the human was vastly outnumbered, and she didn't trust the Poten as far as she could throw it.

"I'm sure we can talk about this," she started as she counted the number of plasma guns that were pointed at her.

Marah didn't receive any reply.

Well, this is awkward, she thought as she rolled on her heels. "I can go first?"

Marah waited with bated breath when suddenly, all the officers collapsed to the ground. Behind the slumped bodies stood Clyna with tendrils of magic swarming from her palms.

"They're not dead, if that's what you're worried about. Just a sleep hex," explained Clyna. The Kosmirian's voice suddenly became flooded with urgency as she exclaimed, "You need to get out of here, now! I'll cover for you, go!"

Marah nodded, thanking the spy before bolting off with the Poten. Her heels clicked against the flooring and for a moment she was worried that the sound was going to give her away but realized that it didn't matter. *Might as well go out with a big bang, huh?*

She expected that once she escaped the alcove that was the Archives, she'd be met with Committee soldiers blocking the exit.

Instead, she was met with no such unpleasantries. The lights were still off, so the rebel spurred onward, eyes scouring for the exit.

She pushed past people, not caring about anything except for getting the Poten to the rebels.

She panted as she just remembered that she had a comm in her ear and people waiting for her cue, "I'm on my way to meet Joven." She lowered her tone, "I got the Poten."

Out of nowhere, Beth appeared next to Marah, trying to keep up with the rebel's pace but failing to, "Nima? What's going on, why are we running and what are you holding?" She shook her head, curls bouncing, "Never mind that, I've been meaning to ask you something."

You have got to be kidding me!

Marah let out a sigh of annoyance as she complied. She owed it to Beth to at least let her speak before she ended whatever friendship they had.

Beth smiled gratefully, "Thanks. I know I haven't known you for a while, so I understand if this might come across strangely."

"The point, Beth," said Marah with gritted teeth.

"Right," replied Beth bashfully. "The point is, I really value our friendship. I know there are some things holding us back, and I want us both to overcome them. Would you like to go for dinner tonight, just you and me? My cousin owns this *noozle* shop and she said that she'd host us for free—"

Beth was cut off by the sound of footsteps and cocked weapons as someone roared, "What are you waiting for? Get her!"

Marah bit her lip, preventing a string of profanities from slipping out of her lips. "I really am sorry, Beth." Before Beth could react, she punched Beth square in the jaw just as a device rolled by Marah's ankle.

When the human looked down, her eyes widened like saucers. Before the rebel spy could even react, the grenade beeped, and then a loud explosion rattled the interior of The Citadel, sending Marah hurtling forward and flying smack into a marble pillar.

The impact of Marah's body against the pillar was rough as she dropped to her back. She sluggishly rolled onto her stomach and huffed.

At least I still have the Poten, she thought as she staggered to her feet among the screams and chaos that unfolded around her.

Someone shouted—who—Marah had not even the faintest of clues, "Take her down by any means necessary, but keep her alive for the love of the Chairwoman! Arrest the rebels!"

Marah came to a stop, watching the rebels do their best to maintain their ground. Each rebel was outnumbered by at least three officers and workers, and Leia was holding up a purple force field over an injured rebel whose face was too blurry for Marah to see. Not too far from the Novan's fight was Clyna being forced onto the ground by London while Kiera and Natira fought only to be met with more resistance.

The two exchanged eye contact briefly as Clyna screamed across the hall, "Take the Poten and run, Marah!"

Marah didn't get the chance to think about what was going to happen to the rebels as coils of white collided into the girl and once again, she went flying.

She felt helpless as she was flung several yards forward, face-first and only had enough time to use her arms to shield her head from the impact. This time, the landing was so hard that when Marah slammed into the ground, her lungs seized, and a spell of dizziness overcame her.

She let out a low groan as a bloodied hand moved to her side where her clothes were now ashy and stained. "Natira was right," grumbled the human as she blinked, dazed, "getting blasted really does hurt." Her glasses had disappeared amongst the chaos, and when she stood despite aching, protesting limbs and cleared the frizzy hair out of her face she realized that that wasn't the only thing gone missing.

The Poten was nowhere in sight.

She exclaimed a curse while turning to look for it, "Where did it go?"

Natira shouted followed with a static-like echo, "Get out of there if you haven't already!"

Another curse slipped out of Marah's lips as the rebel looked behind her, where Chairwoman Kate and the Legionnaires were catching up to her. If she went back for the Poten, she'd compromise herself, but if she didn't, they'd lose the Poten.

Reluctant to do so, Marah sank her teeth into already bruised and bleeding lips and headed toward the exit, pushing past everyone and everything in her way, hating the ache that filled her heart as she left the Poten behind. Everything became a blurry mess of non-stop motion as she pushed past whatever she could, to get to the glass doors that *were so close yet so far*.

"Freeze!" screamed someone behind her.

Marah paid no heed as she practically threw open the doors and took off running toward the alley where she was supposed to meet Joven and just managed to hear the Chairwoman screech, "After her!"

Static filled Marah's ears as someone spoke too fast and too loudly. When she looked up, two rebels were flung through the windows, shattering glass as they tumbled onto the street. One of those rebels was Kiera and she would've gone to help were it not for someone speaking on the comms too fast and too loudly, "Abort mission! We're surrounded! The lights are back on!"

If Marah couldn't breathe before, she definitely couldn't breathe at the fear in the voice, causing her heart to skip several beats. It took everything within the human to not look back as the sound of bullets and sizzling streaks of color continued to echo against her eardrums. Despite the throb that burned in her heart and lungs, she spurred herself to go faster, hoping that no one was around to potentially get hurt in the crossfire.

Glancing at the street names, Marah tripped as she flung herself into an alley, landing sprawled on her hands and knees. She gasped as her skin scraped cement, and moved deeper into the alleyway in case her shooters were coming.

She pressed her back against a wall scribbled in graffiti, panting as oxygen and carbon dioxide filtered through her lungs, allowing the human to catch her breath.

"Where's the Poten?"

Joven was wearing a cloak that covered just enough of his face to be recognizable. Golden glittering rings hugged the Stellan's almond eyes that the so-called Chosen One could not afford to look at.

Marah shook her head, unable to summon her voice. She looked straight ahead of her at graffiti that could only be done by a rebel and sputtered a wheeze, "I'm sorry." She spoke shakily and too rapidly for Joven's comfort as she repeated the apology.

Joven pulled his hood back, and Marah hated every second of her sputtering an answer that neither of them could afford to hear. "Where's the Poten?"

Marah's voice cracked as she looked away from Joven, scared to admit the truth. "I don't know," she finally said after a few deafening seconds, "I had it, then I got caught. As I was escaping it shot out of my hands and I couldn't find it. If I stayed longer, they'd have me." Only as the words pieced themselves together out of Marah's mouth did she realize that she had failed her sole purpose and mission.

We spent so much time planning and waiting, how could we go wrong?

The human cast her gaze elsewhere, her heart lit in all the ways possible that she could never imagine feeling.

Another disappointing grade, huh Marah? Pathetic! You'll never be something great!

The words struck like a slap and Marah flinched. Ashamed, she kept her head down low, vulnerable to whatever reaction she anticipated Joven would have.

She expected him to lash out at her just like everyone else whenever she messed up. Instead, he sat down by her and brushed his fingers against hers.

Marah felt pathetic.

"It's okay. I mean, it's not good, but it's not your fault. You made the right choice, you're more valuable than the Poten." His tone shifted from less calm to choppy and urgent as he bolted to his feet, "Dammit, we need to get back now. They're all alone against everyone and they won't call for back-up and risk more lives. C'mon!" He started to walk past Marah

Marah stood up and grabbed Joven's arm. "Wait." Her tongue felt heavy in her mouth as she struggled to accept what Joven's words insinuated. *I failed my friends, and now they're trapped in a building full of people who want to kill them.* Marah's stomach sank even lower, if that was even possible as she realized that she practically signed their death sentences.

Marah was supposed to be Kosmir's Savior. And all she did was deliver its ruin.

Chapter 28

Location: Long live Kosmir

Marah couldn't help but rub her eyes as water pricked the back of them. She wiped all traces of tears away, not wanting to display them in front of Joven. Marah knew better than to cry because of her mistakes. This was something she needed to fix.

Joven spoke softly despite the tightness in his voice as he stated, "Marah, we cannot stand idle. The rebels, our friends, need us."

"Joven," repeated Marah while pulling him deeper into the shadows, "if we move now, we'll get caught." Her voice was thick with the panic that she was fighting to instill. "I just got out of that hell-hole and faced all of those officers, who are still on the streets."

Joven's jaw fell slack as Marah continued, "We have no way to fight them all."

Joven's conflicted thoughts were evident across his face.

Marah reasoned further, "And if we move now, they'll see us. There's no way we can hold them all back. Plus, there's cameras all over.

They'd find where we're located and then what? Our best bet is to stay hidden and sneak in once the patrols lessen."

"You want us to hide?"

Marah looked down at her shoes. "No one's saying that they want to, but if we don't want to end up like Leia and the others, then we have to be smart, not impulsive."

Joven didn't say anything as he weighed Marah's words. He sighed and retreated further into the alley, "You're right. The minute we're in the clear we have to get back to base."

Marah nodded. "Hopefully that's sooner than later." Not that either of them had a choice. Marah was ready to risk it all to get back to the rebels' base, but if she didn't look before she leaped, she'd end up in a deep, dark well.

Marah sat back down, and Joven followed, tapping his chipped, uneven fingernails against the fabric that rested over his kneecaps, lips set in a firm line.

The human attempted to console Joven and herself at the same time, "I know you're worried about them, but there's not really much we can do."

"I'm thinking about what will happen to them. It's just the three of them against everyone inside. If we sit around, we might be too late in saving them, and the other spies." Joven's voice trailed away as if it was his turn to look away, "If that's still even an option."

Marah tilted her head, "Why wouldn't it be?"

The alien explained patiently, "We lost our leaders in the enemy territory. They're completely defenseless, and knowing Chairwoman Kate," he spat, "she'll execute the three of them." His tone flattened as he paused before kicking a stone by his feet, "If she hasn't already."

Marah could only stare, unable to not think about the idea of her friends' lifeless bodies. If Leia, Kiera, and Natira were gone, what would happen to the rest of the rebels? What would happen to her then? Marah forced herself to remain hopeful as she offered, "If she had, she'd make it public."

If that's even relieving

Joven nodded, and for the next few minutes neither rebel made a sound. The two sat side by side, refusing to meet the other's eyes.

Joven was the first to break both, "Are you alright? You're bleeding a little bit."

Marah brought her cut hand to her cheek where Joven's gaze was and used her sleeve to wipe the blood away, "I'm fine."

He nodded.

The ex-spy pressed her lips shut as she thought of her friends' situation. *Please don't be hurt*, she prayed.

She exhaled, pressing her head against the back of the graffiti-wall, "I know this was my idea, but I really, really feel useless here."

"You and me both."

After a few more minutes of silence, Joven offered, "I may have an idea. How fast can you run?"

Marah flashed the rebel an irritated look, "Are you kidding me?"

Joven raised a hand despite the playful expression that curled his lips, "Okay, fine. If we set up a distraction, we could sneak out and run without them catching us."

"Okay, and how would we set up a diversion?" She held up a hand and added, "Before you ask, I'm not being bait again."

"No need," reassured Joven with a gleam in his eyes, "you know, I never told you what my abilities are."

Marah gave him a pointed look, "Well?"

"Why don't I show you instead?" Joven brought his hands forward with his fingers pointed outward, various colors roaring from his fingertips to in front of Marah, who watched as what resembled her upper half appeared in front of her. As amazed as she was, Marah scoffed at the pixels, "There's no way that's going to work."

It was Joven's turn to look at Marah. "Art can be made in a day if you give me a minute."

"Actually—" The human's sentence remained unfinished as she was suddenly looking at herself.

She raised her left hand and the clone followed suit. She gawked as Joven inspected his work. "How?"

"I'll set it off and it should buy us time to get back to base." Joven curled his hands into a pointed two-finger gesture and flicked the air, and Marah's clone took a step backward.

Marah watched him play puppet master with the clone. "How will it work if you have to control it?"

The Stellan stopped pulling strings. "How fast can you run?"

Marah crossed her arms across her chest and her clone followed.

Joven chuckled, "Like that."

Marah raised a hand and her clone copied. "That is so unsettling. And our plan?"

"You know in the movie *Humans v. Shark* when the sharks recruit the dolphins—"

"I'm sorry, what? Can we watch this later?"

"Yes, of course." Joven paused, eyes revealing the conflict in how to explain to Marah what his plan was. "You know the scene where Luna's doppelganger infiltrates Team Light in *Improfi*? I know you watched this with Natira, it's her favorite show."

"The plan!"

"In short, I'll send your clone out to get chased, and once they go after her, we'll escape."

Marah raised a brow, "And if there's more behind them?"

"We'll check before running." Joven shrugged casually, "If we happen to run into them, I'll show you what else I can do. It won't come down to it though, trust me."

The two took their positions, standing at the very edge of the west of the alley so if someone walked up the sidewalk all they'd see would be the outline of Joven's hood.

Marah held her breath as Joven steered her clone out of the alley and onto the sidewalk. Not even a minute later, someone shouted, "There she is! Get her!" Clone-Marah took off with officers, bullets, and energy forces running after her.

Golden eyes met hazel ones. "Run!"

Once Joven and Marah got inside the rebel facilities, they were met with a herd of rebels huddled around a screen. Marah recognized the woman on the screen easily, with The Committee's emblem over her left shoulder and soulless, white eyes. Chairwoman Kate looked eerily triumphant, which made her sour.

The human couldn't help but scowl at the sight of the Chairwoman. "What's going on?"

Joven hurried over to the monitor, "The Committee is rarely known to make public announcements. And when they do, they are broadcasted to every device across the universe."

Every device all over the universe?

Marah hummed, following the rebel's train of thought, "Correct me if I'm wrong, but for a broadcast to be sent across every device on Kosmir, each device needs a readable signal." She stopped as her eyes widened and she faced Joven, "Can they track us?"

The rebel who was at the monitor's keyboard grimly answered, "Quite possibly. I'm putting up anti-block software, but I don't think they're looking for us."

Wouldn't that be the perfect way to end the rebellion?

An unsettling feeling came over Marah as the blood-red lipped woman spoke with far too much glee for the teenager's liking, "Citizens, as you all may know, the leaders of the rebellion have been captured in an attempt to infiltrate our government and eradicate our way of life." The next sentence Chairwoman Kate spoke sent chills down everyone in the rebel facilities' spine, "And by the order of The Committee," her lips curled upward, "it is my great pleasure to announce that Leia Halim, Kiera Dapolk, and Natira Reyna are sentenced to a public execution later today at The Arena."

Marah's eyes widened and bile rushed up her throat. *If I had brought the Poten like I was supposed to, my friends wouldn't be on death row.* She stiffened; a daunting realization came upon her: *their blood is on my hands because I failed.*

Joven inhaled sharply, and Marah could feel the blow all the rebels took from Chairwoman Kate's words.

A rebel sighed, conclusions were inevitable, "It looks like we're done." Brokenness and disappointment thickened the tedious room, "How can we save them?"

Another piped up, speaking in quiet tones, "We'll have to disperse into the catacombs. Without our leaders, we can't fight The Committee. We're done, at least for now."

More and more faces fell as watery voices began to unanimously agree—the rebellion was nothing more than another lost cause.

A voice aired the contrary, "You're wrong."

Silence fell over the rebels as everyone turned to look at who spoke up.

Even Marah looked around, not realizing—at least, not at first— that she was the one who made the statement. At least a hundred pairs of eyes were on the human, and she resisted shrinking away. Were it some days ago, Marah's throat would have clenched up at the mere thought of being the center of attention.

But, given what Marah had learned and lived through the past several weeks, that had changed. She spoke slowly yet surely, "You're all wrong." She moved her gaze across the room and spoke in a tone that was dipped in incredulity, "The leaders of a cause that you have been fighting for so long are held prisoner, and you are seriously considering giving up?"

Silence.

"If anyone should want to give up and call it a day, that person should be is me."

If everyone wasn't looking at Marah before, they definitely were now.

"I'm not from this world," she continued, voice steady and raw with emotion. "I don't have the things that keep you able to fight, superpowers or special skills. In fact," Marah sighed, "I wanted to give up so many times because I couldn't understand why the Poten chose me," she paused, swallowing thickly, "but here I still am, choosing to stay and fight."

An exasperated voice argued, "So you have been doing this reluctantly?"

Marah shook her head. "What I'm trying to say is that when I was first here, yes. But, once I saw what The Committee did to Artemis, I realized that this fight is worth fighting with as many soldiers as there are willing. Am I wrong?"

Heads shook.

It took the human a minute to find her voice again. "I've been wondering what it means to be the savior that all of you expect me to be. I don't have powers, and I didn't want to disappoint you, though I may have already, maybe even several times. But I now think that's why the rebels needed me. I've seen both sides of this here and in the past, and I'm not bound by the rules of this game." She found herself repeating Leia's words, "It's not about having powers that makes one special, but what one chooses to do with what they're given. I decided to stay and fight, not because it is something I *can* do, but because I know it needs to be done." She looked down at her uniform. "I have been relying on my differences as a human to have me fail, but they've gotten me this far. We need to win this. We need to stand up and get the justice that this planet, and all of you, deserve."

Marah held her breath as she watched her words begin to make an impact on the rebels. "Maybe it's my flawed take on humanity that's making me say all of these things. Maybe it's because I've seen this a thousand times in books and movies. Giving up means that we're allowing Chairwoman Kate and her Legionnaires to continue doing whatever they want. Us, giving up? That's the easy win for The Committee." She stepped forward as she nodded, no longer the clueless follower from her first days here, but something else, something more as she surveyed her audience, "This right here is the fight of our lives. Our own lives, and the lives of our friends. This is where justice happens, and that's not through letting our friends die. Isn't that what a rebellion is supposed to be? The brave, the bruised, aren't we supposed to avenge the lost souls? Isn't *that* why you all have been fighting?"

The silence that ensued made Marah think twice about what she had said.

She lowered her gaze, "If you want to give up, I won't stop you. I don't have that power, nor would I force you if I did. I know what we have to do." The teenager raised her head, hazel irises meeting all sorts of colors as she promised, "And if I'm the only person that's going to stay and fight, that's fine. That being said, I know that you all know that

I'm right. We have to try something—*anything*—to save them." Marah exhaled softly before daring her eyes to look up again. "I don't know about the rest of you," the noirette admitted, "but if this means that I die or we lose out there, I'm willing to take that risk."

She sighed, concluding her words, "So, what are we going to do?"

There was silence, and Marah began to think that she was the only person going to fight for her friends' lives until Joven spoke up, "That was a hell of a speech."

Marah glanced upward to see the rebels staring back and smiling. There was a sense of power that transversed through the rebels as their mood of pain and desperation began to morph with twinges of hope and potency. Realizing what their next move was, they scrambled for their suits and weapons, rummaging for valuable intelligence from their spies, and anything else that could be of assistance.

"There's no way in hell we're leaving you or our leaders alone." "Didn't lose everything to keep on losing."

"This is our calling," rallied Joven, "we're going to stop the execution. Question is how exactly we're going to do that."

Marah Morana stood in front of a mahogany table, bated breath caught at the back of her throat, blaster pressed against the outside of her thigh, and the cape of her suit draped across lithe elbows. Her quiver was strapped across her back, and the fingers on Marah's left hand curled firmly across the metal piece of her bow that she had been itching to hold for some time now. The calloused fingers of her other hand ran over the words of the prophecy that she had never gotten the chance to access herself—until now.

She had never felt so human before. Anxiety was gnawing at her and she imagined she was likely to hear that they were too late, and all of this was in vain. She was vulnerable, yet extremely optimistic, and if that wasn't the epitome of humanity, Marah didn't know what was.

The rebels were due to attack, but there was much to discuss. They had no strategy or insight as to how they were going to go about it and when they turned to their prophecy's chosen one, Marah's answer surprised the rebels. Instead of immediately beginning to devise some plausible strategy to save her friends who were going to be publicly murdered in less than four hours, she locked herself in a room and thumbed through paper older than she was.

Perhaps they understood she needed to know why—why it had to be her all along, before more time or lives were wasted.

It was unbelievably ironic that she, the only human on the planet, was going to be what decided the fate of Kosmir's future. All of this was so much more than a rebellion. This rebellion had shown her what the meaning of life was: it's an adventure.

It's not every day you go from a high school dropout to practically a full-fledged superhero.

The weight of the worlds was on Marah's shoulders as she read the prophecy over and over. Her nerves tingled under her skin, fingers itching to shoot something. Shooting was good. Shooting always unmade the thoughts that ravaged Marah's head. But what?

I know, she smirked, *Chairwoman Kate's face.*

Marah was absolutely sure that the prophecy contained the answers she and the rebels needed. How she knew that, or why, Marah couldn't explain, not even to herself. All she knew was that she needed answers that she couldn't find.

The only other consolation the human had was that she believed in heroes. She had believed in them when she couldn't do the same for herself, and the paragon of change and rebellion was sure that her faith was the only thing that had allowed her to survive up till this point.

She sighed heavily, expanding her chest, and then compressing it. She looked away, hating how her actions doomed everything. *This is all my fault.* She felt like a child, unable to comprehend a lesson—thinking rash and unclearly. Tears pricked the human's eyes as frustration punched its way through Marah's thoughts, causing the girl to wallow about how she was going to fail, and her friends were going to die, leaving her all alone again.

She recalled her own words of hope from minutes ago and wondered if she had adopted the classic human flaw of speaking too soon. "I need to save my only friends!" She sucked in a shaky breath before moving her hands to wipe her face.

She expected that she'd knock her glasses off her face but remembered there were no longer frames slipping down her face. *And to think that I thought I would never get used to them.*

My friends are counting on me, even if they don't know it. She read the prophecy's contents aloud for the umpteenth time, "In the darkest hour, I am the light for I have sinned, wrought, and blessed. For I am unity; one eternal entity, and no army will vanquish the evil pestilence. I am as I am; past, present, and future. I am the eternity."

She reread the prophecy aloud, once, twice, ten times more as she struggled to find the answer that she knew lingered within sacred lines.

"In the darkest hour...."

Well...it doesn't get any darker than your three best friends about to be executed.

"...the evil pestilence."

"Pestilence is the evil," deciphered Marah. *That's The Committee. Obviously. There should be a picture of The Committee next to it in the dictionary.*

"No army will vanquish the evil..."

That means no army can beat it, but what about the unity and eternal entity mentioned?

She sighed, moving on.

"I am as I am; past, present, and future."

Is the I literal or metaphor? Something or someone that has always remained true to themselves?

Marah tried to think of all the times she stayed true to herself against all the odds.

I mean, you did stay true to yourself despite your parents. You've always been you since you've been on Kosmir. You've still been you when you worked with the rebels and you were still you, the real you, when you were at The Committee.

"I am the eternity."

Marah put the pieces of the puzzle together, the blood in her body coursing with renewed hope. *And to think, that the girl with the biggest self-esteem issues, a human in a space battle, is the 'I' the prophecy is referring to.* Then, she began recalling her experiences, aligning her thoughts. "I didn't change as a rebel or at The Committee, the two sides to this story. I grew, but I am still me," mused Marah, eyes flickering with light like they never had before.

Now how does the Eternity fight back?

Realization came over the human as if she had figured out the greatest secret in the universe and dropped her bow, causing it to clatter to the ground. "Oh!" She picked her bow back up and raced back to the main room where Joven wore a creased expression as he separated the rebels into different units.

"I know how we can save them!" she shouted, running toward the rebels.

The entire facility suddenly silenced at her words. Joven whipped around quickly. "Go on."

"It's all in the prophecy," explained Marah excitedly. "We have to sabotage the execution, or at least show The Committee what a real execution is. We bring the fight to them. If The Committee falls here, she exhaled, "by default they'll fall everywhere else."

The rebels exchanged looks and one piped, "Is she right?"

Joven was silent, piecing together what Marah suggested. "How do you propose we show them what a real execution is?"

Marah's eyes twinkled as she looked down at her bow and then at the rebels. "The prophecy states, 'No army will vanquish the evil pestilence.' It also says, 'I am unity; one eternal entity." We are *not* an army. We fight as one united entity. We may be outnumbered and outgunned, but we also know a few things they don't. A good amount of their weapons have been sabotaged, they don't work. If we block all the entrances and exits from the Arena, they can't get into the Citadel, where most of their weapons are. We pick off the officers first since they're the only non-Legionnaire people who'll probably wield weapons, the rest is all ability."

"And the rest?"

Marah paused a moment as she filled her mind with memories from following Leia around in briefings, "Match weapons and powers?" She shrugged, "It's something?"

Her words were more than enough to spark the rebels' eyes as they began pitching their ideas and scrambling for the means to execute them.

"Another thing," stated Marah, looking at her bow with a smile. "As a human, I can confirm from all the books and movies that I've watched and read, we need to be discreet. They won't hesitate to take on all of you. Me? I'm the shock factor. If I make a grand entrance, which I have the perfect idea for, it'll give us valuable leverage of time to save Leia, Kiera, and Natira."

Assurance came over Joven's features. "What do you have in mind?"

Chapter 29

Chairwoman Kate was a woman of many things.

She was a woman of intellect and integrity. She was a woman of fury that thrived within cold ivory eyes, a foreshadowing of the rage that would one day seed and sprout in her heart—something that all the worlds doubted truly existed. She was also a woman of power.

Great power, actually.

Her beloved mother, who rested among meteors and stardust, had once told her that she was a white rose in a garden, destined to stand out. She was her mother's treasured rose, a white seed densely coated in red.

Decades later, her mother stood correct.

Power was a harbinger to glory, and oh, how Kate ascended to be the boldest of roses. Power could be anything, which was what made it so easy for Kate to obtain. A sign of strength in unimaginable forms: the ways genetics determined magic, or the way feet dipped in the soil and shook it loose, and blades cutting through air and flesh with nothing but precision. Power was remarkable.

The Committee was hers. She intended to spread its light across the worlds for eons to come.

First, she needed to demonstrate her ferocity to all the worlds one last time. Sometimes, even family deserved the heat of her heart's flames.

Seated in her office, a mere trophy of her success, she had a lot to think about. However, worries such as infiltrating rebels, Marah Morana managing to live under her nose, and confused soldiers, were all dismissed as she ordered Iris to open the windows more, letting more natural light fill her office. She hadn't bothered to clear the mess that the damned human had made when she snuck in, having more pressing matters than dead officers who were too incompetent for their duties or messy desks. Bent fingers held a pen under her chin as she replayed her statement that would change everything. The rebels would die tonight. They had to.

"Permission to enter, Chairwoman Kate?"

Chairwoman Kate tore her thoughts away from how painfully she wanted her prisoners to die, and toward the mauve-eyed Legionnaire who would have stood indefinitely until the Chairwoman would grant her permission.

"Please, Legionnaire Mizra," the woman greeted pleasantly, or at least as pleasant as one could sound when the rebellion riff-raff managed to break into her premises and pathetically attempt to kill her. Worse, the damned human had slipped right through her fingertips and was off God knows where. "Do tell, what is the current situation?"

Legionnaire Mizra took a seat in front of the Chairwoman, the sword that hung from her belt gently bouncing against the plush engineering of the chair. "Officer Kentar has passed due to the Poten's impact."

"That is most unfortunate," tsked the Chairwoman. "Then again, a human killed him. Pathetic. At the very least, he died for the most noble of causes, wouldn't you say?"

Legionnaire Mizra supplied a nod with a hardened tone, "All thanks to that human." She noted the sharpness in her leader's eyes and inquired gently, "If it is permissible for me to inquire, what are you thinking about?"

"Are the rebels secured appropriately?"

"Yes," smiled the Legionnaire. "I took immense pleasure in watching the horror on their faces as they realized that their plan failed. Breathing in their failure was nearly as satisfying as it was to dampen them of their powers and weapons. Especially the Nantak."

"Excellent."

Mizra was Kate's favorite Legionnaire, partly because of her undying support but also because of how young she was. It was the youth who were truly vicious, something she learned for herself the hard way when she watched her planet burn.

Years later, she understood the weight of those sacrifices, for the term many labeled "the greater good." Unfortunately, her cousin didn't share that same fate.

Chairwoman Kate's lips smiled, a bold bright red that clashed against pearl white teeth as she eyed the sheathed sword that hung from Mizra's belt, "You never disappoint me. Therefore, I will entrust you with a task of utmost prestige."

Mizra closed her right hand into a fist and placed it over her chest as she lowered her gaze, "I am always honored to be of your service, my Chairwoman."

The Chairwoman smiled, one of sinister wickedness, "Find me the most ruthless executioner. A fitting end to my cousin's life, wouldn't you agree?"

Mizra's face mimicked her liege's, "Your wisdom exceeds us all, Chairwoman."

"As it should." Kate stood. "Now leave and fetch me my executioner. I ought to offer my condolences to my cousin."

Chapter 30

Location: If you want peace, para bellum

Leia Halim was many things. Eighteen. Novan. Friend. Orphan. All of those preceded what she was easily identified as: a rebel.

It was in the rebel's blood to never give up, and while some cursed that trait with a string of profanities, Leia saw it as a blessing worth admonishing.

Especially considering how at this very moment, Leia was counting on her blood more than ever.

The Novan grunted while pulling on shackles that chained her hands to metal bars, desperation clinging to the orphan's heart. The rebels had done it all, and yet they were imprisoned, most likely awaiting death.

With thin scrunched eyebrows that couldn't furrow any harder than they already were, Leia resumed her battle with the chains. She could not lay here in weakness. The rebels were stronger than that. She was so much stronger than this.

"Come on!" She grumbled, upper lip curled into a scowl, while pulling on chains once more, the rattling sound filling the room. Leia leaned her head back in frustration, looking down at sore wrists before resuming in vain.

"Resistance is futile."

Leia glared daggers toward the ceiling and ignored the AI as she persisted in attempting to free her hands or get at least a spark of her powers back. "I hate these power dampening cuffs!"

"Resistance is futile."

"Shut up!" hissed Natira, catching Leia off guard as this was the first time that particular rebel had spoken since becoming a prisoner. Her mouth that was trained to be a lock with its mechanical appearance of a frown, had been unlocked with lips wearing stubborn tension. Her eyes, bearing a silver color twitched as she squeezed veiny fingers, itching to rub what little was left of her fingernails against her favorite blade, Ilke. To be *Ilke* meant to be powerful. To be *Ilke* meant to be strong. *Ilke* meant living because what was more beautiful yet miserable than that?

Legionnaire Mizra, who the Nantak had the grace to meet managed to strip most of her weapons but hadn't gotten the chance to take Ilke sheathed inside her leather jacket as she slapped *these damn cuffs on us.*

Her fingers ached from being pressed against metal, which really sucked since her phasing would really come in handy.

The Nantak glanced at Leia, gaze brushing past messy and tangled locks of dark purple, darting straight for the red ichor-like substance that spilled down her cheeks and wrists. For the longest time, then and now, everywhere Natira looked she saw red. Sometimes it was her own blood that left scars with stories she could tell and others she would never tell, or the blood her imagination would conjure of her parents, whose faces she can't remember but always the chilling echo of their last words. Other times red came in the form of the girl with thin lips and huge eyes filled with adventure and curiosity; Ameerah. Or, it was the blood of the boy she dared to fall in love with during her time in a cage, who blessed her with her first kiss—only for her to kill him with a gun to her head. Often, the red she saw reminded Natira of all the children and adults she killed so she could be sitting here today at the mercy of the blood who extinguished Nantak's spark.

It didn't help that the monster who had robbed her of everything and more had put her in a cage once again. It was a cruel reminder of why she was a rebel.

Natira had survived several cages before. She could do it again.

Like the lotus tattooed on her dark skin, she needed to be *Ilke*. *Ilke* would bring *punsi*, revenge.

She murmured a string of profanity as she tried to dislocate her thumbs to free her hands. "Resistance," chimed Iris with a hint of sick satisfaction, "is futile."

Natira would've screamed were it not for the sound of chains rattling for the umpteenth time. "You're going to hurt yourself."

Leia shook her head, and the locks of hair that hung loosely from her braid followed her head, "Got to keep trying."

Natira was quiet. She had been friends with Leia for years and there were times when her stubbornness took over. This was one of those times.

Kiera spoke meekly after a while of quiet that otherwise occupied the rushing blood in Natira, "I hope Marah's safe." She glanced down at her armbands where patches of light green skin neared bluish-black. "I think I saw the other rebels get put in a holding cell, hopefully, they're not beat up too badly."

"Hopefully," whispered Natira. She raised her sleeved arms to wipe her hair out of her face, "If they did get to her, they'd be bragging about it." Her voice lifted, suggesting optimism, "She's smart. I'm sure she got out and is doing something." She fell silent quickly at the sound of clicking heels against marble.

The three immediately stiffened as a voice all too familiar called out, "Yes, I'm sure your human pest is doing something. Though, as Chairwoman, it's safe to say that she's already far too late."

Leia raised her amethyst eyes to the Chairwoman. "Too late for what?" spat the rebel, venom in her words dripping with pure loathing.

The Chairwoman of The Committee wore a vile smirk as she answered, stepping into the cage where the three were being held, "Why, for your extermination, cousin. You three are sentenced to public execution for the crimes of treason and spying on The Committee." She sighed, a sound filled with satisfaction, "You three are like little roaches, creatures that are hard to get rid of, but eventually die."

"*Our* crimes?" tsked Leia. "What about what *you* stand for? You honestly believe that the destruction of worlds is justifiable? Do you have any idea how much blood is on your hands, let alone you inherited?"

She shook her head in disdain, contempt in her eyes challenging Chairwoman Kate. "You disgust me."

"Oh Leia," Chairwoman Kate crooned as she squatted down to meet her captive's eye level, "you say that I like care about your pathetic little feelings. The sacrifice for salvation is often great, but it is not without reward. All these planets are suffering and only we can stop that. Without us, war will rot our universe from the inside out."

"You don't know that!" argued Natira this time. "You and all the ones before you are monsters. You hunt and kill innocents across the universe simply because of their origin? You didn't stop the Black Market when people like me were kidnapped, and you supported all the blood that was spilled there. What about how you torment as many

Stellans as you can simply because their monarchy settled on a seventy-thirty dual-system instead of handing you Stella on a golden platter?"

Chairwoman Kate glanced at Natira, "And yet here you are, once again depending on my mercy. I bet you know that feeling quite well—depending on mercy during all those days at the Black Market." She leaned closer, going for the low blow, "Was I not merciful when I let you bury that boy you loved—and were forced to kill—instead of just tossing his body into one of the toxic waste dumps or letting him sink to the bottom of one of the oceans?"

Natira lunged for the woman, fingers itching to pull out Ilke and rip Kate's heart out of its cage and teach her what begging for mercy and not getting it is like. The heavy chains on her hands kept the Nantak in place.

Kate mimicked sympathy as she diverted back to Leia, "I could've killed you every second you spent here."

Leia shrank away from Kate, a spiteful expression written all over her face.

Kate wore a withering look. "I'm no monster," condescension was thick in her tone, "we are family after all." Soulless eyes and plump curled lips told a different story.

Leia glared daggers as she tugged on chains, the rattling sound as cold as the words that left her mouth, "We stopped being family years ago when you voiced your support to the monsters that killed our family and left me homeless."

Kate sighed, drumming fingers on her thighs as she stood back up and stepped out of the cage. "I hate that you forced my hand like this but have it your way." She continued to speak as three Legionnaires appeared, "I told you this last time I imprisoned you in these walls that you were making a grave mistake by going against me. You should've listened, as I'm afraid that it's now time to exterminate some pesky roaches."

Just as Kate uttered the last word, Legionnaires moved to each rebel and harshly pulled them up despite their attempts to flee.

Natira moved to kick the officer holding her but was punched right in the face, causing her knees to bend sharply and give out. She twisted her shoulder roughly, shrugging the officer's hand off only for her other shoulder to be grabbed.

Chairwoman Kate, reveling in drunken satisfaction, chimed airily, "Darling, you're wasting your time. Not only will your death grant me the satisfaction of putting another kind to extinction, but when the last of the resistance dies, I will finally be able to reign eternally." She added stiffly as the three continued to resist, "I told you three the first time I caught you, you will either serve my empire or be crushed by it."

Kiera, who was silent up until this point, shook her head. "Every empire bleeds. Yours will too. Just because you built Kosmir doesn't mean that you'll keep it just by killing us. People will always stand up for what they believe in."

Kate rolled impatient eyes. She clucked her tongue as she held her hands out, gesturing around the cell, "You think your words hold meaning?"

Natira shrugged against the Legionnaire's hold only for him to grab her elbow instead. "There are more of us ready to finish what we've started. Our execution doesn't harm the rebel cause, they'll finish our work."

Again, Kate rolled her eyes. "I'm not afraid to kill anyone who tries. Besides, who will come and save you? Looks like I scared your human off, the so-called chosen one, if I'm not mistaken."

Kiera argued, twisting roughly against grasp of the Legionnaire holding her, "Kill us if you want. Eventually, justice will be served." The

Zonan's face usually told the hope that came with rebellion, but this time, the weight of all she had dealt with glimmered in their darkest form as she lunged toward the Chairwoman despite the firm hold on her shoulders, "It's screaming loudly, demanding to be heard. Can you hear it?"

Kate only chuckled hollowly, "Brave words for someone who is about to die." She turned to face the Legionnaires, "Take them outside and prepare for the execution. Legionnaire Mizra should have picked my executioner already. Bring the other prisoners too, they should watch their precious leaders perish before they join them."

She turned away from the rebels, calling over her shoulder as she walked away, "I would make your prayers now, darlings. Short and sweet, God has been busy today."

The Legionnaires that were holding the leaders of the rebellion dragged them outside into The Arena, which was now teeming with life as thousands, upon thousands of people sat eager for the blood of orphans who only wanted to make the worlds a better place.

Do they see the blood their masters have served to orchestrate them to be the fools that they are? wondered Natira as the crowds booed and jeered toward them. She ignored them as her former Master had taught her, and doing so came across parties that were quiet, forlorn written under lock and key.

"I'm sorry," she whispered as each rebel was forced onto a white mark on the ground. She moved her feet, wanting to be closer to her friends if they were to part from this world, but the mark she was standing on kept her glued in place. None of the Legionnaires decided to remove the cuffs that dampened their abilities.

She followed Leia's gaze where all their rebels and spies were led out and thrown onto the ground, each with an officer standing behind them to keep them in place. The Novan's face wished to soften, but the leader of Kosmir's rebellion remained strong. If she was to die, she would do so with honor.

But, if Chairwoman Kate and The Committee believed that their execution would go gently into the night, they were terribly mistaken. The golden youth of rebels had screamed silently enough. The worlds and their peoples looked and saw poisoned youth, yet the biggest poison stood on a throne above them all splaying judge, jury, and executioner.

Clyna locked eyes with Leia and brought a chained fist upward, screaming, "Justice forever!" She punched the air as she raised her head, daring the crowd to silence her cries, "Freedom forever!" She repeated herself as she raised her fist despite struggling, "Justice forever! Freedom forever!"

Other captured rebels joined Clyna's cries, raising their heads and fists in unison as they chanted with the might of the strongest army to have ever lived in the world, as officers poorly attempted to restrain them. "Justice forever! Freedom forever! We won't give up!"

Leia couldn't stop the surge of pride that blossomed in her chest. It made the idea of what was to come next a little bit easier since she knew that her fight wouldn't die with her and her friends. Lips waging a war between the saddest frown and the strongest smile, Leia looked over to her friends who had their fists and lips moving. She followed suit.

The officers that were struggling to restrain the rebels had succeeded in pinning them to the ground and clamped gags in their mouths, rendering them silent.

As for the three rebellion leaders, a jolt of electricity crackled beneath their feet and sizzled up across all of their nerves, forcing them into complacent quiet.

Even in death, will they keep us quiet? What do they have to fear? wondered Kiera. The bones in her small nose and round chin tensed, but she forced them to relax for her comrades' sake, a mental assurance that death wouldn't be as painful as they feared. *A helpless death is not one that one wishes to be remembered by, is it?*

The Zonan was stolen from her thoughts as the bane of her existence, with razor-sharp cheekbones and round eyes, emerged and walked to her throne, standing tall. "Today, Natira Reyna, Kiera Dapolk, and Leia Halim are found guilty on the accounts of treason and spying against The Committee and therefore, are sentenced to immediate death." Chairwoman Kate gingerly sank into her seat, features scribbled with smugness mixed with the concoction of venom and eagerness, "Let this be a friendly reminder that resistance is, and always will be, futile."

The executioner emerged, but Kiera never saw who was prepared to take her life as she had her eyes shut, uneagerly anticipating her skull to be cracked open. *You did your best. At least we will be together. We will be united now, Mama and Papa.*

"Three!"

The Novan next to her stood tall as someone began the countdown of their time left amongst the living. Though the life she had lived was not the best, she was grateful for the souls she had met for the strange time life was. She kept her eyes open, standing true to the leader she was. *Someone else will succeed. Someone else has to.*

"Two!"

Natira inhaled sharply as the executioner poised a plasma-ray for her first. She straightened her spine, bracing herself for the blow that would soon come. Disappointment filled her blood like oxygen in her lungs. The last of her planet would be exterminated by the same killers who had eradicated the rest of her kind. *And I never got to avenge any of them.*

At the very least, Natira's suffering as a lone survivor would end. There wouldn't be any more nights unable to look in the mirror or pray on silk mats as her Amma had taught her to.

There wouldn't be nightmares of kiss-turned kills or bloodied chains. She raised her chin, accepting her fate as she spoke the sacred words Nantaks recited upon death.

"One!"

Just as Natira heard the end of the countdown, a large gasp overtook the crowd followed by a clattering sound of a weapon being dropped.

Natira was confused. She was supposed to be dead. A blast was supposed to rip through her heart and take her life.

Kiera, perplexed herself, quietly said, "Look."

Natira followed Kiera's gaze to find an arrow embedded in the executioner's chest. The crowd's murmurings were becoming an uproar as the man's arm fell limp and his knees swayed. When another arrow landed right between the executioner's eyes, he crumbled to the ground. Crowd now a furious uproar, the executioner had been executed.

The entire Arena fell silent as heads swiveled to the balcony opposite Chairwoman Kate's where Marah Morana stood. She looked across the crowd to meet Chairwoman Kate's wide eyes. This was a new Marah, one that didn't depend on the words of others to determine who or what she was.

"Just thought it'd be a good time to say the rumors are true. Yes, I'm the human who is supposed to destroy you all, look familiar?"

Realizing that the rebels' fight was far from over, Natira's smile stretched so wide that the rebels' face began to hurt.

Marah's lips twitched, smirking at the incredulity on Chairwoman Kate's face as she nocked another arrow and released. The arrow sailed to its designated spot and then beeped, releasing a rippling impact that crumbled the balcony, sending it down to the ground, along with the Chairwoman and the Legionnaires seated with her.

Archers emerged from all corners of the Arena, ready for Joven's signal to lose their arrows.

Meanwhile, Marah effortlessly reached behind her shoulder and pulled out another arrow.

Leia muttered, "She's not alone, she brought everyone with her." Additional blasts to the device that kept the rebel leaders' feet planted, deactivated it, and they were free. Blasts of rebel energy caused their restraints to fall off as they realized what Marah was about to start.

A revolution.

Marah shot another arrow—this one attached to a zip line—toward a ledge near her three friends. She then used her bow to glide down to the concrete slab where her friends were.

The Arena became flooded with rebels. Tired of continually playing defense, those rebels who had been captured used the surprise and confusion to throw their captors off and joined the offense their peers had brought to the fight. The youth who brandished hope and resolve stood tall and proud; soldiers ripened for rebellion.

Marah tossed a sack of weapons to Natira, who eagerly strapped them onto her belt. She smirked as she cocked her personal blaster, the weapon humming to life.

Kiera's forehead mark glistened bright blue and Leia's eyes flared with color as energy wisps formed at her fingertips.

The Novan took a moment to ask Marah, "So, what's the plan? And by the way," she grinned as she added, "thanks."

"You're welcome." Marah pulled another arrow from her quiver and drew it back. "As for the plan, we're ending this. Giving them everything we got."

Natira unsheathed Ilke. "I like the sound of that." She turned to Leia, "Boss?"

Leia glanced at Marah who had begun firing arrows with incredible speed and accuracy. "She's calling the shots. Go!"

The rebels within earshot began to take on The Committee soldiers who were pouring in across the grounds from the various seating sections. Abilities were fired up and tossed at the enemy alongside crossbows, guns, whatever could be a weapon in one's hands; both sides hellbent on survival.

Marah remained where she was, turning on her heels as her fingers released arrow after arrow, each one hitting its desired target. She didn't bother looking to ensure whomever she hit was dead. It took all her concentration to aim in the jumbled chaos of colors and shapes.

His back against Marah's, Joven yelled over the cacophony of energy rays spiraling across the ground, "I can't believe this worked! Don't get mad, but how do we know if we're winning?"

Marah replied as another arrow pierced an officer's chest, "If there's less shots coming at you, then you're probably winning."

"Cool." Joven continued to shoot beams out of his hands.

Okay then.

Though Marah had only spent a short time infiltrating The Committee, she had a good idea of who could wield what. So, when a familiar face teleported in front of her to attack, she didn't need to think twice about hitting the soldier with her bow, preventing him from striking her or Joven. She then plucked an arrow from her quiver and wielded it like a blade, shoving it through skin till enemy eyes rolled into infinite darkness.

Marah headed deeper into the fight, shooting arrows left and right. Just as she ducked from a thrown energy blast, something exploded near her, sending her forward onto her hands. As she pushed herself back onto her feet, she found a scepter pointed at her.

Marah reacted instinctively, sliding an arrow out of her quiver and returning the threat.

"Stand down, human." The soldier said as they jabbed the scepter toward her. She ducked under the strike, feeling the tip of the weapon pass through her hair, and lunged forward, thrusting the arrow into her opponent. "Not going to happen."

One down, she mused as she looked at the never-ending fights going on around her between the rebels and The Committee, *and a whole lot more to go.*

She raised her bow, scouring for someone to shoot, when her gaze fell on Leia. Purple energy roared from her palms and was hurled in all four directions, sweeping everything in its path. Watching Leia's energy crackle and fizz around every other second, Marah finally understood why Leia never used a weapon. She was one.

Kiera was leading her own contingent of rebels against Committee workers. She cast out her infamous sleeping spells, and they worked quite well, though some workers put up defenses.

When Marah moved to help, a blurry force collided into her, sending her flying backward and landing not so nicely on the ground.

Marah winced as she moved to her feet, but an invisible shove that sent her crashing painfully onto her knees.

"You're wasting your time. Give up while you still can. Marah." spat the last person the human wanted to deal with.

Marah cursed under her breath as she looked at Beth standing above her with a scepter aimed at her chest. The woman's blonde hair was still as loose and unruly as Marah remembered from earlier, with the only change to Beth being pinker cheeks and red, puffy eyes.

Her tone was raw with betrayal. "Or would you rather I still call you Nima?" Beth pressed on the trigger, releasing a blast of energy that Marah's suit absorbed.

"If you're looking for an apology, I'm not going to give you one. This is wrong, look around you."

Beth laughed, but it was dark and hollow. "Quite frankly, I don't give a damn about your apology. You really think your pathetic words will turn me from my devotion? You *betrayed* me!" She yelled, pressing the trigger repeatedly, "All you did was *lie* to me from the first moment we met!"

That's not entirely true.

Marah was silent, allowing Beth to become frustrated as she realized that the blasts weren't hurting the human at all. Then, Beth thrust the scepter under her chin, forcing the rebel to meet the eyes of her stricken former roommate and friend.

"It's pathetic. I really liked you." Her resolve began caving under the hefty weight of her emotions. "A part of me still does. Surrender. Look around you. You're wasting your life. You'll die. Please."

Marah was silent as she looked around. The Arena was a mess; with fire, blood, and debris. Members of The Committee and rebels doing battle; each side direly trying to one-up the other. Filling her lungs with air tainted by smoke and ash, Marah tasted death. It sickened her. Lives were being taken by those who swore to uphold everything Chairwoman Kate stood for, as well as by those who swore to fight against everything Chairwoman Kate stood for.

It was heart-breaking. To be so young and live through so much.

However, as unfortunate as she may have felt facing Beth and hearing her friends die, Marah still had a job to do. She was the chosen one; with all of her quirks, flaws, acne, and anxiety, she was able to be what no one expected her to be. She had come this far; damned if she did, damned even more if she didn't, Marah was going to do what she learned best—and fight back.

She turned back to face Beth with defiant eyes, "I will not surrender."

Beth's reply was spoken softly with eyes as hard as diamonds, "Then you must die like the rest of them."

Marah's eyes challenged Beth's glare, daring the alien, as she prepared to push off the ground and tackle the Kosmirian.

She never got the chance to.

Instead, Marah watched as Natira ran through Beth, grabbing the weapon before she could fire.

Well, that was oddly very cool…. aaaaand kind of gross.

Beth stepped backward, hands moving across her body. *Probably making sure that everything that was supposed to be there, still was.* Natira used the opportunity to aim the weapon at Beth who raised her hands to her head.

Natira raised a brow, "Relax, I didn't steal your organs. You want mercy?" Beth nodded frantically.

Natira pressed the scepter's tip against Beth's chest. "You were about to kill my best friend. If you want to get mercy, you should give it first." She pressed the trigger, and the damage was done.

"You just, she just, woah," murmured Marah as she looked at Natira and then at Beth's bleeding body."

"Duck!"

Natira pulled Marah down to the ground as a light-blast sailed over their heads and crashed into an officer.

The two turned their heads to find Joven and Clyna leading a group of rebels with weapons and powers ablaze. As he pushed Committee soldiers off their feet, with the light rays emitting from his hands, Joven called out, "We can handle them, you four need to take out the big guys."

Clyna thrust another ball of energy and used the hand holding some form of pistol to point past them, "They don't look very happy."

Marah followed the direction Clyna's weapon was pointing to the debris where the balcony had fallen. Chairwoman Kate had emerged with her Legionnaires out of the rubble. She jabbed a finger toward them whilst screaming furiously, "Kill them! Kill them all!"

Chapter 31

Location: The board where deities, rulers, remnants, pawns,
and knights gather

"Okay, we're still outnumbered. I suggest we take out the legionnaires first," Leia stated, "then go after the Chairwoman together, since she's the most powerful of them all."

Marah mocked a salute, and she pulled another arrow out of her quiver as she eyed the Legionnaires, "I call dibs on the blonde."

Natira scrunched her eyebrows, "You're not smiling. I've never seen you so serious. It's unnerving."

Marah rolled her eyes while drawing her bow. "Says the most serious person in space I know, which out of the many I know, is something coming from you."

While Natira grumbled. Chairwoman Kate, in disbelief that her execution extravaganza was sabotaged in front of her very own eyes, finally caught sight of Marah with the rebellion's leaders and jabbed a finger toward them whilst screaming furiously, "Kill them! Kill them all!"

"So, what about her?" Marah asked, ending Natira's comments. "Are we going to kill her, or do you have other plans?"

"I'm not really sure." Leia breathed out with what Marah detected to be embarrassment, "Chairwoman Kate is my cousin."

"And you tell me this *now*?!?"

"To be honest," the Novan admitted, "we really didn't think that we'd get ourselves this far."

"Fair point." They separated and Marah loosed an arrow straight at the advancing blonde albino, only for it to be shot down by an ice blast.

Marah released the arrow straight for the legionnaire, only for it to be shot down by an ice blast.

"Is that the best you can do, oh great one whom the Poten chose?" She said sarcastically, holding her arms wide, inviting Marah to come forth.

Marah tried again but the second arrow met the same fate as the previous one.

The legionnaire hurled a spear of crackling ice at Marah. With no cover, the human threw herself out of the way before she could get hit with something far worse than frostbite, while the legionnaire continued to advance. Rolling on the debris strewn ground, she quickly regained her feet, although she still had no inkling of what she should do.

Marah slung her bow across her back and charged toward Blondie, when she was brought to a jarring halt by a sudden coldness in her feet. She looked down and stifled a gasp. Ice, that was slowly creeping up her body, glued her feet to the ground, rendering her stuck.

Marah glared at the legionnaire and grunted as she attempted to free herself, but the ice was more stubborn than she was. The closer the legionnaire got, the more the ice inched up Marah's form, now just past her knees.

As arrows were useless, meaning she couldn't use her favorite weapon, she'd have to use another.

The legionnaire seemed more focused on her success than on what the human was doing. Seizing the opportunity, Marah snaked a hand to her thigh, where the blaster Natira insisted she have, was fastened.

Marah managed to grab it before the ice reached it and moved it behind her back.

By now—*Ciel! That's this uppity chick's name!*—was only a couple yards away and the ice had risen past her thighs.

Legionnaire Ciel drawled, "Oh, is this too cold for your mere human self?" Her eyes hardened like the ice that she had trapped Marah in, and her outstretched fingers curled into a raised fist, encouraging the ice to climb up her further and faster. "How pathetic," she sneered. *That's right, keep coming closer.*

The blonde chuckled, now practically toe-to-toe with her enemy. "What a way to go, thinking that you would save your criminal friends, only to be the first to die instead."

Marah raised her chin. "I wouldn't be so sure." She aimed her blaster at the woman's neck and pulled the trigger. Once the legionnaire's eyes fell shut, the ice encasing Marah crumbled like broken glass.

Then, she saw him.

One of the legionnaires Natira was fighting teleported from in front of her to behind her and was about to stab her in the back.

Marah pulled an arrow as far back as her bowstring would permit and then some before releasing it.

Joven and Clyna's troops were now facing an officer without any protective armor who was able to stop everything from penetrating him with a mere flick of a finger.

Despite the rebels' varying slew of powerful manifestations, the barrier refused to falter. The officer's fission energy hurled screeching blasts, bullets, and powers back to those who had originally delivered them. The crackling of energy drowned out the sound of yelps and cries of pain as it was hurled toward a mass of rebels.

The legionnaire now dueling Natira fired heat from his eyes and the Nantak bent backward, gracefully missing the attack.

Were it not for Natira's eyes landing on Marah's back, Marah wasn't sure she'd have noticed the attack in time. "Marah! Hard right!"

She reacted first, then saw the heat blast. Noting the scorched spot where she previously stood. Some resumed firing, while others weren't so lucky. She huffed as she stood, blood splattered wherever she looked, so she turned away quickly, focusing on the war that was assigned to her.

When she did so, she was met by Legionnaire Mizra. The woman's sword was pointed directly at her. "I was supposed to deliver you to Chairwoman Kate a long time ago. Now, I will fulfill my purpose."

Mizra lunged and Marah jerked backward just enough for the blade to miss her throat—barely.

Before the human could process the fact that she was nearly beheaded, she was blocking another pass from the sword with her bow and throwing a punch that Mizra easily swatted aside.

Marah struggled, beginning to go cross-eyed from trying to counter each attack. The woman hit hard and moved fast, dominating the fight. Any punch Marah managed to throw, while trying to avoid getting sliced or impaled, was slammed down, and her toes stepped on before she could even contemplate a kick.

She was so preoccupied with staying upright and minimizing her injuries that she couldn't recall what power the woman had. That was, until Mizra held up a hand as if to mimic surrender, and Marah was pushed back several feet by an invisible force.

"I will get the honor of killing the greatest threat to The Committee." Legionnaire Mizra drawled as she effortlessly dodged everything Marah sent her way, "I wonder what color your blood will stain my hand." She gestured to the sword in her hand that was more of an extension of herself than a separate entity; it was the same look that Marah gave her bow. It was evident that Mizra knew no fear. "Though you are primitive, you are powerful like me."

"Thank you?" Marah was taken aback by the woman's praise, expecting another insult to humanity.

While the legionnaire was talking, Marah managed to put a sufficient amount of distance between them and quickly released another arrow. However, this was no ordinary arrow; it split into three, lodging itself in her opponent's bicep, rib, and hip respectively.

Mizra's face showed the barest of winces before she snapped the arrows' shafts off and let them fall to the ground. Her mauve lips almost smiled, "I see myself in you. Both bound to our causes while living up to the titles we bear."

Somehow, Marah found herself on the floor. The legionnaire swiveled her sword. "There is a reason you are The Chosen One just as there is a reason I was entrusted with handling you." She adjusted her hold on her sword, preparing to plunge it into the girl.

Marah scuttled sideways to avoid the hit, causing the blade to embed itself in one of the chunks of concrete debris that littered the grounds of the arena.

Marah blinked. *Rock beats paper…and alien sword?*

Mizra appeared equally confused, and Marah took the opportunity to skewer the legionnaire with an arrow while the woman tried freeing her blade.

As the arrow sank into her, Mizra swayed slightly, but the human did not want to take any chances. Another arrow joined the first, putting an end to Mizra's fighting days and taking the ferocious light out of her eyes.

Marah exhaled as she turned away from the dead body, "How many more of these guys do we still have to fight?" She ducked as bodies were hurled over her head, some landing on the crumpled balconies.

I'm starting to get tired of all this killing and trying not to be killed.

The human glanced past the bodies lying by Leia, Natira, and Kiera's feet to Chairwoman Kate. The only movement the woman had made since she ordered her Legionnaires to lay down their lives for her and her cause, was to clench her fingers.

From the looks of it, she's pretty pissed.

"What now?" inquired Marah. "The rest of the rebels can hold their own, but we still have to deal with the evil step-sister over here." She winced at Leia's sour expression, "My bad, evil step-cousin?"

Leia raised her voice so said cousin could hear her. "Kate is my actual cousin, unfortunately. Obviously, there is a huge age difference," she spat venomously, eliciting a scowl from the considerably older woman. "Not to mention a difference in our morals. I have them, and she doesn't."

Chairwoman Kate examined her manicure, acting like she couldn't care less about what Leia thought or said about her. Except the old part. It was easy to see that struck a nerve. "Do tell me, Leia, should I feel scared? To be honest, I really don't." She lifted her gaze from her fingertips. "I'm tired of admiring my fingernails and watching my soldiers perish. Let's settle this once and for all. Oh, and family or not, I won't go easy on you."

Leia smirked as she stretched out her arms, fingertips lit, "Good. So, it'll be a fair fight."

"Finally!" Boredom left the Chairwoman's features as she lifted a hand, and a wave of white came rushing for the rebel leaders.

Leia flung her hands forward, forming a force field. "Get behind me!"

Marah didn't have to be told twice as she dove for cover.

White energy smashed into Leia's barrier; a force so intense that it pushed all four girls a few feet backward, with Marah tripping over Natira, who knocked into Kiera. Before any apologies could be muttered, they heard a crackling hum that wasn't from Leia.

Leia struggled to keep the flickering purple energy shield intact from her position on the ground, as white blasts repeatedly crashed into it.

The younger Novan grit her teeth as her fingers skipped across nothingness, conjuring more energy as white clashed with purple, ramping up in intensity. She huffed as another white blast shattered against her barrier. "I'm not sure how much longer I can hold this up," she grunted, straining as more energy leapt from her fingertips.

Meanwhile, the Chairwoman stood, showing not the least bit of effort. Finally, she threw her arms wide and levitated off the ground as power shot and slithered from her fingers, sounding of death and destruction.

"Enough!" She bellowed. "I will not let you get in my way any longer!"

Both the arrow Marah loosed, and the dagger Natira threw, were brushed aside and the two braced themselves as an energy ball was hurled to the ground. The impact was so strong, it took down Leia's shield and sent everyone flying.

The human was once again slammed to the ground, breath stolen from her lungs. She slowly sat up to catch her breath, much like her comrades. She coughed as she watched Chairwoman Kate gracefully lower herself back to the ground, completely unharmed.

Kate surveyed what had become of the Arena. Seeing her legacy reduced to nothing but blood and dust was more than enough to make her own blood boil.

"I will kill you all, one by one," the Chairwoman said, addressing the stunned and fallen girls. "But first," her eyes settled upon Marah, "I was foolish not to have arranged your death a long time ago." She snarled, "The moment I saw your name, I wanted to scratch it off the face of all the realms. However, believing that you were nothing but a feeble human, I decided to not waste my time." She tilted her head, her eyes a poisoned mixture of fire and insanity in her blood churned through Kate's veins, white eyes bent on murder, "You lived on borrowed time. Now, you are going to make up for it."

With the flick of her hand, each of the four rebels were encased in slightly milky translucent bubbles that kept them planted on the ground. White energy licked out from the Chairwoman's fingertips as Natira's pink knife, Ilke, began to rise, its tip pointed straight at Marah.

Marah's heart skipped several beats, realizing the woman's intent as she attempted to free herself.

With the lift of an additional finger, Marah was rendered completely immobile, able to only wait for Chairwoman Kate to deliver her fate.

The rebels scattered across the cavernous space shouted in desperate voices, "Don't! No! You can't! Stop!" But their pleas fell on deaf ears.

""I find it terribly amusing that you came here to ruin the very public execution I had planned, but that it will be you, instead of them, who will be the first to die." Kate flicked her wrist, and the knife was sent hurtling toward Marah.

Marah closed her eyes, waiting for the metal to plunge through her skin and experience the sensation many called death.

Chapter 32

Location: When the mark is hit and power is lost

In all the stories Marah had read, she couldn't think of a single hero who feared fate. It was traditional for heroes to be selfless—worry about only those they loved and protected, and never themselves. It seemed to be a requirement for those who engaged in a world of injustice. Heroes tended to lose: fights, blood, parts of their soul, lives, and hearts. It seemed that despite all they faced, they never gained the fear of what would happen to them.

This was part of what made heroes so appealing to Marah. When her mother threatened to send her away to fix her attitude, when her father left their family, when he would raise a drunken hand to her, throughout the divorce, she had learned to not be afraid of what would happen to her. To the seventeen-year-old girl that Marah Morana was—those stories were everything. Those stories had given her the chance to define what life she wanted. Somehow, it had even brought her to the stars playing the role of hero.

And yet, the human could not force herself to think selflessly, afraid to taste death. She had so much she wanted to do. And, in that split-second while the knife sliced through air in her direction, Marah could not name a single thing she wanted to do more than live. Maybe she was nothing like the heroes that had protected and loved her throughout her whole life. Maybe she was no hero after all. And in that moment, there was absolutely nothing wrong with that.

Marah Morana expected her taste to be swift and quick as her heart screamed, waiting for the sickening silence that would come after.

Except, the feeling never came.

Instead, a shouted protest made Marah open her eyes and cry tore its way through her throat.

No.

NO!

DAMMIT!

Marah's favorite Zonan teleported in front of her, popping the bubble that contained her. A choking gasp slipped past Kiera's lips as her knees buckled, tumbling her backward with the blade that was meant for Marah buried deep within her chest. Keira pulled out the blade and dropped it as Marah moved to catch her before she could hit the ground.

Kiera's face, usually a glowing blue that mimicked snow being bathed in moonlight, was much paler than Marah had ever seen. Sweat glistened on her brow, as tears mixed with the purple liquid that she was already starting to cough up.

Marah's cupped her friend's face. "Kiera," she urged frantically, "what did you do?"

The Arena had fallen into complete silence. Even Kate was momentarily taken aback by Kiera's sacrifice. Hands slack by her sides; her face betrayed no emotion as she watched curiously.

Tears pooled in Marah's eyes. "Why would you do that?" *Why would you give yourself up for me? You're going to die because of me now!*

Kiera only smiled, wincing softly as she placed a hand atop Marah's over her injury. "How could I not?" She opened her mouth to speak again, but only sputtered and spewed more of her life's purple blood.

"How unfortunate," mocked Kate. "Another life lost to your pathetic cause."

Completely enraged, Marah picked up her bow and fired an arrow toward Kate, blinded by anger. Not that it mattered since a wave of white slashed the arrow in half.

She sank back down, not having the heart to care that she missed her shot.

Kiera clasped one of Marah's hands, her almond ones meeting her friend's watery ones. "Because," she rasped, attempting to suck in more air. "You were willing to do all of this and die for us."

Marah squeezed her eyes shut, tears racing down her cheeks in competition with each other to see which would hit the floor the fastest.

How was she supposed to live with the guilt that every breath she took from here on after was at the expense of someone else's life?

Still gasping for air, Kiera used her final moments to absolve her friend. "I can feel your sadness and guilt. This is not your fault," she wheezed. "I still believe in you." She sucked in what was to be her final breath. "Finish this."

Despite the short time they knew each other—and the rocky start to their friendship—Kiera's sacrifice spoke volumes.

Marah helplessly looked over toward her friends, hoping for some sort of reassurance that it was going to be okay. Instead, their faces were riddled with sorrow and kissed with the mark of defeat.

When Marah turned back to face her favorite Zonan, Kiera's eyes were staring blankly at the sky.

"No!" Marah sobbed loudly. As her breath hitched, she closed her friend's beautiful eyes for the last time.

Chairwoman Kate laughed. "There's no need to be so dramatic, you'll all be together soon."

Marah stiffened, and the golden-stained hazel hues of her eyes hardened. This war was waged by the poisoned youth, innocent souls forced to live with broken horrors and tragic calamities that had become so common, society deemed them normal. Hatred had contaminated enough blood; there was no need for it to infect anyone else.

She stood up slowly, drawing back on her bow as she turned her gaze toward Kate. "You are going to pay for this." Her voice becoming steadier and stronger with each word. "You will face justice for the blood of all your victims."

The Chairwoman didn't look the least bit annoyed that she had missed her primary target. If anything, she seemed delighted simply to have killed one of the four, thus riling up the rebels even further.

A day ago, Marah would've been scared of herself for wanting to kill someone so badly. Now, it was all she wanted—she was not only looking forward to getting the job done, but anticipating in the satisfaction that would surely follow. *Screw it. Just because I'm a kid from Earth doesn't mean that I'm weak. Being human is my strongest weapon. Being human lets me be brave in a world where everyone is more powerful than me.*

The results of Chairwoman Kate's actions opened a floodgate of courage within Marah, practically roaring as she completed the draw on her bow, tilting the barest of nods toward the others, who came to stand with her.

The Chairwoman stood plainly, her hands were folded behind her back and her chin lifted higher as her eyes surveyed her surroundings. Her perfectly applied make-up began to melt beneath the sun's glaring rays, though she did not seem to notice or care.

Marah didn't care either. She had a job to do. The whole reason she was brought to Kosmir, perhaps the whole reason for her very existence, came down to this.

Chairwoman Kate now held her hands to in front of her, and power poured from her fingertips. "Such talk for a powerless human." Her eyes lit up like flames ready to burn, "Let's get on with this, shall we?"

We'll see who's powerless by the end of the fight.

Marah turned to Leia, who wiped the last of her tears away and set to building energy up in her hands as she called out to any rebel who was able to lend a hand or two, "Surround her and keep attacking. Three corners, go!"

Marah took her position. This time, when the arrow flew, a crackle of electricity was brought in its wake creating a small hole in the Chairwoman's shield.

In response, Kate merely waved a finger, urging the barrier to thicken.

Marah followed Leia's blasts to a certain spot on the barrier with another arrow, hoping that the combined force would create a hole in the shield. After a few more attempts, they were somewhat successful. Although it was not very large, for a few precious moments, the opening was big enough to allow the rebels to fire with hopes of actually hitting her.

Kate barely flinched, instead strengthened her shield.

Marah was reaching for another arrow when a force field of white surrounded her arm, rendering it motionless. She twisted about, endeavoring to free herself, but the white lingered. Her limb and its white sleeve wouldn't budge, and her predicament was shared by her comrades.

She attempted to slam her arm to the floor, but her limb and its white sleeve wouldn't budge.

Leia managed to flex her fingers, emitting a harsh wave of purple straight toward some advancing Committee members, knocking them all to the ground.

It was just enough to cause Kate's concentration waver, allowing Marah and Natira to break free.

Marah's arrow and Natira's blade quickly joined the spray of other rebel abilities and weapons launched at their nemesis before she could attempt to stop them.

Unfortunately, it was all for naught. Kate simply wiggled her fingers, sending out white sparks that fixed and expanded her barrier, pushing the rebels farther from her. With rage as red as the rivulets of blood running down her arms—*What do you know? A couple of us got her!*—she hurled a pile of rubble over her head toward the rebels. "You have ruined everything!"

Marah ducked as a chunk of concrete sailed past, mumbling, "By any chance, can anyone here do that?"

No," said Leia, "but I can do this." She created two pulsating energy balls, flinging them at Kate's feet, and watching as they climbed up her knees, trying to pull her down. The younger cousin groaned softly, wincing as she stretched her fingers and moved her hands together.

Chairwoman Kate diverted a few threads of her own energy toward that hummed around her legs, dark vanilla clashing against violent violet.

The counterattack caused Leia to stifle a scream as Marah watched blood begin to trickle from the Novan's nose and from the tips of her fingers.

Natira, blaster in her hand, was leading the next wave of attack against Kate's shield, and Marah followed, trying to distract Kate's attention away from Leia. She loosed an arrow with an explosive head, causing a hole to ripple through the shield.

Leia hoarsely commanded, "Brace yourselves!" She pushed her hands forward and splayed her fingers, making the purple energy within Kate's force field erupt. The impact of the power easily took down Kate's shield, but the shock wave from the blast expanded further than anticipated and hit the three remaining rebel leaders.

Marah was thrown to the ground, huffing as she crashed into someone. *How many goddamn times am I going to be thrown onto the ground today?*

Her abdomen ached from the literal pounding it had received over the course of the day. Her arms were sore as she rubbed her scraped and bloody hand on her face, not caring that she was just smearing the dirt that was already there. *If this won't give me acne, I don't know what will.*

She slowly sat up, groaning softly at the pounding in her head. She glanced over at Clyna, Joven, and the other remaining rebels who landed smack on top of leftover Committee soldiers and supporters. Taking advantage of the impact and surprise, the rebels made quick work of knocking them out. Natira had crashed into a pile of debris but used her phasing ability to avoid serious injury. Leia was sent rolling onto the ground, scraping her face along the way.

Despite the rebels' efforts, Kate's shield was once again back up as quickly as it had fallen.

"You have *got* to be kidding me!" Marah huffed as she staggered and swayed to her feet. "I'm too tired for this," she groaned before picking up her bow and helping some of the other fallen rebels up.

As for Chairwoman Kate, the ruler seethed and closed her fingers into fists. As she lifted her hands above her head, Marah, Natira, and Leia rose into the air.

"What the…?" started Marah. White encased her body as she was lifted off the ground. She kicked her feet, trying to break the shell.

The Chairwoman wore a look of madness as she slammed her curled knuckles to down, causing the three to crash to the ground for the umpteenth time.

Marah dropped to the floor rather ungracefully while her friends landed flat on their feet. "The movies make it look so easy," she huffed as she got up to her feet, knees screaming in protest.

If I get thrown against my will one more time, I swear I will scream.

She reinforced the question to whoever was listening, "We are going to kill her, right? I'm definitely in favor of killing, so does anyone mind if we get on with it? This is getting annoying."

"You're telling me," grumbled Natira as she sheathed her knife and drew her blaster. "No one kicks my ass and lives."

"I think we need a new plan," stressed Leia.

"Guys," interrupted one of the rebels, out of breath, "look."

The ground they were standing on began to crack. Marah's eyes followed the crack back to its source. Kate. She called out, incredulity laced in her tone, "Are you out of your mind? You'll kill us all, including yourself!"

Leia crouched down to where the crack had grown and closed her eyes as she placed a hand on the ground. A streak of purple traced over the crack's lines, beginning to pull the crumbling dirt back together.

Chairwoman Kate laughed, her eyes shining with madness and fire as she raged, "Either way I win! If you all die, The Committee will live on! You all just won't be here to see it," she added smugly as she levitated in the air with an ethereal aura.

Leia argued through clenched teeth, "Neither will you!" Her tone was annoyed and gritty, which suggested that the younger Novan was more than pissed. Marah was too, she didn't come all this way to prevent a bloodbath only to be the one *in* the bath.

Marah blurted out the first idea that came to her. "Isn't the Arena and the Citadel tokens of your fortune and glory? You're willing to destroy them? What does that make you?" She raised her confident eyes to meet Kate's dangerous ones, "A coward?"

"Are you insane?" hissed Natira. "Are you *trying* to get us buried alive?"

"Person A talks, persons B, C, and D attack."

Natira's expression shifted with understanding.

More of the Arena began to crumble and snap as bodies were being crushed under falling debris or swallowed by the ever-widening crack in the ground. "At least I won't have to succumb to the likes of you."

Marah shrugged as she lowered her bow but left an arrow nocked. "Well, you don't know that. There's more of us still standing than there are of your Committee. Others are prepared to continue if we die, but from where I'm standing, you look like you're on your own."

Leia lifted her head as her fingers kept closing cracks, "I'm not sure how much more I'll be able to hold. Whatever you're doing, speed it up."

Pulling out Ilke, Natira whispered while Kate fell silent, "Surround her slowly."

The rebels nodded and crept to their positions.

"On my mark," whispered Marah as she looked at the rebels, "give it all you got."

Chairwoman Kate chuckled as she realized that she was being surrounded, "Mere human, is this supposed to frighten me?"

Just as the porcelain wisps of energy glowed brighter, an indication that Kate was about to unleash total chaos, the human shouted, "Now!" as she shot at the woman.

Leia hurled power toward the woman as Natira shot her blaster and threw Ilke.

The other rebels thrust their abilities toward Kate at full force. With the added power of anger and grief, rays of light, energy strings, bolts of electricity, invisible balls of forced air, spears of ice, and javelins of flame shot from fingertips and open palms. Anything and everything the rebels could give to this fight against the woman who had introduced them to death, sorrow, and suffering, they bombarded her with.

It was for Kiera, who lay dead among bodies of the golden youth who wouldn't get to experience the liberation of such dark feelings firsthand. It was for the Artemians, the Novans, the Zonans, the Nantaks, the Litnickians, and the Stellans, all of whom had suffered, and believed that avenging and justice were only dreams.

Overwhelmed by massive attack, Chairwoman Kate's abilities gave way, and she collapsed. As the power from her hands died out, the ground pulled itself back together as if it had never been torn apart. Unable to conjure any more energy, the dictator was completely vulnerable to all forms of attack.

Marah, much like the rebels, erred on the side of caution, keeping her weapon at the ready. It was cruel, vile even, especially for someone who believed that no one deserved death, to wish it upon anyone, but she didn't care for morals anymore. Not after witnessing Kate more than willing to kill her, as well as Leia—her own family—with no hesitation.

She realized now, standing there, that perhaps there were exceptions to the lines between life and death. What mercy had she shown on the battlefield? So, she kept her bow nocked and drawn for the woman who struggled to peel her hands off of smooth stone. Poised to finish Kate off, Marah waited for someone to do something, anything, that would allow Kiera and countless other souls to rest easy.

Instead, Leia raised her hand and curled her grime and blood-soaked fingers to a fist, ordering everyone to stand down.

Remembering her experience on Artemis—*we can't be judge, jury, and executioner all at once*—Marah lowered her bow before shoving the arrow back in her quiver.

As much as Marah wanted to avenge blood with blood, she knew that it had to be done in a fair manner. Not because they'd be like Kate if they did, but because two wrongs wouldn't make a right. Kate was wrong, and Marah realized that the rebels weren't meant to conquer and then sink to the enemy's level. They were supposed to do good. Though the lines between good and bad, or justice and cruelty were often exceptionally blurry, people's morals and actions defined the distinction.

Marah could uphold those lines as she nodded toward the other rebels to lower their weapons but allowing them to keep their fingers near the triggers.

Leia made the first move toward Kate. Marah involuntarily moved forward to follow, but Leia held up a hand to her.

Marah stepped back as Leia approached her cousin, crouching down to ask the wilted woman, "Why are you continuing to do all of this? Look around you," she glanced down at the ring on her thumb as she picked up her cousin's hand, and then at the matching band of their family's crest on Kate's finger, "don't you see all of the hurt you've caused? You don't have to do this; you can change yourself."

Kate withdrew her hand from her cousin, spitting blood on the ground.

"You can better your legacy," continued Leia as hopefulness seeped into her tone as she clasped Kate's hand again, pleading. It was strange to Marah to see Leia attempt such a gesture. Hope was tricky, dangerous.

"No, I cannot," Chairwoman Kate whispered, voice cracked and gravely, as she lifted her head to reveal tears flowing down her face.

Marah was somewhat surprised to see Kate cry; she hadn't expected the powerful Chairwoman of The Committee to be capable of it, especially not over defeat. But, then again, she had been wrong about the people of Kosmir before.

Kate sniffed as she moved a hand to an arrow lodged within her shoulder and yanked it out, blood gushing from the wound. She leaned forward toward her cousin, blood trickling from her lips, "Do you know how many people have died from that war across the universes? Nova lost nearly half its population and fell into an economic depression that took nearly two solar cycles to overcome. Poverty was at its highest."

Kate's eyes glistened with bitter nostalgia of the worst kind, "Before the war was finally over, too many families were separated and there wasn't enough space for all the bodies. And when The Committee came to Nova, promising to end the war that had taken so much of our family, how could we refuse them? Do you remember asking me why we couldn't ever visit any of our family's graves? It was because there was no funeral," she spat, her voice imbued with anguish. She shook her head as she mused, "The Committee promised me what I needed—no more war. The sacrifice of my parents was the price to be paid for joining The Committee," her eyes turned cold, "and I gladly wear that badge of honor. I ended war."

Marah couldn't help but frown at Kate's words. Instead of seeing a cruel, blood-hungry dictator, she was starting to see a lonely, angry orphan. *Understandable motive, but still crazy. You know what normal people do? You go to therapy, not kill thousands, if not millions of people.*

Kate suddenly lunged for Leia's throat. The younger Novan blocked Kate's hands with a purple ball of energy, but the woman continued talking with anger, "I worked so hard for this! I couldn't let others suffer as I had!" Her voice reeked of frustration, "I told you to join me, but you didn't! You brought war and destroyed my Arena and Citadel! This is all your fault!"

Leia's expression was sad. "Even now that you have lost Kate, you are still blind. I want to forgive you, but I can't. You killed and hurt too many people. So, I'll ask you one last time, will you give this all up, or will you force us to kill you?" She held her cousin's gaze, "Those are the only two ways this ends."

Kate scoffed. "I didn't come all this way, spill all this blood for the greater good, to surrender." She spat, "If this war is going to end, it'll be on my terms." Before anyone could react, she yanked Ilke out of her thigh and plunged it right into her own chest.

Kate gasped as she forced the metal as far as it would go into her chest. Marah turned in horror, facing her friends, instead of the sight before her. Many rebels closed their eyes, where as some, like Natira, stared at the dying body of the woman who had hurt them in ways Marah simply could not fathom. She watched as Natira's lips—usually stiff with pure loathing toward Kate—start mouthing words that she couldn't hear. It didn't matter though, because Marah's heart understood the Nantak; she herself hadn't wanted to kill Chairwoman Kate and then she wanted nothing but that.

Leia, whose face was clouded by defeat and disappointment, softly asked her cousin, "Why would you do this?"

Kate replied weakly, "If my sole purpose for living dies, then I shall go with it." She closed her eyes and with her last breath said, "You would do the same."

The human could not dispel her confusion, remaining standing while the other rebels knelt. Watching the Chairwoman initiate her own departure from this world, and seeing rebels hold up their hands while whispering in various dialects, somber melancholy overcame the human who had toppled regime, beat the odds, and saved Kosmir's heart. She got what she wanted, but Marah wasn't sure why she felt the way she did.

Kate had destroyed so many lives and tried to kill them—all of them—and was successful numerous times. These were the very same people who yearned to kill Kate just moments ago, yet now they prayed for her as the light left her eyes. They were praying for her despite everything. *Why?*

As Marah saw it, Kate was someone dangerous because she believed she had been doing good despite everything. This made Marah wonder if the only person capable of killing such a person was themself.

Chapter 33

Location: When the lotus blooms and the sun shines once again

War was an interesting thing. War brought frustration, blood, tears, desperation, and of course, humbling defeat or gilded victory. War brought betrayal for some, love for others, but for Marah—who stood under the sun's light—war made friends out of strangers.

Rays of light shined down on Chairwoman Kate, whose heart had stopped, but whose blood continued to trickle.

Natira collapsed to the ground, unable to fathom how they achieved what she knew to be the impossible.

As relief flooded her system, Marah also collapsed, not even realizing her knees had buckled until her brain registered the white-hot pain as they smacked against the rubble-strewn turf.

She stared ahead, realizing that the rebels had succeeded. *She* had succeeded.

Which meant that everything that the rebels had said about her was true—and Marah found herself proud of that. Then, she spoke the first thought that came to mind: "What now?"

The question was met with silence as Natira pushed herself to stand and approached Leia. It tore the human's heart to see Leia weep for Kate. Then she spotted the rings on Leia's and Kate's fingers and remembered that family was a complicated thing.

And I thought I had family issues.

The Nantak clasped Leia's free hand, exchanging words that Marah couldn't hear, nor did she try to. Allowing the two their privacy, her gaze fell upon the mass of dead bodies surrounding her, those she knew and those she didn't.

She then glanced at her bloodied self and put pressure on her bleeding shoulder, not remembering when that injury happened. The contemplation of her injury's origins didn't last long, for Leia had stood, and like a good soldier, Marah did too. She shifted on her feet, doing her best to minimize the pain she knew was evident on her face.

The other rebels followed their leaders, standing as they waited for their next order.

"So, what's our next move?" piped up one of the rebels.

Leia looked around at what had become of the Arena, debris littering more places than not. Blood stains were everywhere, as were the dead, strewn like the saddest of confetti. Leia sighed at the devastation as she realized they also had to face the conundrum of what revolutionaries do after the need to revolt is finished.

Natira looked down at the woman who had stolen her childhood, "We bury the dead—all of them. And we let the families mourn."

Leia nodded, "We'll have to find a place."

"We could use the Arena as a memorial for all of the fallen," offered Marah. "The Arena stood for The Committee's glory, and now that that glory is gone, it should stand for something else."

"Let the lotus wilt in the beauty of its lake," murmured Natira, agreeing.

Leia nodded minimally, slowly detaching herself from Natira, eyes trained on the ground.

There was a somewhat expectant pause where everyone, defeated and rebel, turned their attention to the orphan Novan—who had been a leader of a battle that no longer required leading—waiting for some command.

It was instinctual, Marah supposed. Soldiers knew how to be soldiers, so it would make sense for leaders to know how to be leaders. Only, it is a strange feeling to come up with a strategic move when the battle is won, and all is left is uncertain, yet not.

When all good comes together to vanquish evil, what comes next for a leader of that good after the big bad is gone? How does one lead once the hoped, not promised, vision has been realized? Especially when that leader believed that they would perish along the way? And without the friends and family who wouldn't be truly dead until lips stopped echoing their names, but were gone nonetheless? There was too much complexity in death when there shouldn't be.

"Let's clean up and bury the dead. Natira, bring the bots to help. I'll debrief the new government."

Marah's eyebrow raised as the Novan wiped her eyes before heading off, "New government?"

"Who do you think has been supporting the rebellion?" answered Natira, dividing the rebels into teams: some for burying the dead while others ensured that those who had surrendered, remained peaceful.

"Leaders, governors, and judges that escaped death were hidden in a secret location. The King of Nova among them."

"We should get started," Natira said as she looked at the dead Chairwoman. "But not this one. Leia will want to bury Kate herself."

Marah stared at Joven's body, soon to be placed in the ground.

He was riddled with bullets and various other injuries as he helped rid the worlds of The Committee.

As they had dispersed to see who needed medical attention, Joven suddenly stumbled to the ground a few feet behind Marah. Before she could reach him, he burst into a hacking fit, realization of what was happening, evident in his reddened eyes. "Tell Pasca that I love her," his words slurring as he spoke slowly to make sure he was heard as blood stained his suit.

Marah had shaken her head, trying to pull him up while shouting for help. "You're going to tell her yourself. Come on, Joven, please don't do this to me." She couldn't lose another friend. "Please."

The human's only consolation was Joven's features suggested that he wasn't upset about being robbed of life with the heartmate of his dreams, or for the fight he had risked his life for dozens of times.

"Tell her," he'd rasped, and Marah's stomach fell again, "I meant every promise and I want to be buried with our ring."

Marah had started to shake her head, but as she looked in his eyes, she saw the truth staring back at her. "I will. I promise."

Those had been her friend's last words.

Natira was silent during the burial process, and Marah could tell that she too, was deeply affected by Joven's passing.

It's not fair.

Marah looked at her friend. "You alright?"

Natira shrugged as she wiped soil off her hands. "Growing up, I've buried so many people. The feelings of heartbreak and guilt never truly go away. But," she wore a small, almost optimistic smile that didn't linger for long, "you learn to live with it."

A soft voice offered, "I'll handle the rest if that's okay."

Marah turned to see the woman whose life she had saved some days ago but couldn't bring herself to make eye contact.

"I'm so sorry, Pasca." Natira said as she stood and placed her hand on the woman's shoulder.

The woman attempted a smile that didn't quite match the water welling in her eyes. She took Natira's position, laying a bouquet of purple lilies at the foot of Joven's grave. After a moment of gazing at her love, she looked up at Marah.

Marah spoke softly, "He's wearing his ring."

Pasca's lips curled a fraction of an inch upward. Knowing Joven died fighting for a cause they both believed in was a small consolation to her shattered heart, but the fact he was being buried wearing his ring, meant his last thoughts were of her. She looked back at Marah and whispered, "Thank you." Pasca favored silence as she brought her fingers to Joven's smooth features. Her fingertips trembled, light and gentle as they barely touched Joven, as if she couldn't bear the experience of touching warm flesh gone cold.

She traced the contours of his forehead, down the arch of his nose, over his cheeks, and to his lips, memorizing the shape and feel of his face.

She whispered, "My Moonshine," as her face crumbled. Scooping up Kosmir soil, she smoothed it over his body until it was completely covered.

Then Marah saw it. A gold ring on Pasca's finger. A fresh wave of tears pricked the backs of her eyes.

"This is war," Pasca spoke in a manner that suggested wisdom beyond her years. "Even the youth die in war. And now we bury the namesake of youth, my beloved Joven," she lamented before shifting her gaze to the human, where teardrops, conjured from a constellation of atoms, raced each other down her still dirty face. "I am not upset, if that is what you are thinking." The hand that didn't wear Joven's promise interlocked with Marah's fingers, "My Joven has returned to his brethren among the stars. He has met the Maker, and that is a journey we all must make, is it not?"

"And until then?" Marah sniffled.

Pasca's eyes shone with weariness, "Until we depart this world that is meant to be a fidelity of justice, we must be strong." She moved her gaze back to the mound of dirt that now covered her heartmate and planted the lilies so that they would continue to bloom to be the most beautiful flowers, "It's what he would have wanted. But for now, we pray for the dead."

Pasca held out her hands and Marah followed, looking at Pasca unsurely.

"Oh, right," the Stellan blushed as she explained, "When someone dies it's customary to give them our blessings. We usually say something based on our cultural practices, but no matter what language we speak, words are still spoken." She raised her hands and Marah followed as she recited softly, "And for every flower that blooms, I will wait to lose my soul to You."

The words resonated through Marah, and she followed them with a soft and quiet "Goodbye, my friend," but she could not bring herself to sit beside Joven any longer. She walked away, permitting Pasca some privacy, and headed over to Natira, who sat silently by Kiera.

Marah knelt on the opposite side of Kiera and made no effort to initiate the Zonan's burial. From the way Natira looked around at

Committee members, rebels, and civilians working alongside each other to bury their dead, the human felt it seemed the Nantak had expected to be the one in need of a grave, not Kiera. She wondered if Natira hadn't been in custody, would the last surviving Nantak have dug her own grave before the battle? She was pretty confident in what the answer was. She leaned back and waited for someone to say something—to say anything.

Kiera had brought her onto this world, but here Marah was, putting her in it.

"I can't do it yet," whispered Natira, burying her fingers in the soil a few centimeters from Kiera's limp ones. "Not without Leia. Maybe not even with her."

Marah spotted a familiar purple jacket a few yards behind the Nantak. Despite their strained relationship, Leia had insisted on burying Kate herself, not wanting anyone else to feel obligated for obvious reasons.

The morality of the whole situation riveted Marah. Kate had planned Leia's death and was about to kill her in cold blood, and yet Leia was the one who would be burying her would-be-murderer honorably. A part of her expected the burial to be tedious as Committee soldiers and officers and rebels buried their own, and yet there was a sense of sobriety. Peace couldn't unite Kosmir, but war, the very cause of consternation for The Committee did. The living buried the dead respectfully and quietly, an implication of who Kosmir's victors were.

The tension was still there, unspoken. Ultimately, all of the pain The Committee created wouldn't perish with Kate's soul.

"Do you think Leia's going to be okay?"

Natira glanced over her shoulder to where Leia sported blotchy cheeks.

"She will. We just have to support her."

Marah hummed, tearing her gaze from cold bodies to where Lizard and other robots buzzed to and from, offering comfort and directions. "It doesn't feel right," she finally allowed herself to admit out loud. "I can't help but feel grateful to be alive, but I know I shouldn't. I wish she was alive," she sniffed, looking down and only down, "she didn't deserve to die. She was a good person, she fought for this and now she can't see it. It feels wrong, she brought me here into this world, and now I'm—we're—putting her in it."

Every second she spent thinking about how she would bring herself to bury Kiera, she thought about their friendship. She had helped her adjust to the rebels, helped her move past Artemis, joked about her predicament with Beth, showed her what the rebels truly stood for, and most importantly, was the first person to truly believe in her.

Marah couldn't help but think about if the cards were any other way. *Would Beth be burying me today? Would Kiera, Joven, and all of these rebels still be alive?*

Natira's features shifted into a look that bore understanding. "You're not evil for wanting to live," she spoke benignly. "Your life is worth as much as hers. You have to remember, Kiera knew what she was doing. She knew the risks." She paused, scooping up a handful of Kosmir that would be a blanket for her best friend and letting it fall between the cracks of short, stubby fingers. The act was as casual as death itself. "To tell you the truth, if it was down to me to save your life, I would've done the same without hesitation."

Marah looked up at Natira.

Natira nodded as clumpy platinum hair blew past her shoulders "I would. You would—you *did*—the same for me. I never got to thank you for that," she saw Marah's expression, "I know I don't have to, but I need to. Thank you, Marah, for sticking with us."

"She's right," said Leia, catching both rebels by surprise as she knelt by Kiera's feet, covered in the remnants of burying her cousin. She exhaled shakily and the tears in the Novan's eyes brought out tears from the Nantak and the human. "Let's do this, together."

They got to it, slowly but steadily.

While they worked, one thing was left to address: Marah going home.

Marah didn't know how to feel about going back to Earth after everything. At first, she'd hated this world, but to sit in the feelings of happiness and friendship, the human felt right at home. There was something about meeting these new and strange people that made Marah feel good about herself and what she was doing with her life.

Something that Earth wasn't able to give her.

Leia pulled back to wipe her hands before continuing to cover her friend. "So, this might seem like a bad time, but we did promise you, Marah, that after the fight you could go back to Earth. Would you rather go tonight or after we finish cleaning up? It's completely up to you."

Maybe, this is where I was always meant to be.

Marah cleared her throat, a smile crawling up her lips, "Actually, I'd like to stay here. Being here, I finally found what was missing in my life. Though maybe we could all go to Earth so I could pick up some stuff?"

Her friends instantly grinned, "That'd be great!"

Marah joked as Natira gave her shoulder an affectionate squeeze, "Besides, you guys aren't that lame."

Natira shook her head, almost laughing, "You too, you're tolerable at best."

"So," started Marah as they finished the first layer of Kiera's grave. "I've been meaning to ask for a while and Kiera said that she'd tell me once we win because I'd only understand then. Do the rebels have a name or are we just called the rebels?"

Leia smiled sadly, "We are the Eternals."

Acknowledgements

If I'm being completely honest, I'd never thought I'd ever get to write end of "Eternals." "Eternals" started as a project in 2019 when I had to write a prompt for my freshman-year creative-writing class and got sucked into this world of aliens, rebellion, and space. And now, it is 2025 and "Eternals" has never felt more real and alive than it has today.

This is my first time properly writing an acknowledgement, so please bear with me.

First and foremost, I'd like to begin by devoting my utter gratitude to my parents. The truth is, were it not for them, this book wouldn't be in your hands, nor would it probably exist. "Eternals" is the product of hundreds, no, thousands, of books bought for me from all the local Barnes & Noble for twenty years of being alive. From reading "Amelia Bedelia," "Henry and Mudge," to both "Geronimo Stilton" and "Thea Stilton," to all the newest YA that caught my attention, every book I've ever read has stayed with me. They've gotten me this far in my life. They've molded me to become the writer that I am, the author I aspired to be, fostered the way I love, read, think, and breathe, and the way I live. My parents have paid for endless AMC tickets, Funko Pop character collections (fun fact: I have six Captain Americas), and quickly had to learn that Sarah on the computer rapidly typing = definitely do not disturb or ask.

Second thanks are in order to my sister and cousin who've been there since day 1. They were the first to know "Eternals" before words had been put to a Google Doc. They've seen this story in all of its drafts, including the very, very first draft—shudder. I still remember all those days when I'd sit and write and they'd insist on sitting beside me, reading and gleefully pointing out any cringey lines or spelling mistakes I made. I'm glad to have shared this journey with them; they always had something nautical and nonsensical to comment on, and I wouldn't have it any other way. Thank you both for believing in me in a time when no one did, being my number one team, and always being eager to read whatever I write.

I also want to thank my best friends who have never not believed in me. I love you so much. I can't thank you enough for believing in me in all of my pursuits, hobbies, and ramblings as "Eternals" took shape from a borderline fanfic to a hot mess, and then a fully-fledged idea ready to fly off into the world. You're the one who let me use you as a sounding board, edited that very first draft of "Eternals," and was there for me when I complained (cried) about the woes of securing a publishing deal for months. You're the ones who I've had the luxury to grow up with. You're the ones who responded and read all my messages whenever I had a spur of a thought worth writing about, helped me with homework (more writing time!), and was always down to go see a movie at the local AMC with me. You paved the way for "Eternals" to get this far. I can't wait to read their fanfics. Seriously, guys, write them. Everyone. Tag me (@sarah._.barahh) on Instagram.

I also have to give tremendous thanks to all of my teachers growing up. There are some teachers who come in your life and leave a mark that's impossible to ignore: my second-grade teacher who insisted that I read every day and let me pick out a book, spurring a life-long obsession, my eight-grade English teacher who one, caught me writing fanfiction in class and didn't read it out loud and two, told me and my parents that I had what it took to be an author, and my high-school creative writing teacher for giving me the tools and resources to figure out how to access the publishing world, and giving me the link of publishing houses that would land "Eternals" its home.

Lastly, but certainly not least, none of this would have been possible without the Between the Lines Publishing team for giving me and "Eternals" a chance when I was so close to giving up. Writing "Eternals" was easy and one of the best experiences of my life. Sharing it with the world? That was terrifying. Luckily for me, I found the Between the Lines Publishing submission call listing a search for stories of feminism, friendship, and the odd. I summoned the courage of facing 50+ rejections, feeling that this would be "Eternals" calling. I'm eternally grateful (full pun intended) for Siân Hyleg and Penny Dowden for seeing something in eighteen-year-old me and "Eternals." I'd like to thank Siân for always responding to my emails so quickly and seeing the vision within "Eternals." Special thanks to Penny for combing through my 424-page Word document, combing through every comment with my Gen-Z incapability of using Word, and bargaining with me to prime into becoming a better writer and thinker.

And, if you've made it this far, I want to thank you for picking up this book off the shelves and coming on this journey with me. You took on a promise I made with this book and I hope I've fulfilled it. Thank you for taking a chance on my name, my premise, and seeing me through the end of it. I hope that "Eternals" has inspired some thought and that you make of it what you will. As we part goodbye, I'd like to insist that you always stay creative and true to yourself. Without readers and writers to form art and be inspired by it, the world would be a much grimmer place.

S. F. Chaudhry is a proud Pakistani New Yorker who lives and operates in Queens, New York. She is set to pursue her BS in Biology and a minor in Creative Writing at Stony Brook University. If you couldn't tell by now, she is a massive fan of action films and loves writing all things fiction. She considers herself a weaver of words and worlds and uses the fictional landscape to unearth what's important to her. "Eternals" is her first published novel.

www.ingramcontent.com/pod-product-compliance
Lightning Source LLC
Chambersburg PA
CBHW010556310726
48969CB00009B/2450